P9-DNA-786

WHO DO YOU LOVE

Also by Jean Thompson

WHO DO YOU LOVE

stories

Jean Thompson

Harcourt Brace & Company

New York   San Diego   London

Copyright © 1999 by Jean Thompson

All rights reserved. No part of this publication may be
reproduced or transmitted in any form or by any means,
electronic or mechanical, including photocopy, recording, or
any information storage and retrieval system, without
permission in writing from the publisher.

Requests for permission to make copies of any part of the
work should be mailed to: Permissions Department,
Harcourt Brace & Company, 6277 Sea Harbor Drive,
Orlando, Florida 32887-6777.

Lyrics from "Who Do You Love" by Ellas McDaniel © 1956
(renewed) Arc Music Corporation. All rights reserved. Used
by permission. International copyright secured.

Library of Congress Cataloging-in-Publication Data
Thompson, Jean, 1950–
Who do you love: stories/Jean Thompson.
p.   cm.
ISBN 0-15-100416-1
1. United States—Social life and customs—
20th century—Fiction.
I. Title.
PS3570.H625W47   1999
813'.54—dc21   98-44378

Text set in Sabon
Designed by Lydia D'moch

Printed in the United States of America
First edition
C E D B

Publication acknowledgments appear on
pages 305–6, which constitute a
continuation of the copyright page.

For Terry Wiggs
who told good stories

I walk forty seven miles of barb wire
Use a cobra snake for a necktie
Got a brand new house on the roadside
Made from rattlesnake hide
I got a brand new chimney made on top
Made from a human skull
Now come on baby let's take a little walk and tell me
Who do you love?

"Who Do You Love"
Ellas McDaniel
(Bo Diddley)

Contents

one

WHO WE LOVE

ALL SHALL
LOVE ME
AND DESPAIR

Scout liked the needle. He liked it almost as much as the high. The tidy way the needle slipped beneath the skin, took its discrete bite, then the thread of pure amazement feeding into you. He liked the precision of it. "What does it feel like?" Annie asked him, back when she still wanted to know such things, when there was still a horrid glamour to it all. "Like something grows inside you," said Scout. "All at once, like a Jack-in-the-beanstalk vine, leaves and stems and purple curling flowers, and it fills you up to your fingers and toes. It's like your head is an organ, and someone plays a chord."

But that was a long time ago, in the good part of the bad old days, and Annie's through with pretty words for ugly things. She doesn't want anything in her life that has to be tricked out in poetry, explained away. She's walking on a beach in Oregon, watching the sun go down. There's a thin watery layer of clouds that diffuses the pink-orange light, spreads it as evenly as butter from one end of the sky to the other. The beach is broad white sand, also smooth enough to reflect light, so that Annie walks in glory without having to think of names for it.

There are other people out on this fine evening, strolling along the soapy edge of the advancing tide, or grilling hot dogs over driftwood fires, and here is a young man exercising his cockatiel. He runs along the sand waving a towel, with the cockatiel flapping behind him. Annie's seen him a few times; they greet each other. "Birdie surfing," the young man calls it. The bird is perfectly tame and won't fly off, but he has to keep an eye out for seagulls. Seagulls are worrisome. This is what Annie wants her life to be now: a procession of ordinary delights.

There's a cliff marking the edge of the beach, with stairs at intervals, and on this cliff edge the town is built up thickly. There are motels and restaurants and houses on minute lots, all of them shouldering each other for space, all of them built of the same weathered cedar or painted pine. The town has strict building codes, aimed at controlling development and preserving a casual beach shack ambiance. The motels all have names like the Gray Whale and the Cove. The shopping district has stores devoted to pottery, seascapes, woven ponchos, hammered brass jewelry, and the like. You can buy jams and honey, locally produced and put up in gold-labeled jars. You can buy soapstone carvings of whales, bleached sand dollars, fudge, pizza by the slice, cookies, and ice-cream cones. There are rentals for roller skates and beach tricycles, and two kite shops. Scout has a job in a bookstore. Annie makes sandwiches in a deli. They've been here two months, just long enough to say *tourist* about other people.

The ocean is no certain color. Steel and slate, gray and blue, reflecting light like metal or lapping up perfectly clear at Annie's feet. It's always too cold to swim in, even now, in August, unless you're a little kid. Up the beach a couple of miles is a cove where people in black rubber wetsuits windsurf and kayak. Annie thinks it's something she might like to try sometime, one of those violent ocean sports, just because it would be so unlike her. She imagines herself encased in a sleek rubber skin, jaunty and exhausted, her hair a shipwreck of snarls, lungs efficiently exchanging CO_2 and oxygen.

Scout, of course, jeers at the whole idea. "Buy me a thrill," he says. "All that equipment. It's the MasterCard high." Annie knows the ocean scares him. It's too large and indifferent, he can't get his mind around it. He has to find a way of dismissing it. Annie allows him this because he needs something to despise, as a substitute for dignity.

The trip from Chicago is something Annie can uncover like a scar on her body when she wants to remind herself that she can do anything. She drove every mile of the way. Even at the end when Scout was well enough to sit up and look around him, she was the one who drove. Her shoulders, spine, and pelvis fused into one unit. She was a machine for driving. The car fed its energy into her, and she powered them on. Her fingertips drew in every mile of road. Her feet tickled. The road became her drug. Iowa was black night, and Nebraska sunrise. Headlights pricked out of the darkness, then just as suddenly extinguished themselves. They made Annie start, although she knew perfectly well this was paranoia, mental gymnastics, a trick she used to fuel them across the country on black wings. No one knew where they were. No one would know where they were ever again.

She muscled the accelerator down. In the back seat Scout moaned and sweated. Annie bought him cartons of milk, milk shakes and jelly doughnuts—the only things he could eat. Even then he puked a couple of times, so the back of the car was full of wet sour paper. At gas stations Annie pulled Scout to his feet and made him use the bathroom. She waited under the banks of humming lights at convenience stores. The lights reflected ten thousand cellophane-wrapped surfaces with crazed precision. Rows and rows of hygenic, appalling food. Sugar highs, caffeine highs, preservative highs. It was a place where you might find yourself reasonably contemplating armed robbery, or dying. Annie thought, *I could drive away right now. Somebody else will come along and take charge of him if he sits there long enough, the police, somebody, it won't matter, finally, who it is.* But she waited until Scout appeared, looking if anything a little worse, smelling a little more, his junkie's breath, his poisoned sweat, his rash-bearing skin, all of him collapsing into nothingness and bad air. Annie opened the back seat door for him and they drove off.

Scout is twenty, Annie twenty-one. Scout is small, like a jointed puppet, an assemblage of stick arms and legs. So small that once, in high school, he found a Cub Scout uniform in the Goodwill bin, complete with neckerchief and hat, and it fit him. So did the name, which stuck. Scout has a mouse's face and little intelligent mouse eyes behind his wire-rimmed spectacles. Annie is half a head taller than Scout, but thin, and when they stand together they might be brother and sister, or at least members of the same brittle species.

Is Annie pretty? She doesn't think so, particularly. And she's not the kind of girl who gets told it very often. Sometimes, though, she leans close enough to the mirror to see, just out at the edge of her vision, not her reflection, but a kind of shadow cast by her face. She sees a landscape of pale and dark in the liquid shine of her eyes and the grain of her cheek, distorted, mysterious, beyond beauty. Like looking at the moon through a telescope, or an eggshell under a magnifying glass. When she pulls back from the mirror, it's only a face, common and clumsy, no cause for marveling or delight. One reason she loves Scout is that he doesn't notice or care about people's faces.

Back in Chicago, in the good part of the bad old days, they used to walk down to Belmont Harbor to look at the boats. It was always windy, or that's how Annie remembers it, windy gray or windy blue, wind ruffling the water, shivering the well-tended strips of grass, making them dig their hands in their pockets and hunch their shoulders. Scout said the lake was nothing, just a big cold bathtub. It couldn't take you anywhere. What was the point of a boat if it always came back to the same place? (He hadn't yet seen an ocean, hadn't had the chance to be disheartened by one.) The lake was small potatoes. A poisoned fishbowl, an industrial sink. They should reverse the plumbing and flush it all clean. They should blast a hole in the ass end of Superior. Like those crazy old explorers who tried to get to India by way of Duluth. Another crazy thing was ore barges. Tons and tons of rock, floating on water.

Annie let him talk, though she didn't agree with what he said: the lake was bottomless and shoreless and seemed fearsome enough to her. When Scout talked, she made small noises in her throat as a kind of acknowledgment, so she didn't have to pay close attention, or pretend one thing he said followed from another. Scout was the most intelligent person she knew, even when he said stupid things. Ideas kept coming out of him; everything he saw got turned into ideas. She was flattered that he talked to her. She knew Scout better than anyone else in the world did, because he talked to her so much. He imprinted himself on her, until his ideas took up space in her head and her own voice always seemed to be asking a hopeful, anxious question. In bed when he locked his body into hers, gulping air and crying out, tears came to her eyes. The tears had nothing to do with pleasure or pain, only the closeness, their two red hearts keeping exact time. She thought being in love was the most important thing she could ever do.

When Scout was high, he stopped talking. His thoughts were too slick and elegant, his ideas too big, like the slow turn of a planet on its axis. Annie wouldn't touch junk. Never. It scared her more than not doing it scared her. It was another thing without boundaries or measurable depths. When she felt herself wanting to do it, it was to keep from being lonely, and so Scout couldn't smile and tell her she didn't know anything: "Junk ain't no tea party, toots." Annie suspected he liked her not doing it. He wanted to have something he withheld from her, something too big and bad and sad for her.

Whenever she didn't want to do it, she felt guilty and dishonest. It meant a part of her was still not in love and wouldn't follow where he led. Because there is that about her. Something stubborn and mutinous and impatient, or perhaps merely practical, that makes her think *Yes but* when he talks. Something that will not love him without judging him. Just last week, walking on the Oregon beach, Annie found the clean bleached skull of a seagull. Wedged at the back of its throat was a tight metal spring, of the sort used in mousetraps. She thought the part of her that refused to be in love was like that spring, like the sounds she made in her throat instead of words. Something that wouldn't go up or down, just got caught in her.

The first time they walked out on the beach, they were timid, as if someone might shoo them away, smell the city or the fear on them and determine they had no right to be there. People were flying kites in the buoyant air—wonderful kites, kites stacked on kites, ingenious flying cantilevers made of geometric Mylar shapes in neon and black and paint-box colors, trailing cellophane ribbons. There were kites that suggested bats or spaceships or dinosaurs, others that resembled nothing at all, only some idea of flight given whimsical form. Annie laughed out loud at them. The laugh sounded odd, squawking, as if she'd swallowed a bird that was now squeezing its way out. It embarrassed her. "Aren't they something," she said rapidly, to cover up. "I mean, there must be all these people who work day and night just thinking about . . . kites."

She meant it was wonderful that people engrossed themselves in something so innocent. It seemed hopeful to her. She thought of all the kites that hadn't been invented yet, or even imagined. She thought that in this new life she might become a water conservation officer, or a mapmaker, or something just as blameless, just as absorbing.

Scout looked solemn and confused. He gaped up at the sky, then at the ocean. His hair was still damp from the shower, combed thinly across his skull, and he'd put on a clean shirt. Shabby, convalescent, scrubbed, he didn't belong there. You might as well take a pigeon out of its concrete roost. Annie didn't want to feel sorry for him; it would be one more weakness in him. "We could get us a kite," she said in a coaxing voice. "One of those big ones, with all the strings, like driving a team of horses."

Scout was still looking out at the ocean, as if he expected it to stop moving eventually. She touched his arm. "Scout?"

"Jesus," he said in a quiet, flattened voice. He rubbed at his nose with the back of his hand, then turned away, his eyes averted and noncommittal. Annie's heart sagged. He didn't like it, and she couldn't fix it for him, not a whole ocean.

But then he reached out and spun her by the shoulders. Annie squealed. The sand made them stagger crazily. The wind blew Annie's long hair into both their mouths. Scout whooped. "We'll get a big goddamn mutha kite. It'll eat all the other kites."

Annie wanted to say that wasn't the point of a kite, but she was out of breath from laughing. Then Scout loosed her and sprinted away. Dizzy, she squinted after him. The sky tilted into the ocean. Scout was running straight into the water, arms outstretched. Ankle-deep, knee-deep, with his pants legs sogging and his shoes weighted down, legs pumping, getting nowhere, as if mere stubbornness could turn the ocean floor into a sidewalk. A green wave slid toward him and hit him waist-high. "Hey," called Annie. "Hey dummy." It was important that she be there for him to ignore.

Finally he waded out again. He was grinning. His fingernails were blue and pinched. "You're nuts," said Annie. He looked pleased with himself, perhaps because he'd alarmed her. He peeled out of his wet shirt and swung it around his head, like a stripper.

"Glad you're feeling better," she said mildly, which was her way of reminding him where they'd come from, and why.

Annie stooped and dug up a sand dollar, the flat cracked portion of one. She was glad she had something she could use to ignore him back with. She wondered what the thing that lived inside looked like, and how it grew this pleasing cool flat shape. She liked the delicate fossil print, resembling a blossom, or a five-pointed star, or an outstretched hand. She supposed there was some biological reason for the pattern, but she preferred to think it was pure whimsy, like the stripes on a kite. She said, hefting it, "This is great. This place. Everything about it. The cops ride bicycles. They look like kids whose parents buy them fancy bikes."

Scout didn't answer. They were laboring back up the cliff. The sand slowed them. Scout's bare chest was covered with big knobby goosebumps. The glee had worn off and he was sullen and shivering and glum, as if someone else, probably her, was to blame for his being wet. Annie wanted him to say he liked it here. She wanted him to say anything at all. It wasn't fair that she had to keep doing and saying everything, waiting not to be ignored, calling him back from deep water.

When they reached the top, he brightened, as if he'd only wished to punish her for enjoying something on her own. "We did it, cupcake. We discovered the Pacific Ocean."

"Uh-huh."

"What's with you?"

"Nothing." The only thing she could openly accuse him of was running into the ocean, and that didn't seem like a real grievance.

"You worry too much," Scout pronounced. It was what he always told her. They were the same people in a new place. It had been stupid to think anything else.

"Come on, lighten up." Scout's hand in hers was colder than cold. Kissing, she tasted the salt on him. It tasted like tears, only cold. She hugged him hard. His bones were shivering and electric. What was the difference between too much worry and too much love?

The needle always looked clean, no matter where it had been. Nothing could be cleaner than its thin bright nakedness, its silver eye, its spike. Scout let it fall to the floor. His eyes rolled back in his head like heavy silver pinballs. A piece of indifferent Chicago sky hung in the window. The room smelled of gas and sugar, a closed, wintertime smell. There was a color television and a bean-bag chair and a sofa. The chair was dark orange tweed with black welting. Annie hated that chair. It was the single ugliest thing she knew. It absorbed every stink and puddle. It was an altar to ugliness. The needle lay in a fold of its orange hide.

"Scout," she said. A giggle slid out of him. The television was on, a tiny idiot noise, bathing the room in garish candy colors. When Scout's eyes opened again, the colors reflected off them. "Scout?"

After a while he turned toward her. His teeth were scallops of dim light. "Yaas," he said. "Speaking."

"You OK?"

His eyes were sugar yellow. His mouth made an O, for OK. When his eyes closed again, Annie turned the television off. She sat and watched the piece of sky grow black. In the kitchen the gas stove burners were turned on for heat. She could hear the blue gas whispering. She heard the city noises, traffic and catastrophe, muffled by distance, like a lion's yawn. This was Annie's secret: she liked these times. Because it was just the two of them, and he couldn't get away. Because he couldn't say things with his needle tongue, and she could say anything she wished. "I love you." She said it small because there were already so many secrets filling up the room.

Scout said she worried too much. He only shot once in a moon. He could handle it. *Yes but.* The *why* of it kept itching her. Scout's real name is Edward. He grew up on the South Side, praying to the Polish saints. Their sweet faces were garlanded in roses and lit by candles in pink glass holders. It was the wrong kind of heaven for him, too grave and pastel, smelling too strongly of his mother's hand cream. He wanted more commotion and sweat. He liked alleys and brick dust and gravel and old paint cans; he liked streetlights and the politics of sidewalks. Heaven got turned upside down for him, as it does for a lot of people, and he was curious, bored, resentful. His father drove a bakery truck and the house was always full of stale or staling bread, sacks of butter cookies, doughnuts, coffee cakes dyed a staring yellow. Wasting food was a separate category of sin, involving thrift and ingratitude. Annie thinks Scout is always angry, or at least never very far from it. Like he's been cheated out of heaven and can't find anything important enough to take its place, and maybe that's what junk is. Junk lets you float right up there with those gilded antique saints and choirs of sugar angels, high and mighty. Junk turns all their fussy ribbons and their cotton-puff clouds into grandeur; junk is God. By the end, though, Annie doesn't think Scout's reasons are any smarter than any other junkie's. By the end it's no longer a matter of reasons.

In Oregon they live in a cottage, which is another way of saying converted garage, closer to the highway than the beach. It's a part of town that's home to the waitresses and grill cooks and garbage haulers, everyone making a summer living off the beach. The cottage is paneled in dark uneven boards. Moss grows at the base of the foundation slab. Ferns surround the garbage can. There's a matchbox kitchen, a loft for sleeping, and a shower stall with snails. Their jobs are simple and undemanding, time in exchange for money. On free afternoons they go to the Laundromat and the grocery, like ordinary people. Scout brings home serious books by dead and living philosophers, inquires into the nature of consciousness, or of politics. Annie brings home the ends of turkey rolls, avocados, and slices of cheesecake. They become friends with one of their neighbors, Phil, who delivers soft drinks to vending machines. Phil supplies them with Nehis and Dr. Peppers, and some evenings the three of them set chairs outside the front door and drink beer together.

"Say you like it here." Scout and Annie are in bed, and rain drills against the cottage walls. They are surrounded by water, like a ship at sea. Annie puts a finger in the corner of Scout's mouth to pry the words out. "Say it."

"Don't like all the rain. Being snail meat."

"You like the bookstore."

"I love selling cat cartoons to grandmas."

"Sco-ut." Annie sighs, a cinematic, exasperated sigh. She waits for one of them to get serious. After a minute Scout says, "You want me to say I like being straight."

They listen to the rain, its multitude of voices. "Well, do you?"

Scout's ribs expand and sink. Annie feels his breath in her hair. "I miss it sometimes. I miss the bigness of it. You know?"

Annie nods. Sometimes she misses her own holy pain. Saint Annie of the Spike. Our Lady of Dolors. The one thing she could always count on was that righteous misery. Who is she now? Somebody sadder but less miserable.

"I'm white bread," Scout says into her hair. "I floss my teeth. I watch *Wheel of Fortune*. I'm boring."

"So is dead boring."

"You want me to say you saved my life. You think like that, don't you? Like an old-time movie."

She doesn't answer because he's right, he can always see through her. Scout goes on in a kindly, mocking voice, "Sure I like it here. I'll like anything you say. After all, you saved my life."

They are silent but the rain keeps talking, subtle and persistent, bubbling up from underneath, invading the house with fronds and jellied creatures, filling their dreams with water-words: *secrets, secrets, sleep.*

In the bad part of the bad old days the phone rang and rang. Annie said, Hello, hello? The phone was black and dense and listening. The ghost calls only came when Scout wasn't home. They scared her, and she got so she wouldn't answer at all, just cried and let the phone ring. The television was broken. Annie cried over that too, as if it were a pet. She thought it might be Scout on the phone, checking up on her. He was calling from junk heaven to tell her what it was like, saying ecstatic things in a frequency just out of her hearing.

Or maybe the caller wasn't Scout at all, but someone he owed money to or had stolen from, someone he'd brought around. The people Scout brought around were not friends. They were all involved in commerce and betrayal. They had faces like the dulled blades of knives. One day Scout brought home a man named Ace. Ace sat with his hands between his knees, picking at his fingernails, tapping his feet and grinning. "Ace has a car," said Scout. "We could go for a ride."

"Where to?" asked Annie. They didn't do things like go for rides.

"Anywhere. Or just you and Ace could go."

Ace kept grinning his grin. He could have been any age from thirty to fifty. Junkies all looked the same to Annie, like old newspapers. Ace glanced at Scout and wiggled his eyebrows. "Hell of a ride," he said.

Scout was edgy, keyed-up. "Come on," he said to Annie.

"Go yourself, if you're so excited about it." Annie got up and went into the bathroom and shut the door. She wanted to stay in there until Ace left. She didn't like him. He had a smell to him, a chicken-bone smell.

Scout opened the bathroom door. "Do you *mind*," Annie said, but he wasn't paying attention to things like that. Scout's lips had a dark cracked rim around their inner surface, like someone with a fever. He said, "You got to help me."

Annie looked around the bathroom, thinking he meant something right in front of them, aspirin or a towel. "What do you need?"

"Help me with him."

"Help you what?" said Annie, but Scout just stood there, impatient, persistent, sly, like he was waiting for her to get an especially good joke. Then everything in front of her eyes changed, as if the light had cracked along with her comprehension, and she could not distinguish between the water running from the tap and the rust stain it followed like a river in its bed. "No," she said, then she screamed it, striking out at him.

Scout caught her hands in his. "Listen, I'm into him," he said, as if he had merely explained things badly. "I'm way into him. See?"

She screamed again and looked for things to throw. He backed out the door and she kicked it shut after him. "Jesus, this is *important*," he shouted. "Am I getting through to you? Huh?"

"I have the scissors in here," she announced, and waited. After a while she heard their feet receding down the stairs.

The phone rang. Annie opened the bathroom door and watched it ring. When it stopped, she went into the bedroom and found a duffel bag and a backpack. She filled them with her things. She put a loaf of bread and three 7-Ups in a paper bag, thinking she must be forgetting something. She'd stopped crying by this time. All those tears. There were rust streaks beneath her eyes.

It was late, past midnight when she left. The sidewalk was lit with its pink streetlight moon. There were cars parked against the curb, pink and gleaming where the light hit them, shadowed below, lunar and motionless. She took two steps onto the pavement. Her own shadow swayed beneath her, then froze. Behind her in the closed apartment the phone was ringing. Her fingers shook in the locks. The door banged open. "Hello," she said to the silence.

She lay down on the bed to wait for daylight. *God god god.* Unlike Scout she had no childhood saints to beg or curse, and God was only a vague, woolly face, like an angry sheep. Then it was colorless dawn, and she opened her eyes to find Scout lying next to her. Dark thick strings stretched from the corners of his open mouth. Annie poked him and he swallowed.

"Get up," she said. She pulled the sheets from underneath him. They were flecked with the trails of old blood from his arms. "Get up." Scout moaned and fell to his knees beside the bed. Something metal hit the floor. Annie stooped and picked it up.

Scout was doubled over, junk-sick. Annie shoved the keys under his nose. "What are these?"

"Car."

"What car? What did you do?"

The phone rang and kept ringing. Annie screamed and backed away from it. She pulled Scout up by his armpits. He retched and coughed. "What car, where?"

It was a little white Ford, the kind of car no one ever noticed or missed, a car she assumed had a long pedigree of theft. It had been new not so long ago. Now a puddle of bilge rocked on the floor, and the trunk was punched in at the lock. (It would get them as far as Umatilla, Oregon, where the engine seized up and they sold the tires for bus tickets.) Annie nudged the car along the city streets, then into expressway traffic. Moving, anonymous, observing all speed limits. She looked into the rearview mirror at Scout's bent knees, pointing up, then at her own stupefied eyes. Scout hiccuped. It was nine A.M. The Seagram's girl on the billboard above the Tri-State smiled her white and gold smile, like another kind of saint. "Good-bye," said Annie, which was as close as she could get to prayer.

Gift shops on the Oregon coast, the ones specializing in piety and bad taste, sell the Mariner's Prayer, wooden plaques decorated with nautical-looking ropes, and anchors formed into crosses. The prayer asks for calm seas and benevolent winds, guiding beams from the heavenly lighthouse. People here keep pleasure boats at the harbor marina, or haul them on trailers down to the beach. Sometimes at an evening high tide you can watch half a dozen boats riding the surf in. They shoot out of the water and bump along the sand to the trailers, and it's a matter of skill for them to see how precisely they can aim. There are always little social groups of people around to assist and cheer, families driving off together in the dusk toward supper.

Their neighbor Phil has a brother who has a boat, an eighteen-foot skiff, the *Lazy Day*. On a clear evening, a sunset with a little scoop moon already in the sky, Scout and Annie walk down to the marina to see it. Annie is disappointed at how plain the *Lazy Day* is. No cabin, just a kind of hatch you can kneel into, an anchor on a winch, motor, fuel can, pump. Nothing else. Scout and Phil are having a serious conversation about draw and displacement, and Scout is nodding, like a man deciding whether or not to buy a car. "Taking her out this weekend," says Phil. "Come on along."

"Naw," says Scout, and Annie understands that the boat scares him just as the ocean scares him. "You and Annie can go if you want."

Annie glances at him sharply, but he's only poking around the boat slip, not looking at her, meaning nothing.

"It's not much of a boat," says Annie, just to be making conversation, as the two of them walk back home.

"It's a real boat. Not some bullshit floating RV. You ever hear of Thor Heyerdahl and the *Kon Tiki*? The Polynesians? They sailed the whole damn ocean in canoes. Canoes."

"Mhm," says Annie.

"You know what would be cool? Staying out all night in a boat. Like the fishermen do. If we went up on a cliff right now we could see their lights. The longer you look, the more you can see. Like stars."

"*Stella maris,*" says Annie. "That's Latin. It means 'star of the sea.' I forget where I know that from. It just popped into my head."

Scout's still going on about fake-o cabin cruisers and the fake-os who own them. Annie watches the moon, thinking you could make a kite that looked like the moon, and says uh-huh, because she doesn't care one way or another. Boats are just something to talk about for her. They aren't things she has opinions about.

But Scout brings home books on navigation and shipbuilding and naval warfare. He talks knowledgeably about reefs and currents, riptides and swells. He spends a lot of time with Phil, tending to the *Lazy Day*, learning to talk like a sailor. He's disappointed when he finds out you need running lights and a radio to sail at night.

"Why don't you ever go out in the boat?" Annie asks him. "What's the point if you never go out?"

"I will when I feel like it."

"I mean all you ever do is talk about stuff. Oh, never mind."

Scout is watching television, something with laughs in it, though his face is fixed and stony. Annie says, "I'm sorry if I hurt your feelings."

His face doesn't change. He's waiting for her to keep talking, apologize more, act interested. He's waiting to daunt her with some weary parade of facts. Annie looks at Scout and sees a sulky, big-headed child with glasses, his hair combed into an uneven peak, lower lip stuck out like a blister. He looks small and furious and absurd. She recognizes that she is seeing him without love. She recognizes this in the space it takes her not to speak.

Finally Scout says, "Oh for a life of deeds, not words. The smell of Old Spice. The swordfish mounted over the fireplace."

"Just for once don't talk that way. It's ignorant." Maybe she's never really loved him, only the image of her suffering self, reflected in him.

"You know so much. Tell me one damn thing you know something about."

"You," says Annie. "I know you." She's just said a terrible thing: that she knows him and doesn't love him.

They're both quiet. Then Scout says, "Right. Me."

Sometimes she pretends that Scout keeps talking. *Don't sweat it. God's the only one who loves us perfect, and God isn't getting through on the phones. The rest of us love what gets us high. We end up hooked on all the wrong things. Gotta fly. Over and out.*

But of course he says nothing at all. Two days later Scout doesn't come home for dinner, and Phil, who gets stoned every morning before work, and collects beer cans, and who is bewildered to discover malice in anyone, comes to tell her the *Lazy Day* is missing.

So Annie walks in glory in the watery sunset, watching the incoming tide. Bits of kelp and clamshells rinse in and out. At the place where the sky meets the water is a star that looks like a boat, or a boat that looks like a star. They won't find Scout, he'll make sure of that. He will have worked out a way not to be found, just to prove to her that he knew what he was talking about. All along he needed her to prove things to, and to be afraid for him. Annie says, "Scout." Even his name will be buried at sea. Annie thinks he'd like the idea. In a little while she'll go home and be sad about everything, but not just yet.

THE LITTLE HEART

Somewhere in Missouri the grass began to look hopeful. The trees budded and the winter clouds that had followed them all the way from Wisconsin softened and purpled, smelling of rain. Benny rolled down the car window and tested the air with her fingers. "Spring," she pronounced, then wrinkled her nose, as if spring were a dish needing more salt. "Give or take a few ice storms."

Pete, who was driving, only nodded and bore down on the road. He tended to be serious about driving. Benny wanted to call his attention to the leaves, the first chubby unborn clumps, invite him to watch their progress into full leaf as they drove south. She reminded herself severely that such instructive, proprietary remarks made you a pain in the ass, and people could see things for themselves. In the same way she had to avoid telling too many droll stories about her previous trips south: the Devil's Triangle around Senatobia, Mississippi, where she'd had two separate automotive breakdowns. The amusing incident with the New Orleans customs agent. Hotels she'd stayed in, meals she'd eaten, who she'd been in love with at the time and whether they'd been happy or angry, blissful or falling apart. Why should he care? She was mortally afraid of boring him, of becoming one of those nostalgic old broads who preened over their ancient glamour. Or so it would make her feel. Benny knew very well that she was glamorous—a glamorous, suspect, outlandish woman.

Sometime tomorrow, a couple hundred miles south, it would be warm enough to peel off their socks and regard their solemn toes. They'd feel the sun freckling their poor dusty winter skins. They'd even sweat. There would be redbuds and willow ribbons and azaleas, everything she remembered. It did not seem unreasonable to imagine this sort of happiness. It seemed like something you could allow yourself.

"Do you want me to drive?" she asked Pete, because he was stretching his spine, raising his legs then putting them down in exactly the same place, like a horse in a stall with nowhere to move. "Are you getting cranky?"

He raised his eyebrows, his quizzical face, the one he made whenever she fussed over him. He said that he was fine for now.

"In my youth," said Benny, "I aspired to drive myself everywhere. I think I was trying to prove something."

"Your car tracks to the left. When's the last time you got it aligned? Or have you ever?"

"I did once. I forget when. It always runs fine no matter what I do. I drive better cars these days. I find better drivers." She patted his knee. Idiocy kept spewing out of her. She didn't care. She was that happy.

"I think," said Pete, "that I will start calling you embarrassing pet names in public. Watch me."

"I dare you," said Benny. Oh, he was perfect. He knew when to ignore her and when not to. She was besotted with him.

Benny was a sculptor. She constructed large projects that sat in the plazas of large office buildings, bright steel beams and arches that jutted and curved and vaulted in the city airs. Witty, postmodern versions of monkey bars and totem poles. She was praised for creating the illusion of motion and energy out of heaviness and mass. Benny had tried to imagine Pete's face, the beautiful muscled grooves of his body, in plaster, clay, bronze, polymer, stone, discarding each in turn. No charcoal or oils. Maybe photography, straightforward stuff. She wouldn't want to settle for anything less than actualities. She wouldn't want to lose him in some artful image.

She had a pet name for him she would never say. *My little heart,* she thought. Little dalliance, circumscribed folly. Pete was twenty-six. Benny was forty-four. It was the last chance she would ever have to be besotted.

Benny did not look her age. (But then neither did Pete, who would get carded in bars for the next ten years.) She'd kept her figure, through nearly abusive discipline, and she hadn't gone crepey at the neck or eyes. She wore pretty shirts and jeans and funky, intricate jewelry. A handsome woman with dramatic, angled hair and a vivid mouth. The survival of her good looks—she allowed that there were moments, lights in which they'd even improved—gave her forebodings. It seemed like something that would have to be paid for sooner or later. She mistrusted the elegant apparition surfacing in her mirror, that amazing construction, her best art. Most of the time she felt none of the things she looked to be—smart, wry, knowing—as if she'd deceived herself as well as age, gotten too clever by half. Underneath it all she was merely a fond, foolish woman. She was a fraud waiting to be found out, just as age would catch her up eventually. Sometimes, perversely, she even looked forward to letting it all go, surrendering to corrugated skin and a thick waist. No more infernal vanity.

She would be shrunken and sexless and dignified, like Georgia O'Keeffe.

They spent the night in a motel in West Memphis, Arkansas. It was their first motel together. Pete wandered the room, switching things on and off. Benny tested the mattress, which was large but thin, like a slice of inferior bread. They ate dinner in the motel restaurant, which had crushed red velvet on the walls and gilded swag lamps with electric cords kinking through their festoons, and heroic menu prose ("zesty . . . robust . . . he-man portion").

"Cheeseburgers," declared Benny. "This is just fodder. We'll eat in New Orleans. Everything there's voluptuous and unwholesome. We'll fit right in."

The waitress came upon them then, stretching a polite face over Benny's remarks, which had been audible. She inscribed their zesty tangy crispy order and went off to enlighten the kitchen.

"You don't have to keep saying things like that," said Pete. "You don't have to make jokes."

"I don't ever know how to act around you. Motherly. Doting. Worldly wise and tolerant."

"I'm not an audition. You don't have to act. Drink your drink."

"You're wise beyond your years. Beyond mine too. I'm drinking, see?"

That night in the motel bed, the mattress cover puckered beneath them, like a skin gone loose from countless such rubbings. The smells were daunting: chilled breath of circulating air, musty pillow, furniture polish, an impersonal man-made stink that was probably the carpet. The strange room orbited around them, eclipsed, finally, by their own breath and skins. Later, Benny lay awake while Pete slept. She did not think there would be any sort of happy ending to the two of them. There would only be an ending. It appalled her to think of how much she was risking, if she did not keep some part of her wits about her.

The next day's driving went faster. They both liked Mississippi, finally someplace truly alien, with its red clay and pine jungles and balmy air and the little towns of softening boards. "Look at these hills," said Pete, marveling. When he lifted his chin to gaze around him, light touched the rim of his iris, turning it to green glass.

Benny, who was driving, decided to venture a story. "Once, about this time of year, I was driving home, north, with Stephen."

Pete nodded. He knew all about Stephen, which one he was— one of the husbands.

"There'd been a freak snow, six or eight inches. The roads were glazed like a skating rink. They didn't have any plows, of course, and only a few loads of sand to dump on the bridges for traction. I can't remember how long it took us to go how many miles, all the mythic details. We saw cars and trucks gone off the road, down at the bottom of the hills. And you'd see the same people inching alongside you for miles. There was one woman driving by herself. We kept passing her, though of course there must have been times we stopped and she passed us. She kept looking over at me. She looked like somebody trapped in a leaking submarine."

Pete made the sort of obliging, respectful noises one made in the presence of such stories. Benny saw again the woman's face, white and stiff as paper, terrified, alone. How many times in her life had Benny worn that face herself. In cars, or standing at darkened windows, or hurtling out of restaurants, or, on one occasion, thrashing up a hillside in a rainstorm, with mud sucking at her shoes. All those lost, black, betrayed times when she'd stood on some slippery edge, trying to decide whether or not she wished to throw herself over. And always there had been enough reason not to. She'd saved herself for revenge or consolation or some absolutely final calamity.

She supposed the woman in the car had survived also. Benny didn't remember if the storm had actually killed people. She thought of the woman now as a cautionary tale in this fat and happy time, when she herself was giddy in love and with a clear road ahead of her. Someday that woman's face would fix itself in her mirror, there to stay.

Pete had his own stories. Once he'd crashed a motorcycle, once he'd been arrested in Mexico, once he and some friends had gone rock climbing in Utah and watched smoke begin to curl around the base of their mountain, like the steaming edges of a bowl of soup. When Pete told his stories, he was animated but private. His eyes fixed on the air before him and he moved his shoulders back and forth, like shadow boxing. He told his stories in order to relive them, while Benny was always too aware of herself standing in front of a story, using it for high drama or sympathy. Pete was so straightforward, so without stratagems, so exactly as he appeared to be, she kept searching him for dark complications. So far she'd found none. He was clear all the way through, like a glass of water.

Her mind busied itself with the notions of clarity and substance, the nearly mathematical concentration that sculpture brought about in her. He had triggered some commotion in her regarding light, transparency, weight, and air. . . . He was speaking again, and Benny returned her attention, a little guilty at neglecting him.

"Isn't it weird," he said, "how the worst times make the best stories."

"These days," said Benny, "I want to know how the stories end first. Did you think you were going to die up on that mountain?"

"Wasn't time to think about it," said Pete, a truthful but unsatisfactory answer. He was a scientist, getting an advanced degree in microbiology. There were times he was all too empirical.

The hotel in New Orleans was an 1840s townhouse restored to near-modern comfort. It had elegant stairways and a patio with ferns and palms dripping into a brackish pool. "Like it?" asked Benny. He had to like it. She couldn't stand it if he didn't. Panicked, she realized he would have to like the whole city, everything about it, in proper measure.

"It's perfect," said Pete. "It reminds me of an old movie house."

"Lie down with me for a minute," said Benny. She couldn't say a word more. These days tides of feeling either ripped through her at unpredictable moments or dropped her like a poleaxed cow.

Once she'd even fainted at a party, which was embarrassing but not as bad as it could have been. She was sitting at a table and slumped heavily onto her leaning arm. It felt like falling for miles through black space lit with whistling stars. There were times with Pete when Benny wondered if she was in love or suffering neurological distress, or if the two were akin.

They sat in an oyster bar looking out from the shadowed interior, with its sweat-polished wooden chairs and tables, and revolving fans and humid frying smells, to the bright street. The sun flattened everything, like an abstract painting—white cement and masonry squares, black oblong shadows. Pete wanted to see the river, so they strolled through the tourist crowds and portrait painters and street musicians and a rank of carriages and patient mules wearing straw hats, past the stores selling pralines and fluorescent necklaces and mammy dolls and T-shirts and edible panties, out to the Decatur Street walkway and a view of the brown water. As always, the river made Benny think of soap and metals. The Father of Waters. The National Sink. "It's all sort of like a big sleazy Disneyland, isn't it," said Pete. Benny was glad that he seemed amused by the sleaze, or at least he didn't think less of her for it.

They were holding hands, a little self-consciously, because they'd never done it before. Back home the layers of gloves and mittens made it seem pointless, and they had not known each other in any different season. Pete's hand curled in hers like a pet, or a child's hand. Benny had a sudden unwelcome vision of her son Marcus, a fifteen-year-old who lived with his father in Arizona and did not like her much anymore. When he was a little boy he'd clung to her in crowds, hobbling her knees and crying wetly into her legs. She remembered his weight in her arms the way a mouth remembers tasting.

Now his child's terrors had grown a sullen skin, and he disapproved of his mother for being handsome and quirky and accomplished. That is, for everything others admired, as well as for liking to drink and divorcing his father and enraging him with her every word. Sometimes he shouted at her, things like "Jesus, do you have to *laugh* like that?" At one time he'd fitted inside her like the meat of a walnut; now everything he did and thought and said was in perfect opposition to her. When Pete no longer wished to touch her, she'd know it right away. How that felt.

This time the dizziness began in her skin. She was sweating everywhere all at once. Her legs stopped moving. It seemed she could not sweat and walk at the same time. Her hand fell to her side and she closed her eyes, feeling herself majestically tall and toppling, a tree being felled. "Timber," she said, or tried to say. She could still see the image of the street behind her eyelids, reversed like a negative, black with exploding white spots.

Then the moment passed, and she righted herself. "Ben?" Pete was steering her toward a chair at an open-air cafe; she wanted to tell him it was one of the bad, overpriced ones. There were tears in her eyes, called up along with her skin's weeping.

"I was thinking of Marcus," she said for an explanation, not wanting to go into the rest of it. "When I saw him at Christmas he'd shaved the sides of his head. There were boils on the back of his neck and he was wearing an army jacket—a camouflage jacket, with no shirt underneath. I swear he had makeup on, black stuff under his eyes. This is only the part of him that *shows*. What do you think he actually *does*?"

"What? Slow down. Don't try and talk."

"I asked him what he wanted for Christmas. He said bolt cutters."

"Shh."

"He's disfigured himself so I won't love him. He thinks that'll do it."

She did stop talking then. The sadness leadened her mouth. She understood entirely why her son had to try to separate himself from her. Her love for him could stop her in her tracks in the street, and had turned him into a scarred freak. She could never restrain it, keep it damped down, contained, channeled, her love a network of spiky veins, a river of blood spilling over its banks.

She told Pete the sun had gotten to her. She was fine now, just tired. She smiled her tired smile. Pete was studying her, as he did on occasion, with the same face he must use for peering into microscopes. She was so far outside of his previous experience that she might as well be an escapee from a bestiary. She saw that he was making allowances for her, deciding not to worry yet. And surely there was nothing to worry about, just these little blips of dread and foreboding, age, loss, death, change of life, end of life, hysteria, brain tumor. Calamity descending as blinding light or blinding dark, as heat or blizzard. She grinned it all down. It was true that she was tired.

And by evening, after a nap, she felt much better. At dinner in the superlative restaurant, she gobbled happily through the expensive menu. "Will you still love me when I'm fat?" Benny asked, and Pete said he'd think about it. She wanted to remember everything forever, except you never did, and that was what her art was for her, the thing that kept you from dying entirely because it forgot nothing.

Afterward they wandered mazily outside, through a courtyard of azaleas and shaggy climbing vines, the mingled smells of swamp, river, ocean. On the streets crowds circled and shuffled. They circumvented a man carrying a tuba wrapped in duct tape and, farther on, an old woman dressed in a silver motorcycle helmet and a trailing witch's gown. Her long white hair hung down beneath the helmet like something spilled.

Benny threw her head back to the sky. She was at least a little drunk. She imagined aiming herself straight up, like a rocket. She said, "I have had to invent my whole life out of nothing. I mean I didn't have a clue. A sculptor, what was that? It was the last thing on my mind. Nobody tells you how to be a madwoman who hangs out in foundries. Or lugs around oxygen tanks and won't stay married. Nobody tells you how to live that kind of a life."

"What?" said Pete. He was looking out at the crowds as he walked, giving her the edge of his attention. "Well, it all paid off, didn't it?"

He meant, reasonably, her commissions, grants, reviews, credentials. All the things that validated her, that could be produced on demand. "No," Benny said. "I mean my *life*." She was a rocket, a neon dragonfly; she was in a nearly oracular state of drunkenness. "You are the most beautiful creature. Hush. You are. I'm crazy about you. Throwing caution to the winds here. Do you know I've been menstruating for longer than you've been alive?"

He was waiting politely for her to stop. Benny thought it served him right to be embarrassed; he deserved it for being a man and always making too much sense. That seemed funny also. "Let's head out on the town now," she said. "Let's mix it up."

In the morning Benny woke up with a hangover that aged her ten years. Her eyes fell open to a blurred view of Pete's untroubled shoulder rising out of the humid sheets. She had spent some measurable portion of her life watching men sleep, as if their sleep was a code that could be cracked with patience.

In the bathroom she applied hot and cold waters, aspirin, mouthwash. She looked brittle and post-operative. She left a note for Pete and went out in search of coffee. It was early, not yet eight. Workers were hosing down the sidewalks, which smelled of bleach and garbage.

Shakily, inhaling coffee steam, Benny concluded that she had to stop drinking so much. Drinking always dredged up the messy and inconvenient heart of her. She had a heart like a Twinkie, full of oversweet goo, yes, a real junk-food heart. She needed prudence, the middle ground—some balance between caution and fear, love and death, weight and nothingness—but already she was confusing things. In any case she would watch her drinking.

That afternoon they sat on the hotel patio, under the shabby palms, yawning over the newspapers. The air was so warm and dank, it was nearly molten. Pete too felt hungover and convalescent, which cheered Benny some.

The hotel's proprietor, a juiceless old man in bedroom slippers and with a belly like a cantaloupe, stopped by their table to determine if they were worth being nosy about, if they were exactly what he thought they were. He had one of those puddingy southern accents, the kind that always sounded fake to her, too much like the movies, except it was the real thing.

Pete was polite to him, as he always was to annoying people, or maybe he did not find them as annoying as Benny did. She sat behind her sunglasses, not bothering to talk. Benny thought the old man's curiosity was natural. She tried to see the two of them, her and Pete, the way other people must. They were like one of those puzzle pictures that shifted perspective each time you looked at it. Were they mother and son, or lovers, or something else entirely? One or both of them was always throwing the image off, putting it out of focus, looking too old or too young. Some haze of sex surrounded them, interfering with radar.

The landlord, having asked them all the pointless questions he could think of regarding weather and travel and sightseeing, limped off, disappointed. Benny yawned. The air was milky with humidity. "Old nuisance."

"He's harmless."

"I don't like being gawked at."

"You just don't like it from close up."

Benny glanced over at him, trying to decide if she had to take offense at that, and decided he had been only funny. "What is it you like about me anyway? I bet all your other girls were cheerleaders."

"You're wrong about everything," said Pete, unperturbed.

The next day was their last full one in the city. There were the plantation tours, and swamp tours and cemetery tours, but all they had to do was mention them to run out of energy. Pete surprised her by saying he wanted to go to the aquarium. It was a new, state-of-the-art aquarium, with hundreds (or perhaps it was thousands) of species, instructional exhibits, the works.

"Won't it be crowded?" Benny asked. The thought of crowds and galloping children made her feel languid. But she was curious about the things that excited Pete. Sometimes she missed that in him. He was so even-tempered as to seem phlegmatic, at least by comparison to herself, which, she noted, was hardly a norm. Perhaps he was merely a normal, pleasant young man who was amused and bemused by her, and that ought to be enough. What depths, what core there was in him was everywhere displayed, like the heart of light itself.

The aquarium was a marvel, she had to admit, a fish palace made of echoes and glass and space. There were grottos and great halls of arching concrete, filtered sunlight and blue underwater glow. The air held whiffs of kelp, mold, and brine. The crowds were just as bad as Benny had imagined. They pressed you up against the glass like the fish bumping the edge of their tanks, so that there were two habitats, one air, one water, carved out of the same space. Certainly it made her feel creature-like and edgy to be so jostled along.

A transparent tunnel led them to the first exhibit. Overhead fish cruised in the glassy span, darting flickers of yellow and purple, like underwater parrots. Rays with flattened mouths, flopping turtles. Light bubbled through the glass and water, dazzling her. With an effort Benny squinted upward, wondering what it was about this place that so oppressed her. Claustrophobia? Or so much furious, thrashing life on both sides of the glass?

Pete read every exhibit label, unlike Benny, who kept pushing in and out of line, looking for places to sit down. She knew he wouldn't mind if she wandered, or even acted uninterested, as long as she was there. She watched the jawfish, which were like big pale goldfish, heaping up piles of pebbles, and the uglier blowfish with their blind-looking eyes. In a separate, freestanding tank, a school of blunt-faced aluminum-colored fish swam round and round in a mad circle, as if in hectic pursuit. What was the point? she thought wearily. You thrashed about and declaimed and made mistakes and then you made them all over again. You loved people too much or not enough. She couldn't remember ever feeling so tired in her life.

Pete joined her, giving the aluminum-colored fish an alert, dis-interested look, steering her toward the next hall. "Rain forest," he read from the guide. "How are you holding up?"

"Fine," she said automatically. "The gift shop sells seafood cookbooks. Doesn't that strike you as sick?"

"If people want to eat fish, they need to conserve the oceans. Makes sense."

"It's morbid."

"It's only food," said Pete lightly. They gazed into a tank full of horrid twining eels, green, faceless, gouged mouths collapsing in on themselves. Benny couldn't catch her breath. The rain-forest room was a net of gray moisture. "These fish from around here?" she heard a plaintive voice ask from the crowd. Benny gritted her teeth. She was not going to give in to her body's distress, not here, where if you went down you might molder and rot, get pitched out in a black plastic bag like the rest of the specimens.

She could go to a doctor when she went home and get her brain scanned, her fluids desalinated, her glands squeezed. Have the kind of tests that made you feel you were being autopsied. There was a tank of surprisingly mild-looking piranhas; there were loops of snakes and tiny little poisonous frogs like china figurines, black with turquoise mottles. Everything in the place could kill you. Eventually she would go to a doctor, who would tell her she was imagining things. But eventually doctors told you things you didn't want to hear—that you were dying and had been all along.

Thinking it cleared her head, as if the world slowed and emptied itself, as if she'd said "so what" and was free now to move on to other matters. The world had become the space before her eyes, and she was suddenly attentive. A young man who was not her child was leaning against a square of glass, and a shadow self reached out of the glass to him, joining hands. He couldn't see the reflection but she could. He was looking into a tank of sharks, small brown sharks like a pack of dogs. The sharks passed behind the reflected face; it wavered, then grew visible once more, holding steady. It seemed a remarkable sight to her, the beautiful shadow and the ugly fish existing in the same plane. Then the young man turned and smiled at her, his perfect smile, real once more.

Benny smiled back and pointed to the door. She would go on a little ahead, it was understood.

She wanted to register everything: these children smudging the glass, that lovely flower-faced young woman dressed in white, the sort of young woman the young man would fall in love with someday. Penguins and electric eels, knife fish, flashlight fish, lumps of coral, mermaid's purses, paddlefish, alligators. Catfish and sturgeon, snakes and crawfish. All the creatures of the seas and mires. In her own body she felt an itch and a flutter, as if the creatures swam and flopped and glided within her too. Extraordinary feeling. She was full to the brim. When she walked, she splashed. Tomorrow, driving home, wave after wave of spring would follow them north.

MERCY

Beowulf had something cornered in the back garden and was letting the world know about it. It was mechanical, indefatigable, neighbor-aggravating noise—the sound of a dog in ecstasy. Quinn set out across the yard to shut him up. The morning was gray, foggy, and the shifting mists made it hard for him to see all the way to the fence. Beowulf's excited tail and rigid hindquarters were circling a small pale lump of fur. A cat, Quinn thought at first, but moving closer, he saw it was a possum.

A youngish, underfed-looking possum. It was hunkered down in a corner of the fence, its long mouth hanging open, hissing. Not all possums played possum, Quinn knew. Lucky for this one it hadn't tried. Beowulf liked to toss them around by the neck until they were well and truly dead, not just pretending. Stupid animals, possums. Ugly too, thought Quinn, surveying this one. Unclean, rat-like, yellow-drab fur, naked tail, little glittering eyes and pointed snout. It looked like it was made up out of all the leftover parts no other animal wanted. The foggy morning must have made it feel invisible, safe, or else it was hungry enough at the end of the long winter to be incautious.

Quinn got himself between Beowulf and the possum and caught the dog by the collar. Farther down the fence there was enough space between the boards and the ground to allow the thing to escape. The possum's mouth gaped again, panting, baring its teeth, not yet aware it was out of danger. What did possums eat? Insects, grubs, garbage? There was nothing on earth as useless as a possum. But it pleased him that it was ugly and useless, and that he had saved it anyway. It was a completely gratuitous act of mercy.

"Cut it out," he said to Beowulf, who was still barking, twisting the collar tighter and choking himself. Quinn dragged him across the waste of shredded-wheat grass and frozen mud that was his yard in February. Spring was weeks away, but he always felt hopeful this time of year, waiting for the promise to be kept.

Once he got Beowulf inside the kitchen, the dog turned his attention to his empty food dish, batting it from one corner to another with his nose. He was a three-year-old black Lab, and food was his god. He'd go to fat if Quinn didn't watch him. "You're a complete moron," Quinn told him. "And a big fat slob." He could have gone on berating him affectionately, but there were times when the sound of his solitary voice irritated him. As if people would be able to tell by looking at him that he had most of his important conversations with a dog. When it came time, they would probably bury him with a dog.

He worked nights, a city cop on the graveyard shift, so mornings were the time when he took the dog to the park, did errands, and cleaned up around the house. At noon he put Beowulf out in the yard and laid himself down in bed, hoping for no more possum invasions, or at least, none he couldn't sleep through. He woke a little after six, showered, fixed himself dinner, and watched television. This was his normal routine. Thursdays and Fridays were his days off, and then he got himself off track trying to stay awake during daylight, so as to feel more like the rest of the world.

He got to the station with enough time to read the log and the new reports before his shift began. DUIs and domestic complaints, car accidents, the constant high and low tides of drugs. A sixteen-year-old kid had climbed forty feet up a high-voltage tower and threatened to jump because his girlfriend broke up with him. He'd been talked down and taken into protective custody, a psychiatric hospital.

"You should have seen this guy," said one of the second-shifters, reading over Quinn's shoulder. "He had purple hair and a nose ring. And his girlfriend had a shaved head."

"They should get back together. Definitely."

"It's this Kurt Cobain thing. They all want to kill themselves now."

"Why don't they save it for day shift," said Quinn. This was a running gag, a rivalry. Day shift was traffic stops and senior citizens who hear noises in their basements. Things heated up after dark, and graveyard was when the bars closed, the drunks drove, and the crazies came out to play.

Quinn had been on graveyard for four years, since his marriage ended, and there was no reason for him to be home during normal hours. He was used to it by now; it even suited him. This smallish city, with its sized-to-scale crimes, suited him. Homicides and truly ghoulish happenings were infrequent. He was glad for that because he did not wish to become inured to such things. At the same time he knew that ordinary human meanness and folly, the kind he saw on a regular basis, were what wore you down and took the air out of you.

Last week he'd been called to an all-night grocery for a shoplifting complaint. The manager and a stockboy had the guy up against a wall at the back of the store, like another sort of possum. A little crowd had gathered, as much of a crowd as you could get in such a place at one A.M., leaning over their shopping carts. The shoplifter was a tall man with a bald head and a fuzz of gray curls around his ears. A red birthmark on his forehead, like a bruise on fruit. Something off-center, misshapen about his mouth.

When Quinn walked up, the manager stepped aside. "Cat food," he said, in tones of disgust and disbelief. "Joker has about ten cans of cat food up his sleeves."

"Let's see," said Quinn, taking a step forward and patting him down. "Would you remove your jacket, sir?"

The jacket was blue nylon, slick at the elbows, the kind of generic garment sold in racks of fifty at the Farm and Fleet. The shoplifter allowed the coat to be taken from him. Cans dropped from the sleeves like silver dollars and rolled across the floor. "What's your name?"

The shoplifter looked glassy, dazed, his face pulled into a knot by the misshapen mouth. The ranks of fluorescent lights overhead cast no shadows. It was always unblinking noon here, noon on some ugly planet. A drizzling sound made Quinn look down. A puddle collected beneath the shoplifter's pant leg, spreading across the tile floor. The front of his trousers darkened.

"Jesus Christ," said the manager, and sent the stockboy for a mop. The little crowd of watchers dispersed in a hurry, not wanting to see more.

"Tell us your name," Quinn said again. "Nobody's going to hurt you." The man was damaged in some way, simpleminded, that was clear enough.

"Tiger." It came out *Thigoo,* as if his tongue took up too much space in his mouth.

"That's your name?"

"Tiger had kittens."

Quinn looked at the manager, who shrugged in an irritated

way. Quinn said, "You want to file charges?" He was thinking of the man's wet pants, of having to put him in the squad.

"I want all the weirdo idiots in the world to stay out of my store."

In the end the man went shuffling off into the night, back to wherever lives like his were lived out. Quinn was glad he didn't have to learn any more about him. The job made you accumulate all sorts of dispiriting knowledge: what implements people used when they beat their children, which of the town's motels rented rooms no questions asked, how the bones of a broken nose could protrude through the skin, where people went when they wanted to trade a stolen VCR for a twenty-dollar rock of crack. There were times Quinn regretted all the other kinds of knowledge he might have acquired, if only he'd led a different life. How to grow orchard fruit, perhaps, or be a really good mechanic.

Tonight was a Monday, and he could expect a slow shift if people stayed home and behaved themselves, if nothing much burned or collided. He didn't feel like chasing crack heads or being cussed out by both sides in a fight. He'd never been injured on the job, although there were times he'd come close, times he'd had to suck it up, run, stick his face in the dirt, push the bile back down his throat, times he walked up to a car he'd pulled over for a traffic stop and could quite clearly imagine a gun held just below his line of vision.

It was still cold and clouded over, a dead sky that reflected no light. Quinn balanced a cup of coffee as he patrolled. The city was divided into eight zones, each of them covered by at least one squad, with two or three more cars at large, able to provide backup as needed. Quinn's beat was the far northwest section of the city, encompassing the shopping mall out on a spur of the interstate, the semi-slums that surrounded it, a handful of stores that sold tires and discount carpets and power equipment, and one brave subdivision of pale brick ranch houses with forests of sticks planted in the front yards.

He cruised the shopping mall, locked down tight, like a city abandoned long ago by a tribe of concrete worshippers. Dispatch sent him to check out a report of loud music, gone quiet by the time he arrived, and someone who'd driven off without paying for gas, also gone. By two A.M. he was beginning to feel cautiously lucky, too soon, it turned out, because Dispatch came back on with a report of a woman being threatened by her teenage son.

Weapons? he wanted to know, but Dispatch was vague, could only provide him with name and address. The woman had called 911 and said her son was acting crazy, screaming at her, she was afraid of him. Drugs, Quinn thought. Pain-in-the-ass kids on drugs. He was only a mile or so away and he kept the radio connection open until he got there. Bonnie Livengood was the woman's name. Mrs. Livengood and her little boy Gary.

The house was one of a line of small bungalows, each set on its fringe of lawn only a few yards back from the street. It was stucco, some uncertain pastel color, the walls damp-stained. Such houses were never meant to be anything more than boxes with roofs, even when they were built thirty years ago. The streets had names like Rainbowview and Sunnyside and Queensway, names which fooled nobody. A neighborhood of people barely making it, or not making it. People who kept ungainly dogs chained to their front porches, who had the diseases of poverty (TB, goiter, impetigo), who might steal or might just as often be stolen from. All in all, a neighborhood that Quinn would find himself visiting on a regular basis.

In one house on the block a television flickered blue behind the front window. Everything else was dark and quiet except for the Livengood household, which was sending out an overamped bass throbbing, a menacing, subterranean noise. Lights were on, not two A.M. lights, but the wide-awake sort, almost as obtrusive as the music. A new-looking black Camaro sat in the driveway, and Quinn pulled up next to it, keeping his engine running.

He rang the bell, then knocked. This close the music had words in it, or shreds of words. Not rap, but some head-banging techno-punk heavy-metal crap. He knocked again, louder.

The door was opened by a thin, redheaded woman in a pink T-shirt and sweatpants. The mother, he supposed, though she looked too young for that. "Mrs. Livengood?"

She opened her mouth to speak, but just then the music took a jump in volume that Quinn wouldn't have thought possible. She shook herself convulsively, like someone trying to shake off flies, turned, and stalked to the back of the house. A moment later the music stopped, leaving a stinging silence, and half the lights went out.

"FUCKING BITCH!"

Gary Livengood charged out of the dark bedroom, heading for the kitchen, but stopped short when he saw Quinn. He was fifteen or sixteen or seventeen, a tall skinny kid with his hair cut in bristles. "Goddamn fucking bitch," he said, not willing or able to shut himself up entirely, but sounding more tentative. Quinn relaxed a notch. The boy was nothing to worry seriously about.

The mother came back out then, looking edgy and somehow pleased with herself. "Don't think I raised him up to be so nasty," she said. "This is his own idea."

The boy folded his mouth into a line and shoved his jaw out, a ludicrous face that made him look even younger. Quinn addressed him. "Were you threatening her?"

"No."

"I'd like to know what you call it, then."

"What did he do?"

"Put his fist through the bathroom wall. You can go see it for yourself. Then he started in on the furniture." She indicated a three-legged chair propped against a wall, and a sofa cushion disgorging its stuffing like fuzzy cauliflower, things Quinn might have taken for normal household features. The rest of the room was dim, disordered, either as a result of the fight or because it was always that way. The woman—Bonnie, he remembered—pointed out the wreckage with a spiteful, nearly triumphant air. She wasn't young, as he'd first imagined, but she was one of those women who still kept some part of the girl in them. Thin white arms, hair in a ponytail. It increased Quinn's impression that he was refereeing a child's argument, something the two of them engaged in on a regular basis.

Quinn turned to the boy. "What's this all about?"

"She took my car keys."

"Like he needs to be going anywhere this time of night."

"It's my car! I paid for it!"

"When you can afford to keep gas in the tank and get the muffler fixed and pay for the insurance, then it'll be your car."

"God," said the boy. "Somebody ought to hit her."

"That's enough of that," said Quinn.

The woman asked Quinn, "You have any kids?"

"No ma'am."

"You should give thanks for that," she said, her mouth shaking. "You should get down on your knees on a daily basis."

"God," said the boy again. He seemed unable, just then, to come up with anything worse.

"He was a darling baby," the woman said. "You know what he used to tell me? 'I love you, little mommy.' Isn't that the sweetest thing?"

The boy gave Quinn a sideways, hateful look, although Quinn knew it had nothing to do with him, only with the boy's shame and impotence and messed-up self. He knew how he must appear to the boy, and to everyone else who found themselves having to answer to the law in their own living rooms. A face that only went along with a uniform, a symbol of the arbitrary power that someone or something held over their lives. He said, "Let's step outside a minute, Gary."

"What for?"

"I want to talk to you. Come on. Grab your coat."

Neither the woman nor the boy was pleased with this, he could tell. They'd wanted something grander, something involving more noise and threats. The woman started slapping at her pockets, looking for cigarettes, ignoring them both, as if Quinn had sided against her.

Quinn held the door open and followed the boy out. "Let's sit in the car," he said, and when they were both settled, asked, "How old are you?"

"Seventeen. Almost." The boy dragged the words out of some vast reserve of boredom. He was tapping one hand on his knee, as if he was still listening to the music and the conversation was only a distraction. But Quinn had made up his mind to speak as if he were being listened to.

"You go to Central?" The boy dipped his head, still tapping. "A junior, huh?"

Another nod. Something theatrical and unconvincing about his disinterest. He probably had pot or worse back in his bedroom and didn't want it found. All the wise guys, all of them doing imitations of sullen rock stars who were imitating James Dean, though they probably didn't know that.

Quinn said, "What do you aim to do with yourself when you're all through with school?"

"Move out."

"You have some kind of a job in mind?"

The kid shrugged, meaning that even if he knew what he was going to do, he wouldn't tell him. Quinn saw often enough what happened to kids like this one. If they were lucky they went into the service and stayed alive long enough to grow a brain. If they weren't lucky they accumulated enough small and large trouble to land themselves in Joliet or Stateville. He said, "How smart are you?"

"What?"

"Simple question. You think you're smart?"

"I do OK."

"I don't just mean school. I mean not-screwing-up smart."

"If you think I'm stupid, just say so."

The boy's voice had a challenging, gladdened edge to it, as if he'd in fact been told this any number of times and was now on familiar turf. The ugly haircut showed the bumps and ridges of his skull. Quinn thought it was possible he was neither ugly nor stupid, had only adopted the pose as a kind of protective coloration.

Quinn said, "You have to be smart enough to figure out which fights aren't worth getting into. Like with your mother. Like letting things get this out of control."

"She's crazy. She fucked up her life already so now she wants to fuck up mine, just to keep her company."

"So don't let her. Don't get into it with her."

"It's my car! It's my name on all the papers!"

"Fine. But don't tear up the house. If I have to come out here again, we'll go down to the station. Now you better get yourself inside to bed. You have school tomorrow, right? Ask your mother to come out here a minute."

The boy stayed put a moment longer, not sure things were really over. Then he shoved his way out of the car and into the house, taking his time, just to show he didn't give a shit about any of it.

Quinn waited for Bonnie Livengood. This was one more occasion when he had a choice of doing too much or too little, pretending anything he said would make a difference. Of course the boy would pay no attention. He would sink or swim on his own.

The passenger door opened and Bonnie Livengood climbed in. The dome light showed her to be wearing a coat made out of some blanket-like material, red, with a vaguely southwestern, vaguely Indian pattern. She shivered and huddled inside it, turning the collar up. "We couldn't talk inside?" she asked, her voice flat and displeased.

"Gives everybody a chance to cool off."

"Freeze, you mean."

"Tell me about Gary."

She only shook her head. She was working her way up to a good mad, like the boy. "Where's his father?"

"It was what you call a starter marriage."

"Beg pardon?"

"Human beings are getting more and more like the rest of the animal kingdom. The males only come around in breeding season." She turned to look at him. "My opinion."

"You're entitled to it."

"What's that supposed to mean?"

"Why don't you just tell me about Gary."

"You think this is easy? Calling the cops on my own kid? Having some total stranger walk into the middle of my shitty life?"

The radio crackled then, Dispatch asking him to check in. Quinn reached for it, told them he was still on scene, settled back in the seat. The silence held. He fixed his gaze on the house, noticed that someone had driven a car into the front wall and left a big soft-looking gouge in the stucco. He was waiting to see if the woman would start in again, wondered if she'd been drinking.

But she only rubbed at her eyes with the back of her hand. "What time is it?"

"Almost three."

"So if I fell asleep this second, I could get almost four hours of shut-eye before I go in to work."

"Where do you work?"

"R and K." Quinn gave her a questioning look. "The vacuum cleaner place. Over by Target. Somebody's got to work there." She only sounded sullen now. She yawned. "Wish I was a cop instead and got paid for shooting people."

Quinn thought there was something brittle, unpredictable about her. Not alcohol, he decided. Exhausted nerves, maybe. "Has Gary been in trouble before?"

"Yes. No. Nothing big. Drinking beer on the golf course. Driving around with his yahoo buddies after curfew. I don't want to talk about him. I'm sick of him."

Quinn reached for his clipboard and asked her the details of names, ages, social security numbers. Bonnie Livengood was thirty-eight, she said, making a little wry mouth. "Is this all stuff you're going to put in the newspaper or something?"

"It's only for my report."

"I was just wondering. I'm way beyond caring who knows how old I am or how I look or anything. You get to that point."

"You look just fine." He immediately regretted saying it. It would sound either false and perfunctory, or else overpersonal.

She hadn't heard him, or perhaps she chose not to. She said, "Cigarettes. I would be out of cigarettes at a time like this. That child never lacked for food, toys, anything. Even that stupid car. I did everything one person could. Now what. You tell me."

"Any signs he's using drugs?"

She shrugged. "Wouldn't surprise me none."

"There are some social services I can refer you to if you'd like. Family counseling. Youth programs, drug education. That sort of thing. If you'd like to give them a try. Sometimes it can help." When she didn't answer he looked up from his clipboard and saw that she was asleep.

She hadn't moved or changed position, but her head sagged against the headrest, heavy, pinned back by gravity. Her mouth drooped open. Quinn went to put a hand on her shoulder, wake her up, but stopped himself. Let her rest. She'd wake herself up in a minute. He finished with his report. Checked with Dispatch. Nothing doing out there. He spent some time on the radio with the other squads, just bullshitting, thinking the sound of voices might wake her, but she slept on. The idling engine sent its steady warm breath across them. If he'd wanted to he could have driven off with her, carried her sleeping through the sleeping city, returned her to her own door without her knowing any of it.

He studied her, the small-boned child's face with the overlay of fine wrinkles around the eyes. She must have been pretty once, was still pretty around the edges. Her bright hair was pulled back so you could see the clean gloss of it.

He'd never been a good sleeper himself, even before he started working nights. He'd doze, wake himself on and off, as if sleep were a shallow sea he was unable to completely submerge in. Sometimes he got up and watched television. More often he simply lay awake, floating on the sea's surface. His wife hadn't liked him watching her while she slept. "Don't do that," she'd say if she woke up and found him at it. "Don't look at me when I can't tell you're doing it." When he'd asked, reasonably, what possible difference it would make, how she'd even know, she said, "Just don't. It's creepy. It's like being in some vampire movie."

His wife was always coming up with complicated reasons for being mad at him. She was a PE teacher at the high school, a tall girl with slim strong legs and a pirate's grin. After school and on weekends, she played in volleyball and softball leagues, and coached a gymnastics club at the Y. Quinn spent a lot of time in gyms and ballparks, rooting her on. After the games all the people on the teams, and all the husbands and wives, went out to the taverns. Sometimes they got together for picnics or birthday parties. Quinn got along fine with everybody. There was always a lot of laughing and carrying on and easy friendship, the kind you get with drinking.

Driving back from these occasions Quinn and his wife would be quiet, regretful. If they had to spend too much time together alone, they got into fights. The fights were about nothing at all, things like what he'd meant by using a certain tone of voice, and whether or not he had been ignoring her when he turned on the television one night last week. His wife told him he was "unwilling to work on the marriage," and he told her that sounded like something out of one of her dopey magazines and that he hadn't thought getting married was like a job. He knew she was disappointed with him, but couldn't say so plainly. He was disappointed too, after the first year or so. They were irritated with each other for being ordinary and unexceptional, as if they had been promised more. Neither of them had known one thing about each other, or themselves. His wife was superficial and childish, full of mysterious grievances, but he could remember a time when she'd seemed infinite and desirable. He was a fool and he deserved a fool's comeuppance.

After the divorce he lost touch with the people from the sports teams. His wife remarried and moved to Chicago. He did not often find himself thinking about her, except at times like these, when his life slowed down, seemed to sag between two points, an inconsequential past and a weary future. He was not really conscious of the woman next to him, did not realize he was staring at her, or that she had opened her eyes and was staring back at him.

"What happened?" she asked.

"Nothing. You fell asleep."

She sat up, passed a hand over her hair to straighten it, gave him a last mistrustful look, and got out of the car. She let herself in the front door of the now-quiet house. He waited a few minutes more. He half-expected her to come back out, finish their conversation. But the house stayed as silent as a closed mouth. Quinn backed out of the driveway and drove off.

And that was the inconclusive end of things, at least for that night. Spring arrived, tentative and muddy. Grass emerged from the cold earth. Quinn measured time by shifts and shifts' ends. It was a night in late April when he answered an accident call west of town, on a two-lane country road bordered by farm fields.

An ambulance was already there, as well as a fire-and-rescue unit and two other squads. A new-looking black Camaro lay humped and misshapen on the far side of the ditch. It had rolled at least once, by the look of it. The hood was buckled and the roof creased, so the car sat right side up, but gaping, cockeyed, crazed. The rear axle was knocked loose and the body of the car rested on it like a broken toy.

Quinn set up his squad to block the road at the near end of the scene and watched from a little distance the fire-and-rescue team trying to cut through the crumpled metal skin of the passenger side door. It was taking longer than they wanted it to; one of the paramedics was reaching in through the smashed windshield, working on whoever was inside. When they finally did get him out—a kid in jeans and a T-shirt—Quinn heard someone saying it was his face, couldn't they do something about his face? A few dozen yards away from the wreck was a body covered with a blue plastic sheet. A second ambulance had arrived and was backing up to it in an unhurried way.

Quinn walked over to another officer. "What have you got?"

"Two white male juveniles."

"No shit," said Quinn. As if they were ever anything else. He asked about the boy who'd been pulled out of the car.

"He hit the windshield coming and going. He might make it. Car smells like a damn brewery."

Quinn said nothing. There was nothing he could have said that would not have been obvious, inadequate. He turned away from the wreckage and the halogen-lit ambulance crews. The sky was blind and black after the lights. The fields were newly planted and bare. The air smelled of gasoline and scorched rubber. He felt angry and unquiet, as he always did when such things happened, at the stupid waste of it all, wasted life, love, grief. He stayed until the ambulances left, and the tow truck fastened the wreck back together with chains and hauled it off, and the road was swept clean of sparkling glass. He was the last one to leave, and he walked back to his car along the shoulder of the dark road. He kept thinking there should be more you could say. Something like prayer but that wouldn't embarrass anyone.

He hadn't recognized the car. He didn't recognize the name of the dead boy the first time he saw it. It was the end of his shift and he was back at the station, blinking in the morning glare, finishing up his paperwork. He stared at the name, his eyes trying to tell his brain something. Once it registered he looked up at the officer standing next to him at the counter. "I knew this kid."

"What kid?"

Quinn pointed to the paper. "Shit," the man said respectfully, and Quinn explained himself.

"I went out on a call a while back. His mother and him were having a ruckus."

The man said Yeah? He asked about the accident, what had happened, and Quinn spent some time telling him. He would have liked to talk about the boy, his dangerous, absurd fury; how when Quinn had seen him, he'd instantly thought of him as doomed, even expendable; how that obscurely shamed him now. He wondered who'd called Bonnie Livengood. Probably someone from the hospital. That was the way they usually did things.

That evening there was a brief death notice in the paper, saying that funeral arrangements were incomplete. Though Quinn watched for it, he didn't see any other obituary. Three or four days after the accident, he drove past the house. He'd never seen it in daylight. It was just as small and dispirited as before. The exterior was a chalky, light-orange color, an unnatural shade he associated with certain medicines from his childhood. There was no car in the driveway and the curtains were drawn. He wasn't even sure why he was there. He wouldn't have gone up and knocked or anything.

The next week, on his day off, he went to the R and K Vacuum Service. It was a storefront in a flat-roofed building on the outer orbit of a parking lot. He opened the door and stepped inside a crowded, hutchlike space full of people and talk, six or seven people, none of them Bonnie Livengood. The walls and floor were jammed with vacuums and vacuum parts—hoses, belts, bags, brushes, all manner of plastic appendages—a brief impression of disproportionate clutter.

At the tiny back counter three men were laughing over something. "Help you?" one of them asked Quinn, and he made his way toward them. They were sitting on chairs and cardboard boxes, listening to a radio. There was an ashtray with a cigarette burning down, a can of 7-Up, the sports section spread open, as if they were all gathered chummily around a bar. Quinn asked if Mrs. Livengood was working there today.

"Miss-us Livengood," said the man behind the counter,

drawling the name out. He had a red, pitted complexion and blond unconvincing hair, like a wig. He tilted back in his chair. "Hey, Bon?" Turning around to Quinn he said, "She's probly in the bathroom."

Quinn nodded. He waited, letting them look him over. It didn't seem like the kind of business that needed half a dozen people to run it. Most likely some portion of them were pals, buddies, who hung around the place helping the owner waste time. At the front of the store an old man in a brimmed cap and work clothes was watching suspiciously as a woman pointed out the attractive features of one of the vacuums. All the machines were used, reconditioned, their squat or elongated shapes like the robots in old black-and-white science fiction films.

One of the other men at the counter asked, "You from the insurance company?"

Quinn said no. The blond man took a drink of 7-Up. "She's been waiting on some insurance guy."

"That so."

The man addressed his friends. "She keeps thinking they're gonna pay out full price. I say no way. We're talking serious lawsuits here."

Jackass, thought Quinn, not with any personal feeling, only as a kind of classification. Bonnie Livengood walked out from the rear of the shop. She glanced Quinn's way, paying him no mind. "What?"

"You got company."

He indicated Quinn. She looked him over again, not recognizing him. He hadn't expected her to. Even if he'd been in uniform, she might not have. "Help you?" she said. She was dressed up, in a white blouse made of some tissuey stuff, and her hair was held back with two gold clips. There was makeup too; it made her look prettier, in a way you might not expect a bereaved mother to look.

The men were listening. There was no way for them not to, and no easy way to move her into a private conversation. "I was one of the police officers on the scene of Gary's accident. I just wanted to tell you how sorry I am."

She was staring at him. He felt a dull, embarrassed heat spreading through him, but he kept plodding on. "The EMTs and the rescue people are the best there is. I know they felt really bad they couldn't help him."

Her face didn't change, but her lower lip tightened and her eyes went shiny. Quinn said, "I'm sorry. Sorry to upset you further." He nodded and aimed himself at the door.

But she stepped out from behind the counter and caught up to him. "Hold on a minute. Sonny?" She addressed the blond man. "I'm taking off."

Sonny made a face of owlish surprise. "Are you now."

"Yes, and don't give me any shit." To Quinn she said, "I have to get my purse." And disappeared again to the back of the store.

The men kept silent. Quinn made his expression flat, impassive, his cop's face. He wondered just what sort of idiot he must look like. He tried to convey, by his casual boredom, that this had been his idea, his intention all along, as perhaps it had been.

Sonny put out his cigarette in the ashtray. "Hell. Let her go. She's too messed up to get much work done anyway."

"If you ever was to move your behind three feet off that chair, I could take your talk about work seriously," said Bonnie Livengood, returning. "Come on," she said to Quinn.

"Nice talk," said Sonny. "I just meant, nobody broke your arm. You didn't have to come back until you felt like it."

"So I felt like it."

"And now you feel like leaving. Well sure, princess."

"I got you caught up. Try and keep it that way."

"She doesn't understand kindness," said Sonny to Quinn. "It's wasted on her."

She gave Quinn a see-what-I-put-up-with look and smoothed her skirt over her hips. All of them watched her. When they were almost to the door, Sonny called out, "So I guess you're in police custody." The other men were tickled by this. "You really a cop?"

"Yeah," said Quinn. "Is that really your name? Sonny?"

"Oh, he's deep," said Sonny, addressing his friends. On the way out the door Quinn heard one of them say, "Get his badge number," and a last snort of laughter.

Then they were outside, adrift, Quinn wondering what he was supposed to do next. "You have a car?" asked Bonnie. "Let's go somewhere. I can't stand this place."

Quinn opened the passenger door for her. It was hot for May and the inside of the car sent off waves of airless heat. He suggested a restaurant nearby. Once they were underway she said, "I'm sorry I was so nasty to you. That time you were at the house."

It pleased him that she had finally remembered him. "You were just upset."

"I'm a terrible person. Ask anybody. I can say the most terrible things." She angled the air-conditioning vent so it bathed her face. "What's your name?"

Quinn told her. She said, "You already know everything about me."

"No I don't."

"I mean from your report. What did you say about me?"

She seemed apprehensive about this. He said, "It didn't talk about you at all. It was, 'Mother reported son damaged wall and furniture during argument. Deputy mediated.' That sort of thing."

That satisfied her, or perhaps she lost interest. The neck of her blouse showed how thin her throat was, a little softening pouch of skin at its base. He found himself staring at it, as if it explained something about her. She said, "Would you tell me one thing? About Gary. Did he look really bad? Before they cleaned him up, I mean."

"He wasn't bad at all," Quinn lied. "You'd be surprised how people can come through an accident like that. Sometimes you wonder why they aren't up and walking around."

She wasn't looking at him, but out the window at the new,

lacy trees. "Don't worry about me crying on you or anything. I'm all dried out for now."

The restaurant was one of those dressed-up hamburger places, with booths and shaded lamps overhead. It was late for lunch, almost two, and except for the bored waitress, they had it all to themselves. Bonnie lit a cigarette and looked around her, as if trying to make up her mind about the place. Quinn, short on sleep as always, drank coffee. He should be saying something soothing, human and comforting, but nothing came to him. She was too aloof and edgy for him to find any purchase for his sympathy. He'd expected something different from her, though he wasn't sure what.

She blew smoke at the ceiling and followed it with her eyes. She said, "My family's from Kinmundy. Ever been there?" Quinn said that he had not. "You're not missing much."

He waited while she took a drink of iced tea. Her lipstick left a perfect pink half moon on the rim of the glass. "It's sort of like a slum out in the middle of nowhere. It's where we buried Gary. He got an aisle seat in the Methodist churchyard. It would've really pissed him off. He hated the damned town. So do I. But Mom has these plots there. I'll probably end up there too. Unless I decide to get myself cremated. What the hell. They can vacuum me up with a Hoover."

Her voice was rising. Quinn said, "I don't think talking like this is going to make you feel better."

"Who says I want to feel better?"

She glared at him, then slumped back in the booth. "Forget I said all that."

"It's OK."

"I'm not handling this real well."

"Give yourself some time."

"Fine." She waved her hand. "Let's talk about something else, then. Not Gary. Not this minute."

He cast about for something else. "What is it you do at R and K?"

"I'm the bookkeeper. Accounts payable, accounts receivable.

The bookie. That's what he calls me, Sonny. He's so busy selling bullshit, nothing else ever gets done around there. The place is a joke."

"Why don't you go somewhere else? There's probably lots of other bookkeeping jobs."

"Oh, I don't know. You just get used to certain things," she said vaguely. "How about you, you like being a cop?"

"Yes." She raised her eyebrows, meaning that he should go on. "I'm good at it. I like doing something I'm good at."

"You like being the one who locks up the bad guys and finds lost kids and fights for truth, justice, and the American way of life."

"You're making fun of me."

"Disguised as Clark Kent, mild-mannered reporter for the *Daily Planet*."

"Most people," said Quinn, "wouldn't want my job. They wouldn't want to deal with the fifty-seven varieties of scumbags walking around out there. They wouldn't want to carry out the law the way I have to. They want everything to be a TV show."

"I was just teasing you. Oh come on, don't be mad. I know you're a good cop. When you came to the house, you were very polite."

Their food came then, and he didn't have to explain or deny how he felt. Bonnie had ordered some kind of salad plate, composed of cantaloupe and tuna and those pinkish-white tomato wedges that taste only of refrigeration. She ate slowly, taking care to lay her silverware down between bites, like someone who had been taught this was good manners. Quinn managed his roast beef sandwich more clumsily. He'd never been shy with women, had always been able to joke, chat them up, make them like him. But he was having trouble now. Part of him was still in his cop's skin, noting facts. Part of him was silenced by the enormity of her tragedy and his irrational, useless guilt at not having prevented it, said or done something more about the boy. And yet another part of him remembered her as she slept beside him, the strangeness of it, as if he had entered her dream, or she his.

When she was done with her food, which hadn't seemed to interest her much in the first place, she said, "I'm not anybody's mother anymore. That's the hardest thing. I don't have any other kids. I won't have any more. All of a sudden that part of you's gone." She regarded Quinn. "You don't have kids, right?"

"That's right."

"Wife?"

"Not anymore."

"Mind my asking why not?"

He did mind, but there wasn't any way to say so without sounding grudging, as if his privacy was more important than hers. "Nothing gruesome. We just—I mean it really was nothing. It was like when you start talking to somebody at a party, and after a while you realize you're stuck with them and you're bored."

Again she seemed to want him to say more. "I don't know why we got married to begin with. Because she wanted to, I guess." He tried for a joke. "There are eight million stories in the Naked City, and I'm not one of them."

"You should have kids," she pronounced. "You still could. I bet you're younger than me. Besides, men can make babies even when they're eighty or ninety, as long as they can keep pulling the trigger."

The waitress was lounging toward them with the check, and Quinn didn't want to debate the point. He'd always thought he would have children. There was no good reason why he and his wife had not done so. At first they'd been in no hurry, and later, when they were having problems, it was one more thing that receded from them. An imaginary loss, compared with her real one. "You ready?"

She went to the ladies' room and he waited for her at the front door. When she came out she stopped to light a cigarette. The shoes she wore had high heels that made her legs look long and precariously elegant. He liked the way she looked, although he recognized that his wife, for instance, would have looked down on her, her discount-store clothes which imitated clothes that were not themselves entirely fashionable. She walked toward him, not hurrying, her gaze fixed on something distant, giving him time to look her over. He recognized this as a kind of flirtation, although it was hard to tell if he was meant to be anything more than an audience for it. He held the door for her and they stepped out into the wide white afternoon.

"Where are you going?" she asked when he'd started the car and was out in traffic.

"Taking you back to work."

"I don't have to go back today."

He weighed this. He knew he was meant to move things along somehow. "You need a ride home?"

"Sure."

Quinn changed directions. He wished she lived farther away, so he'd have more time to sort things out. He was trying to focus, stay alert. He should have been asleep hours ago. Bonnie said, "That was the only car we had that ran good. My other one needs a whole new transmission, and I can't get it fixed until the insurance money comes. It's sort of a trade. My kid for a new transmission."

"You shouldn't talk like that."

"Like what."

"Trying to make jokes. You don't have to act tough all the time."

"I'm not *acting* anything. Is that what you think?"

Too late, he tried to backpedal. "I know you're just trying to be brave. . . ."

She was crying. "Hey," he said. "Come on." She shook her head. The tears squeezed out of her closed eyes.

"I can't keep *doing* shit like this. I have to get up and go to work every day. I couldn't even pay for the damned *funeral*."

She was crying hard now. He looked for a place to pull over. They weren't far from her house, and he settled for a convenience store, a place that he knew because it was always getting robbed. He parked in a corner of the lot, away from the parade of people gassing cars and buying their afternoon twelve-packs. People who had an arrestable look to them, no matter what they were doing. One or two of them glanced over, curious, but Quinn stared them down. "Hey," he said again. He touched her hair, shoulder. "I'm sorry. I should have kept my mouth shut."

"Kleenex," she said, recovering a little, opening her purse. "You'd think I'd have Kleenex."

Quinn found some in the back seat. The parking lot, he noted, was filthy. Cigarette butts, candy wrappers, pools of spilled soda, flattened and anonymous wads of colored sugar. Didn't they ever clean the place? He concentrated on feeling indignant about this. When she'd blown her nose and was silent, he said, "Sometimes I think I'm helping when I'm really not."

"You didn't do anything." She didn't sound entirely convinced.

Quinn backed out into the street. He was going to just shut up from now on. He asked her if she still wanted to go home, and she said she did. They were only a couple of minutes away. There were worse neighborhoods in town, Quinn knew that, but Bonnie Livengood's depressed him because of its deliberate, even spiteful ugliness. Who had thought to paint the house that medicinal orange, Quinn wondered, pulling up to it. The house next door to it was bright blue, and the one next to that was a trailer.

In the driveway she said, "Come on in a minute."

He must have looked hesitant. She said, "What do I have to do, call 911 again?"

"I thought you'd probably seen enough of me."

"If you really want to help me, come in."

The front room was different than he remembered, barer. Couch, chair, TV on a stand, not much more. He'd thought of it as cluttered, but there had been the three of them and an argument to fill it then. He stood behind her while she set her purse down and stooped to remove her shoes. "Want a beer?"

"No thanks."

"Back this way." She led him, padding in her stocking feet, around a corner, where he caught glimpses of a bathroom, green and dimly glowing like a swimming pool, and a room that must have been hers. She stopped at a closed door and pushed it open. "This was his. Gary's."

The air was stale from being shut up, and it still smelled of him, or so Quinn imagined, sweet and acrid, like an animal's burrow. The room was an amalgam of kid's stuff and other, more adult and sinister items. Baseball cards, posters of Michael Jordan, also of bands who used death, the commercial representations of death, to sell music. Books of matches, pyramid of empty beer cans. There was a mussed bed strewn with items of clothing, more clothes in piles on the floor. A stereo with oversized speakers mounted in the corners. A set of dumbbells and a stack of car magazines. An unidentifiable papier-mâché item, painted blue and green, possibly meant to be planet Earth.

Bonnie said, "I'm going to get some trash bags." Quinn started to ask a question. "I want to clear everything out. I can't handle it alone."

"You're throwing everything away?"

"I don't know yet. This is just the next thing I have to do. Are you going to help me?"

Quinn stripped the sheets off the bed and put them in the washing machine, and bagged up the dirty clothes as she directed. Bonnie sat on the bare mattress and dumped the dresser drawers one by one, sorting through them. Quinn hoped that the boy hadn't left behind anything too gamy or distressing. She said, "That other boy? He's still in the hospital. I think that's almost worse. Having to wait."

Quinn remembered what Sonny had said about lawsuits. "Have you talked to his family?"

"They told me not to. The insurance company." She held up a square of colored cloth, an embroidered patch. "This is from his Cub Scout's uniform. Isn't it funny, him keeping it all this time?"

Quinn thought there was a difference between keeping things and simply not throwing them away, but he didn't volunteer this. She said, "He was supposed to stay home that night. He promised me up and down. I called him twice to check on him. I was at a friend's house," she explained, and Quinn nodded, feeling he was meant to understand or approve something that he did not. "So the last thing he told me was a lie."

"He didn't know it was going to be the last thing."

"I guess not."

She was dry-eyed and composed, and again Quinn thought she was trying to show him how well she was handling things. She said, "I have to find his pictures from when he was little, so you can look at them. You've never seen a cuter kid. He did all kinds of great little kid things. He had a pet hamster named Millie. He fell off his bike a hundred times. Made me valentines every year at school; I still got them."

She said, in a sharper voice, "I don't want you, or anybody else, to remember him as just this troublemaker."

"He was only a kid," said Quinn. "He would have grown out of it."

"What were you like when you were his age? I bet you didn't raise Cain all over town."

"Sure I did."

She smiled. He hadn't seen her smile before. "I don't believe that."

"My nickname was Mad Dog."

"Oh, please. You."

"How about Killer?"

She was laughing along with him. He thought there was something complicit about their laughing together. She said, "Well, I guess you didn't turn out so bad."

"Thanks."

Now their silence seemed complicit also. He yawned in spite of himself. The warm room was drugging him. Bonnie stood and sorted through a pile of CDs. "I should give these to his friends. He would have liked that. I'm going to get some pictures of him framed up too, maybe along with a poem or something." She took out one of the CDs and turned on the stereo. "Travelling Willbury's. He had a few I like."

Quinn recognized one of the songs, the happy chorus, singing it was all right, all right, everything was all right. A high, sweet, true voice on solo, the voice of a male angel. "Roy Orbison," he said.

Bonnie nodded. They let the music fill in the gaps between them. When the song was over she shut the stereo off. "He's dead too, isn't he? Roy Orbison."

"I'm pretty sure."

She went back to her seat on the mattress, gloomy again. She said, "I am trying very hard to remember the good things about him. Not just when he was little. Even right up at the end, when we had fights. We used to order out pizzas and make fun of stuff on TV. He could do all the voices. We'd laugh and laugh. He knew me better than anybody else in the world did, or ever will. He would have thought that crack I made about the transmission was *funny.*"

There was no right thing to say to that, so Quinn held his peace. The room was so small, even when they were on opposite ends of it there wasn't much space between them. Quinn was standing over her, close enough to see the part in her hair as she lowered her head. He followed the clean white line into the bright tangle of her hair. He was trying to tell the exact place the part ended, trying to see each individual hair distinctly. He supposed he was tired. When she raised her head and caught him staring at her he felt confusion, even panic.

She stretched out her hand. He took it and drew her up to

stand next to him. She stepped in close, so that his mouth now rested where his eyes had been. His body and his mind were operating on different circuits, shorting each other out. The fatigue had been shaken off, jolted loose, but he couldn't entirely believe or participate in what was happening. He was glad they had stopped talking. He was aware of her small breasts, pressing against him, aware suddenly of her shape and smell and the feel of her thin blouse sliding beneath his fingers. He wanted this. His mind caught up with his body, which was already in motion.

"Not in here," she said, and led him into her bedroom. Here the curtains were drawn and the light was shadowy. A fan in one corner stirred the air. She stepped to the side of the bed and began undressing, not looking at him, as she must undress every day, whether or not there was someone else there. When she saw him watching, she said, "See anything you like?"

"Everything."

By the time Quinn had wrestled his own clothes off, she was lying on her side, her head propped up on one elbow, the pose of a hundred bad paintings redeemed. Her body was pale and wavering, like a source of light. He was nervous about his erection, didn't trust himself to keep it, so he rushed things at first, choosing to be inept rather than fail entirely. She allowed this, raising her hips to accommodate him. My God. This felt fine. More than fine. He registered a kind of pious gratitude for the way things sometimes happened without anyone, least of all him, planning them.

They ended up afterward with her still beneath him, and she wriggled to let him know he should shift his weight. "Sorry." He located his knees and elbows, moved to one side.

"Quit being sorry all the time."

"I'm not," he said, or imagined saying, but sleep was closing over him like a mouth, and her hair was sifting across his chest, and he felt too good to argue.

She poked him in the ribs. "Don't fall asleep."

"Not."

He woke up without knowing how long he'd slept. The light in the room was the same, but he felt too clearheaded to have just dozed. Bonnie had pulled the sheet over her and was curled up with her back to him. He looked around for a clock, couldn't find one, surveyed the floor for his clothes, then swung out of bed. He hadn't paid any notice to the room itself before. Now he saw that the walls were papered with a pattern of spattered roses, pink and crimson and unlikely blue. There was a closet with an accordian-pleated door half off its track, a jumble of clothes peeking through. A dresser with the usual woman's things—perfume bottles, dinky bits of gold and silver, a stuffed monkey perched on top of the mirror.

"You going somewhere?"

He sat down beside her on the edge of the mattress. "What time is it?"

"Almost six."

"Shit. I've got to let my dog out."

"A dog," she stated.

"Yeah. He's been in all day." Quinn bent over and kissed her on the neck. "I could come back."

"What kind of dog?"

"Big black dog. His name's Beowulf."

"What wolf?"

"Beowulf. It's the name of this old poem we had to read in school."

"A poem about a dog?"

"No. Beowulf's the hero. He kills a monster." Quinn was finding it hard to remember much detail. "He saves his people. It's a weird old poem. Nobody liked reading it. Naming the dog after it was supposed to be funny."

"Here we are back at funny again."

She was smiling, which he took as a good sign. She stretched beneath the sheet, her arms over her head. Another inch would have shown her breasts, which Quinn wanted to see again. But he hesitated to pull the sheet away and settled for kissing her. "I really do have a dog." Jesus. He couldn't believe himself sometimes.

"A police dog."

"Now who's being funny."

They kissed again, this time with a little more behind it. Quinn lingered, his skin filling up with the warmth and scent of her. When he sat up again he said, "Are you OK?"

"Now why wouldn't I be?"

"I was just worried you might be feeling down about everything."

"You mean about my boy?" She rolled away from him. "There's nothing about you that's going to make me feel any better or any worse about that."

"I wouldn't want to make you feel worse."

"Then quit worrying about me."

She sounded sullen, as if there were some boundary he was not allowed to cross. He didn't want to leave things on that note. So he said, "You're the prettiest little thing."

"Right." Not believing him.

"I mean it. First time I saw you, I thought you were a teenager."

That made her turn and smile. "Even if you're lying, that's sweet. A cop. Now I guess I've done everything."

Quinn got himself dressed. "I'll call you," he said, and she pretended to throw a pillow at him, meaning she didn't believe this either. "I will," he protested. "I'll call tomorrow."

"You better. Now go take care of that dog."

It was still light outside, the sun declining behind a heat haze of rose and gray. The day felt unnaturally long, as if this same sun had bobbed up and down more than once while he'd slept. He couldn't have imagined any of it. He wondered if she had watched him while he slept. He hoped she had. He liked the idea of it.

Beowulf greeted him with distracted affection, then rushed outside to pee. Quinn wandered the house, unsure if he should go back to bed or stay up. He settled for taking the dog on a walk through the twilight streets. His body felt light and dispersed, like the mild air. He would have liked to remain entirely within it, but his mind kept turning things over. Maybe they should not have done what they'd done, or at least not so soon. Women got funny about such things, he knew, brooded, felt guilty, got mad at themselves and then at you. He still didn't understand why she'd let it happen, even made it happen. He was willing to admit that he didn't know one thing about her for certain.

The next evening he called her at six o'clock. He didn't have to work that night and thought maybe she'd like to go out and get some dinner. He tried again at seven, and a little after seven, and again at eight. He stopped trying at a quarter to ten. There wasn't an answering machine, just the phone's steady drilling. The next day was Saturday. You never knew if people worked on Saturday or not. He didn't call in the morning, figuring if she wasn't working she might want to sleep in, and then it was time for him to sleep, and make the transition to his workday self.

Saturday night was always busy, and more often than not bad, as this one was. There was a shooting in one of the housing projects, a woman whose shoulder was torn open and who lay on the ground screaming and writhing like an animal in a trap. A crowd had gathered, grown people and children both. Quinn didn't like to see children there but they were always present, staring and solemn. Then there was the man who'd shot the woman. He'd thrown the gun in a ditch and hid under a porch. They dragged him out by his feet, a figure from a nightmare, trailing clouds of spiderwebs and stinking with sweat and blood, cursing like the lost soul he was. Quinn was the one who wrestled him quiet and cuffed him and drove him in, and after that there was a burglary, and after that two drunks who'd sideswiped each other in a parking lot and were having a contest to see who could act more sober.

By sunrise Quinn was bone-weary but keyed up. He drove past her house, imagining her asleep inside her rose-printed room, wishing he could let himself in and lie down beside her. Instead he went home to his own restless sleep.

All the following week he tried to find her. The phone was never answered. He took to driving past her house at night as he patrolled, telling himself it was on his route anyway, though by the end of the week he didn't bother even trying to believe it. There were never any lights. Twice he came back after he got off work and knocked on the front door. He thought she might have gone back to her family in Kinmundy; he looked it up on a map. It occurred to him that she might have tried to call him but had forgotten his name, which would be unflattering but understandable. He worried that something might have happened to her, the kind of thing that seemed to happen to people who'd already collided with tragedy and were accelerating downhill through illness, depression, accident, more and more bad luck.

He hadn't wanted to show up at the vacuum store again and deal with the odious Sonny. But he couldn't think what else to do. He thought he could wait outside before the place opened, catch her on the way in. Or if she didn't show up, that would tell him something too. Of course he'd look pathetic and obvious, a little dog chasing after her. But as before he had a sense they had left a conversation unfinished. There was an entire constellation of feeling in him, things that kept surprising him, like stars you didn't see until you'd stood for a long time in the dark. He thought he would like to have children, a family. It wasn't the sort of thing you could count on, but it might happen. So many kids had it rough these days. He thought he could do a lot for a kid.

Quinn waited until Tuesday morning, since Monday was never good for anyone. He parked at one side of the lot, but there wasn't any hope of hiding, and besides, he didn't like the idea of it. The weather had turned cool again. A little rain blew through as he waited, and left the parking lot covered with oily, rainbow-edged puddles. People were already arriving at other shops, opening doors and setting up for business. R and K Vacuum, it seemed, operated on a more relaxed schedule. The sign on the door said business hours began at nine. At twenty to ten a big slow-moving Buick turned into the lot and parked in front of the shop. Sonny was driving; he opened the door and unloaded himself. Bonnie got out of the passenger side. She walked around the front of the car but stopped when she saw Quinn standing there.

Sonny didn't recognize him, Quinn could tell. Then Sonny saw Bonnie looking over and squinted in Quinn's direction. His ridiculous wig-like hair—except that no one would ever buy such a wig—turned from one to the other, then back again to the woman. They were about twenty yards away. Quinn saw Sonny say something to Bonnie, sliding his mouth sideways. Then the two of them headed his way across the space of damp pavement.

Bonnie looked down to avoid the puddles, dropping a cigarette underfoot. She was wearing a denim jacket over a sweater and a little red skirt. She looked mussed, not quite awake. "Well this is a surprise," she said.

He could tell in that instant that she didn't want him there, didn't want to see him, and everything had been a mistake.

Sonny said, in a jolly, sneering voice, "Uh-oh. It's the sheriff."

"Why don't you go on in," Bonnie told him. "I'll be there in a minute."

"Maybe he needs himself a vacuum."

"I'll ask him."

"Our motto: 'It Sucks.' "

"I'll see you inside," Bonnie said, and waited as he took his time getting up to the front door and opening it.

"How've you been?" Quinn said.

"OK, I guess." She wasn't looking at him but beyond, at the traffic moving through the intersection.

"I tried to call you."

"Well. I guess I haven't been around that much."

There was a space of silence, when they could hear the sound of tires on the wet road. She passed a hand through her hair. "I bet I look like roadkill."

"You don't."

"Thanks."

Quinn saw Sonny come up to the front door and lean into the glass, watching them, then retreat. Bonnie followed Quinn's gaze and turned. She said, "He gave me a ride to work."

"None of my business."

"That's right. Look." She sighed and shifted tones, from brusque to patient, explanatory. "I'm not trying to be this real bitch."

Quinn said nothing. He wanted to get it over with.

"You're really a nice guy. You didn't ever do anything that wasn't nice. But—"

"But you don't like nice guys."

"Maybe not. I haven't made a habit of them, that's for sure."

He was ready to turn and go when she said, "You'd always be reminding me that he was dead. Every time I'd look at you, I'd think of it. And you'd all the time be asking me how I felt and if I was all right and did I want to talk about it, and the truth is I don't want to. Not just so you can hear about it. It's my business and I'll handle it my way. I don't need some cop telling me how I should feel."

She reached into her purse and came up with what had to be her third or fourth cigarette of the day. "You smoke too much," Quinn said, just to be saying something.

"See? One more reason it wouldn't work out." She smiled nicely, in a no-hard-feelings way.

"Don't let me keep you from work."

She dismissed this by rolling her eyes. "Oh, him." A moment later she said, as if she'd been thinking it through, "He's not so bad. Once you get used to him."

"You could have told me."

"It's kind of an off-and-on thing." She shrugged and smiled again.

"You mean, it's on whenever you want to run somebody off. How convenient."

"Oh *fuck* you. You think because we screwed the one time you

can show up here and make all these *judgments*. Christ. I felt sorry
for you. You and your sad-sack face and your stupid badge. It was
a mercy fuck, OK?"

He opened his car door, but before he could get himself inside
she'd grabbed hold of it, put herself in his way. "That came out
wrong. I just said it because you made me mad."

"I think we're done talking."

She released the door but didn't move to let him pass. "I told
you I was this terrible person. You can't say I didn't warn you.
That's one thing about Sonny. He's known me years and years. He
doesn't expect me to be any different than I am."

He thought he would have to stay there, trapped and listening,
but she stepped aside. She said, "If I was you I'd arrest me just on
general principles. I really do think you're nice. Say something."

"I'm sorry if I interfered."

"There you go with that 'sorry' business again."

Much later, after he had met and married his second wife, and
left the force, and had become accustomed to his new happiness,
he was able to see that moment more clearly. She might have been
cruel, but she had not been unwise to cast him off. He had only
wanted to fill himself up with her grief, because it would take up
more space in him than his own imperfect grief. Because it would
allow him to feel what he needed to feel, as the unquiet, damaged
lives he encountered night after night allowed him to cry or rage
or bleed as they did. It had been a time in his life when he could
not have said to himself, "I am in despair," and still have kept
himself going.

But he didn't know that yet, or that things would get better,
or that he would not always feel his shame like a sickness. He
started the car, and she gave him a little fluttering wave, and the
rain dropped like a curtain over the windshield glass and blurred
the red of her skirt. She made a pantomime of dodging the rain,
turned, and disappeared into the shop. He had been set free from
something, although that was another thing he did not yet know.

HEART OF GOLD

The furnace was ready to quit. It groaned and kicked and la-
mented every time it woke up. Its asthmatic breath filled the house
with dust. "Pussy," said Ginny, exhorting it. "Nya nya." Ice crept
up the windows. Sunlight struck frozen rainbows in the ice, un-
earthly crystal violets and greens and blues. The phone wasn't
working. The television was. Gene Autrey and Roy Rogers were
talking about the good old days, the singing cowboy days. Back
when fistfights were clean and villains were swarthy and girls knew
how to faint and a string orchestra lurked behind every boulder.
"A bill of goods," Ginny said. "Maximum bullshit." She always
kept the volume turned down so she could make wisecracks.

Gene and Roy had grown old and prosperous. They owned

real estate, baseball teams, hotels, broadcasting networks. They wore dude clothes, just like in the movies, cowboy hats and embroidered shirts and bandanas and fancy tooled belts. They were the only old men in America who could get away with dressing like that. Gene and Roy both looked pretty good. They'd taken care of themselves, made the right investments. They were wrinkled but hale, and their dentures gleamed. Their past was glorious, their future serene. "Capitalist swine," said Ginny. "No. I didn't mean that." The stage set was made up to look like a western ranch, with cactus and longhorn skulls and wagon wheels and Mexican serapes and such. Gene and Roy talked for a little while, and then the movies came on, movies like *Rocky Mountain Rhythm* and *Loaded Pistols*. The movies were all pretty much the same. With the sound turned off, they were even more the same. There was always singing. When the cowboys sang to them, the girls looked blissful, like this was the most natural thing in the world.

Ginny heard Annemarie's truck tires crunching on the packed snow all the way in from the road. She heard Annemarie come in through the kitchen, stamping the snow off her feet and rustling grocery bags. "Yo," Ginny said, not turning around.

"It's nine A.M.," Annemarie said, meaning the dope.

"Want some?" Ginny held out the pipe. Annemarie sat down on the couch beside her, frowning at the television. She frowned at the pipe too, but took it.

"What is this?" Meaning the television, this time.

"Melody Ranch Theater. They show all the old westerns. It's great stuff. I'm delving into the archives of my soul."

"Sure."

"These guys. Don't you remember them?"

"We didn't have television until I was twelve," said Annemarie. "My parents were communists."

"The girls always fell off their horses and the cowboys rescued them. It really did a number on me in my formative years. Watch this."

On the screen, a young Gene Autrey made Champion rear up, for no reason except to show off. "Men," said Ginny. "Always doing wheelies."

Annemarie stood. Ginny heard her in the kitchen, opening cupboards and rattling the groceries from their bags. "I'll do that later," said Ginny. "Don't worry about it, OK?" When Annemarie didn't stop, Ginny sighed and hoisted herself off the couch.

"Go ahead, watch your movie," said Annemarie. "I can do this."

"I've seen it already. I've seen them all."

She watched Annemarie move back and forth, putting everything in the right place just like it was her own kitchen. Annemarie wore white cotton turtlenecks and serious sweaters, the kind that still looked a lot like sheep. She kept her dark hair in a braid and her face scrubbed. She was neither pretty nor unpretty. You looked at her face and saw straight through it. That "whole-wheat look of yours," Ginny called it.

Annemarie worked at a counseling center for battered women. She found the women lawyers and jobs and safe beds to sleep in. She talked calmly to police and doctors. Ginny thought it would be the worst job in the world. It would be like getting beat up twenty times a day, and you'd hate everybody. Annemarie said you couldn't allow yourself to hate. The violence was all learned behavior, generational patterns. "Social worker talk," Ginny said, but she couldn't dismiss it. What if Annemarie was right, and you weren't supposed to blame anyone? Most of the time Ginny felt guilty that there was not more wrong with her anyway.

Ginny saw the women clearly in her mind's eye. It shamed her somehow to admit she thought of them so often, as if that was as bad as beating them up. The women were missing patches of hair torn out by the roots. The women had lips like torn plums. There would be other things that didn't show. Their bodies had become like foreign countries to them, strange landscapes, something they had to move within warily. Annemarie said the women had to learn not to be victims. How did you do that? It wasn't on television. She couldn't imagine herself being Annemarie, in this or any other life. How could you unlearn the ugliness of the world, stare it down, not see yourself in every brutalized face? It was some failure of nerve or compassion that depressed her even more to contemplate.

Annemarie asked Ginny if she'd done anything about the car or the phone yet. Ginny said there was a guy from the garage who was supposed to come out and look at the car, maybe today. And she could always phone from the landlord's, if she had to.

"The landlord's a mile away," said Annemarie. They were back on the couch. The movie was over, and commercials for E-Z Chord guitars and custom-built wheelchairs filled the screen with color.

"I think about getting the phone fixed," said Ginny. "But there's nobody I want to talk to anyway."

"I meant for emergencies."

"Look, after a while shit ceases to be an emergency. After a while it just turns into your life."

"You could maybe clean this place up a little, you know?"

"Gene Autrey was the best. Roy Rogers was all right, but then he teamed up with that dope Dale. I took it personally. My first betrayal."

"It's freezing in here. You run out of LP?"

"No. I'm just afraid the furnace'll blow up. Quit worrying. I'm fine here. I'm going back to the land. I want to get a dog. Maybe a horse too. The cats are all right, but if I bring them in the house, they poop all over. I want to have lots and lots of animals."

"Being Rima the Bird Girl is not a career. OK. Do whatever you want. Be fine if you want. I'm sorry."

"I'll pay you back for the groceries," said Ginny.

"Don't be a jerk."

"It's winter. It's a good time to hide out. Get that look off your face. Nobody's beating me up."

Ginny stood to turn the TV off. "Why did you do that?" Anne marie objected. "Maybe there's something else on."

"All I can stand are old movies. I don't know how anybody watches the news."

"You want someone to rescue you," said Annemarie. "But the only one who ever shows up is me."

Ginny watched Annemarie's truck until it was out of sight. The winter-cleared fields were perfectly flat, and there were no obstacles to vision; still, you could never see for any distance. Snakes of wind-driven snow blew across the plowed surface of the road. The wind had picked up when the snow stopped. When the wind died down, the snow would begin again. That was the pattern. The car had been dead for two weeks. The phone had been out for one. That was another pattern.

She realized she hadn't said anything to Annemarie about Jay, hadn't taken the opportunity to bitch about him. Jay was Ginny's rotten husband. They were getting divorced sometime. It was one more thing that had to be fixed. Not talking about Jay gave her a sense of something left undone, like leaving an item off the grocery list.

It wasn't that there was anything new or worse to say about Jay. Everything had already happened. Jay was a real estate developer. He built condos and sold them to buy other condos, and got bank loans to pay other bank loans. The ball was always rolling. There were always people calling, the buyers and sellers and builders and accountants, important people. It had all seemed exactly like the real thing, to Ginny at least. She hadn't paid enough attention. She hadn't paid any attention. Why should she? There was always enough money. Always the excitement of the next deal cooking, the big one that was going to put them over the top. Now she supposed it had been a greedy, unthinking life, with no one to blame but themselves. Along the way Jay bought a lot of cocaine to sell, but that was the one thing that didn't get sold.

When the ball stopped rolling, a lot of things stopped. Jay

owed everyone money. Ginny found out that she owed people money too, people she'd never heard of. It was amazing, the things they could do to you if you were married to someone like Jay. The lawyers were in charge of their old life now. None of it had anything to do with Ginny anymore.

Every day she practiced hating Jay. It was something to do, like stomach exercises. Jay had lied to her along with everyone else. She'd loved him up until almost the exact minute she'd decided to hate him. When the phone still worked, he'd called a few times, from Florida and the Virgin Islands, places he said he had to go to get away from the drug dealers. The dealers didn't mess around, they'd break your face open, slit your throat, worse. Did she remember the kid they found in the vacant lot, set on fire with gasoline? The picture in the paper, that embarrassing black wet mess, the body. That was the dealers. There had been people following him, wrong numbers at night, all those times he couldn't sleep. He'd wanted to tell her but he was so ashamed, it was all so crazy by the end, when he couldn't eat without puking, when every shirt he put on his back felt filthy. He was worried sick about everything, worried about her. It still wasn't safe for him to talk long. Did she understand?

The calls came either late or early. Jay never had much time to talk. All the urgency and hurry reminded Ginny of the old days, the big deals, except that now the news was all bad. "I never meant for any of this to happen," said Jay. "You can believe that at least, can't you?"

"I guess so," said Ginny. She was cautious about agreeing with him. It was too much like salesmen. They always asked questions people had to answer yes to. Is this the lady of the house? Apartment nine?

"I know I can't expect you to trust me anymore," said Jay. "I know I've got a long way to go before that's even a possibility." Somehow it seemed as if in fact he did expect it, as if his saying this was what she was supposed to want.

Ginny poked at the phone cord, knotting it around her finger. She didn't know what it was about the calls, how all her righteous anger backed up on itself, wouldn't fit through the line, and instead of saying what she wanted to say, she found herself listening for what she wanted to hear.

"Jay? What's it like down there. I've never been anyplace like that. An island."

"Hot. If you walk around barefoot, the tops of your feet get burned. It's so hot you can't see straight. Even the shade is hot. The trees are all wrong somehow."

"It's cold here," said Ginny. The fields across the road flooded when it rained, shallow pools that were beginning to ice over at the edges. The water looked dirty. It reflected the dirty sky. When the wind blew over its surface the water stirred a little, like cold soup.

"Is it a nice house?" said Jay. "Are you OK there? Honey?"

Spitefully, she kept silent.

"I got in over my head," said Jay. "That happens to people."

"It happens to dishonest people."

"I owe you a lot of explanations."

"Don't use that word to me."

"What word?"

"Owe. You still doing stuff?"

"I can't hear you."

"Never mind," said Ginny. "I have to go now."

"I love you," said Jay. "You figure it out."

She could remember loving him. Most of the time she tried to forget it, so she could hate him satisfactorily. It seemed you ought to be able to make up your mind whether you loved or hated somebody and not keep wimping along between the two, doing neither of them right. She couldn't decide which was more gratifying, the notion that Jay had plotted ruin and betrayal from the beginning or that he used to be somebody worth loving and she hadn't been a total idiot for doing so. When the phone first went out she panicked. It meant Jay couldn't call, couldn't help her make up her mind. Now she liked it that way. She didn't want him trying to talk her into and out of things anymore. Every so often this last week she picked up the phone just to reassure herself it was still broken. There was nothing more silent than a dead phone.

Ginny pulled her boots on and took the new bag of cat food out to the barn. She dove into the cold. It was exactly like immersing yourself in water; you were cold everywhere, all at once. The ice had frozen into blue ruts between the barn and the house. You had to watch your step. Ginny imagined herself sliding, smashing into the ground hard enough to break a leg or knock herself out. Trying to crawl as far as the road. Fingers and toes already dead, frostbitten. Her body piling up drifts on the windward side, a little clear space to leeward. When they found her, weeks later, she would be something nobody would want to see, like the boy who burned.

But of course none of this happened. She reached the barn and slid the heavy door back just far enough to squeeze inside. The barn was dim and smelled comfortably of old manure and hay dust. It was better inside than out. Outside you could see all its angles softening, waiting to collapse, its boards a patchwork of paint and weathered wood and air. The cats came as soon as they heard the food bag open. There were four or five of them, as far as she could tell. There was always the chance that more hid in the loft, came out only when she wasn't there. The cats were wild. They seemed to come with the property and existed whether or not anyone paid them any attention. While they ate, Ginny ran her hand over their rough black and gold and tiger fur, feeling the greedy swell of their ribs, hearing the small tearing of teeth. When they were done with the food, they escaped and finished ignoring her from different corners. If she died in the snow, would the cats eat her?

The barn had four box stalls, fenced off with boards. The boards were rubbed smooth or chewed in places. Depressions in the clay marked the spots where the horses had stood, or lain, or pawed. Ginny tried to imagine the horses. They wouldn't be anything like Champion or Trigger or Buttermilk or Sweetheart, those glossy, heroic animals who kicked at villains and nuzzled the cowboys on cue. No, these horses would be shaggy and stupid and patient. All day they would stand patiently, their hoofs rotting in the wet straw, gazing at the smeared windows. They'd rub their tails raw and eat their own manure out of boredom.

The sky looked like it could snow again. Clouds were piling up on the western horizon, layer on layer of indistinct darkness. Ginny couldn't decide if she wanted the garage man to come or not. If the car was fixed she'd have to drive somewhere, talk to people, earn and spend money. The roads would be bad for days and days, weeks even. Ginny thought about Annemarie driving back to town, intent on the road, the snow snakes twisting under her tires.

She wasn't as brave as Annemarie, never had been. She thought it was because Annemarie never expected things to be any better than they were and was not outraged when they were every bit as bad as you could imagine. Annemarie called her a romantic. That meant you didn't want to face up to the real world. Amen. The real world made her lose heart. She knew what people meant by that now. Losing heart was when you were afraid of everything. It was stupid to be afraid of things like dying in the driveway. Or maybe you wanted to die in the driveway so people would feel sorry for you, but you didn't really want to die. You just wanted the sorry. You wanted things to be over, one way or another. At times Ginny felt something rise up in her throat, wet and thick, as if the last shreds of her heart were loosening. She'd try and force it out but it wouldn't come. It crept back into her chest and squatted there, and wouldn't let her do anything right.

The garage man did come. It was midafternoon and a little snow had begun to spit from the sky when a tow truck, bright red and yellow like a circus car, slowed at the driveway, idled, considering, and then pulled in. Ginny watched from the window. She saw the garage man, dressed in jeans, jacket, and cap, get out and trudge up to the front door, stamping his feet a little for warmth. That tickled her. One of the things she liked about men was that they never wore enough clothes in cold weather. She'd forgotten. *Get ahold of yourself.* So she'd have to talk to him. No big deal.

She met him at the door, holding it open in case he wanted to come inside. But he stayed on the porch, hands jammed into his pockets. "Hi, the car's out back." Incredibly bright. Some people kept theirs in the basement. "I had somebody jump the battery but it didn't help." She always tried to sound like she knew what she was talking about with cars around men. It made her feel less ignorant. Who was she trying to fool.

The garage man nodded. He was older than she expected, a grown-up. Usually it was kids, teenagers you saw cruising around in the wreckers, hair in their eyes, radio blaring, indifferent to all the dead cars in the world. "This weather, there's nothing wants to run," he said. He bobbed his head at her and trudged down the porch stairs.

Ginny watched him from the window. He leaned over her car's engine, hooked up cables, prodded and adjusted. The tow truck idled, a constant vibration she could feel through the glass. It was comforting to know that some machines ran the way they were meant to, that people could make them behave. The furnace rattled weakly beneath her. She couldn't tell if it was getting ready to quit or blow up. There was a fireplace in the living room, if she had to use it. She could dismantle the barn, burn it piece by piece.

The garage man slammed down the hood of Ginny's car and walked up to the front door again. This time he did come in to confer with her, standing politely just inside the door. Careful to keep his feet on the square of rug laid down for a doormat. She could have laughed. As if there was any surface in the house you could ruin. As if she lived that kind of life. *Stop it.* Some edge of giddiness was creeping up on her, making her feel she might do or say anything, embarrass them both. She readjusted her face, attempting to look properly anxious about the fate of her car.

He was saying it was not her battery. "Maybe the alternator, or the starter. Hard to tell." He had one of those flat, country voices. A big man, bulky, trying not to take up too much space. Snow was melting into his dark hair at the edges of his cap.

Ginny waited for him to tell her what it all meant, the car talk. When he didn't go on she said, "Can you fix it? I mean, is it a big thing?"

He said that maybe it was and maybe it wasn't, and if it was the one thing it could be a hundred or more, and if it was the other it would be a hundred or less. With new parts, that is. Sometimes you could get rebuilt, but he wouldn't recommend it. Anyway, he'd tow it in for her. She wanted it towed, didn't she?

"I guess so," Ginny said. Somehow she hadn't figured on that, his taking the car away. It was stupid, but if the car wasn't there, she knew she'd feel worse. Another thing she wouldn't have anymore. She wasn't making sense. She thought the garage man was looking at her oddly. Did the house still smell like dope?

"We can take a look at it, give you an estimate before we start work," the garage man said. She nodded. Eminently reasonable. All she had to do was agree. She felt thick-headed, slow, like she was moving underwater. Agree and he'd go away and take the car with him. "Ma'am?" He was the one looking odd now, his face too wide, like she was seeing him through some kind of lens. Then she was sitting on the floor, staring up at him. For the life of her, she couldn't have said how she got there.

Something hurt. Her back. But not bad. Vaguely, she felt that it should feel a lot worse. The garage man was bending over her, offering his hand. She didn't want to get up. Getting up meant you had to admit you'd fallen down in the first place. She closed her eyes. Through the floor she felt the furnace shuddering, a cranky, grating sound. "I think the furnace is broken," Ginny said, without opening her eyes. When she leaned her head back, there was a wall.

Jay was outside the window. He was wearing beach clothes, a shirt with parrots, and shorts. His nose was sunburned. The sun had turned his hair almost white. The snow fell in big swarming flakes, and the air was white too, a soft diffused light. Jay was laughing. The cold didn't bother him, or else the white air was as hot as the sun on the beach. "Look," said Jay, scooping up handfuls from the ground. "Snow."

Ginny opened her eyes. There were sounds underneath her, metal scraping metal. He was doing something with the furnace. There was a pillow behind her back now. She didn't like to think of anybody seeing the basement. It was full of the landlord's un-loved furniture, nests of old paint cans, mouse corpses, rotting can-vas, spidery pipes. The upstairs wasn't that much better. You could maybe clean the place up a little.

She heard his feet on the stairs; then he was peering around the corner at her. She wished she was still dreaming, oblivious. Was it too late to pretend?

"How you feeling?"

"Stupid." She'd fainted. Just like the goddamned movies. She watched the window. The snow was the way she'd seen it behind her eyes. It whirled and whirled, making the window a blank white space. She wanted the snow to keep falling so she'd never have to get up again.

"Glass of water?" he offered. Ginny shook her head, not looking at him. The floor was cold. She guessed she couldn't stay there forever. The sweatpants she was wearing were somewhere in between clean and dirty.

"That furnace had a loose belt," he said, and this time she did look at him.

"You fixed it?"

"Tightened the belt. That should do it."

"All that noise. I thought it was blowing up."

"Nah. Just cranky."

He was still in the doorway. "Snow," he said, nodding at the window. "Funny how something can be so much in the way, then disappear like it never was."

"Funny," she agreed. Wind banged the loose storm door, and the ceiling creaked. The roof would blow off and the house whirl away through the snow, the two of them rattling around inside it like a couple of beans. Anything could happen and not surprise her. "Thanks for fixing the furnace," she said. "That was really nice. You didn't have to."

"Glad I could help."

"There's the fireplace," Ginny said. "I guess I wouldn't freeze."

"You'll want to clean that chimney out first. You could start a roof fire, worse. Back up carbon monoxide into the house."

"You're kidding." Amazing. She really couldn't do anything right.

"I've seen it happen." They were talking now like it was the most natural thing in the world for her to be sitting on the floor. Like the white window was a movie screen they had come to watch, they had assembled here for just that reason and were chatting before the show started. Then he said, "Look, I'm just waiting for it to let up a little."

"Sure."

"Once it lets up, I can get through. That wrecker gets through most things."

He looked at Ginny once, then away, back to the window. He had a broad, dark face, the features a little flattened, as if the mold that stamped out faces had slipped a bit. But a solid, good-looking man, she'd noticed it right away and stuffed it down, afraid that she had noticed such a thing. She wondered if she should introduce herself, ask him his name. It would be almost flirting. It seemed important not to do that, not to scare him away. They watched the snow for a while, then Ginny said, "There's probably coffee. . . ."

"I'll get it." He went into the kitchen, started making his noises there.

She supposed she really ought to get up. She padded into the bathroom. She looked like shit. She splashed cold water, which didn't help anything. This was just how you looked after a while, when you didn't bother with mirrors. Annemarie was the only woman she knew who could wear her lack of vanity like a medal.

The rooms smelled like coffee now. Ginny sat on the couch waiting for him to bring it in, like a guest in her own house. Of course it didn't feel like her house, if that made any difference. The house she'd lived in with Jay was full of blond wood and glass, expensive things. It felt like her house, but it wasn't there anymore. She wondered if Jay missed living there, if it was anything he let himself think about.

She leaned closer to the window, until her face touched the cold pane. She'd seen him clearly, what was it she'd seen? Jay in the snow. Now that seemed ominous to her, as if it were a piece of news, something that had reached her instead of phone calls. *Jay?* She searched the whiteness for him.

"Looking for something?"

The garage man was behind her, holding two mugs. "My husband," Ginny said, and saw his face change, retreating. "He's not here," she said. "He's not coming."

"Snowed in someplace?" He was afraid of saying something wrong, she could tell, something you shouldn't say to a married woman.

"Sort of," she said, wondering why she'd brought it up. She took the coffee he held out to her. "Thank you."

The coffee was hot. It didn't have any other taste. The garage man was drinking his down fast. Ginny was afraid he'd leave soon now, snow or not. "Actually," Ginny said, "I don't know where he is. He ran off. He got into a lot of trouble with drugs and ran off."

He looked sideways at her, then out the window. Embarrassed? Disgusted? "That's a rough one," he said.

They both watched the snow, which had changed in quality from large flakes to small, sleety ones, as if someone had fine-tuned it. With his cap off, he looked older. Older than she was, at least. Hair creeping back on his forehead. A furrow above his nose, a little crooked line. He looked like someone who worked hard every day, busting his knuckles on rusty bolts, breathing in gas fumes. Men used their bodies just like tools or machines, until they wore out. And it was no wonder that a woman's body, to them, was just another balky piece of equipment, something you had to kick and curse until it obeyed. Ginny felt the dizziness wash over her again, like ink blotting out her vision. It occurred to her that although she could imagine the battered women with nightmare clarity, she had no picture of the men who beat them.

No. Not him. He was her cowboy. "Are you married?" Ginny asked. She could say anything to him now that she'd said that first thing.

"Yes," he said. Looking almost guilty about it. Was it something you weren't supposed to ask people?

"Kids?"

"Two boys. A couple of pistols."

"That's nice. We were going to have kids. All those normal things." The roof of snow was lowering and the room seemed dark. Ginny switched on the lamp next to her, and a little world of rosy light sprang up around them. You didn't sit with a strange man alone in a dark room. The unwritten code of the west. Fight fair. "I guess I'm glad now we didn't. This is no place you'd want a kid to live."

His eyes strayed from the window. She tried to see everything he saw. The floor rolling with dust, the clouds of stink that rose almost visibly from the upholstery. Ginny said, "He was a wheeler-dealer. My husband. He was always one step ahead of everybody else. Until the drugs. The drugs made him think he had a ten-mile head start."

She wished he'd say something. Laugh even. It was hard to talk to cowboys. They could sing better than they talked. He'd been so nice to her, she just wanted it to keep happening for a little while longer. Oh Lordy. There was a different movie in her head now. The snow fell up to the eaves, no one could get in or out for days. They strung a clothesline between the house and the barn to feed the cats. She cooked the meals. He fixed the fireplace. The first night they were shy and slept in different rooms. After that they did it like rabbits. He was actually quite intelligent. A man of deeds, not words.

She was both ashamed and excited to be thinking like this. *Faint again*, the part of her that was not ashamed said. *Fake it. Make him touch you.*

"My husband," Ginny said, not knowing yet exactly what she would say, just wanting him to stay, how did you ever get a man to stay? "My husband," she began again, hoping to think of something funny, something that would make him feel sorry for her. She didn't know her lines. The girls in the movies didn't really belong there. They were just an excuse for the cowboys to sing. It was all fake anyway. Even the horses were fake. Roy Rogers grew up in Ohio. His real name was Leonard Slye. "I had this dream about my husband," she said finally. "I dreamed he was happy." That was what it meant, she decided. No vengeance even in dreams.

"I keep thinking a plow's got to come by soon," the garage man said, as if that was the conversation they'd been having.

"It's OK," Ginny said. "I mean, you're not in the way." She couldn't decide if she wanted him to stay because of or in spite of his being a man. Touch him. Easy. It was supposed to be easy.

"This guy, your husband," he said, surprising her. "What line of work was he in?"

"Real estate," she said cautiously.

He nodded, as though she had confirmed some private suspicion. "All right if I use your phone?"

"It doesn't work. Nothing in this house works."

The phone rang. The bell had a weak, dribbling sound. Ginny and the garage man stared at each other. "Excuse me," said Ginny.

The phone was in the kitchen. "Hello?" Static. The voice at the other end was tiny. "Jay?" She could hardly hear him. He sounded like the ocean in a seashell. "Talk louder. Where are you?"

"That's not important."

"Every time you call you get farther away."

"What?" said Jay. "Listen, sugar. I need a favor."

"A favor," said Ginny. She heard the garage man in the next room, coughing and shuffling his feet. Trying to make enough noise so he couldn't be accused of eavesdropping, she guessed. "It's money, isn't it?"

Silence. She thought maybe the line had cut out. Then he said, "I was thinking, maybe you could sell some of my stuff. My camera."

"What camera? I don't know where any camera is."

"Goddamn it, Ginny. Don't tell me you lost my *camera*."

"I guess I wanted you to be a good person," said Ginny. "I want someone to be who they're supposed to be."

"I can't hear you."

"Never mind," said Ginny. She turned on the kitchen light. Shadows raced to the corners of the room.

"Or you could say the camera was stolen," Jay was saying. "Get the insurance money. Would that be such a big deal?"

"Ma'am?" It was the garage man, making a break for it. "You want that car towed in?"

"Who's that?" asked Jay.

"A silent film star," she said to the phone. "Happy trails."

Everyone had gone. The car was gone. The phone was off the hook. Ginny sat on the basement steps. She was listening to the furnace. It had a good sound now, steady and peaceful. The flame of the pilot light was blue, like wood smoke. It was her campfire. She had to be the cowboy. There was no one else left. She thought of Gene and Roy, preparing for sleep in their mansions, laying down their decent old men's bodies, rising up in dreams to gallop through clouds and once more live blameless lives. Knowing right from wrong, sure. Even the horses knew that. "Giddyup," said Ginny. She sang a song about the snow.

WHO DO YOU LOVE

It was an itch in her mouth. She had to say it. "I love you."

His eyes were closed. The lashes fluttered, a brief, involuntary code: SOS.

"You don't have to be embarrassed. Relax. Hey, it's just me. It's just how I feel right this minute. You feel any way you want to."

"I feel fine."

"Well that's good. It's fine to feel fine. Don't mind me, I'm just happy."

He laughed and patted her arm. Then he picked up the arm by the wrist, as you would a sack, and moved it off his chest. He pushed the bedsheets aside and stood up.

"Where are you going?"

"Bathroom."

She listened to his footsteps, then the gargle of the plumbing. He wasn't coming back to bed. Well, OK. She hopped up also. He was sitting at the kitchen table, reading the *TV Guide*. Annoyed, she imagined, at the lack of morning newspapers. She would offer to go out for them. She would offer to subscribe. What was the matter with her? She wasn't even sure yet if she liked him very much. "Hungry?" she asked brightly.

"Not really."

"Belgian waffles. Steak and eggs. Fresh-squeezed juice. Home-made jam. Denver omelet."

"I'm not that hungry. Honestly."

"I want to smother you with food. Smother you, then lick it off. Just kidding. I'll make coffee. So you're one of those no-breakfast guys."

"Sometimes I eat breakfast. But why disturb the sleeping beast that is my appetite."

He said it so it was funny and she could smile. She had to remind herself that she'd really only said one wrong thing.

They both had coffee. She fixed herself toast. She was ravenous. She was almost impatient for him to leave so that she could eat all she wanted, something sickening and unbreakfast-like, cold spaghetti or a whole box of Girl Scout cookies. They talked a little about work and something else that didn't matter. She was looking at him, trying not to be obvious about it, like taking little sips from a glass of water. She was trying to put all his different faces together. His ordinary daytime face, and the one that hung overhead in bed like a blurred moon, and now this rumpled morning one. It didn't matter what she looked like. He wasn't watching her.

"What are you thinking?" she asked, the next time there was silence. "What are you thinking about, right now?"

"Women are always asking you that."

"And men never tell you."

"Well, women always want you to say, 'I was thinking about you, darling.' Or, 'About us.' Anything else is a wrong answer."

"No, no," she protested. "Whatever you say is fine. Anything at all. Spill it."

"Well I *was* thinking about you."

"Uh-oh."

"It wasn't anything bad. Why would you think it was bad? I like you. It's just that sometimes you—"

"Interrupt people. Finish their sentences. Talk too much. Try too hard."

"We just need to take things slow," he said, not unkindly.

"Oh yes." She was happy, relieved that it wasn't anything worse. She knew everything else would be easy. If that was the worst thing he was going to say, she could sit there patiently, smiling, agreeing to everything, waiting for him to leave. Once he was gone, she could do whatever she wanted. Cry, stare at herself in the mirror until she was as ugly as she chose to be. She would call herself *idiot, fool, jerk, cunt.* She waited with perfect serenity, curious, even, as to how he would extricate himself.

"Well," he said finally.

The woman's name was Judy Applebee. She was thirty-two years old, and she worked in an office that coordinated human services for the city. The office directed programs for latchkey kids and meals for the elderly, hotlines for battered women and drug addicts, ghetto basketball leagues, emergency shelters, urban mini-gardens, home winterization assistance. There were programs to help the deaf get telephone equipment and to aid the illiterate in filling out tax returns; others that gave horseback-riding lessons to crippled children or provided them with foster grandparents, or served Thanksgiving dinner to recent immigrants. There was an enormous patchwork of such services meeting the city's large and small, real and imaginary human needs.

Judy's friends would say to her, "It must be rewarding to make an impact, to really help people with their problems." Judy would shrug and say she supposed so. Her friends thought this was modesty, one more proof of how virtuous her work was. But Judy knew better. Her office did not solve anyone's problems. It only took the edge off misery so that misery could be endured. Her job was not to eradicate poverty, but to tend and manage it as you would a crop. Her job was to make poverty more tolerable. Sometimes she imagined the city's misery as water backed up in a dam, passive but threatening, and herself as a kind of engineer, monitoring the pressure, opening sluices and closing valves. If you supplied one old woman with transportation to the doctor's, the teenage prostitutes or the Vietnamese refugees living in church basements would somehow be appeased. The soggy wave of human suffering would not crest that day. Often she felt there was no point in giving people what you thought they needed, when they would never get what they wanted. They wanted fish fries, new automobiles, Florida vacations; they wanted their cancers to shrivel and their children to thrive. People wanted good luck. They wanted the lottery, not human services.

And if you were serious about changing anything, you would shut the office down. Allow misery to become intolerable, let it boil over the lip of the dam and come down hard on everything. Of course, she and those like her would be the first targets. The poor hated the doling out and apportioning she did, the grudging gifts of half a mouthful. They hated waiting in line, they hated being orderly and deserving. Since when did *rich* people deserve what they had? They hated the office itself, the neat walls and airless corridors and stink of thrift about the place, meant to convince them how little there was to give. They would destroy it gladly. Judy was unsure why it gave her such satisfaction to imagine this. She supposed she felt guilty for having problems less monumental than those she saw at work, inadequate, unworthy problems.

She was a pretty woman, although she knew she had the sort

of looks that would not hold up forever: fair, fine-boned, brittle. She had long nervous hands and a quick smile. "Judy dresses like a social worker," her friends said despairingly. Her light hair was long and artless, her nails were blunt, her shoes merely comfortable. She attracted men who would have been uneasy with a more decorative woman. With these men she had serious conversations about whatever the men wished to talk about: politics, technology, literature. She usually agreed with them. There was no reason not to. Those things hardly mattered to her. She agreed with them so they would like her. She was always too anxious to be liked, she knew that. People could tell, and then they secretly despised you for it.

She was often unhappy for no reason at all. What right did she have to be unhappy? She was stern with herself about this. She was healthy, well-fed, a citizen of a highly developed nation. Each day she consumed more of the earth's resources than some people did in a year. She had family and friends. Why should she spend whole evenings weeping into a towel? Or dug into a nest on the couch, watching the most inane, grating television she could find, sunk in idiocy and uselessness until she could loathe herself properly? It was true that she was alone. None of the men she agreed with had amounted to much over time. She thought she would like to have children. Of course she was not unique in any of this. So many overeducated women her age were alone that it hardly seemed worth complaining about.

Once she swallowed a handful of Valium and drank most of a bottle of red wine and waited for something to happen. She was pretty sure she wouldn't die, but if she did at least she would not be around to reproach herself for it. She supposed what she wanted was to wake up in a hospital, surrounded by concerned friends and efficient nurses. "Judy, we had no idea," her friends would say. The nurses would hush everyone, tell her when to chew, swallow, roll over, sleep. She would sleep as long as she wanted in a white gauze world. She would be helpless.

She had fallen into a muddy, thick-headed dream when the phone rang. It kept on ringing. Since she was not dead, she had to answer it.

"Judy?" The voice was so small it fit in her ear. "Honey? Did I wake you up?"

It was her mother. "Kind of," Judy said. She couldn't hear herself say it. Her voice dropped into the silence like a stone in a well.

"Honey? Your phone must be going out."

"No, I'm here." Judy tasted the inside of her mouth. It tasted dead, even if the rest of her wasn't.

"Maybe it's my phone. We got a new phone for the den. Nothing ever works the way they say it will. How are you?"

"I'm dying."

"Darling, don't talk like that," said her mother briskly. "Everybody has those days."

Judy felt sweat rolling under her clothes, everywhere all at once. She leaned over the edge of the bed and vomited, thin sour purple vomit.

"Dying never helps anything," her mother went on. "Cheer up. Most people are just about as happy as they make up their minds to be. You were always such a happy child."

"No I wasn't. I was afraid of everything."

"Hold on," said her mother. The phone exploded in Judy's ear, a series of bludgeoning sounds. Her mother came back on the line. "That's much better. Darling, I should let you get some sleep. It's good to hear your voice. Call us. We worry when we don't hear from you."

"Why?" asked Judy. Then it was morning. It was fifteen minutes before the time she usually got up for work. The vomit had dried on the floorboards by her bed, leaving a small tidal pool of food particles. So that much had really happened. She wasn't sure about any of the rest of it. She was afraid it had, and that her worst fears were confirmed. She was emotionally invisible. It made no difference what she thought or felt or said. Others looked at her and saw what they had always seen. They thought she was happy. Most people were just about as happy as other people decided they should be.

She went into work that day. There was no reason not to. She threw up as soon as she got there. The path between her head and stomach was a subway line traversed by shrieking incessant trains. It was that day she had an insight. She did not feel compassion for the poor, or even that much guilt. She envied them because they were allowed to be unhappy. She was interviewing a client. The client's name was Mrs. Sturgis.

"And how have you been?" She marveled to hear herself, sprightly, banal, her lips twitching in a passable smile. Was there no part of her that was genuine?

"Praise Jesus, no worse," replied Mrs. Sturgis, belligerently. Mrs. Sturgis had breast cancer and bone cancer. Parts of her body kept dropping away. She wore a sticky blond wig to cover her bare scalp. Her pale eyes were flat with pain. She had four children, two of whom were diabetic, and a husband who drank. If you wanted pure suffering, she was perfect.

"We need to update your profile," said Judy, wondering just what combination of fear and hope and calculation allowed Mrs. Sturgis to praise the deity. "Is your husband working?"

"Oh, *him*," said Mrs. Sturgis, twisting her clamp-like mouth tighter.

Judy waited, but this was all the eloquence Mrs. Sturgis had to offer. Judy was used to dragging answers from her. It was as if Mrs. Sturgis begrudged letting any more of herself be taken away, even words. "Well, when was the last time he worked?"

"Know when he says he worked," said Mrs. Sturgis, meaningfully. She shifted her fatty shoulders. Her bosom shifted a moment later, like a sack of sand. Before the cancer she had probably been big, fleshy. Now she was sucked dry.

"Well, we have to put something down."

"Put down I never saw any money. Him and his stories."

Three months, Judy wrote, recognizing this as a new, danger-ous edge she was approaching: indifference, arbitrariness, spite. In similar fashion, she dealt with the questions about the children's doctor and Mrs. Sturgis's prescriptions.

Mrs. Sturgis sat, squat and unblinking. This was what was left of a human face, after you shoved it around enough. Her skin was freckled, dusty, worn thin. She looked impossibly ugly and she knew it. She saw it in other people's faces. Her own stare only reflected that back again. Oh God this woman, Judy thought, sick with feeling. How could anyone have problems compared to hers? How could you have problems if they didn't show? How could you refuse to pity Mrs. Sturgis? But I do. Judy's head was grinding and her stomach clenched. I do refuse, she said inwardly. I dislike and fear you.

"Coffee," said Mrs. Sturgis, out of nowhere. "Isn't coffee bad for you?"

"It's not particularly good for you."

"They say it gets into your brain," said Mrs. Sturgis severely. "I'm giving it up."

Judy waited for one of them to say more. When that didn't happen, she stared at Mrs. Sturgis, who stared back. There was nothing particularly rude about it. They could have been two cats.

Of course she should have agreed with Mrs. Sturgis. Should have told her of miraculous cures effected by caffeine-eschewing sufferers. Told her it would keep her last few healthy cells from peeling away. Chat her up. Be human. Here's your chance. Judy said nothing. That was how she knew she must hate Mrs. Sturgis. It must be hatred, when you withheld something that cost you so little.

"Well, that should do us," said Judy. A marvel of folksy cheer, she was. She reached for a paper clip, and then another. "Did you get your vouchers? Your receipts?"

She watched Mrs. Sturgis begin to gather her vinyl handbag,

her rain boots, her lumpy brown overcoat, and finally her body, that loose bundle of treacherous parts. She rolled and heaved and limped. The office humanely provided Mrs. Sturgis cab fare for her visits. The trip to and from the cab would probably kill her.

In the midst of her preparations, Mrs. Sturgis paused. "Doctor said I have a nervous bowel," she announced, a little grandly.

"Oh dear."

"It's a sensitivity thing," said Mrs. Sturgis.

After she'd finally gone, Judy went to the window. It was November, and the sky was thin and watery, the wind steady. Old newspapers and smaller, gaudier trash skittered along the sidewalks. The city was scoured by wind. People too were caught by it like so much garbage. It was a long time before Mrs. Sturgis emerged four stories below. Her coat flapped in the wind like something broken. One hand was clasped to her head and it threw her off balance, slowed her even further. Judy realized she was afraid her wig would blow away. And even this did not move her.

Judy watched Mrs. Sturgis until she stumped around a corner out of sight. She was tingling with hatred. It exhilarated her. People expected to be hated here, and now she could oblige them. She hated them because they were ugly, ill, hopeless—all the reasons you ought to pity them. Pity was only failed love. Pity exhausted you. Hatred made you feel powerful. You could never pity anyone enough to do them any good, but you could hate them all you wanted. She went back to her desk, feeling much steadier, and worked calmly through the rest of the day.

"I hate to see you so unhappy all the time," he said.

"I'm not," Judy protested. "I'm only unhappy when it makes sense to be. When something goes wrong or just when I get tired of being happy."

"Tired of being happy. Why would anyone feel that way?"

"Well, sometimes I do. Nobody has to believe it."

They were sitting at Judy's dining-room table. She'd cooked

dinner and, as usual, she'd made way too much food. Broccoli sagged in a volcanic lake of crusting cheese sauce. The cooling steak seeped blood.

He pushed his chair back from the table. She knew he would leave now. Once he'd eaten everything he wanted, he'd leave. No one was ever hungry enough to stay as long as she thought they should. But he said, "Have you ever thought about going to see somebody?"

"What do you mean?" She knew exactly what he meant.

"Like a counselor. Somebody who's good at thrashing out problems. Sometimes it helps to have somebody you can talk to."

"I'm talking to you. Right now."

He smiled and lowered his eyes. Mistake. He didn't want to be her therapist. She wouldn't want him to be.

Still, she couldn't let it go. She asked him just what sort of problems he thought she had.

"Like I said. You aren't happy."

"Happy is an attitude. It's not something you have to have."

"Sure it is. Why not."

"Character building."

"That's stupid. Look, drop it. Forget I said anything. You know, this was one of the top ten great all-around meals. Maybe number five. No, four."

"You can't do this. You can't tell me how sick I am and then leave."

"Did I say sick? I wish I could stay, but I only keep upsetting you."

"Bullshit."

He said, "I'm so stuffed, I don't think I'll need to eat again for a week."

After he'd gone, Judy ate the rest of the broccoli and two pieces of pecan pie. She did the dishes, soaped them carefully, and scalded them clean. She was not the sort of woman who threw dishes. She tidied the rooms, switched on the stereo, and turned off all the lights. In the darkness the stereo hummed green. There was a red dot of light to show the power was on.

The record was an old one. It was old when she got it, at a garage sale. The date, if there was one, had rubbed off the jacket long ago. The musicians looked mid-to-late hippie. The music was full of feedback and concussion. She always played only one song. Nowadays it was the only record she played. She sat on the floor with her arms clasped around her knees, watching the red and green. The beat thumped. The guitars grabbed notes and held them far out in the empty air, like coming for a long, long time.

> *Who do you love?*
> *Who do you lo-ove?*
> *Come on and take a little*
> *walk and tell me*
> *who do you love?*

The singer had a hoarse, throaty, bad-boy's voice. The song made her feel she was on the brink of something dangerous, a high cliff or a dark pit. She turned the volume up one more notch past what she thought the neighbors would bear. The record was scratched, and silvery balls of static jumped from it. Still the sound came through, urgent, menacing, hard. All the other love songs were sugary. She supposed that was why she liked this one. Judy wondered where the singer was now, if he'd grown pouchy and middle-aged or died from cocaine or something. She wondered if he was even the one who'd loved someone, or just the person who wrote the song. It didn't matter. Somebody had once loved somebody else, and the echo of it still reached her ears. Judy gripped her knees harder. "Who do you love, who do you love," she sang along under her breath, faking it. She knew she didn't love anyone at all.

The psychologist asked her what she saw as the main problem in her life. "I cook too much food," Judy said.

———

She was looking for another job. The psychologist had suggested it. Or rather, since he was not the sort of psychologist who gave advice, he put it on her list of life decisions. He talked about burn-out and making positive changes. Judy thought it was a nice way of saying that she herself was beyond hope, but she could at least get it together at work. And burnout was just another way of saying you hated people.

For a while Judy was excited about the idea of a new job. She updated her resume, she read the want ads. She considered going back to school. She imagined herself emerging with a new degree, a new woman, barking orders and building empires. Then she realized she did not want to be anything in particular, at least, not enough to work at it. When she considered what would really please her to do all day, she thought of making deliveries for United Parcel Service. She liked the idea of driving a van busily from place to place, wearing a neat anonymous brown uniform. People would be glad to see her because she brought them things. She stopped sending out her resume. She tore up her list of life decisions.

One evening, shopping in an expensive store, she wondered what it would be like to work in a place where people had lots and lots of money. The store was decorated grandly for Christmas. Small trees with Italian lights perched on columns. The vaulted ceiling, three stories high above the main floor, glittered with glass and silver globes, silver stars and bows and swags of silver roses. The carpeting smelled of perfume. The Muzak played the very classiest sort of Christmas carols, medieval arrangements performed by harpsichord, oboe, and flute. Everywhere were soft heaps of things, expensive surfaces.

"Can I help you?"

She had strayed too close to one of the counters and a sales-clerk appeared to guard it. The clerk was as splendid as the rest of the store. All the clerks were like that, pretty women who dressed like rich ones. Judy stared at the clerk. She was young, younger than Judy, with a prim, small-featured face. She wore a high-necked gray dress, severely fashionable, which made her look like a long gray tube. Her hair was white blond, short stiff curls—sheep's fleece in a storm. Silver shells hung from her ears. The face was painted raspberry, slate, blue, mocha. Amazing. To think that this face and Mrs. Sturgis's belonged to members of the same species. Judy watched the face begin to crease and pucker, and realized she had not answered.

"I'd like—" She cast about her. She seemed to have washed ashore in small leather goods. Her eye took in ranks of billfolds, coin purses, cigarette cases, eyeglass cases, in sober brown calf, red and navy and turquoise and gray and butter yellow leathers, paisley and embroidered fabrics, the hides of exotic animals—too much of everything. "—to look at wallets," Judy said, and the salesclerk turned noncommittal once more. It was a sort of code. Anyone too dazzled to get the words out would be hustled through the door.

The clerk handed over wallet after wallet, waiting while Judy pretended to examine them. The clerk's fingernails were polished, ten raspberry crescent moons. The nails tapped, out of rhythm with the medieval carols. It was plainly a boring transaction for both of them. No one would expect it to be otherwise. If she were a salesclerk, no one would expect her to pity or love or hate the customers.

It was then that she caught sight of her own face in one of the ever-present mirrors. She should not have been surprised. She looked the way she always looked in such stores. Her hair was as lank as if she'd sprayed it with a hose. Her face was bare, shiny, more unnatural somehow than the clerk's layers of cosmetics. The flesh was spread unevenly over the bones, like cold butter on bread. Her best sweater sagged at the neck. Her waistline was sloppy. Poor self-image, the psychologist said, but that wasn't the half of it. She was so ugly that she would not ever be allowed the luxury of treating anyone with indifference.

"I'd like to see that one." Judy pointed, and when the clerk's back was turned, she flopped one of the wallets into her open purse.

This is a suicide attempt, Judy thought. If anyone had seen her they'd wait until she reached the door to arrest her. She knew that much. There would be phone calls, lawyers, disgrace. "Judy, we had no idea," people would say, but not to her face.

The clerk saw nothing. She had the kind of face that saw nothing very easily. A few moments later Judy said, "I'm afraid I just don't see the kind I want." Ridiculous statement. She couldn't have imagined any other possible kind of wallet. The clerk looked nearly as bored as she would have been if Judy had bought something.

"I like your hair," said Judy, surprising both of them. She felt powerful in her ugliness, like Mrs. Sturgis, forcing people's eyes to her.

The clerk touched a hand to her hair, as if to remember just what shape it had taken. "Thank you."

"Is it expensive?"

"You mean—the perm?"

"I guess so." She was stalling for time, not wanting to leave and reach the door. "I keep meaning to do something about mine."

Judy giggled, and touched her own hand to her hair. If she had a wig, like Mrs. Sturgis, she could take it off.

She imagined the clerk was hesitating between polite escape and polite small talk. But the clerk leaned toward her and shook her head violently, raking her fingers through her white curls. They blurred in the air like a miniature snowstorm, then settled back into place undisturbed. "Look," said the clerk. "See what you can do. Everybody in the world should have hair like this, but in all different colors."

On the way out Judy forced herself to slow down, dawdle, pretend she was interested in silk scarves and crocodile handbags. She eyed the doors. No one official-looking waited there, but she knew these people made every effort to be unobtrusive, to look normal, as she herself did.

Even the music sounded expensive, Judy thought as a swell of it lifted her toward the triple bank of glass. She walked to meet them, head up, like the last scene in a movie. She kept a little smile in one corner of her mouth, ready for the moment when the hands descended on her. She would arch her eyebrow, questioning. Some mistake? Afraid not, miss. They would find the wallet. And after that there would be other hands.

Beyond the glass the city dusk lay like a blue pool. The carol was one of the stately ones, "Adeste Fideles," maybe, a triumphal march. The glass swung toward her.

And then she was outside. Nothing had happened. Without the frame of warm light the street was only dark. She leaned up against the rush of the late shopping crowds, and touched the wallet inside her purse. Of all the things to steal, an empty wallet. It was like a bad joke. Nothing had happened. She was still invisible.

He said, "I want to help you. I really do."

She had been crying steadily for ten minutes. The lights were already out. She kept crying to keep him awake. "Help me do what?"

"Feel better about things. Enjoy life."

"Like one big goddamned Pepsi commercial."

"I truly think there's something chemically wrong with you. One of those drug things."

"Caffeine."

"Huh?"

"So what's wrong with *you*? What's wrong with a man who can fall asleep while someone's crying?"

"Am I asleep?"

Judy raised herself up on one elbow. "Why do you want to help me?"

"Because you need it."

"Not good enough."

He yawned and pulled the sheet over his head. "Nothing's ever good enough for you."

"Do you love me?"

The sheet stopped its billowings. He exhaled. "Does it matter so much what I say?"

"I guess not."

They were both quiet then. After a while she heard his breathing lengthen. The body under the sheet relaxed into sleep.

This time she cried silently. Tears ran down her throat and burrowed into the sheets. With great caution, she twitched the blankets away from him. Little by little, until she had uncovered him down to his feet. Her eyes had adjusted to the dim underwater light from the hall, and she could see him clearly. He looked blue. Like something newly born or newly dead, fished out of the depths.

The house was chilly, and she put on a sweatshirt, sweatpants, thick cotton socks. Goosebumps were forming on his legs and arms. Funny how skin led this independent life of its own. She thought of Mrs. Sturgis's skin, thin as Kleenex, bombarded by radiation from outside, cancer from within.

She padded out to the kitchen. She sat down at the table, pulling the chair up hard, thump.

Bastard.

She slipped on her shoes, fetched her coat and gloves and keys and wallet. She thought about shooting him, buying a gun and shooting him, or setting the bed on fire, and knew she would settle instead for some small meanness. She turned on the stereo, set the volume on high, and positioned the record. She was out the door and at the elevator when the first crash of music reached her. She imagined she heard it falling all the way down the shaft after her.

It was past midnight, and no one was on the street when she stepped outside. There had been a hard frost. The ground was covered with it and the sidewalk glazed. Rings of frozen vapor surrounded the streetlights. Her street had trees and boxy hedges and buildings that sat like fists on little squares of lawn. It was considered a safe neighborhood. All that meant was that people left you alone. What was so safe about that?

She set off walking. She was still crying a little, weak, sick, furious, not caring what happened to her as long as it was his fault. This is a suicide attempt, she thought, aware she was being childish and that nothing she did made sense anymore. She would freeze to death or be raped or murdered or all of these and that would make her happy.

Of course, if you walked far enough in any direction the city provided you with an unsafe neighborhood. On the larger streets cars still rolled through the path of their own headlights. From time to time one of these honked at her, or someone shouted something from a window. A tavern sign winked out on a corner as she watched. Across the street two little Puerto Rican boys, out too late, chased each other down the broken sidewalk on skateboards. A thin sleet began to tap. Not too far from here the real decay began, warehouses as tall and black as vertical tombs, gangs of rats, steel gates pulled across steel doors, blind windows.

By her elbow, a voice said something in hard, efficient Spanish.

Judy's heart billowed up, then fell back to her knees. A woman sat in a doorway. You could tell it was a woman by her voice. Her face was grimed black, her eyes were white and veined, like cracked eggs. A knit hood was pulled down over her head, and a baseball cap over that. The rest of her was layers of flapping rags.

Judy bent closer, close enough to catch the smell. "Do you speak English?"

"Shit."

Judy regarded the face. The mouth gummed and spat more Spanish. What was it she kept trying to see in faces? Something human.

The Puerto Rican boys had crossed the street and racketed up to them. Their skateboard wheels cut trails in the frost. "Eh, it's Grandma," one of them said. He might have been as old as eleven, thin and woolly-haired. He danced with cold and excitement. "Grandma say, give her a dollar."

"Grandma nasty," said the second, smaller boy. "She piss on herself."

"Talk nice, dickface. Lady, Grandma say she hungry."

"Grandma say, Piss on everybody!"

"How do you say that in Spanish?" Judy asked. The old woman's tongue kept darting in and out of her mouth, a surprising pink. She didn't look at any of them but addressed the cement. The smaller boy giggled and retreated. The older boy took it up again, sounding almost patient:

"A dollar."

"You should go to a shelter," said Judy. Which of them did she mean? The cold was making her thick-headed. She felt as if they were the only people awake in the city and everyone else was iced in sleep. She wondered about the boys, if they had stolen the skateboards, if that was what they had instead of homes. "Ask her if she wants to go to a shelter," she said, but at the same time her hand closed around the wallet in her coat pocket. She drew it out, seeing the older boy's green eyes come closer, realizing two things simultaneously: that the boy would take it, and that it was the wallet she had stolen, still empty except for its protective leaf of tissue.

Something collided with the back of her legs, hard, at the same time the boy snatched at her hands. The next instant they were flying away on the skateboards, calling to each other in shrill, excited voices. The sleet was coming down in a fine curtain now, and their figures blurred in the distance, dissolving.

The old woman was laughing into the curb, a sound full of ancient spit. "Yes, funny," agreed Judy. "Joke."

She started back the way she'd come, back to the man who did not love her. Well, OK. She didn't particularly love herself yet. When she reached the apartment her legs were as numb as stumps, her hair full of ice. The city birds were calling, their voices small in the gray air. She opened the door cautiously. He was asleep on the couch, the blankets dragged into a cocoon around him. The record lay in two pieces on the floor, a perfect jagged crack, like something in the comics.

She had begun to shiver. She peered over the edge of the blankets to look at his face. Sleep made it appear slack, as if some pin that held it together had come loose, and anger, amusement, indifference—all the things that made him recognizable—had dropped away. Human? Yes, she decided, and her shivering increased, her heart started up like a drill in her chest, painfully, dangerously. There was no reason not to love anyone.

two

OTHER LIVES

FIRE DREAMS

Everybody lives two ways. The first is simple, the second less so.

It's Sunday afternoon. The firemen are washing the fire trucks, sending great streams of water into the air and filling the gutters with soapsuds. It reminds me of elephants taking baths. Other firemen are sweeping out the firehouse, or trimming weeds with a snarling electric wand. Sunday afternoon is when they do this sort of thing. The fire station is at the entrance to the subdivision, so people driving to and from Sunday errands can gaze approvingly at the firemen. *Volunteers,* people think, impressed.

I live next door to the firehouse, which is an aluminum-sided building with a flagpole. I live in a disreputable corner of an exemplary neighborhood. You reach our subdivision by driving a few miles down the highway, past a shopping center and a couple of superannuated farmhouses. It is nearly always Sunday afternoon here. It is the sort of neighborhood that real-estate agents enjoy touring with clients, pointing out its virtues from their pneumatic front seats. The lawns are groomed with military precision, and the houses sit on them like closed mouths. If a garage door opens, it reveals the organizational splendor of hardware-store advertisements: tools on pegboards, lawn chairs on hooks, garden-hose caddies, sparkling concrete. There is always a ball of some sort, either aloft or smacking on a sidewalk. There is a child on a bicycle and a dog barking at nothing.

At night no one lives here. That's what you'd think. The lights are out by ten, except for the ornamental lampposts in one or another front yard, throwing arcs of light on the white, white gravel of flower beds, on the acid-green grass. In a darkened room, a blue aquarium sends up bubbles, and fish circle their plastic coral, castles, mermaids. Everyone is asleep, or at least invisible. You try to imagine sex, anger, insomnia, grief. But everything is too well hidden, muffled behind layers of glass and draperies and silence. The night is unacknowledged.

But some nights the siren sounds. Men rise up from their beds, not yet awake, still dreaming of fires. Their hearts are large with excitement and hurry. Dark figures lope across the grass, calling to each other. The fire trucks go screaming out onto the highway, most often to some country district, returning a couple of hours later to fill the night with unnatural light and noise. This is when I hear them. I can sleep through the siren, but the laughter of the men wakes me, and I go to the window to watch. The men take their time folding the hoses and maneuvering the trucks back into place. The night is over but they linger, reluctant to let the excitement go. When they do return home the more anxious of the wives will be waiting up for them, offering coffee, asking, Was it a bad one? Was anyone hurt?

The husbands shake their heads. No big deal, they say,

yawning. It was a trash fire. Or a field fire. More yawning. Jeez, I'm beat. And they go off to bed for a last hour or two of sleep. The wives are left feeling they've been cheated.

I'm imagining that last part. I live alone, a suspect woman in a neighborhood of families. How would I know what the wives and husbands say?

There is always something happening at the firehouse. The firemen keep busy with raffles, yard sales, fund-raisers of all sorts. They have an annual pancake breakfast (spring), and a chili supper (fall). At these events, the firemen's wives don aprons and serve up food on plastic trays. I've eaten it, trying to be a good neighbor. On pancake day or chili day, the cars start arriving early. All day long, the hungry and sociable disembark. Inside, people sit at long tables drinking milk from cartons or iced tea from sweating plastic glasses. It's a friendly group. Everybody knows everybody else. The firemen's wives bustle importantly in the kitchen. They are stern, competent women, managing their children with efficient threats, wrinkling their noses over cigarettes, scrubbing and disinfecting energetically.

I sit at one of the tables ruminating over my milk, chewing thoroughly. Even while eating I maintain a pleasant, neutral expression—someone willing, though not anxious, to make friends. But no one talks to me. My solitude embarrasses them, and finally me. The pancakes accumulate in my stomach like a stack of mattresses; the chili solidifies. Eating this food is a ritual for me, the way eating the heart of bear was for Indians. If I eat my neighbors' food, will my house grow as sleek and prosperous as theirs?

My house is, I'm sure, a grief to them. It is a survivor of pre-development times, a shabby bungalow that must have been unimpressive even when new. It is the sort of house the real-estate agents refer to darkly as "rental property." The gutters sag. The paint blisters. The flowers in my odd garden—daisies, golden yarrow, orange cosmos—have a weedy, overgrown look to them. I live somewhere between halfhearted effort and eyesore. My plumbing sweats. My driveway is bald in patches. My lawn distresses everyone from April through September.

The lawn is how I met Clark. To explain: I have too much lawn, a third acre of dispirited grass punctuated by thistle and dandelion. I wish it would turn brown and stunted. Either that or come up in wildflowers, a meadow. Anyway, I was trying to mow my lawn. I usually try, and get just so far before I give up and hire someone else to finish it. This time, I couldn't get the mower started. Each time I yanked at the thing, it barked and stopped short of turning over. Each time, I swore and bruised myself against it. I couldn't win and I couldn't hurt it. The muscle in my shoulder felt torn. Sweat was growing on me like fur. I considered going berserk, then straightened my back and called, "Hey, could you help me a minute?"

That was Clark. He was next door at the fire station, dragging boxes out to the trash. I didn't know him then. He's blond, and all summer long he looks boiled from the sun. A spare, rangy man who walks with a hitch, as if his shoulders were out of line. You don't think there's any size at all to him until you stand up next to him. I don't know what I looked like that day. Pissed off, and wearing something I could cut the grass in.

Clark approached, looking startled. Or maybe it was just his blond eyebrows. "I can't get this mower started," I announced. I wanted to say the goddamn, son-of-a-bitch mower. I wanted to sound tough. I was embarrassed about asking for help.

Clark didn't say anything. He never says much of anything. He stooped over the mower, gave it an experimental tug. I felt better when it wouldn't start for him either. Another yank. This time he was getting his back into it. The mower kicked and coughed. Greasy smoke erupted from it in a steady stream, turning the grass blue-black. It was genuinely alarming, as if I really would need a fireman in a minute. Clark shut the mower off. We watched it bubble blackly to a halt. "You put oil in it lately?" he asked.

His voice was light, flat, perfectly Midwestern. If he was laughing at me, I couldn't tell. I figured out later that he wasn't.

"Too much, huh?" I said, regarding the oil pooling on the mower's surface. I felt as mortified as if shit had poured out of the thing.

Clark wiped his hands on a nearby patch of weeds. "You'll have to drain all that out," he advised me. "Drain it out and start over. How much oil you put in there, anyway?"

"Oh, I really don't know." I shrugged. I'd put in most of a quart, but I was damned if I was going to admit it. "Thanks for your help."

He said it was no problem. We introduced ourselves. He lived just down the street, he said, pointing. I knew which house was his. When Clark cuts his grass, he uses a riding mower. Afterward his lawn has a pattern in it, perfect diagonal stripes. The diagonals knocked me out. They indicated either compulsiveness or artistic nonconformity, I couldn't decide which.

"Night before last, I heard the sirens," I said. "Was it a big fire?"

"Night before—Oh. Nah. Not really."

"Where was it?" I persisted. I was tired of not knowing things. And I wanted to keep him talking.

"County Line Road. This house trailer. Nobody home. We think it was electrical."

"Electrical," I repeated. I didn't like to hear things like that. As if the walls of all houses were threaded with mutinous wires, twining like ivy, conspiring against you.

"I hate a trailer fire," said Clark. "Those things burn like cereal boxes. People shouldn't live in them."

The line of sunburn under his eyes darkened. Talking about fires seemed to energize him. He brushed the sweat from his forehead with the back of his hand. He looked strong. I imagined him climbing tall ladders into smoke, swaying with the high-pressure stream of water. "Where should they live, then?"

"Pardon?"

"Some people can't live anywhere else. That's what trailers are for."

Clark looked at me, visibly thinking. You could see different thoughts tugging him this way and that. His nose twitched. His eyebrows converged. He was trying to figure me out, why I lived the way I did, alone and out of place. He looked guilty, embarrassed. "I guess so," he said. Then, "You should get a dog."

"Pardon?"

"A dog. Nobody bothers you when you have a dog."

"But nobody bothers me now," I said.

Clark shrugged. "You never know about people."

"Maybe not," I said. He was alarming me. I wondered what it meant when someone looked at you imagining how easily you could be hurt.

"Don't worry," he said. "We keep an eye on you from the firehouse. We watch out for things. Remember to drain out that oil." He ducked his head and smiled a quick, jerky smile.

It was more than a week before I got the grass cut.

I take a walk through my neighborhood. Who here would do me harm? It's twilight. The lawns are velvet, and kindly yellow light spills from the windows. On the next block are the Holidays. That's what I call them, though it's not the name on their mailbox. As regularly as a grade school, their house displays the trappings of the season. Festoons of paper hearts a month before Valentine's Day. Then eggs and bunnies, then patriotic bunting, then jack-o'-lanterns and witches. Turkeys in November, Christmas an explosion of lights and plastic Santas. Every night, the premises are lit up like a prison yard.

The Holidays are bizarre, but they're not the sort of people Clark warned me about. Their eccentricities are too well displayed to be dangerous. They have no secrets. They are nothing to fear. They are a skin turned inside out.

At Clark's house there is a gap in the drapes and the color TV is alight. From the sidewalk it looks like a luminous marble, or like the earth seen from space. Someone's head is visible, resting on a chair. From the back I can't tell if it's Clark or Mrs. Clark or their son. Mrs. Clark is a tall woman with amorphous hair. I see her only from a distance, tending to garbage cans or lawn sprinklers. I imagine what she and Clark say to each other: *The roses need fertilizing. Did you fix the window? The washer? One gallon latex semigloss white. Kleenex.*

Their boy is about ten. Blond, like Clark. I've never talked to him, though I've seen him often. He speeds down the sidewalk on his bicycle, coming up behind so fast and so silently all you feel is the sting of the air blowing past you, a whirring like an insect. Sometimes the boy looks back. To see if he's frightened you? I don't know his name. I see him with other such boys, calling out to each other from their bicycles, shouting taunts. The boys are restless, shrill, bored. They pedal the bicycles furiously, as if this might make them grow up faster. They argue over baseball games and handfuls of coins. They set off forbidden firecrackers. If there were large enough trees here, they would build tree houses. Instead, they erect backyard tents, which they inhabit all summer long, reading comic books with flashlights, filling their mouths with soda, Oreos, bubble gum in the shape of robots. Restless, shrill, by turns languid and hyperkinetic, they seem to me both alarming and hopeful. They are unformed; they are not yet respectable.

"What is it you like about fighting fires?" I ask Clark one afternoon.

He shrugs. He either doesn't want to answer or wants me to pull it out of him.

I anticipate this; I'm ready to be patient. "I mean, I'd be scared."

"Nah."

"Come on. Aren't you afraid of what could happen?"

"A chemical fire. You worry about those, sure," says Clark.

We're standing on my front porch. I'd ask him to sit down, but that would startle him, make him take flight. Standing, we can talk all day.

"You go into a warehouse, farm shed, place like that. You don't know what all's in there. Things start popping, they could be caustics, explosives, anything. Stuff's like nerve gas. Go in without your air, you're cooked."

"I never thought of that," I say. "That would be bad, all right." Then, craftily, "The lumberyard. You must have liked that one."

Clark grins his sideways grin. It's as if one side of his mouth is trying to hide the other. "It was something."

People drove to the lumberyard fire as if it were a parade. There was never a question of putting the fire out. It burned hot and clean, a rolling orange flame in the shape of a ragged paintbrush. People crowded against the barricades, wanting to get close enough for it to feel mildly dangerous. Six fire companies were there, talking into radios, marching around the perimeter in their heavy rubber boots and coats. (Are they really rubber? I'll have to ask Clark.) When the roof went, it didn't happen all at once, the way I thought it would. It seemed to take a long time, and it made a noise like a waterfall. Who would have thought fire could sound like water? We watched the roof sink in on itself, making a hole in the great flame we'd almost come to believe was solid. New flames licked up from it, new sparks somersaulted through the air. The firemen watched too, no longer pretending to do anything. We were all in love with it. We didn't want it to go out. I had a vision of us feeding the flames, of people scurrying to bring it fuel, tossing microwaves, minibikes, Mr. Coffees, La-Z-Boys into the fire. The heap of things grows. The fire consumes golf clubs and toaster ovens. And everyone is peaceful and content, watching.

Recollecting myself, I say to Clark, "No one got hurt either. That's important."

Clark nods, looking pious. "That's the real satisfaction of this job."

I say, "What would you do if there weren't any fires?"

He's looking at me, and everything about him is completely still except his eyes. His eyes are fixed on my face. They are moving him closer without his taking a step. The late-afternoon shadows pass over us like breath. He says, "Once in a while I . . ."

At the same moment we both hear it, that small insect whine of gears. Clark's son coasts by on the sidewalk slowly, balancing on his bicycle pedals in a sort of parade rest. One hand hoists something to his mouth, something purple on a stick. His face, turned toward us, staring, is elongated by the labor of sucking. He resembles a little blond horse. The pedals click; he's gone.

"Getting late," says Clark. "Been nice talking to you."

I sit on the porch after sunset. It's suppertime, TV time. If you were to invade the grid of privacy fences that mark the back yards, those fences within fences, a stockade of houses defended against themselves, you'd see families bathed in the light of the cathode ray. An enormous car passes by. It's some mutant species of Lincoln, bronze and caramel, metal made to resemble wood, and so long it seems to bend around corners. The tires are white, the glass is tinted the color of tobacco. There are little chrome crests, crossed swords, miniature banners, scrolls. The car has a calculated heraldic look, as if it was inspired by an old Robin Hood movie. It rolls majestically down the street and out of sight.

Things begin to go wrong—little things at first. A bicycle disappears from a back porch. A garbage can is rolled into the street. A mailbox is knocked off its moorings. People are puzzled, then outraged. Neighbors regard each other warily over the fences. Small mischief, but it does a disproportionate amount of damage. The polite theory is that outsiders, deprived and envious youths from less fortunate districts, have invaded us, but in reality everyone suspects everyone else's children.

Then the Holidays are victimized. Someone heaves a rock through the picture window where they have displayed, in the sweat of August, a Halloween witch. The next day a repair van pulls up in their driveway along with a somber car, most probably the insurance agent's. When the window is replaced it's left vacant, as if in mourning. Who would do something so mean-spirited? So petty? So audacious?

"I would," I say to Clark. "If I thought I could get away with it."

We're eating peanut-butter-and-jelly sandwiches in bed. Peanut butter and jelly is all we could find in the kitchen. The television is on and we're hitting the remote switch: talk shows, baseball, Japanese science fiction. I like Clark better with his clothes off. The pattern of white and sunburn reminds me of the pattern in his lawn.

"I hope the siren doesn't start," I say. "I hope you don't have to jump up and go fight a fire."

"I don't care. Everything can burn down."

"You don't mean that."

He rolls onto me, fast, so his weight pushes the breath out of me. On the television, a cardboard Japanese city sways and totters. The tiny screams are blotted out by Clark's warm mouth on my ear. He breathes peanut butter. "Don't be so sure," he whispers.

Evening. I am walking my dog. The dog is an elderly spaniel with jowls, and pouchy fat dangling from him like an udder. The dog's name is Snoopy. "Good dog," I say to him, making conversation. "Good Snoopy." He looks up at me with sorrowing, red-rimmed eyes. He reminds me too much of my shabby furniture and mismatched plates. Still, I enjoy walking him. A dog gives you an excuse for a walk. It's a kind of camouflage, as well as protection. With a dog, no one suspects you of nosiness or idling. You become less visible. Clark was right. No one will bother me.

We're rounding the corner toward home when I hear the sirens. The trucks are just pulling out, swaying as they make the turn. The men holding on behind look precarious and small. The sirens recede in the distance, like sound falling down a well.

By the time we reach my yard, the fire trucks are back. No noise this time, no flourishes. The men drop off the truck and walk away quickly, as if embarrassed. I look for Clark but don't see him. "What happened?" I call to one man, a man with a blue T-shirt and a potbelly. Not all the firemen are in good shape, like Clark.

The man gives me a look. "False alarm," he says curtly, and points his stomach down the block toward home.

It rains for a week and no one can cut the grass. When I let the dog out he squats miserably at the edge of the yard. He has a constant smell of old rug. My neighbors worry about their sump pumps and garage roofs. At night we sleep in a world of water, the sound of it soaking into our dreams. Clark's sunburn is fading. I tease him about it, tell him I'm going to get a sunlamp and adhesive tape and burn my initials all over his body like tattoos. But he's gloomy.

"I'm not happy," he says. "I'm tired of being a fireman."

I look at him, startled. "Why?"

"I don't know. There aren't any good fires now. It's just not the same."

"Maybe people don't appreciate you? They take you for granted?"

"It used to be enough," Clark says mournfully, "keeping things clean, staying alert. Now, who cares?"

"I've done this to you," I tell him.

He lets his hand graze my breast, tries to make a joke. "I didn't know how much I was getting into."

"You were happy before you met me."

"But I didn't know I was happy. What good did it do me?"

I don't have an answer for that and he mopes on home, his shoes squishing with rain.

I think the whole neighborhood has been infected with discontent. A mailbox sags on a broken hinge. Hedges grow leggy. A door slams, cutting off the sound of an argument. There's nothing good on TV. When the rain pauses from time to time, low clouds remain, pressing the smell of swamp into everything.

One night, just after I turn my lights out, I hear something beneath the bedroom window. Whispers, someone giggling. The dog snores undisturbed at the foot of the bed. I creep to the window. "Chicken," I hear a voice say distinctly. A boy's voice. "*You* do it, then," says another. "Go ahead. It was your idea, big shot."

Just then the dog awakes and, snuffling with confusion, hurls himself at the window, baying. They are so young their voices are still girls' voices when they scream. They bolt away across the wet grass too fast for me to see their faces.

Clark's son's name is Cliff. I ask Clark about him and he says, "Funny kid. Won't talk anymore. Ask him a question, he looks out the window. Name, rank, and serial number, that's all you get out of him these days." I tell Clark it's just the age he is, a phase.

I sneak up behind Cliff when he's on his bicycle. I have to hide in the shrubbery for hours, as if it were a duckblind. I wait for the whir and click of his gears, then spring out, wrestling his handlebars to a stop. "Gotcha."

He topples off his bicycle but lands on his feet. Even now, he only looks me in the eye for a moment, then his face closes up again. Tough kid. "Gimme my bike," he says.

"What were you doing under my window?"

"I didn't do nothing," he says, addressing the air to the left of my head.

"Bullshit." The great thing about ten-year-olds is that you don't have to watch your language. "I caught you red-handed."

"You can't prove nothing."

"I don't have to. Look at you. You have one of those naturally guilty faces. You ought to do something about it. Otherwise you're going to spend your life in police lineups."

He takes this as a compliment. Pleasure fleets across his face, then he flattens it again, looking sulky.

"Nice talking to you, Cliff."

"Call me Spike," he says, coasting down the sidewalk.

The rain stops, but in its place is a glaring, no-color sky. Everything feels sticky, everyone is stupefied with heat. "Dog days," I tell

Snoopy. He's wrapped himself around the toilet and he lies there, panting shallowly.

I'm in the bathtub. I've been there all morning. I'm trying to shrivel myself up entirely. Skin is the enemy in this weather. Then I hear the peculiar moan and wrench of the plumbing, which means next door the firemen are opening a hydrant. An unmistakable sound, invasive and guttural. As I lie in the bathtub, it feels like someone is goosing me. I dress hurriedly and go to the door.

It's a strange sight. The firemen are lined up in military formation, at attention. In spite of the heat, they are wearing full regalia: hats, boots, gloves, long shaggy coats. Each fireman clutches a bouquet of wilting back-yard flowers: petunias, snapdragons, zinnias. The fire chief is reading from a small book, and when he closes it the men, on cue, drop the flowers into the stream of water making its way along the curb. They stand for a moment with bowed heads, then they troop inside. It looks curiously like a funeral, though for no one in particular.

It's evening, and not one breath cooler. Clark has heat rash on his stomach. He scratches it ferociously, leaving clawed red crescents.

"I wish you'd stop that."

He gives me an ugly look. "I thought that was your whole philosophy. If you have an itch, scratch it, and damn the consequences."

"Guilt-tripping. I should have known you'd get to that."

His face turns the color of his inflamed skin, and red seeps into his eyes. He draws in his breath. "All right," he says. "I'll take my share of the responsibility."

"I hate that word," I say. My turn to sound bitter. I know it's all over and I've lost something.

"Things were better before," he says. "Everyone knew who they were and how to behave. We didn't have secrets. Everything was out in the open."

"You'd better get on home," I tell him, wanting him gone now.

He bounds through the room, snatching up his clothes. He's

that grateful to be leaving. At the door he hesitates, seems as if he's about to shake my hand. Kisses me instead. "I'm sorry," he says. "I'm not the man you thought I was."

"Remember to put something on that rash," I tell him.

It's Sunday afternoon. We all have our jobs to do. The firemen are painting the trim on the firehouse. They have erected scaffolding, a kind of exoskeleton, around the building. They haul buckets up and down, or they take turns standing back to admire their work. Clark is perched on the topmost rung of the scaffold, showing off. He is painting the very highest board. It looks as if he were painting the sky. The muscles in his reaching arm form one long arc. Reaching, reaching . . . the scaffolding begins to shake and clank, threatening disaster. Finally he steadies himself and climbs down, grinning, as though he knew all along he wouldn't fall.

Next door I'm doing laundry. I'm hanging all my best underwear on the back-yard clothesline, pinning it carefully so the wind puffs everything into anatomical shapes. On the other side of the back fence children are playing with cap guns and making realistic dying noises. They are very young children, but they know exactly how to do this. After a time, bored with dying, they begin a ritual, listless argument. Did not. Did so. Did not. Did so. Bored with this too, they let it lapse. "I know all four swear words," one of them announces.

There's a scent of autumn in the air, something smoky. When night comes, pockets of mist fill the low places. The mist is like smoke. The smoke is like mist. Dreams become almost visible. In Clark's dream my house is on fire. The house has grown a second story, and he has to climb a ladder to save me. Everything is a total loss. I'm endlessly grateful.

Cliff, the son of Clark, dreams that he comes home from school to find his parents' house in ashes. He parks his bicycle on the sidewalk and scuffs through the wreckage thoughtfully. It was sort of a dumb house anyway, he thinks. "A terrible tragedy," someone says. "But you know, I presume, that they weren't your true parents."

In my dream, flames surround the fire station like a crown. They hiss and snap and shudder. But, as in a dream, nothing is consumed. Burning and burning. I keep trying to wake up. Things could go on this way forever.

THE WIDOWER

The doorbell rang, and Campbell's wife shouted from upstairs that she was in the middle of shaving her legs, could he get it? She had a habit of announcing things that Campbell would rather not hear about. He put his newspaper down and went to the front door. At first he saw no one there, only fat green treetops, blurred and wavering behind the high glass panel. Stepping closer, he saw Dr. Flynn pacing the walkway below the porch, interrogating the flowers.

Campbell watched him. Dr. Flynn stooped and fussed with something. They hadn't kept up the flower beds, what with all the other work the house needed, and besides, they were ugly plantings. There were lots of cabbagey hostas, which Campbell had never liked. Bells of Ireland and starved-looking salvia. They were going to dig it all up and put in something more updated, something else for Flynn to object to. They'd bought the house from Flynn three months ago. Flynn was a widower. His wife's damp ghost hung on, in the garden and elsewhere. Flynn hung on. It was a package deal.

At the house closing Flynn leaned across the gleaming conference table, a pouchy old man in a golf shirt and seersucker pants. "I understand you're going to paint the living room."

"That's right."

"Paint, as in new color?"

"Sort of a gray," said Campbell.

"More eggshell than gray," said his wife.

"We had a top-notch decorator in when we redid the house the last time. And that decorator chose the perfect color for the living room. Wedgewood Blue. It's designed to take advantage of the natural light in every season."

"It needs painting," said Campbell, wanting to put a stop to this sort of thing.

"But why change the color?"

Campbell surveyed the assembled realtors and mortgage officers, their smoothly listening faces. What the hell. He was never going to see any of them again after today. He said, "I guess it's like dogs. You have to pee on the bush to get your scent on it."

The doctor sat back in his chair, fascinated into silence. In the car on the way home, Campbell's wife said, "I can't believe you said that about dogs."

"Yeah. Don't ask me where that one came from."

"We don't even have a dog."

"That's not the point."

"I feel sorry for him. I mean, he lived there about a hundred years. I bet that was his wife's favorite color, Wedgewood Blue. Maybe we shouldn't paint it after all."

"Let's not start, OK?"

"I just think it's sad. What if we live there all our lives and then one of us dies? I think it would be very hard to let go. I completely understand how he feels."

It was not difficult to understand how Dr. Flynn felt because he told them. "It's like cutting off your own arm." Had Flynn ever cut off anyone else's arm? No, he had been a different kind of doctor, a pathologist. They were viewing the house for the first time. Campbell's wife and the realtor were down in the kitchen. He could hear them opening cupboards and disapproving, knowledgeably, of the linoleum. Flynn and Campbell were upstairs; Flynn had him cornered. "My daughter's been after me to sell. All the time with the nagging. They want to move me into one of those retirement places. Death camps. Wheelchair farms. Do I look like I need a wheelchair? I passed my last driver's exam by a mile. Aced it. The death camp has handles in the can so you don't fall down. I bet every time I go in there, I'll think about falling down. Wouldn't you?"

Campbell studied the ceiling. There was a water stain in one corner. Leaky roof? One more thing. The plumbing hiccuped. The furnace looked like a carbon-monoxide dispenser. The house would need every imaginable repair. There was a smell to it, a smell of mattresses slept on until they were nearly a part of the body, like a gland. Smells of talcum powder and long-dead cats and the gluey remnants of old medicine bottles. He could not imagine living there. He smiled briefly at Dr. Flynn, already thinking ahead to the next house on the list.

"I bet you two got married not too long ago. Am I right or am I right?"

"Beg your pardon?"

"You and your wife. You have that first-house look in your eye. That major-purchase gleam. Hotcha."

"We're in a condo now," said Campbell. In fact they'd been married eighteen months. He had waited until he was thirty-three to get married. Now it was time to establish themselves, incur serious adult debt, think about starting a family. You needed a house before you could do anything.

"My wife and I were married fifty-one years. She died of an aneurysm. Something in the brain just goes snap crackle pop."

"Sorry to hear that." Weren't these people supposed to leave while their houses were being shown?

"She didn't suffer one second. She was down in the basement doing laundry. I heard the noise she made when she fell. And I knew right then what happened. Don't ask me how. I just did. But I didn't go downstairs right away. I was eating a bowl of soup in the kitchen, and I finished eating and rinsed the bowl in the sink and wiped the table. Isn't that the damnedest thing?" Flynn's mouth crumpled like Kleenex, and his eyes squeezed out little tears. "It was one of those times you know your life's about to change forever, and you just want to put it off for another couple minutes."

Campbell was sure that Flynn had told this story before, probably told it to everyone he met. There was a self-satisfied quality to his mourning, something ritualized and relishing. But hearing it was still invasive, a swarm of death and grief and the confusion of the heart making itself known.

"I hope it doesn't put you off the house."

"Not a bit."

"Knowing she passed away on the premises. A natural death, of course."

"Excuse me," said Campbell, stretching his ears for sounds from downstairs, then nodding and hurrying away.

The realtor confirmed that the house had been on the market for some months. "He'd probably consider a low offer," she said coaxingly.

"You could do something with that house," said Campbell's wife. "The floors would be beautiful if you stripped them and refinished them. And that bay window. They don't build them like that anymore."

"Why not?"

His wife and the realtor gave him a distant, pitying look. They seemed to have bonded together, excluded him, already decided what sort of house he would spend his money on. He was reminded of his wedding, all the preparations and fuss, which he had unwittingly set in motion, and which then had moved far beyond his control. The realtor was a glossy middle-aged woman who dressed in outfits. You kept noticing different bright-colored parts of her: shoes and necklaces and scarves and handbags. Campbell sometimes confused her, in thought, with his mother-in-law. The realtor sent them calendars and greeting cards. She never said house; she said home. Campbell supposed she was good at what she did, but he still disliked her for her veneer of purely commercial manners. They had been house hunting for some weeks now. They were looking for what the realtor called a "starter home," meaning not much money. It was a difficult market, the realtor said, but it was as if she meant the opposite, as if she was consoling them for a personal failing.

"I was talking about craftsmanship," said Campbell's wife. "Nobody's into craftsmanship anymore."

"I thought we'd pretty much decided on a new place."

The realtor said, "Older homes have so much more character. Buy cheap enough and you can use the money you save to remodel."

"Then we wouldn't really be saving money, would we?"

Another of the pitying, excluding looks. Campbell said, "His wife died in the basement."

"What?"

"Flynn's wife. She dropped dead doing the laundry. Right in the middle of the rinse cycle." He turned to the realtor. "I guess he didn't tell you."

"That's really gross," said Campbell's wife. "What did she die of?"

"I think he said blood poisoning."

"Yuk."

"Nothing contagious," said the realtor coldly.

"I think it gives the place more character," said Campbell.

They looked at three more houses that day. By now Campbell had learned to translate real-estate prose. *Cozy* meant "small," *wooded acreage* might border a landfill, and so on. You could count on a certain level of disappointment. The realtor dropped them off at their condo, with a fresh stack of brochures and listings, those glossy, full-color, nearly pornographic depictions of houses—homes!—arranged in their most airbrushed, concupiscent poses. Campbell threw them all bottoms-up on the coffee table and went to stretch out on the bed.

"Why do you have to be so mean to her?" demanded his wife, following him into the bedroom.

"She always has lipstick on her teeth."

"Don't you want to find a house?"

"What do you think she wears to sleep in?"

"You're impossible," said his wife, sitting on the edge of the bed and pulling off her shoes. She was a pretty wife. She had slim white feet, high-arched and curvy, with pink-painted toenails. Her behind rested on the mattress next to him, sweet and cushiony. He reached out and walked his fingers up to it.

"Stop that."

"Come over here."

"No. I'm mad at you."

"I'm sorry. Come over here so I can show you how sorry I am."

She threw a pillow, then bounced on top of him. "Let's pretend the bed is a great big haystack," she said.

They forgot about Flynn's house. Every weekend they looked at houses, sometimes with the realtor, sometimes on their own. They stalked the suburbs with maps and the classifieds. They saw houses they liked, but all of them were out of their price range. There was nothing in their price range that didn't seem utilitarian, cramped, entirely wrong. Perhaps they would be better off staying in the condo, at least for now. But that made them feel gloomy, as if they had lost momentum, and the promise of their future was diminishing.

Then he came home from work one day to find his wife with the phone to her ear. "Guess who had a heart attack." His own heart floated loose. "Oh I didn't mean anybody we knew. Remember that old man with the house?"

It had been a mild heart attack, but his daughter and the doctor ganged up on Flynn. The house was too much for him. The stairs alone would finish him off. Flynn had become what was known in the ads as a "motivated seller." They could get the house for a very reasonable price, if they were quick about it.

Flynn had lost weight. His arms were thin as knotted string. His nose stood out like a beak and his mouth hung open, laboring. He was sweeping the front walkway when they arrived, dragging a broom across last fall's leaves. He started toward them but they breezed past him and into the front hall. Campbell had to give the realtor credit for that. She smiled her big smile and waved her big wave, not breaking stride. There was a great deal to consider if they were serious about the house. They went from room to room, trying to decide what would have to be remodeled right away, what could wait. There would be contractors and inspections and bids and permits.

"Tell me you're going to love it," his wife pleaded. "You have no idea what a difference skylights can make."

Campbell only shrugged, not wanting to abandon the leverage his resistance gave him. But he was beginning to feel excitement at the grand scope of the project, how absorbing and all-involving it would be. The house could be made over in their own image, freed from Mrs. Dr. Flynn's net curtains and brocades. He stepped out onto the back porch, breathing in the mild spring air. It was a quiet neighborhood, gentled by time. There were shade trees and trim shutters, green lawns and birdsong. Campbell was a practical man, unwilling to trust anything that could not be handled or counted, but standing there on the porch he had a moment of pure vision. His life would take root here. This sky would be his sky. He would stand on this spot more times than there were counting, and each time would be both the same and different.

Flynn limped around the corner of the house, the broom tucked beneath his arm, hobbling him. He sat down on the bottom porch step, out of breath, purplish nicks showing in his skin where his glasses had slipped. He twisted around to look up at Campbell. "Goddamned cardiologist. He doesn't know which end he poops from."

"I'm glad you're feeling better," said Campbell, although the remark raised the question: Better than what?

"Everybody thinks I should hurry up and die. Move on, clear out, save them a lot of trouble. I say, they have me confused with somebody else. Doctor Donald Duck. Quack quack. The man graduated at the bottom of his class. I looked it up. So. You going to buy the place?"

Campbell said that nothing had been decided yet. In fact they were considering the lowball offer the realtor had suggested.

"Where are you going to find trees like this? I ask you. I planted that hackberry myself, when we first moved in. Now look at the two of us. The tree's twenty feet tall and I'm just an old stump."

Campbell couldn't think of the right remark to finesse Flynn's belligerent self-pity. And he didn't want to start admiring the landscaping, in view of the lowball bid. He was relieved when his wife came out onto the porch. "There you are. Hi, Dr. Flynn. How's your poor heart?"

"Broke in a thousand pieces."

"What happened?"

"There are still such beautiful young women in the world, and I just remembered I'm an old man."

His wife smiled. She had a knock-out smile. "I bet you're not all that old."

"Seventy-five on my next birthday."

"Well that's not *old* old."

"I thank you for your kindness. Your husband is a lucky man. I hope you two end up living here. I'd like to think of another happy couple taking our place."

"What was your wife's name? I want to know."

"Caroline. My Caroline. If you'll take an old man's advice. Treasure each other. Let each day be a pearl you string together to make the necklace of your lives."

"That is so sweet," said Campbell's wife. "Why don't you ever say anything that nice to me?"

"Oh come on, Monica."

"I think your Caroline was the lucky one." She smoothed her skirt, which was light and spring-like, reminiscent of petticoats and milkmaids, and went back into the house.

Flynn bent double to hoist himself up from the porch step. He winked and made a tasting shape of his mouth. "Yum yum."

It took some doing to get the house at a price they could manage. Flynn may have given them his blessing, but he only reluctantly gave ground. Once again Campbell was forced to admire the realtor. She cajoled and bullied, flattered and pushed. Flynn didn't want to believe that his basement seeped, or that the kitchen was no longer at the top of its form. He accepted their third offer, but with an injured air, as if by rights they owed him more.

As soon as they moved in, Flynn began making his suggestions. The phone rang importantly. Flynn, garrulous and helpful, reading pages from his owner's manual to them. They should be careful of the drains. He had always avoided using harsh chemical products in the drains. He'd left the blister pack the soap dish had come in, should they ever need to mail it in for repairs. There was a file of his correspondence with wallpaper companies, trying to match the paper in the upstairs hall. When Campbell fixed a leak in the toilet, he found the 2,000 Flushes had been labeled: Replace 8/1. Flynn, of course, would calculate the number of flushes per day. He called to caution them about the kitchen storm windows, which were tricky. They'd see what he meant.

"He's just lonesome," Campbell's wife said. "I don't mind talking to him."

"How long are we supposed to put up with this?"

His wife was going through a stack of decorator magazines. She spent most of her time these days in the Talmudic study of such magazines. "What are you afraid of?"

"I'm not *afraid* of him. He's a pain in the ass. He's senile."

"What does it cost to be nice to him? He's old and sick. I never knew you were such a cold person."

"The man has a daughter. She can be nice to him. She can keep him leashed."

"You're being perfectly hateful." She pushed the magazines aside to glare at him. Now he'd done it.

Perhaps he was afraid. Not of Flynn, but of the stale, used-up past that had once been Flynn's future. He wanted to feel that his own life was newly minted, unique. He would not be beholden to anyone else's dead dreams.

He had to promise his wife that he would be nicer to Flynn, hoping, of course, that he wouldn't have to act on it. But here was Flynn again this fine summer morning, making yet another farewell tour. Campbell opened the front door. Flynn, still absorbed in the flowers, waved without raising his head. He'd gained back some weight, and his skin had lost that old-newspaper color. His heart was probably good for another decade.

Campbell went down to him. Flynn said, as if they had already been speaking, "You know you got snails in here?"

"I guess that's not good."

"I hate snails. I hate their slimy little sucking mouths. You know what kills them? Snail Away. You get it at Ace Hardware. One box'll last you forever."

"We're going to be digging it all up anyway. Putting in some

other stuff. Ornamental grasses and coneflowers and bee balm."
Flynn looked uncomprehending. "Sort of a prairie look."

"What do you want to plant a bunch of weeds for?"

"Then we're going to put in some nude statues. Just joking."

"Very funny. I hope you and your jokes know CPR. Come see what I brought you."

Flynn led the way to his car and opened the trunk. "Spare parts for the water softener. I forgot I even had them."

Campbell regarded the dusty cardboard box and the useless-looking, knuckle-shaped bits of plastic inside. Flynn waved a technical diagram, much-handled, ringed with coffee-cup circles. "Special system. I had it put in myself."

"Dr. Flynn."

"You just try and get the replacement parts for a custom system."

"We have to talk about something."

Flynn's mouth pursed, his eyelids batting dryly. Had he ever been a handsome, or even an average-looking man, back before his face raisined up? Possible, but there was no evidence of it now. Veins in his forehead stood out, green and webbed. His teeth were wearing down, like an old picket fence. The man was pitiful. But of course, he counted on being pitiful. "The house is ours now. We live here."

"You're making a point?"

"We don't need your spare parts, or Snail Away, or anything else. Just a little privacy."

"You're absolutely right. I've been a terrible old pest."

Campbell kept himself impassive. Flynn said, "It's not so bad. The Death Camp. Excuse me. The Home." He spotted a neighbor, called out a morose greeting, as if from exile. "I got my own little apartment there. Kitchen, everything."

"I'm glad you like it."

"I didn't say I *liked* it." Flynn brooded. "You know who else lives in that place? About three hundred old ladies. Each and every one of them wearing a hair net."

"You won't be lonely, huh."

Flynn looked out from under his eyelids, a lizard-like movement. "Mr. Campbell, I have to make a confession."

"No you don't."

"When I told you about my wife? How she died? That wasn't the exact truth."

"You really don't have to tell me."

"I was almost glad to see the woman go. All those years together. My God. You get like the gorillas at the zoo. Sit in a corner all day and scratch."

Campbell tried to close the trunk, but Flynn's hand was still in the way. Flynn said, "I've never told anybody else this. They'd think I was crazy. But I know she wanted me to go first. I used to watch her rubbing cold cream into her hands after she did the dishes, staring out the window, rehearsing her widowhood. I don't blame either of us. It's just the way you start thinking. I'm not saying we had a bad marriage. Not all wine and roses, but not bad. She was a good manager. Hardheaded. She wasn't much of a cook, but I learned to eat what was put before me."

Campbell's wife appeared in the front doorway, wearing green shorts and a white shirt with the tails tied above her navel. She waved extravagantly.

"That was another thing about my late wife," murmured Flynn. "She didn't have an affectionate nature."

Campbell's wife tripped down the stairs to meet them. She gave Flynn a hug. "You have to come see the kitchen. They just got done with it and it's perfect."

Flynn, beatific, climbed the stairs with her while Campbell lagged behind. He felt obscurely betrayed, angry at Flynn for pretending to be something he was not all this time. You couldn't trust anyone, anything, least of all time, which would sneak up on you like Flynn himself, limping but relentless.

The remodeled kitchen was full of blue-and-white tile, Shaker pegboards, shining glass, and copper. His wife stepped aside so Flynn could admire it fully. Flynn took it all in, patting his mouth with his hand. "Amazing. I hardly know the place."

"I hope you like it," said Campbell's wife anxiously.

"I think Caroline would have liked it," said Campbell. "In fact, I'm positive she would have."

"This must have cost you folks a pile. Here I practically gave the house away because I thought you were young and struggling. I should have held out for the big money."

"I want you to like the changes we're making," said his wife. "I want you to know that this house will always be cherished. We'll raise our children here. We'll love it as much as you did. Dr. Flynn?"

Flynn's face searched the ceiling. His mouth opened and closed, fish-like, and one hand groped at his chest. He looked like a man acting out *heart attack* for a game of charades.

"Call 911," said Campbell, catching Flynn as his knees gave, lowering his bony weight to the floor. Flynn's head banged backward against the tiles, and his heels drummed. What were the mechanics of a heart attack, Campbell wondered dreamily, even as he moved in efficient shock, issuing orders and unbuttoning Flynn. Something electrical went wrong, didn't it? Then the heart muscle fluttered, and the blood went limp, puddling. There was a noise coming out of Flynn now, not a voice but a noise, the chest as a sack of air, forced out through the mouth.

His wife rattled the phone back onto its hook. "Oh God. I've never seen a dead person before."

"He's not dead," said Campbell, though Flynn was doing his damnedest to make a liar out of him, bluing as he spoke, eyeballs rolling back in his head. Campbell found himself thinking, with the same drifting detachment, of Flynn's wife, pitched face first into the laundry basket, scattering detergent like pale green snow. It was the kitchen that killed Flynn.

But no. The paramedics came, with their crackling radios and oxygen tanks and matter-of-fact heroics. They knocked at Flynn's bare blue chest, got his heart started again, threaded tubing through his nose and rolled him out to the ambulance. "Go with them," Campbell's wife told him, giving him a little shove. "I have to try and find his daughter. Wouldn't you want someone there with you? Go."

Campbell drove behind the ambulance, squeezing through red lights in its wake. He felt the adrenaline charge of the last half-hour's events. He would have liked to retell it to someone, explain everything: how Flynn's heart had gone flat-line, as the EMTs said, stopped entirely, and had been struck by artificial lightning, revived. He would have liked to talk about the feel of Flynn's skin as the tide of blood retreated from it, its pudding coldness, how, as he'd unbuttoned Flynn's shirt and groped for a heartbeat, he'd thought once more of snails. But there was no one to tell. And there were things he would not have wished to relate, his mingled feelings of guilt and irritation. He might have wished Flynn dead, but only in some antiseptic, impersonal way. And now, as punishment, he was stuck with Flynn's not-quite corpse, at least until he could hand it off to someone else.

The paramedics moved fast. By the time Campbell pulled up to the emergency room, Flynn had already been magicked inside. Dead, or semi-live? No one seemed able to tell him. At the admitting desk Campbell said, "He's a doctor. Was." But no one knew Flynn, no one had heard of him. Had Flynn been brought to the wrong hospital, been misfiled? The clerk hustled away with a clipboard. Campbell wandered off to the waiting room, which was filled with people arranged in poses of stoic distress and boredom, as if they were all waiting for a bus that would take them somewhere none of them wanted to go.

He called his wife, who wanted to know how Flynn was, was he going to be all right? "I don't know. They can't find his social security number."

"What?"

"He's back somewhere they won't let me in. Did you reach his daughter?"

"She's at her son's softball game. They were going to go get her. What an awful, awful thing. He won't really die, will he? First George Burns, now this."

When Campbell got off the phone he asked a nurse about Flynn. "We've got him sedated. You can go sit with him if you want."

"How's he doing?"

"You'll have to talk to the doctor," said the nurse forebodingly. Campbell followed her back to one of the treatment rooms, feeling he was doing so under false pretenses.

The room was tiled in green, like a shower stall, and lit by fluorescent lights. It would make anyone look dead. Flynn still had the oxygen snake up his nose, and he was plugged into an amplifier and speakers. At least that's what it looked like, though Campbell supposed it to be some kind of heart monitor. It gave off a little red winking pulse. Campbell sat down on a bedside chair. The nurse drew a curtain around them. Flynn's breathing whistled in and out of his nose. He looked diminished, even soiled. His hair floated in wisps above his skull, like molting feathers.

He had never watched anyone die before, and he didn't want to start. Here was the end of all Flynn's work and worry, his custom water softener and decorator paint jobs and storm windows. It all came down to this. They really should have bought a new house.

Flynn's eyes opened and fixed themselves on Campbell. Campbell stared back at him, unable to produce the right sounds, even the right face. Flynn's mouth unhinged. He was trying to speak.

"I'll get the doctor," said Campbell, standing up and batting at the curtains. He couldn't find the place where they joined together.

"Sit down." Flynn's voice, weak but clear.

"Your daughter's coming. She'll be here in just a little while."

"I killed her."

"She's at a softball game, Dr. Flynn. They went to get her."

"I killed my wife."

Campbell sat. The sick man plucked at the covers, trying to get his hands up to the oxygen tube. "Pillow," he said, meaning that Campbell should raise his head. Flynn exhaled. "That's better. Christ. ER rooms are all slop."

"I don't think you should try to talk."

"My deathbed confession. Listen up."

"You're going to be fine."

"What I told you before? That's not how it happened. The truth is, I killed the woman."

"How about I get you a glass of water. Or a Sprite or something."

"I'll tell you how I did it. Shrimp."

Campbell shut his mouth, fascinated into silence.

"She made a big spiteful thing about how she was sick of cooking. How she'd had to put food on that table every night of her life for fifty years, blah blah blah. So I started cooking. She was allergic to shrimp. I put canned shrimp in the meat loaf. In spaghetti sauce. I could get away with it in macaroni and cheese, if I used a real strong cheese. Then she'd holler at me for the way it tasted. I just kept forking it down. Smiling away inside."

"You can't kill somebody that way. Macaroni and cheese."

"At first you get reactions like hives. Gastritis. It's at the higher doses you get your full-blown anaphylactic shock. Airways closing up, that sort of thing. The day she went, I made gumbo. I told her it was imitation crab." Flynn started to cough. His face pleated like an accordion. Clusters of little red veins seemed to burst into flower on both cheeks. He said, "Chart."

"What?"

"Where's my chart. I want to see what they gave me. I feel like hell."

"They said it was a sedative."

"It's not working. What is this place, the VA? I should be at Mercy. She would have killed me, if I hadn't gotten to her beforehand. I'm telling you, it was a nuclear first-strike situation. The woman hated me. She convinced herself I was put on earth to blight her happiness. She worked me over with a dull knife for the last thirty years. I bet that's how long your mortgage is, isn't it? Thirty years?"

"Why are you telling me this?"

"You think you got away with something on that house. I saw you looking at each other, winking behind my back. You thought you put one over on me, and I was too stupid to figure it out."

"The house was a business transaction."

"Monkey business," Flynn jeered.

"We haven't done anything to you. You didn't do anything to your wife. You need to calm down." Campbell was growing alarmed. It was the medication, whatever they'd given Flynn. It was microwaving his brain.

Flynn had another coughing fit, punier this time. "Funny thing about allergies. People can acquire them sudden-like, and not even know until they have a reaction. You allergic to anything, Campbell? Anything you have to watch out for when you sit down to dinner?"

"That's enough."

"Your wife a good cook? She make you apple dumplings? Cherry pie?"

"Shut up, OK?"

"The trouble with you yuppie types is you think you can buy everything. Buy me out and live happily ever after. Buy yourself a cute little wife. How much she set you back anyway?"

"I love my wife," said Campbell. The room seemed to be tilting away from him, growing hot, as if the air was running out of it like a liquid.

"Sure you do." Flynn let his head sink back into the pillow. The matter now bored him.

"You're a sick, bitter old man consumed by jealousy," said Campbell. But Flynn was just that instant dead. The heart monitor was shrilling away.

There was a squeaking of rubber shoes running down the hall. A nurse and a doctor in scrubs pushed the billowing curtains aside, then redrew them so that Campbell was now out in the hallway. "Rats," said the doctor.

The nurse said, "I don't want to say I told you so, but I told you so."

There was some other whispered talk that Campbell couldn't make out, then the doctor emerged from the curtains, drawing them closed behind him so that Campbell was unable to see in. "I'm sorry. When there's that much damage, there's really nothing we can do."

"I understand."

"Would you like me to send for the chaplain?"

"What for?"

The doctor looked at him oddly. "He wasn't a relative or anything," Campbell explained. "He just had his attack in our kitchen."

There was a commotion out by the admitting desk, a woman's raised voice. The doctor sprinted toward it and Campbell followed. "What do you mean, you don't know? Is that your job, not knowing anything?"

The woman was sunburned and stoutish, dressed in a pink T-shirt and shorts and a visor. She only sounded like Flynn. She had a square, jaw-heavy face and black, overcooked hair.

The doctor went up to her and spoke. The woman's face turned soft and bleared. The doctor motioned Campbell forward. Campbell took his time.

The daughter's name sounded something like Mrs. Babylon, though that couldn't be right. Campbell spoke his own name and murmured that he was so sorry. "I was with him when he went. It was very peaceful." He felt rotten, low-down rotten. Mrs. Babylon was crying into a paper napkin. Campbell guided her to a chair. The doctor had disappeared, to fetch the chaplain, Campbell hoped. He waited until the woman calmed herself and blew her nose. "Can I get you some coffee or anything?"

She touched her visor, as if she'd just now remembered it was there, then stared at Campbell, as if she was only now seeing him. "You're the guy who bought the house."

"It's a great house," he said, a little too enthusiastically for the occasion.

"Poor Daddy. I never should have made him move. I feel like I killed him."

No, I killed him, Campbell thought but did not say. I yelled at him and he died. The two of them sat in silence for a time, Mrs. Babylon applying her paper napkin now and then. Campbell looked her over, trying not to be obvious. A healthy, well-fed matron who probably went in for the League of Women Voters or community theater or other public-minded groups. He felt sorry for her now, lost in her purely private grief. He touched her bare, sunburned knee. "Is there anyone you'd like me to call for you?"

"Thanks. I'll get it together in a minute. Oh boy. You just never know how it's going to hit you. Like when Mom went. That was so sudden, we were all just numb."

Campbell leaned forward. "She had a stroke or something, right?"

"Is that what Daddy told you? Poor man. He couldn't own up to it."

Campbell tried to pry his tongue loose, failed. "She choked on something she ate. Daddy was devastated. Him, a doctor. If he'd only been there, he could have saved her." She rested both hands on her knees to help her rise, a gesture that instantly recalled her father. "I have to call my husband. I have to get him to bring me some *clothes*."

Campbell kept his seat in the molded plastic chair that pitched him and everyone else waiting there into that bus-station posture of slack discomfort. The room was quiet, as if grief and death and fear were only allowed behind the white curtains. There was nothing keeping him there, but he didn't leave yet. He knew his life was about to change forever, and he wanted to put it off for another couple of minutes.

MOTHER NATURE

The dog had some kind of allergy that made him chew his skin down to bacon. We'd tried cortisone, everything. Then there was the water line, which was leaking again. Somewhere deep down in the subterranean clay it was sending out streams and tributaries that rose to the surface of the lawn in green puddles. The redbud was drowning, probably already dead at the roots. The dog looked at me with his suffering doggy eyes, asking, Why is there evil in the world? Is free will an illusion? The water company sent me nasty letters, saying they were going to cut off my service if I didn't get the leak fixed. There were two or three other sustained crises in progress, mostly involving money.

I kept expecting life to get, if not better, at least more dignified.

Less cluttered up with things like trying to get the backhoe guy to return my calls. I wanted a little breathing space. I wanted maybe one day a week when I could spend twenty minutes thinking about the state of my soul, or anyone else's. What my daughter Lily wanted was to put the dog on a vegetarian diet. You can do that, feed them cans of formulated rice and soy and kelp and whatnot. Lily was fifteen and puritanical about food. But I thought it would be one more rotten thing to do to the poor beast. The dog loved those treats shaped like little steaks or drumsticks, anything made out of red dye #40 and chicken by-product meal. On my worst, most jagged days, I'd stop at the Casey's Mart and get Snausages for the dog, a fatty doughnut or a cookie for me. It cheered both of us up.

I loved the Casey's Mart. I was a little embarrassed about that, as if I was supposed to be above liking such places, but in fact I wasn't. I was always there, buying gas or newspapers or some kind of junk. Unlike other convenience stores they kept the place clean, and you didn't feel like you might get raped in the parking lot after dark. I liked the truck drivers who pulled in off the interstate to get their smokes and Mountain Dew, and the kids with their fistfuls of grubby change, and whoever it was that bought the shotgun shells they kept behind the cash register. I liked the clerks who worked there, the lady with the Jesus tattoo on her wrist, and the gap-toothed black guy, and the two or three others who were always hanging around the counter, gossiping and making absorbing personal calls on the pay phone. I even envied them, because they seemed so clubby and comfortable and because I did not know the entirety of their lives. In the same way there might be people who drove past my house when I was out watering the flowers, the late-summer reds and golds, snapdragons and sunflowers and nasturtiums, the dog lying, fur side up, in a (dry) patch of sunlit grass, everything glowing and peaceful, people who would envy me. You couldn't chase them all down and explain what was wrong with you.

Lily's father, Buffalo Bill, hadn't lived with us for years, not since Lily was seven. We never saw him. He lived in Florida and worked for a car rental company. He spent his days sweating through his white shirt, tapping a sweaty computer keyboard, craning his neck to loosen his tie, smiling his polite grimacing smile to customers while he toted up mileage and weekend rates and a million million useless numbers. At least, I hoped it was that bad. He sent Lily postcards of ocean sunsets, seashell jewelry, tins of saltwater taffy, crap like that. Money, forget it.

Poor Lily. I was certain she was damaged in some way, either by his absence or by the simple fact of him, though she was too cagey to let on. Once I asked her if she ever wanted to go see a counselor, just to talk about things. She looked up from her homework. "What things?"

"Kid things. Secret addictions. Resentments. Anything you can't tell your rotten mother."

"There's no need to be pathetic, Mom."

"I just want you to know you have resources, if life gets icky."

"Why do I have to keep telling you, I'm fine."

"How can you be fine? You're a teenager. Your father's a warthog. Your mother's a high school English teacher."

"Maybe you're the one who ought to see a counselor, Mom." She gave me a little grin and went back to her books and her E-mail and her phone calls, which was where she lived her real life.

I gave up and returned to my bag of Cheese Curls and the TV movie. She was a smart girl, Lily, on track, impatient with emotional messes, ready to unleash herself on the world. She wasn't pretty, which saddened me. I think she decided early on that she would be objective and disinterested instead. Nothing fazed her. She knew everything; all the kids did these days. There was nothing you couldn't see in a movie or read in a magazine: AIDS, condoms, drugs, herpes, date rape, incest, you name it. I wanted to believe she was inoculated by all this knowledge, that she'd never make a wrong or hurtful choice, that she'd always soar above trouble. At other times everything about her life seemed brittle and precarious to me, as if I'd raised a caterpillar in a glass jar and was now sending a butterfly out to try its wings on the expressway.

I worried that she'd grow up smart and lonely. She'd work training dolphins, or writing computer programs for mathematicians, something obscure, brainy, self-involved. My disorganized and fractured life had set a terrible example. I should have done a lot of things differently for her, been wiser, braver, more patient, more everything. I should have found her a better father. Of course at the time I thought he was fine. I was in love and all that.

Love. I used to love Bill. Now he was dryer lint. A flake, a bozo. The man was born to be inconsequential. Ask me if I missed him. But I missed the being-in-love part, the sweetness of it, whatever it was that let you maintain your delusions. I suppose it was possible that Bill had been a better person then. Maybe I had been too, back when I believed you only had to make up your mind once about a thing: good guys, bad guys, God, no God, politics, war, money. I used to have everything figured out. I was so purely arrogant, so armored in absolutes. I missed some of that certainty. At least delusions were better company than the weariness and fear that we all soaked in nowadays. Anyway, the marriage had gone bad, or soft, like a fruit, and while I'd long since come to terms with it, it remained my first great failure. You don't plan for failures. Nobody does. They make you cautious, turn your heart stingy.

Lily would have said, and often did, "Mom, your attitude just sucks."

I was at the Casey's, where you have to understand I never see a single person I know from any other part of my life. It's like a zone of invisibility. I could walk in wearing pajamas if I wanted and not attract any particular attention, no more so than the counter clerk I saw one morning, helping her child eat ice cream out of a carton for his breakfast. In fact I'd just come from school and was looking pretty good, if a little shopworn. I was standing in line at the register, waiting to pay for my Starlight Mints, gazing, in a vacant way, at the long mirror above the counter.

This is what I looked like: Hair I'd dyed sort of red this time. As usual it was somewhere between short and long. I'd start growing it out, hoping for luxuriance, but it would get thick and brambly, and I'd give up and hack it off. I'd taken to wearing a lot of black these days, hoping it would make me look thinner, or cooler, anything. But maybe I should go for something a little more tailored? Less of the flapping-crow effect? My face always looked the same to me, by which I meant, I was familiar with its different weathers, took them into account, but it was always the same face, or so I flattered myself. My skin had held up pretty well, and I hadn't grown chins, or pouches under my eyes, or anything really grim. How funny, I was thinking, that over time you were reduced to these few square inches of eyes and forehead, nose and chin, one's only true kingdom.

Right there in the Casey's I had the strangest sensation. It had to do with the hair on the back of my neck rising, and any thoughts I had emptying out like a sink with a slow drain, and an inability to move my eyes. There was a face next to mine in the mirror. A man's face that smiled at me in the glass and spoke my name: "Suzanne."

"Godalmighty."

"I didn't think you recognized me," he said, turning away from the mirror and grinning at me.

"Ray. Shit."

We hugged and stuff. The counter clerk and the other people in line were looking at us tolerantly, waiting for us to get over it. "Old friend," I explained, as if any of them cared. Ray paid for my mints and his orange juice and we walked outside to the parking lot and looked each other over again.

I said, "You won't believe what I was just thinking, the second before I saw you. About how faces change and don't change over time."

"Yours hasn't. You're still beautiful."

"Oh pshaw," I said, hugely delighted, embarrassed, unable to really look at him, study him, let my face show what I thought of his. "What are you doing here?"

"I live here. I moved back three weeks ago."

"Three weeks," I said, meaning, why hadn't he called.

"You're not in the phone books. Are you gonna be mad now? Want me to go away?"

"Follow me home. I'm just around the corner."

I didn't wait for him to agree but got in my car. I needed a minute to catch my breath. It was too much all at once, seeing him. I watched him pull up behind me, his turn signal clicking along with mine. Ray's car was a new-looking Camry. There was a general aura of prosperity about him, I'd caught that much. I remembered when none of us could afford new cars, any kind of cars. Bill and I used to go everywhere on bikes. Carried groceries home in those gnarly cotton sacks.

When he got out of his car in my driveway I said, "Fourteen years. That's how long it's been. I figured it out."

Ray was looking around him. "All these flowers. I could have guessed you lived here."

"It makes up for the inside," I said, unlocking the front door. "Lily's not home yet. She has orchestra practice."

"Lily's just a *baby*. What's she doing in an orchestra?"

"Playing first-chair flute. Sit down or something." I'd talked us all the way in the front door, but I was running out of breath, and there was still the nervous space between who we used to be and who we were now. The dog came padding up to us and sniffed Ray over. Slobbered too, which Ray pretended to find endearing.

"Barkley, you're a pest. Shoo." I opened the back door and shagged him out into the yard.

"What's the matter with his skin?"

"They don't know. I'm going to try acupuncture next. I'm serious."

"I thought you didn't like dogs."

"That was Bill. I got Barkley after he moved out. Barkley's his replacement."

It eased something between us to have mentioned Bill. Ray handed me my mints, which I'd forgotten all about. "I'll make us some tea. Or maybe we should have a drink. Do you still drink? I don't assume anything nowadays. Everybody's in twelve-step."

"A drink would be fine."

"I have some pot too, but I have to hide it from Lily."

I brought out a bottle of wine and glasses. I sat us down at the dining-room table. It was a solid table, the kind you could dig your elbows into, negotiate treaties at, good for long sessions. The afternoon light came in at the window behind me, lighting up the grain of the blond oak, filling Ray's brown eyes with sun specks. I looked at him then, finally. "You still look like Pancho Villa."

"It's the mustache," Ray said, poking at it as if it were a bug he was trying to get to move. "It'll probably outlive me."

"God it's good to see you." I was drinking the wine. I wanted to drink it all down, get sloppy and exuberant. I felt as if some part of me had been restored, as if I had been restored to myself. The part of me that could be reckless and beautiful and sure-hearted. "You might have written," I said, keeping my voice light. There was no point in spoiling things.

"I didn't write anybody. I was lost in space."

"Not good enough."

"I was real messed up. Mad at everybody. Even you and Bill. Because you had each other, you were happy."

"Happy," I said, giving the word an ironic weight in my mouth.

"You were."

"We all were," I said, and we were quiet, remembering.

Two acres of meadow with a thin belt of woods at the north end. Most of it level ground, except for a low spot that collected rain. The trees were hardwoods, oak, maple, walnut, sycamore, with scrubbier growths of mulberry, buckthorn, and unidentifiable brambles. There were deer in the woods, raccoons and possums and skunks, and once we saw a red fox, his tail flagged and high, racing across a field of new snow. There was a vegetable garden, fenced off with five-foot wire that kept out everything but the chipmunks, and a falling-down barn and a blue-painted farmhouse. The house had a front porch and a stained glass window of the humble kind, squares of thick red and blue and yellow set around the edge of the frame. You could sit at the table, this very same oak table, and watch the afternoon sun pick out the colors one by one, like a clock striking red, blue, yellow, then the lamplight and the long dusk and the curtains drawn, and the night worlds, one within the walls, one without.

Ray said, "I was really afraid to see you again. I thought you'd be mad. Or worse, just be polite and not care one way or the other. I didn't want to call you. I wanted to just show up, like I did. I followed you from the school. I watched you haul your books into the front seat and kick the door shut. That's when I knew it was really you."

I didn't want to start talking about the real or the spurious me. So I said, "Tell me where you've been, what you've been doing."

"Long or short version?"

"Short, for starters."

"You already heard it. Lost in space. I hitchhiked out to California. I wanted to do something romantic and legendary and self-destructive, sort of like Peter Fonda in *Easy Rider*. The closest I came was getting stranded in Green River, Utah, with a bunch of speed freaks, but that's the long version. OK. I wound up in San Francisco, joined the party, dealt a little coke, lived like a dirtbag. Worked some dopey jobs. Cleaned up my act, got into computers, got good at it. Made some real money. Moved to Seattle. More computers. Hooked up with some bad investments, got my clock cleaned. And voilà."

I was laughing. "So what in the world . . ."

"Am I doing back here? I left out the married and divorced part. That was the bad investment. One woman chased me out of here, another chased me back."

"How long were you married?" I was just amazed, listening. I felt like I hadn't been anywhere, done anything.

"Five years. I know. You're pissed because you didn't get invited to the wedding. It was real small."

"Did you—do you—have any children?"

"Nope. I got out clean. Just as well. I hate to think what a mess I would have made of a kid."

"Here's mine," I said. I heard the front door open; Lily, no doubt curious about the strange car in the driveway. "We're in here," I called, and when she appeared in the doorway I said, "Lily, this is Ray. You won't remember him, but he lived with us when you were little."

Ray had gotten to his feet, which seemed not just polite, but courtly. He needn't have bothered. Miss Lily, looking her primmest and most disinterested, said, "How do you do," and sniffed us over. I tried to see her as a stranger might. Her square jaw and limp sandy hair, the eyes set just a little too far apart. God help me for this unsparing critical vision, this constant silent mother-worry. For I never *said* anything, not since our unfortunate conversation about makeup. She didn't wear any, kept herself as utilitarian as a little Marxist.

Ray smiled at her. "We go way back, Lily. I was in the room when you were born."

Lily gave him a look of fascinated horror, then turned to me. "What did you do, make a party out of it?"

"Sort of." Hell to pay later on, I knew. "How was rehearsal?"

"The stupid oboes kept splitting their reeds," she announced with satisfaction. "I'm going to practice, OK?"

"Good, that way we can talk about you." She left without rising to the bait, and a little while later we heard her flute, playing something complicated and slippery, full of trills and arpeggios. She played the way she did everything else, accomplished, effortless.

Ray said, "She looks a lot like Bill."

"I guess so."

"That doesn't sound very . . ."

"I know how it sounds. It's not that every time I see her I think of him and I love her any less, or differently, I can't imagine such a thing. It's just that I ought to know her better than anyone else in the world and I don't, really. She's supposed to be half my genes, right? But sometimes it feels more like fifteen or twenty percent."

I stopped myself. The conversation was too close to our old level of intimacy, intimacy that we hadn't yet re-earned. You couldn't just pick up where you'd left off. I said, switching gears, "You haven't said what you're doing here. I mean for work, a job. Do you have a job?"

"I'm freelancing. Doing a little systems consulting."

"Jeepers."

"All it means is I go around and tell companies how to upgrade their computers, how to train their people on them, that sort of thing."

"Are you rich or something? Lookit those shoes."

"Nah. I just have this yupped-up job."

He smiled at me. He was still a good-looking man, Ray was. Even if he was no longer the skinny kid in jeans and army surplus T-shirts I'd known, the kid with the bandit black hair and the devil in him. He was solider now, and his hair was wearing down at the edges, like a lawn does with too much foot traffic. But he still had some of that dangerous, girl-eating charm; probably wouldn't ever lose it. You had to allow for that when you talked to him, watch yourself, sort of like not looking into the sun during an eclipse. I said, "So why are you really back here?"

"I need a reason?"

"You could be anywhere. This place is Podunk. Nobody ever comes back."

"It's not so bad here," he protested. "You get so you miss real weather. The change of seasons and all that."

I just waited. He said, "The divorce was a dogfight. There were a lot of times I wished I could call you, or anybody else from the old days. But I couldn't because I'd cut everybody off, which I know was a shitty thing to do, but I had my reasons, mainly having to do with being such a sick puddle of puke when I left here. Then the floor got yanked out from under me one more time, and I wanted to be back. Don't give me that look."

"What look?"

"The 'you're a sniveling opportunistic self-absorbed twerp' look."

Well, maybe that was part of what I felt, but there wasn't any point getting into it. He was just sitting there, looking into his hands. I thought that if he'd shown up in some other trouble, hungry or broke or even on the run from the law, a bank robber or a mad bomber, I would have taken him in, helped him, rallied to his side. This shouldn't be any different, should it? But I said, "What if you hadn't gotten divorced? Would I ever have seen you again?"

"Maybe. I don't know. But I always knew this was where my life was best. Where I was best. When we were all here together."

I realized I could no longer hear Lily's flute. The sun was pouring in, laying a path of blaze all along the old table, showing up every nick and burn in its surface. I heard the dog scratching at himself outside the window, a rhythmic, thumping sound. I was going to have to get up soon, give him his medicine, make a round of phone calls, think about cooking dinner, take up the load once more. I said, "I don't think that much about the old days."

"I do. I could tell you what was in every room. Every beautiful, cruddy room."

I heard Lily behind us in the kitchen, running water, moving things around in the cupboard. And while it shouldn't have made any difference to me that she was listening, while she wasn't making a secret of it and had every right to be in her own kitchen, still it seemed to make us self-conscious, even false. Ray said, "You remember the time we killed the chicken?"

"Oh God. That chicken."

"I hooked up a hose to the truck's tailpipe and tried to give it carbon monoxide poisoning."

"We wanted to be humane."

A pause. Lily was doing something with the microwave, opening and closing the door every few seconds so the bell kept dinging and dinging. Ray said, "I should get going," just as I said, "Stay for dinner."

"How about a rain check?"

"Come on. I'll open a few cans or something."

He laughed, but he was already standing up, drawing himself together. We talked a little more, traded phone numbers, hugged again at the door. It was just as well he wasn't staying, we both knew it. "Good-bye, Pancho Villa," I said.

"Adios, Mother Nature."

I waved from the doorway as he drove off. Lily was still skulking around in the kitchen. I went in to face the music.

"Are you getting hungry?" I asked her. "How about stir-fry?"

But she wasn't going to be put off that easily. "What was that guy doing hanging around when you were . . . *giving birth?*"

"He was holding one of my legs back."

"God, Mom." She looked at me with that peculiar fifteen-year-old loathing that makes you think of tragedy queens on the nineteenth-century stage.

"He lived there. You were born at the farmhouse, you know that."

"You didn't have any doors in that place? Was he like, your roommate? I didn't think people had roommates after they got married."

I could have told her a few crisp facts about my marital status at the time of her birth, but I just said, "He and his girlfriend lived with us for a while."

Lily began pulling vegetables out of the refrigerator: mushrooms and bok choy, scallions, a red pepper, some lumpy zucchini someone had given us, bean sprouts. We ate like squirrels. We started chopping everything up, not talking now, and I thought we were done with the topic. Then she said, "What did he mean, Mother Nature?"

"It was a nickname. Sort of a joke."

"I'll say." Lily snickered. She can't forgive me for hair dye, processed sugar, chlorine bleach, that sort of thing. She didn't ask me anything more and I didn't volunteer anything. I don't think children have a right to know everything about you.

Sixteen, seventeen years ago? Christmastime, and we'd put up a tree in the big bare living room. A splendid, oversized tree; we'd gone out and cut it ourselves. It smelled great. We'd decorated it with popcorn chains, foil stars, and those old-fashioned bubble lights you can't buy anymore because they burn things up. We had a litter of tabby kittens in a nest in a dresser drawer, and Ray swore I was sitting in the rocking chair, knitting, although I don't remember that. I'd just baked bread, you could smell that too, and set the loaves out to cool. Ray had come home from some night at the bars, half lit, walking with that little bop step that meant he was in a drunken good mood. I don't know where Buffalo Bill was, maybe asleep, and Gina? Probably in the studio. "Oh Lordy," said Ray, rocking back on his heels. "Here I am, all nasty-ass drunk, coming home to Mother Nature."

So that was the joke. We made jokes about things like that; bought myself a farm, way out in the country, spent time in the hayloft with the mice and the bunnies, ha ha. We weren't Marxists or Christians or anything organized. Just a few friends who wanted to build a refuge, a place where we could leave our make-do jobs behind, touch something real on a daily basis. I know what people think of that now. I know what I think of it. But I'd forgotten the honeysuckle that grew along one wall of the barn, the old-fashioned weedy kind of honeysuckle, sweet and rank at the same time. You could get drunk just smelling it. You could pinch the end of the blossom, draw the stamen through it so it brought a drop of nectar with it, and you drank the flower like a hummingbird.

I put the memory back where it belonged. It wasn't any help to me now. I called the backhoe guy again and left another message. How did you get to be somebody like that, I wondered, somebody who didn't have to pay attention to phone calls?

The next time I saw Ray, we met at a coffee shop they'd opened up in a defunct movie theater. Two underemployed-looking kids stood behind the counter, dishing out lattes and espressos. They'd tried to fancy the place up with old movie posters and glass-topped tables, but it still had a cavernous, vacant look, the look of a small-town enterprise with hopeless ambitions. Outside the windows the trees were full of autumn light. A few cars poked along the Sunday streets. Ray was quiet, fidgeting with his cup. It was funny how his new face, that is, his older face, was now the one that seemed familiar to me. It was as if we'd reached some agreement, some truce with the time that had passed.

I said, "I've been thinking about Bill. You guys were closer than he and I ever were. You did all those buddy things together. Always screwing around with the truck or the well or something in the damned barn."

"You sound jealous."

"I was jealous. Anything he did with you was fun. Anything I wanted him to do was a chore. He was just better at being friends, friends with men."

"Most of us boys are. Sorry."

"Not you," I insisted. "You were always good with women, you liked women. I don't just mean sex. Liked their company, appreciated them."

"You think so? Thanks. Look where it got me."

"Are you going to tell me about this wife?"

"She wasn't at all like Gina."

I'd known he was going to say something like that, something about Gina, that the wife had been either like or unlike, smarter or not as smart, more or less than Gina.

"She was—she is—a nice levelheaded girl. Law school. Civic-minded. Works on political campaigns, gives money to Public Television, that sort of thing. She looks sort of like Sharon Stone on a bad day. We had it made. Until she fell in love with somebody else."

I murmured that I was sorry. Ray got up to get us more coffee. He said, "At least this one didn't die on me."

I watched him walk up to the counter, where one of the kids refilled our cups, managing to slop some of the coffee into the saucers, fumble the change, and in general look like he'd rather be writing alternative journalism. I felt sorry for kids these days, I really did. I couldn't imagine them believing anything they did would make a difference in the world. Right or wrong, we'd believed that. What could they believe in now? There was nothing that couldn't be sneered at, dismissed, seen through, as if we'd used up all the good things years before. But I expect that's how every generation feels about the one that comes after. Was it how I felt about Lily? I didn't have time to consider it because Ray was back.

I said, "I wonder what would have happened to Gina, who she'd be today. If she'd still be painting."

"Her parents wanted me to send them all her canvases. But I kept the best ones myself. I still think they're good. She was the real thing. She would have kept it up, gone places. And I would have hung on for the ride. That's what I tell myself. I guess it doesn't matter what I tell myself."

"Do you know anybody who's still together from back then? I don't. I'm sorry. I'm trying to make you feel better, in some weird way. I'll quit."

Ray smiled, one of those curdled smiles. "She would have looked the same, I bet. Except she would have cut her hair and had her ears triple pierced. I still can't talk about her much. I wind up feeling like Edgar Allan Poe and Annabel Lee."

So we talked about something else, his work or mine, I don't remember. It had been a long time since I'd thought much about Gina. My only dead friend. Unlike the rest of us, she'd simply stopped, hadn't aged or changed, been disappointed in herself or the rest of us. Although *stopped* is too easy a word for lymphoma, for dying that way, and for the chemo and radiation that bleached and poisoned her. After she was diagnosed, she'd had to move back home with her parents. None of us had anything like benefits, health insurance. It didn't take long, six or seven months. She was dead before any of us believed it was really happening.

When she was in the hospital and it was clear she wasn't going to leave, Ray flew to Pennsylvania, stayed with the parents, who didn't want him there but couldn't get out of it. While Gina lay in her hospital bed, her body whittled down to the mechanics of respiration and excretion, her body that was now only a device for the production of pain, Ray slept, or didn't sleep, in her old bedroom, surrounded by her schoolbooks and spelling-bee medals and the watercolor landscapes she'd done in eighth grade. There was none of her newer work, those strange, silvery canvases she'd painted up in the attic studio of the farmhouse.

I hadn't known any artists before Gina. I'd thought they were all, you know, artsy: pallid and bored and contentious. But Gina told jokes, the cornier the better. She took her turn at cleaning the bathroom. Art was just work like any other kind of work, she said. Anybody who claimed otherwise was striking poses. Of course it wasn't as simple and straightforward as she made it out to be, and neither was she. If I spent my time shelling soup beans, or dyeing yarn with beets and onion skins, or some such intricate domestic project, Gina was taking photographs of the dead raccoon we'd found on the road, or painting every door in the house orange. Once she did a series of nude self-portraits with condom wrappers glued to the canvas. Her parents, who had bought her books on Mary Cassatt and wanted her to get a degree in art education, hardly recognized the odd little elf she'd become.

In the end, of course, the cancer turned her into something no one recognized. And Ray had been there to see it, struggling politely with the parents over who got to sleep at her bedside. Unable to comfort each other, though they pretended to, like the funeral where, Ray said, they'd played Lutheran hymns and the minister talked about Gina getting her angel wings.

We'd finished our coffee. I was waiting for one of us to declare an end to the afternoon, get up and go. And I still wasn't certain if Ray and I could be here-and-now friends, or if we were just going through the motions of a nostalgia convention. I said, "It all seems so long ago. I don't just mean we're older. Somebody told me once that every cell in the body changes in seven years, and it's been twice that. I'm a different person now. A dull person."

"Says who?"

"Says me. I don't know what the hell I used to think I was. But I always believed my life was important, that things like community and trying to keep the world sane and genuine were important. We didn't plug ourselves into the TV every night, or buy loads of plastic K-Mart glop. Well, maybe I still don't, but I'm pretty much like everybody else now. That's what I mean by being dull."

Ray was shaking his head. "I don't believe that. We're still the people we used to be. So we don't raise goats or buy flour in fifty-pound sacks anymore. We had something important. We had each other."

"It didn't last that long."

"Nothing perfect ever does."

"You remember it differently than I do," I said, irritated. "You're idealizing everything."

"And you're dismissing everything."

I wanted to pick a fight with him, prove he was wrong. It hadn't been perfect. We'd fought about things, made mistakes that had damn near cost us the leaky roof over our heads. When Bill and I finally sold the place in the grand wreckage of the divorce, we hadn't lived there for years, and we all but lost money on it. But before I could get myself wound up to speak, Ray said, "How about a walk? It's too nice an afternoon to sit around inside with these alienated youth."

He was right; it was a beautiful afternoon. The sun poured its honey light through the maples. Heaps of gold leaves covered the lawns and sidewalks. We walked through a neighborhood of tumbledown houses at the end of the gravel alleys, the unprosperous edge of the commercial district. I had always liked these shabby little houses, would have been happy to live in one of them if I didn't have a child to worry about. I'd have a birdbath in the yard, like this one, or blue-checked curtains like those. I suppose they reminded me of the farmhouse. There was still something in me that loved simplicity, and the dream of a humble life.

Ray said, "Remember the first Thanksgiving we had out there? When you made three different kinds of pie?"

"Why is it that the only thing anybody ever remembers about me is food?" I was still mad and wasn't going to concede to anything.

"You know it's not. But what's wrong with saying you're a terrific cook? What's wrong with talking about the good times?"

"It's just talk. It's nothing we can get back again."

"When I say, 'Remember Thanksgiving,' I don't just mean you made great piecrust. I mean we sat down together to food we'd all worked to put on the table. I mean we loved each other. Don't tell me that's just living in the past."

He was still walking along beside me, not looking at me. I felt something like vertigo, the present sliding into the past and back again, his now and his then faces blurring. God, he was still a good-looking man. I said, "I have to get back and mark some quizzes."

"I'm sorry. I didn't mean to upset you."

"Look, Ray, you show up after all this time, towing a bad marriage and whatever else, and I don't know what you want from me. How I'm supposed to fix it all for you. I really do have to get back home."

That night Lily asked me, "Is that Ray guy your new boyfriend?"

"No. He's a friend of your dad's."

"I didn't know Dad had any friends."

"Sure he did. Does. He was always a very sociable person."

"So why does he come see you and not Dad?" continued the annoying child. "I hope you've thought about AIDS and stuff."

"Did you give Barkley his medicine?" She smirked at that, lame dodge that it was, but she said yes, she had.

He was looking a little better, poor cur. Less raw, and he hadn't lost any more hair. I called him and he waddled over to me, smelling me to make sure I was still the same. He was getting arthritic and white around the muzzle, getting old. I didn't want to think about that, the inevitable descent into geriatric problems, deafness, kidney failure, incontinence, then the final trip to the vet and his eyes glazing over, fixing on nothing, this comical black and white fur turning into something you were afraid to touch because it was dead.

What was wrong with me, why was I doing this to myself? The dog was wagging his tail, happy, he'd never have one thought about death, about time past or time lost. I scratched his ears and he tilted his head, leaning into it. "What?" I said to Lily, who was talking again.

"I said, Ray wouldn't be my real father, would he? He's pretty hot."

"Lily!"

"OK, OK." I think she knew she'd gone too far, that even a smart-ass kid whose favorite entertainment is mother bashing has some limits.

I was allowed to be shocked, at least technically. I'd never slept with Ray. But we'd talked about it. We'd all talked about it, right from the start, had an actual meeting. Should we try to ignore the inevitable sexual attractions and tensions? Repress them, acknowledge them, act on them? Lily would have found it instructive, if nothing else, the four of us sitting around debating whether monogamy was really just a way of ensuring property rights, one more capitalist flimflam.

And what had we decided in the end? That whatever happened, we wouldn't keep anything a secret, which still seems like a good resolution to me. And if nothing ever happened, maybe it was because we didn't want to sit through another such meeting. It wasn't a bad way to keep things under control, I'm convinced, setting rules for unruliness.

I took a shower and got myself ready for bed. The bathroom mirror was not my friend. It showed all the soft pouches and failures of my body, all the battles I was losing, pound by pound, inch by inch. Lily was wrong, I didn't want a boyfriend. I needed a husband, someone who'd been here all along and would have gone to seed right alongside me. Well, it was too late for that. I turned off the light and went to bed.

I finally got the backhoe guy on the other end of the phone, had to be nice to him, even, because I needed him for the job. It took another round of phone haggling to get the plumber lined up. But here they were, finally, the backhoe like a giant yellow insect tracking across the lawn. It dredged buckets of runny mud out of the hole in the ground, while the plumber, who turned out to be the surlier of the two, stood around in his rubber gaiters waiting to descend into the muck. He was mad about something, something about me having plastic piping instead of copper, as near as I could tell. It wasn't the sort of thing I felt personally responsible for. I kept trying to make pleasant conversation with him, but he only muttered and kicked at the clods of dirt at the edge of the excavation. Once he'd climbed down there I tried to ask him how it looked, how bad it was.

"Can't say yet."

I gave up on him. The backhoe guy, who was standing next to me, an interested but disinterested party, said, "I seen them like this where I had to dig all the way back to the house. Every time they tried to splice the pipe, it split on them." The plumber worked for forty-seven dollars an hour, the backhoe guy for fifty, with a two-hour minimum.

Cars had been slowing down to watch, and a few kids had

come up on their bikes. There was something festive about an excavation. Ray pulled into the driveway, got out, and walked over to us. "Mind if I join the party?"

"It's more like a graveside service," I said. I wasn't sure if I was glad to see him or not.

Ray said how-do to the backhoe guy, the way men nod and sniff each other over, then he admired the backhoe itself. He asked if the rig was new, and the backhoe guy said no, he'd had it eight years but he tried to keep it up. Not that it earned any money sitting in the driveway looking pretty, and Ray said he had that right. They agreed it was a good thing the rain held off. You didn't want no cave-ins. The backhoe guy had seen any number of them. The two of them were jawing away like old pals. Ray squatted down at the edge of the hole. "Is that three-quarter-inch pipe?"

"Yeah. What's left of it."

"I've never seen a plastic fitting on a joint like that."

"Different, ain't it? Whoever put it on in the first place must of been different too."

They all got a good laugh out of that. By now I wasn't sure if Ray had come over to see me, or to hang out with his buddies in the skilled construction trades. Nobody was paying any attention to me, and I decided I might as well go back inside. I was in the kitchen unloading the dishwasher when Ray knocked and let himself in.

"Got anything to drink?"

I didn't turn around. I said, "There's iced tea in the refrigerator."

"Plain water's good enough."

"Water's the one thing I haven't got right now."

"Oh. Yeah."

"I don't suppose either of them said how much this was going to cost me."

"The plumber's almost done. It shouldn't be that bad."

" 'Not that bad' on a schoolmarm's salary can still be pretty bad."

"I'm sorry."

"Don't be. Poverty is the last link to my idyllic past."

"I should have stayed in Seattle. All I ever do is make you unhappy."

I turned around then. "No. Nothing's your fault. I just don't know what to *do* with you, Ray. Every time I see you I have to think about everything I ever screwed up, then and now."

"What did you screw up? I don't see it that way."

"Yeah. Look. Why don't we just say nothing turned out like it was supposed to. Not me and Bill, not Gina, not most of the damned twentieth century. Certainly not my life."

"You know anybody's that did?"

I didn't have anything to say to that. I went past him to the front door, where I could see the backhoe on the move again, this time scraping dirt back into the hole. The plumber was over by the side of the house, using the garden hose to wash the mud off his legs. The water was already back on, then. Maybe the bill wouldn't be too high. Maybe the house wouldn't wash away, cave in on itself, explode.

Ray was still in the kitchen, washing out the glass he'd used for iced tea. That killed me, that he felt he had to wash the glass. "You have water now," he said. "Let it run for a while to get the air out of the line."

"I haven't been very nice to you. I'm sorry."

He shrugged. He looked so hangdog. "I should've called before I came over."

"Will you come back tomorrow night for dinner? Please. I really want you to."

"I don't—"

"Seven o'clock. I need to do this, OK? For old times' sake."

I went to the grocery and bought eggs, butter, and sour cream. Whole milk, for a change. I ravaged the produce section: potatoes and lettuces, artichokes, baby carrots, raspberries, lemons. I picked out cheeses and olives, almonds and chocolate. When I got everything home, Lily looked in the refrigerator. "There's all this meat in here," she said accusingly.

"You don't have to eat any."

"What's the occasion?"

"Ray's coming for dinner tomorrow."

Lily didn't say anything, just poked around in the refrigerator some more, then shut it without taking anything out, so as to demonstrate how unsatisfactory my purchases were. But she wouldn't leave the kitchen, kept skulking around. "What," I said.

"I was just wondering. . . . Mom, do you think sex is gross?"

"No. But a lot of people want you to think it is. Because they're afraid of it."

"Oh."

I was trying my damnedest not to say, What brings this on? What is it about a lamb roast? The next thing she said was, "Mom, if I was having sex, would you want me to tell you?"

We'd never had quite this sort of conversation before. About sex, sure, the names for everything, the basics, the usual cautionary pronouncements. This was something new. "I'd probably be able to tell, or guess. But yeah, I'd want you to tell me."

"So you'd probably tell me if you were, right?"

Oh, she was sharp, my Lily was. She gazed back at me, all calculated innocence. I could have said adults were different than children and I was responsible for her, not the other way around. I could have talked about privacy and setting boundaries, any of those old traps that parents set for themselves. "Right," I said. "No secrets."

I left school early the next day to start getting ready. I seasoned the lamb with lemon and rosemary and garlic, scrubbed the little red potatoes, tied the carrots in bunches to steam. I'd almost forgotten how much I enjoyed cooking a grand meal, enjoyed it for its own sake, not just because it was for my loved ones and how happy it would make them, all that crap women are supposed to feel. I toasted almonds and ground them up, sifted flour, caramelized sugar. Brushed rounds of bread with olive oil and set them under the broiler. Took the cheeses out so they'd be at room temperature. I'd probably scare everybody with all this food.

I dressed in what Lily, when she was smaller, called my gypsy clothes: a long tiered skirt, velveteen shirt, silver dangle earrings. I didn't care if they dated me; I liked the way they made me look and feel. When Lily came home she looked me over skeptically. I hadn't had all that many dates, boyfriends, over the years, hadn't ever made this much fuss over any of them.

"What's this?" she asked, wrinkling her nose.

"Raspberry almond torte. It's bad for you. Have a rice cake."

"Do you want me to go over to Belinda's or somewhere tonight?"

"Why don't you just set the table for Mommy, sweetheart."

When Ray arrived he brought flowers, a sleeve of pink and white lilies. I sat us down in the living room, poured the wine, and set the artichoke pâté, the brie, and the garlic toasts in front of us. "Everything looks terrific," he said, meaning it but straining for enthusiasm. We were both a little keyed up. "Where's Lily?"

"Sulking. It scares her to see me having fun. It doesn't have anything to do with you, she likes you. She thinks you're hot." Ray groaned.

When I called Lily to the table she managed to look unfestive, even unwashed, in an old sweatshirt, with her hair skewered up in a bird's nest and her glasses drooping over her nose. She rather ostentatiously ate some salad, nibbled at a carrot, pushed the potatoes around on her plate. "Not hungry?" I said cheerily.

"I thought you guys were hippies. I didn't think you ate a lot of fancy stuff."

"We're reformed hippies," said Ray. "We can eat bacon, anything."

"Why does it have to be lamb? It's creepy. It's like eating babies."

"The flesh of the young," I said, pretending to spear her arm with a fork, "is regarded as especially succulent." She gave me a cold, you're drunk look. Maybe I was, a little, enough not to care.

Ray said, "Actually, Lily, we couldn't afford to eat like this in the old days. We had plenty of brown-rice casseroles. Of course, they were good too," he added loyally. "Your mother's the best cook I know. A genius."

"Thank you, Ray. I so seldom get compliments these days."

Lily said, "What I don't understand is why you all had to live together. That's weird."

"We thought traditional family structures were too rigid and patriarchal," I murmured, serving Ray more lamb.

"You mean, one of those marriages where the husband actually lives with you?"

"What's in the potatoes?" asked Ray. "Is it Gruyère? They're delicious. Everything's delicious."

"She thinks it's my fault that Bill abandoned us. And that I've ruined her life by sticking around to raise her."

"You know what she does all the time? Pretends to eat salads and stuff, then sneaks over to the Casey's for pizza and dough-nuts."

I said, "When you were born we were so excited; remember, Ray? This kid was going to be raised right. The product of radical ideals and enlightened values, not to mention a sound diet. She was going to be perfect."

"Sorry to disappoint you," said Lily, with a little of her old spiteful flair. She was glowering at her plate. "God."

"She didn't learn language like that from me. I never took her to church. Nothing's perfect. That's my point. Not you, not me. Not the good old days."

They were both looking at me. I guess I'd spoken with the sort of drunken, magisterial tone that makes people afraid to disbelieve you, at least for a moment. "Though I must say," I continued, "that this lamb is pretty close to perfect."

"The sacrificial lamb," said Ray, pouring more wine with a flourish. He looked addled but happy. "Lily, more milk?"

"No thanks, Uncle Ray."

Now it was our turn to stare at her. After a pause I said, "I was about to say, I can accept falling short of perfection. It's a coming to terms, maturity sort of thing."

"Whose idea was it to name me Lily? I'd really like to know."

"She wants to change her name to Pocahontas," I informed Ray. "No. To Fleur."

"I even brought lilies tonight," said Ray. "What do you know. I hadn't even thought of that."

"We wanted a name that meant something, something in English. Not 'she who wields the spear' in Old Norse. I guess we all decided on it. You were everybody's baby. We took turns feeding you, changing you, rocking you to sleep. Your dad made a cradle for you. He sanded and finished it himself. It had these little birds and animals painted on the headboard. Gina did that part. The paint was probably toxic. We didn't know any better."

Even while I was talking I felt my eyes tearing up. I wished I knew what happened to that cradle. It was really sweet. I remembered Bill making it, how much he fussed over it, giving it coat after coat of shellac, calling me out to the barn to admire it, me with my big belly that made me feel like an ocean liner, the two of us laughing when I tried to navigate: hard astern, hard to port. On the way back to the house we stopped and looked up at the white stars, arms around each other, breathing each other in. It was cold, but we'd be warm as soon as we got inside. The house's winter smells: wood smoke, coffee, pine soap. The swaybacked bed heaped with quilts, our legs tangling in the center, rocking each other into slow sleep. And a hundred hundred other memories, each of them jumping up and clamoring to be recognized. Here was Lily, newly born, coming out bright red and screaming, and Bill's face looking down at her, everybody weeping and cheering, the ghosts of our younger, better selves.

"Mom?"

"I'm sorry, baby. I'm just crying because you made us all so happy."

Through the opal blur of tears I saw Ray getting up from his chair and starting toward me. I hurried to get up too. "Who's ready for cake?"

Lily slithered out of her chair, escaping, muttering that she didn't want any. Ray blocked my path to the kitchen. "Why don't we hold off on the cake for a little while?"

"You have to admire it. It has enough sugar to put you in a diabetic coma."

"It looks terrific. I'm not hungry."

"You know what my problem is? I always think food can fix everything."

"Come here," he said, although I was already close enough for him to drop his arms around me, pull me toward him into the kitchen, where we kissed amid the fine wreckage of the dirty pots and pans.

Ray drove, and we held hands across the gearshift. October was closing down, winter closing in. The corn and bean fields were all harvested by now, and the two-lane road divided vast bare acres of stubble. There was an occasional hedgerow, or a concrete bridge over a twisting creek, a distant woods, the bare treetops looking tangled and smoky against the overcast sky. I hadn't driven out here in years. I told Ray that for all I knew the house had been torn down, plowed under, converted into a grain elevator. He insisted we had to go see for ourselves. All right, I said, though I wasn't looking forward to it.

"It's still there," Ray said as we came over the little rise that had always meant we were home.

"It looks empty," I said as we slowed, then pulled up in the old driveway. In fact it looked as if it had been empty for some time, one of those semi-derelict houses that could pass for haunted with a little imagination. The roofline sagged, and loose shingles littered the yard. An upstairs window gaped, broken, and someone had taken a shotgun to the front door, just for fun, leaving a trail of blisters in the soft wood.

"Sad," said Ray, but I didn't really think so, which surprised me. We climbed the steps and pushed the front door open, walked across the bare planks of the floor. The little stained-glass squares were still in place, although one of the blue ones wobbled when I touched it, like a loose tooth. I think it would have bothered me more if the house was still in use, occupied by some normal and prosaic family. This way I could think of it as a kind of archaeological site, like Stonehenge.

We went through every room. Drafts cruised around our ankles. Water had come in through the roof, stained the corners rusty. There was a hole in the drywall of the old bedroom, a circular pattern of cracks, as if someone had gouged or kicked it in. Pink insulation trailed from it. Mice were probably using it for nests.

We ended up on the back porch, looking over the sunken, weedy spot that used to be the garden. I said, "It's funny, but being here, even with it all falling apart, makes it easier somehow. Easier to say yes, we were happy here. To trust being happy. Do you know what I mean?"

"You were the one who held everything together. The one we all counted on. The foundation."

We didn't say anything else, just watched as the descending sun found the edge of a cloud and emerged like a red jewel caught in the distant treetops. Then, because it was getting cold, I reached for Ray's hand again, and we walked back to the waiting car.

ICE ANGELS

We were headed straight into bad news. The snow had begun sixty miles back as something light and sifting. It raced across the highway in curving snake shapes and slid harmlessly beneath the wheels. By the last exit it was sticking to the road in patches. Just a few miles farther and the pavement turned solid white. The wind was stronger now; it blew at right angles to the highway, kicking up loose snow, filling the air with it. I was driving, hunched up against the wheel as close as I could get. Holly said, "I told you, check the forecast."

"What difference would that have made," I said. I didn't want to be having a conversation right now. It was hard enough just trying to see where I was going. The car was a fourteen-year-old

Buick LeSabre, rump-sprung and slick-tired. It handled the road like a boat, an oceanliner, a blimp. At least the road was flat and straight. Interstate 57, the most boring highway in the world, a concrete zipper up and down the length of Illinois. I couldn't see past my nose, which is just a way of saying things, but it was near true. Maybe in other weather there were trees and farmhouses and billboards outside. Right now there was only this blind and shifting cloud come down on top of us.

"Can't we go any faster?"

"You want to drive?"

"Just a thought," said Holly. She slid down on the seat until her knees rested against the dashboard. "I never want to see snow again."

"Then you're headed the wrong direction."

We were on our way to Chicago, to try something new. We knew this girl Vivien we could stay with for a while. We needed a change of scene. One of these days we were going to wake up and not be young anymore. Why not Chicago? You could have a life in Chicago. You could have something resembling *fun*. Didn't we deserve something better than bad luck and worse men? Once we got to Chicago, things would change. We just hadn't counted on the getting there being so hard, like all the bad luck was coming along for the ride.

I saw a car up ahead. I wasn't going fast, but I was gaining on it. When I realized it wasn't moving, that it was some distance out in a field and I was following it right off the road, I over-corrected. The Buick fishtailed. The wind pushed us back the other way, but it was a moment before the wheels grabbed and held the road.

"That was close," I said cheerily. I was shaking a little from the adrenaline, and my stomach was clenched like a fist. "God, I wish I had a cigarette."

"You don't smoke."

"Well I wish I smoked."

A line of fence posts emerged from the snow, connected by sagging wire. "This sure would be an ugly-ass place to die," said Holly, gazing around her.

"Oh hey thanks. Thanks for the vote of confidence. Get a grip, would you?" That was how you had to talk to Holly sometimes. She could be so pathetic.

The next thing she said was, "I wish the radio worked."

"So we could get the highway death toll?" I had no patience with her.

"You're about as funny as a crutch."

"I never understood that expression. Why a crutch? They couldn't come up with something else unfunny?" I decided to get off the road at the next exit. But exits were few and far between out here. I couldn't even remember the last town. It had some dopey name that made you know you'd never want to go there. I flicked my eyes over the rearview mirror, hello. Neither of us is pretty, Holly and me, not strictly speaking, though I like to think we have our moments. Holly is sort of blond, and spotty. I'm dark, that's about all there is to say. Hair falling in my eyes in spite of all the clips and rubber bands in the world. My mother used to tell me, "Jeanine, you always look like you need to be scrubbed clean," and other helpful things. Vivien says looks aren't the most important thing in Chicago anyway.

The left lane was drifting closed. There were little hummocks of blown snow and long fingers of snow reaching toward the centerline. I hadn't seen a snowplow. Not one. What was the matter with people anyway, the ones who were supposed to be taking care of things? Wasn't that the way it always went, nobody pulled their weight, kept their promises, gave a shit. This was how I was thinking when the Buick hit another slick spot. It galloped along for a few dozen yards, me tapping the brakes the way you were supposed to, the way every driver's-ed class told you, no good. Holly started making a yipping sound. The Buick slid majestically, following its nose along the right-hand shoulder, then a lumpier ride down the slope of the ditch, and a pretty good crunch when we landed.

I gunned the motor, just to be doing something. The tires whined and dug in deeper. I said, "This is fucked."

"I don't guess we could push it out."

"Guess again."

Now that we weren't moving, the snow seemed lighter, prettier. It landed on the windows so you could see the crystal structure of each flake. I put my fingertip up to the glass and picked out one snowflake. The next minute it was obscured by more crystals, and turned into a heap of uninteresting white. Holly said, "We could make ice angels."

"What?"

"It's when you lay down and move your arms to make wing shapes."

"You mean snow angels."

"If you say so." She wiggled her door handle. "This is stuck. It got jammed or something."

I unlatched my door and cracked it open, not that we were going anywhere. I closed it and shut off the engine.

"Why'd you do that?"

"Save gas. We only run it when we get cold."

"I hope it starts again."

I just looked at her. Holly said, helpfully, "If you have a candle and a coffee can, you can make a stove."

"Somebody'll stop. They'll see us and stop."

Holly pointed out that we hadn't stopped ourselves for the car we'd seen off the road, and I said there hadn't been anyone in it. But Holly said we hadn't known that for sure, and I told her to just drop it. We sat in silence for a while, until Holly said she was cold. Big surprise.

"Well I'm cold too. I'm just not being a giant baby about it."

"Why is it you have to be so nasty? You're just ill-tempered," she pronounced. "It wouldn't hurt you to try and be nice to people."

"Is that what you owe your success in life to." I admit it was a snotty thing to say. The situation was not bringing out the best in me.

"There's no talking to you when you decide to be ugly."

I looked out the window long enough to track and lose a dozen more snowflakes. "I'm sorry."

"Beg your pardon?"

"You heard me."

"You know, the rest of the world won't put up with your mouth the way I do."

I let that pass. I watched the highway. Nothing moved on it, only the ghost shapes of the howling snow. After a while Holly said, "Jeanine . . ." Meaning she was still cold.

I sighed. "You can be cold now or cold later."

"Just turn the heat on."

"First we gotta make sure the tailpipe's clear of snow."

"Oh, OK."

"That's so the exhaust doesn't come back in the car and we die of carbon monoxide poisoning."

"I *know* that."

"So let's go."

"My door doesn't work," Holly reminded me.

I opened my door and wriggled one leg out. The wind stung my eyes and made them tear up. The first step landed me halfway up to my knee in snow. "Shit." Behind me in the car Holly giggled. I hopped the rest of the way out and slammed the door behind me.

It was cold, icy, blasting cold, but for some weird reason I felt better out here. I felt free and brave and lonely. I imagined myself walking away from the car and into the storm, walking and walking down the frozen road without direction or thought, until my legs gave out. I wanted to imagine a time that things would be so bad, you were allowed to give up.

Instead I walked around to the rear of the car, bracing myself against the doors and the fender. As near as I could tell, the snow stood only a few inches on the level ground, but the ditch had collected it in a deeper trough. The car looked like it had landed in the snowbank like a bird in a nest. The left front wheel had an odd angle to it that I didn't want to think was the axle.

My jeans were all wet by the time I reached the tailpipe and scooped a clear space around it. Not one thing I wore stood up to this weather. What had I been thinking? It was February, February in Illinois. I popped the trunk and hauled out my backpack.

"What's that for?" Holly asked, when I got back into the car.

"Help me find some dry socks." I pumped the gas pedal and turned the ignition. The Buick always started. It was a classic boat. The vents blew cold air at first, then warm.

"Jesus, you're shaking."

I'd thought it was the engine, but it was me. I peeled off my wet socks and put on new ones. Heat crept into the car gradually. My jeans dried to damp, at least the top side did. I was still sitting on wet. The windshield wipers moved in lazy arcs, clearing a space in the whiteness. I felt drowsy, like my blood was turning to syrup.

"Jeanine?"

I roused myself. "What?"

"It's really creepy that nobody else is out here."

"It's the interstate. Somebody's always out here." I hoped that sounded logical. It was beginning to creep me out too, like maybe the rest of the planet had been destroyed by aliens and we were the only ones left. It was after four, and it would be dark by six. We only had about a quarter tank of gas. I didn't think we were in serious trouble yet. But that was probably true of most people who ended up dumb and dead. They didn't see things coming, just sat there like chumps in a bad movie, while whatever-it-was snuck up behind them and the audience hooted.

The wind picked up a notch. It was so strong I imagined I felt the car rock, even sitting down there in the ditch. We're from Centralia, that's southern Illinois, and too small a place to even have a decent blizzard. Holly had a broody look on her face. I thought she was still worrying about the car, but what she said was, "I'm not so sure about this Chicago thing."

I said, "We been through all this before."

"It just seems so lowlife."

"Nobody's making you do anything," I said. I knew she just wanted me to talk her into it again, that's the way she is. Holly and I go back like forever. I can't remember not knowing her. Plus we're sort of related. Holly's dad married this woman Lila that my one stepfather used to be married to. Both our families are totally fucked. We got our periods the first time exactly one week apart. The times she drives me crazy I remind myself of all that history, which is something different from loyalty. I said, "Look at Vivien. She's OK with it."

"I still want to try and get a real job first. Like at a travel agency, I bet that'd be good."

"Sure. You can do that if you want."

She dug into her purse to find her compact, ran her tongue over her teeth, and smiled into the mirror. Then sighed. There wasn't going to be any travel agency and she knew it. "Doesn't it bother you though? Honestly."

"I expect I'll get used to it. Just lie on your back and spread your wings."

"What if some of them are creeps?"

"You make it sound like creeps would be something brand-new and different."

"You got an answer for everything, don't you?"

"There's a car coming," I said.

I laid on the horn, but the car was already stopping. Its yellow headlights pointed down at us, and you could see how fast the snow was whipping around in them. I got out and made my way along the ditch. So much for dry socks. It was a state trooper. I saw the light bar on his roof and his Smokey Bear hat as he came out in front of the squad car.

"Don't you know this road is closed?"

The first thing he said. Not hello, how are you. "What did you do, drive around the barricade?"

"Wasn't any barricade when we came through."

He did ask if we were all right then, and I told him we were. "Who else is down there?"

"Just my girlfriend."

"Go tell her we need to get a move on."

He went back to the car to squawk into the radio. Holly and I got the suitcases out of the trunk. The trooper gave us a hand, helping us scramble out of the ditch. "Where are you two headed?"

"Chicago."

"Well, I don't guess you're getting there tonight." He got us into the back of the squad car, then went to take a look at the Buick.

Holly stamped her feet to get them warm. "This is weird. It's like we've been arrested."

I guess it was, sort of. You could see all the scuffs and scrapes on the backs of the leather seats where people had kicked them, and it smelled like a bus station or some other public place, whiffs of hair oil and cigarettes and feet. I wondered if the doors were the kind you couldn't unlock from the inside, but I didn't try them because I didn't want to know. I didn't want to think about the Buick's axle either.

Smokey Joe got in behind the wheel and turned around to look at us. "OK back there?"

"Fine and dandy," I said. He had a military haircut, you could see the shaved edges of it, and a tidy mustache. There was a plastic cover on his hat, which always looks silly to me, like a rain bonnet.

"You're lucky I spotted you girls. You could have been down there all night."

The last thing we felt was lucky. And he had that reproachful tone in his voice, like we'd set out on purpose to screw up. I said, "Just where was this famous barricade supposed to be? Because we sure didn't see one."

"Onarga. There was a twenty-car pileup and two semis jack-knifed, so we closed the northbound lanes."

"We must of come through right before it," I said. I could tell he didn't believe me.

He wrote something down, studied it, then clicked his pen shut. "You live in Chicago?"

"We're moving there," Holly piped up.

"That so."

"We're going to cosmetology school," she informed him. Like he cared. It was one thing we'd been telling people.

He glanced up at the mirror then, at our draggled and funky selves. "You mean, hairdos and such."

"Yeah." The air went out of Holly's voice, so it was almost a question. "Where are we going now?" She sounded all pitiful. You'd think we'd been picked off an ice floe on our way out to sea.

"I'll take you up the road to the high school. Red Cross is setting up a shelter, you can stay there tonight."

Holly was dumb enough to be pleased about this. I wasn't, but I was too whipped to think about tomorrow, when I'd have to put everything back together again. The trooper shifted the car into gear and we inched down the highway. It wasn't a good feeling to see the Buick in the ditch like some kind of giant roadkill, but I was glad not to be driving, or worrying about driving. I figured Smokey Joe would get us through, with his big-ass Crown Victoria and his new tires and his radio and his no-doubt-full tank of premium. The blessed heat came shooting out of the vents. On the other side of the window the world turned into snow, and the snow into feathers, a sky full of silent birds.

I guess I dozed off, because when I opened my eyes the car wasn't moving and the air outside was navy blue. I couldn't tell where we were, either the same middle-of-nowhere road, or one just like it. Holly was still asleep, sagged into the corner of the seat with her mouth half shut. The engine was running and the radio was making its talky noises, but Joe was nowhere to be seen.

I got out of the car—the doors worked after all—and stepped right back into the weather. *Cold* doesn't do it justice. The darkness gave everything a mean edge. There wasn't as much snow coming down, but the wind was blowing like the devil and the road was as white and iced as a wedding cake. There was another sheriff's car idling nose to nose with this one, the way you always see them. I guessed Joe was off in the other squad, gossiping.

The front passenger door was open and I let myself in. I figured, why not ride in style? It was actually my first time in a cop car, believe it or not. Vivien said getting arrested was no big deal, just a game you had to play with the law, like hide-and-seek. I didn't see why it had to be a crime in the first place, and why it was always men who made the rules. Why call a whore a whore, except that some man set it up that way, so he could blame her for everything?

Trooper Joe must have seen me get into the front seat. He came right back over to see if I was up to anything, like stealing his extra bullets.

I said, "Could we stop someplace and get something to eat? A McDonald's maybe?" Red Cross food was probably bean soup and macaroni.

He shook his head. "Sorry. The McDonald's is in Kankakee. The road's not plowed that far."

"Well, will they do that anytime soon?"

"First thing tomorrow morning, I'd guess."

He had one of those dry types of humor. "And when do you think they'll get my car out?"

"Tomorrow, probably."

That meant we were going to be stuck a whole day in some pit of a high school gym equipped with somebody's screaming kids and Styrofoam cups of bad coffee. Absolutely nothing was going right for us.

Trooper Joe was studying me from under his hat brim. "Where is it you're from?"

"Centralia. Ever been there?" He shook his head. "I wouldn't bother. The place is a cosmic hole with three inches of water in the bottom."

"What were you doing there, you in school?"

"I'm nineteen," I told him. I'd been through with school for a while.

"But you're going back to school. Cosmic . . ."

"Cosmetology." I looked over my shoulder at Holly, who was still out like a light. "That's right. How much farther to this exit?" We were going about two miles an hour.

"Just a little ways. When do your classes start?"

"What?" I was watching the taillights up ahead, small red dots falling down a long tunnel.

"When does school start?"

"Whenever we get there. It's like, rolling admission." I wished he'd just leave it.

"I suppose you've got ID to show you're eighteen, you and your friend."

"And what if we don't," I said, just to string him along.

"Then we'd have to contact your parents, make sure they knew where you were."

Well, my mom hadn't known where I was since I was about fourteen years old. "We're legal," I said. "Better you should worry about something more important, like where we're going to eat."

"You do have a driver's license, I hope."

Here was one guy who couldn't take a hint. I dug around in my pack for my wallet. "Here," I said, waving the license in front of him. "Happy now?"

"I'll look at it when we're stopped."

"Suit yourself." I couldn't see the other squad car ahead of us any longer, only the deep white ruts where the treads had passed. It was spooky out there, like being on the moon, like all the gravity had spun off and we were about to drift into black space. It felt like the cold had gotten down deep inside me. I tried to fall asleep again, but I was awake behind my closed eyes when he spoke up again.

"You in some kind of trouble back home?"

Eyes open. "What do you mean?"

"Just wondering."

"Mister, the only problem I had back home was being born there in the first place, thank you very much." I relaxed some. It wasn't like he knew anything about me.

"You see so many kids these days that're just lost. No real place for themselves. Fallen in among thieves, like the Bible says."

"You some kind of Christian?" I looked him over. I'd fallen in among Christians before. They were always these white-bread types. It never fails.

"I believe in the Kingdom of Heaven, if that's what you mean. Maybe you have trouble getting along with your folks. Maybe boyfriend trouble?"

"Boyfriends," I said. "You're right, they're not worth the trouble."

"Now that's pretty cynical, young lady." He shook his head and laughed some, and I laughed a little too, just to be polite.

The truth was, I never had real boyfriends, if by that you mean ones that would call you up on the phone and buy you birthday cards and shit. We were never popular, me and Holly. We were too much, too wild for the goody-goods. We did just fine without them. We had our own lives. Holly was even married for a while and had a baby, though that didn't turn out so great. And I had my share of fun along the way.

Of course, after you get yourself a reputation, you're stuck with it. Somewhere down the line I decided that I didn't care what they said about me. And whatever names they called me I was going to carry like a flag. I was always smarter than them anyway, those clodhopper boys with their raw hands and meanness, and the prissy girls. I knew I was going to leave them all behind the first chance I had.

"So," Joe began, and I sighed, waiting for the preaching to start. "Tell me what you do believe in."

"Beg pardon?"

"You must believe in something."

"Is it like having to have a driver's license?"

"Seriously."

I thought about it for a while. I didn't go in for anything like astrology or tarot cards, if that was what he meant. Not Satan or vampires or past lives. I wasn't a Buddhist or a Jew or a Scientologist. What else was left? I said, "I never really bought into anything much. I guess I believe in what I can see with my own two eyes."

He nodded, like I'd said the right thing. "That's the difference faith makes. You can see a lot more."

Not continuing this conversation was not an option, in the present circumstances. "Like what sort of stuff?"

"Glory," he said, pointing to the windshield, as if there was something else out there besides deep freeze and misery. He laughed some, and there was a moment when I wondered if they let anybody who wanted into this job. Then he went back to being Mr. Serious. "You got somebody you need to call? Tell them where you are?"

"My friend in Chicago that we're staying with."

"Is she going to this school too?"

"Yeah, she does."

"What made you decide to be a hair person?"

"What made you decide to be a cop?"

"I asked first."

"I thought I could make a living at it. I thought it would be a challenge." Lord, but I had to keep spinning them.

"I guess it was the same for me. Plus I like driving."

"That's fortunate." As if he'd reminded himself, he squared himself up to the steering wheel. Then he had to get on the radio, so no more nosy questions, I was glad for that. I wondered what he'd think if he knew what me and Holly were up to. He'd shit bricks. Someday it would be a story we'd tell, how we got this police escort, two honored citizens of the State of Illinois.

I couldn't believe it, we were finally getting off this road. There was an exit, and we were headed up the ramp. I reached over the seat and shook Holly to wake her up. She mewed a little, protesting. Just off the exit was a giant truck stop, an acre of rigs, bright lights lifting out of the snow. "Where are we?" asked Holly.

"Gilman," said Trooper Joe. Like that was a name that meant anything to us. "We'll get you fed here, OK?"

"We're purely grateful," I said, meaning it. The truck stop looked like a shrine to me, its red and white and yellow lights promising hot coffee and every other good thing. Snow was blowing across the parking lot, but we pulled right up front, where I guess the law was allowed to park, and scooted inside. Holly and I ran straight to the ladies'. Along with everything else, I'd been having to go for the last hour.

The bathroom had that industrial-strength fluorescent lighting that makes anybody look like the unburied dead. I groaned into the mirror and ran water over my face. The light reflected off ten thousand yellow tile squares, off the chrome and porcelain and mustard-yellow stalls. It was the ugliest place in the world and I fit right in. Holly came up to the sink next to me. "I don't want to go to Chicago."

"Good. 'Cause we can't get there."

"That's not what I meant."

I turned the water off. "What's all this?"

"I want to go home. I'll take a bus or something."

I looked at her. She wouldn't look back. "What is it, you're tired?" She could be like this when she was tired.

"You think I never have a real thought in my head, don't you?"

"I beg your pardon? Did I say that?" My heart was going. I could feel it shoved up under my ribs.

Holly leaned into the mirror, poking at her face. She said, "I never figured out why Chicago was supposed to be such a good idea. Oh I know. The money."

"Yeah, the money. Duh."

She picked up her comb and put it down. "You think you're so smart. Well, maybe you are. But I know I've got my own dumb limits."

"What's got into you, princess? You're all of a sudden too good for me?" She was starting to piss me off.

"I guess I don't want to do something real crummy to myself."

"Oh, like I do?"

"Yeah," she said, without much of anything in her voice. "Somehow you think that's different from having somebody else do it." She yanked at her hair with the comb. "I'm hungry, you coming?" When I didn't say anything she shrugged and walked out.

There was somebody in one of the stalls. I waited until they were done and had washed up and left. There were dark circles under my eyes. My hair crawling every which way. I could feel the safety pin that held my bra together in front. I hoisted my back-pack up and swung it into the mirror. Three, four times. One of the straps came loose, but something heavy inside smacked the glass and made a spiderweb crack in one corner. I kept on swinging it. The strap went flying and the pack fell to the floor, spilling wads of clothes I'd put in clean but now looked like nothing you'd ever want to wear.

When I went out to the restaurant, Holly and Trooper Joe were sitting in a booth, all homey-like. They made me sick. I sat on Holly's side, because I had to sit somewhere. "I ordered you a Coke," she said.

I just read the menu. The trooper had taken his hat off and you could see his neat hair. He was younger than I would have thought, but dressed in the uniform of a grown-up. It was odd, all that squinting light after the dark of the car. Through the windows the storm looked distant, tamer, nothing you could imagine killing you.

The waitress came and I ordered something. "Cheer up, you two," said our trooper. "Things could be a lot worse."

"It's got to be zero minus eighty out there," said Holly.

"It's a bad one," he agreed.

"Is this Red Cross place likely to have TV?"

"I guess it's possible."

"I just thought there might be something on."

She might have been somebody I'd never met before. I ripped open some crackers and started eating them. The waitress brought the Cokes. "Hey," I said. "I want coffee too."

She didn't like my tone, I could tell, but she fetched the pot. "You're welcome," she said, like this was the world's biggest put-down. She was a hefty type with hair cut like a kid's, the bangs combed straight down.

I said, "Everywhere you go, there's people who are under-appreciated."

"Where'd you find this?" she asked the trooper. "Somebody tie it to your bumper?"

After she'd left Holly said, "Then you wonder why nobody wants to hang around with you."

"I'm not asking anybody to. Especially not some crybaby I have to take care of every single minute."

"She's mad because I said I wasn't going with her," Holly told Trooper Joe. Like they were the ones who'd been lifelong friends.

"Just put a lid on it. You don't need to go telling everybody our business."

"Maybe I'm tired of you telling me what to do." She was full of sass, really pleased with herself.

"You getting a kick out of this?" I asked Trooper Joe. "I hope it's a good enough show for your trouble."

"God, Jeanine, give it a rest. What's he going to think?"

"What do I care what him or anybody else thinks? They can kiss my ass."

Nobody said anything then. The noise of the restaurant swelled up around us, though I guess it had been there all along. I clamped my jaw down. But it was like I couldn't keep it that way. "He believes in the Kingdom of Heaven," I said. "He's going to pray for us."

"I think that's real sweet," said dumbshit Holly, just like he'd given her a corsage.

"Oh, grow up. You know what I think? He's looking for some action. Those holy types are the worst. I bet we end up in the Waterbed Motel, not any Red Cross shelter."

"She's crazy. She don't mean it. She says horrible stuff all the time, just to get to people."

"After all, cops are human too. Human nature being what it is. Everybody needs something to wipe their feet on."

The waitress came with the food, and we all shut up then. Trooper Joe looked like one of those faces carved on Mount Rushmore. We watched the plates come down and land in front of us like flying saucers. Mine had some chicken on it and fried potatoes. The steam and the food smell came up from my plate but they didn't touch anything hungry in me. I was trying to see myself up in Chicago with Vivien, or back home in places I used to be, but nothing came to me. I wasn't going anywhere, not really.

Holly and Joe were eating their food in silence. I said, "I didn't mean any of that."

Holly said, "Next time you might consider not saying stuff in the first place."

"Right." I saw the fat waitress yakking it up at another table, smiling now, like she'd forgotten all about me.

"You never know when to quit, do you?"

"Sure I do. Excuse me a minute."

I got up and threaded my way through the tables, which were full of truckers and other people trapped by the storm. At the doorway I stopped and looked back at them. Holly was leaning across the table, talking. She was probably telling him everything in the world, and making it out to be my fault. He'd probably like her. They might even end up together.

I pushed open the door to the outside and started walking,

past the gas pumps and the parked cars and the still-idling rigs, past the concrete and the reach of the lights. Somebody honked at me but I didn't turn around. The exit was slick from people's tires and I could skate a little. The snow had stopped and the wind didn't seem near as strong. Once I got to the highway itself it wasn't near as hard walking as I was afraid. It was even pretty, in an odd way. The sky was black and moonless and the wind had heaped the fields with all sorts of snow shapes—scallops and ridges and smooth white cliffs. It gave off that light that fresh snow does, like it's reflecting invisible stars.

I was walking north, because it seemed a good idea to continue the way I'd set out. My face and ears burned and I felt myself shrink inside my clothes. But it wasn't so cold that I couldn't keep walking. I was thinking nothing in particular, I was done with thinking and all the feeling bad. And that's when I saw them. The ice angels, the glory of the sky.

They marched right down from the heavens in waves of color, arcs and ribbons of beautiful light. There was blue flickering into violet, and violet into pink, and bursts of gold. I heard their voices, an electric hum like the singing power lines make.

I lifted my face to the sky. They whispered and danced above me. If I was seeing things that weren't really there, I didn't mind. It was the first time ever that the world had produced a miracle for me and me alone. The snow glowed with reflected colors, blue and gold and rose. I took off my glove and let the light play over my bare skin. I held up my hand to admire it. I swear on my life, it was the absolute most beautiful thing I'd ever seen.

THE AMISH

My father came home from the war to a household of girls and women. There was me, my mother, and my sister Carol, born while he was away. It was 1967, which was early to be coming back from Vietnam. More people were going there than returning, as is the case in any war. And the great acceleration, the downhill plunge, was just beginning. You have to remember none of us knew how anything would turn out.

While he was away I kept a few memories of my father that came to represent him, the way a photograph comes to replace the real person after a time. He is mowing the lawn, marching his infernal noise from one end of the yard to the other. There are the smells of engine and hay, and the shaved path, and the gold-rimmed afternoon, and the casual ease with which he subdues the grass. Another time he's sitting at the kitchen table drinking beer and making my mother giggle. He is pretending to be a cowboy. He keeps calling her ma'am and saying things like, "Godamighty, ma'am, what I'd give to keep my boots under your bed." I liked it when he charmed us that way. I liked it whenever he made us admire him.

There were the letters he wrote us, telling us he missed us and that we should be good, but anyone could have written those. When he finally returned, we were all shy with each other. My mother explained that he was very, very tired and we shouldn't bother him. We seemed to confuse him, as if he could not remember acquiring us. He moved carefully around us and wrapped us in silence the way you'd wrap pieces of china. Our plush bunnies and hair ribbons and stiff-wigged dolls amazed him. It was as if he had forgotten the names of such frivolous things, or was trying to puzzle out what they were really for.

"What was it like in the war?" I'd ask him, before I stopped trying to ask him things. I was ten. I was a nervy, clever kid, a show-off. I'd ask to sit on his lap, because that seemed like something you were supposed to do with fathers, something I'd seen on television, maybe. But we never got the hang of it. I'd balance on the blades of his legs and we'd sit that way for a while, like a ventriloquist and dummy.

"It was hot," my father would say, or, "It rained all the time." If pressed, he'd say there were jungles and monkeys, but that was as close as he could come to making the war a story for children. He was a tall freckled man with a sandy crew cut, good-looking in a noncommittal, American-man fashion. Except that now the skin over one eye was taut and shiny, and pulled the eyebrow up along with it. He said a monkey bit him, but he wouldn't say how. He'd left the army with a forty percent hearing loss, so that much of his silence was turned in on himself. Once, later in his life, I heard him telling another man about being pinned down for two days by rocket fire. He and his platoon had lain on their backs at night and pissed into the air, and tracer bullets would light up the arc of their falling water.

We were living then in Douglas County, Illinois, where my mother's father ran a farm-implement dealership. My mother had served out my father's Vietnam time there, clerking in the office. My father was going to work there too until he could decide what to do with himself next. Douglas, or Dumb-Ass County, as kids said when they wanted to taunt you, is midway down the eastern half of the state. A thin rectangle without any sizeable town in it, though it does contain the junctions of several main roads, rail lines for the Illinois Central, Union Pacific, Norfolk and Western, and CSXT, and portions of the Kaskaskia and Embarrass Rivers. At one time it must have seemed like a good idea to make a county out of it.

My mother had grown up there, and it was logical that she return with me and the new baby to wait out my father's absence. He was regular army, and had been since before I was born. We'd lived in New Jersey, and in California, and in Texas. Those were the places I could remember. When we arrived in Illinois it was late winter, an important time in the agricultural calendar. The television was full of commercials for seed corn and herbicides and scours preventatives. Enormous tractors, their treads many times my height, stood in ranks in my grandfather's graveled lot. Also discers, drills, and balers, sharp-toothed and lethal. The tractors smelled richly of oil, their paint was bright impervious red or green, and I made some connection between them and the machines of war my father dwelt among. I couldn't imagine our side losing. Although at the same time I envisioned my father slipping beneath the wheels or grinding gears and being lost to us. Accidents like that were always happening. Men and boys smothered in grain at the elevators, or lost their arms in pickers. Machines seemed to win every fight.

Life without my father settled into its own routines. My grandparents doted on us. I had school to contend with, new friends to impress or bully. The town we lived in, Tuscola, was the intersection for three of the rail lines, including the grand City of New Orleans train. The next stop on the line was Arcola. "Arcola, Tuscola, Coca-Cola," my grandfather said to make us laugh. From any house in town you could hear the trains, their whistles at night or the thunder of two empty boxcars slammed together.

At one time you could take the train from one little town to another in any direction, but that was long past. Now the trains carried seed corn and chemicals, loads of rebar and girders, and people drove everywhere. The roads were laid down straight as tape through the cornfields and beanfields, and in summer when the corn was overhead you nudged your way up to blind intersections. To measure distance you anchored your vision to the grain elevators that poked up above the horizon. Carfuls of teenagers barreled up and down the county roads, engaged in wars between rival high schools, painting their names and class affiliations in dripping black on the highway viaducts. You could measure the vigor of each class by how far their range extended. Often enough there were accidents, and the papers would print pictures of the dead from the high school yearbooks.

There was bingo at the American Legion Hall, and the catfish supper at the VFW. There were sidewalk sales in the spring and fall, with sparse racks of merchandise set out to sun. There were cafés full of chapped old men eating pie, and there were shade trees, and frame houses like my grandparents' with broad plank porches and panes of wavy blue and red glass mounted above the front door.

Twenty-five miles to the north was the state university and its enormous swarming population of suspect young people. We drove there sometimes to go to movies or eat at the Steak-n-Shake. The campus was pretty enough, green lawns and rosy brick buildings trimmed with marble festoons like a wedding cake. But it was nothing you could trust. It bred seditions and rowdiness, and people like my grandfather resented each new crop of privileged smart-asses, and the professors who knew too much about all the wrong things. The university diminished us in some way; it was oblivious to us. "Look at *that*," my grandfather would say, nodding over the steering wheel, inviting us to scorn. "Which is the rooster, which is the hen, eh?" The students sprouted hair and leather and fringe and bandana headbands, drugs and riots, a general uncleanness. They were against the war, or at least enough of them were for me to hate them too. (It was years before I would admit to wanting to resemble them in any way.) I had heroic daydreams in which I confounded and shamed them with crushing remarks.

To the southwest, around Arthur, were the Amish, who went to no wars. They were farmers, mostly, though with their large families it was getting harder and harder to leave each son enough land for subsistence. More and more of them were working as cabinetmakers or carpenters, hiring outsiders to drive them to their jobs in forbidden automobiles. They themselves rode in buggies that clipped along the county highways with orange warning triangles on the back. The men wore beards and flat-brimmed hats and suspenders; the women, long blue or black or violet dresses skewered up the front with straight pins. There was no mistaking roosters and hens with them. Sometimes the women would come to town to shop at the discount grocery, buying great lots of generic milk powder, flour, and soap. They wore thick black wobbling shoes and white net caps. Their hair, what you could see of it, was skinned back tight in a way that made my own scalp throb. Inbreeding, people said, had given many of the Amish extra fingers and toes, though I never saw that myself. They were strange in enough other ways to be gratifying. They spoke a German dialect that was full of mutterings and trills, and whenever I saw any of them I stared, trying to puzzle them out, wondering if they had secrets worth keeping.

Somewhere overhead, tethered above everything like a great balloon, was the war, where my father did things too brave and terrible for us to know.

After a while I didn't think of my father that often. There was only the weight of dread that something might happen to him. My mother's married life had been composed of equal parts dread and patience. She waited for my father's orders to take us from base to base, for his death or return, and finally for him to love us all in the way he ought to.

My mother wore her dark hair long and straight, in bangs, like one of the college girls. She was a young-looking mother, with thin wrists and ankles and opaque white skin. Once we reached Illinois it was easy for her to live much as she had before, as a girl in her parents' house. Lots of her old school friends remained in town, women who had married or divorced or married-divorced-married all over again. She went shopping with these friends, or over to their houses for coffee. Or she went out in the evenings to drink old-fashioneds and smoke cigarettes in the taverns, which in small towns are like an extension of your living room.

Some nights she accompanied her wilder friends to Chanute Air Force Base, almost an hour's drive, and the bars that catered to the flyboys, the trainees. These were young men with shaved heads and leather bomber jackets, full of drink and swaggering and lonesomeness. They were thirty or sixty or ninety days away from the war. They were learning about jets, which were intricate beyond the dreams of wizards, and fear, which was simple. My mother always came back early on these nights, airy and demure, tucking her chin to keep the liquor on her breath out of our faces. I don't believe she was unfaithful to my father on these occasions, only because later, when that did happen, I could tell.

My mother believed in love, the yearning, holy sort that glorified men and let women bask in their own suffering and sacrifice. It was what had allowed her to endure a life with my father, his prolonged absences and casual presence. All her women friends believed in love of that sort, even the ones who had cast off their husbands. It was only the husbands who had proved themselves unworthy of love, too small-scale to support the weight of it. It made the women furious to think how they'd been deceived, how inadequate and contemptible these men had been all along. Myself, I would rather live a life dedicated to greed or cruelty, words which at least can't be mistaken for anything else.

When my father returned, his dress uniform hung in the front-hall closet, as if he might need to pull it on at a moment's notice, like Superman, and rush back to the war. The uniform was splendid, with loops of braid and buttons and his sergeant's stripes, and the red patch for the Big Red One, and the crossed rifles for the infantry. The medals were like miniature flags, bars of colored thread that supported the star and the heart, for his bravery and his wounds.

He slept a lot at first, like a new baby. That was probably the best time we had with him, when we could tiptoe in and sneak looks at him, all humped up in the sheets. Or when he came down to the kitchen and my mother cooked blueberry pancakes and sausage, foods he was reputed to crave. We watched him eat. We wanted to see him transported by it. "Great," he said. "Sure not army chow."

After some time had passed, I began to wish, without really admitting it to myself, that my father would return to the army, or rather, to some other place where we wouldn't have to worry about him. We'd grown so used to his absence that it was awkward and inconvenient to have him taking up space in the bathroom, or falling asleep on the couch with the television turned up too loud. He never told jokes anymore. My sister or I hurled ourselves at his knees; he braced himself against us. He never yelled or scolded either, even when he was supposed to be minding us and we pulled things off the refrigerator shelves or fought. Because of his deafness, he always seemed to be listening to something at a great distance. It was anticlimactic for the war to be going on without him, as if they had not needed him that much in the first place. He must have felt the same way. Without his uniform he looked diminished, incomplete, like my paper dolls in their decent uninteresting underwear. I'd expected him to be a multitude of wonders, a live-in circus, a constant soda-pop fizz of glamour and attention, and I felt cheated.

We lived in our own house by then, a few blocks away from my grandparents. My father had been home for almost three months when one morning my grandfather stopped by to see my mother. I was home from school with a cold. I was glad to see him; I was already bored with being sick and turning my tongue red with cherry cough drops. My grandfather had on his office clothes, the neat creased slacks and the belt with the silver eagle buckle, a white shirt and windbreaker. He was a big man with heavy shoulders and a stomach built up from a lifetime of righteous eating, and a mouthful of perfect china teeth, acquired the same way. "How's the sick heifer," he asked, and I pretended to be mad about being called a heifer. Then he said, "Sweet pea, why don't you play upstairs while I visit with Momma."

I didn't mind that. I could hear everything through the heating vent in the bathroom. I settled myself on my stomach on the bath room rug, with my elbow wedged against the toilet. I heard my mother moving around with the coffeepot, rinsing and filling, and then there was the coffee smell. "What's Don doing this morning?" she asked. Don was my father.

"The usual. Answering the phone and saying it's for me. Admiring the view."

"Oh Dad," said my mother.

"You'd think he'd have some pride. He has a family."

My mother said something about things taking time.

"Acts like he's got all the time in the world."

"It's not a line of work he'd have chosen for himself," said my mother. "Maybe that's part of it."

My grandfather said, "I just want you to know you and the kids will always have a home here. You will never lack for anything."

"You think he'd do that. Let us starve. Thanks for the vote of confidence."

I went galloping down the stairs then. I said, "Grandpa, come see my science lab. I got a science lab with a real microscope, and Carol can't play with it."

"Don't race around," said my mother. "You have a temperature."

"It has slides of bacteria and viruses." I dragged my grandfather into the living room to admire it.

That night my mother and father had a talk. They waited until I was supposed to be asleep. "We don't have to stay here," my mother said. "What's one place or another to us? That's never mattered."

My father didn't answer right away. Then he said, "This isn't so bad. Where do you want to go instead?"

"Nowhere. Anywhere. Wherever would make you happy."

"I'm happy enough."

"Sure," said my mother. "I can tell. That's why we never talk. Have sex. Because you're so happy."

"What you mean is you're the one who isn't happy. Leave me out of it."

"Goddamn it, Don. Everybody around here is trying so hard for you. They really are. And it just rolls off your back."

"Nobody has to do anything for me."

"Then do something for yourself. Show some initiative."

"Initiative," said my father. "Whenever they said that in the army, it meant a lot of sorry bastards ended up dead."

They were in bed, talking with the lights off, and my mother got up to use the bathroom. It was a kind of conversational strategy, since she didn't really have to go, and only ran water in the sink. I saw her when she opened the door. The light was on, and she was looking in the mirror. She wore a nightgown she'd probably bought for my father's return, white and silky, like a slip, with thin straps that crossed in the back. The nightgown embarrassed me. It made her look like someone not my mother. She yanked at the straps and squared her shoulders. For some reason I thought of my father's army uniform. She turned off the bathroom light and went back to their room. "You're not the only one in the world who has it tough," she said, but by then my father also was pretending, to be asleep.

My father began to skip work at the implement store, mornings or afternoons or whole days. He'd take the car and be gone until dinnertime, and sometimes he'd miss that too. My mother served up pork chops and applesauce to us like a waitress with a grudge. My father started wearing his old fatigue shirts, army green, with his last name, Baer, stamped across the breast pocket. He grew out his hair until it covered his ears in little blond tufts. He grew a mustache. All that winter we heard his footsteps late at night, a soft dragging sound accompanied by the breath of the furnace. I knew my mother was awake then too, listening. Crescents of shining ice rimmed our windows. Trains wailed and echoed in the frozen air, as if they were falling away down a long tunnel. Beyond our walls was the desolate night, and within our house was this unquiet darkness, dense and watchful.

My mother went back to doing bookkeeping for my grandfather, bringing work home with her. She had precise, methodical ways and an orderly sort of intelligence disguised as simple tidiness. (In years to come she would work as an office manager for a law firm, and do well for herself.) She sat at the kitchen table in her hooded sweatshirt and jeans, her pencil making crisp 4's and 7's, elegant 3's and 6's. My sister and I would be in the living room, watching television and eating pizza rolls. I liked those times, the sameness of them, knowing exactly where she was and what she was doing.

If my father came home then, it spoiled things. The car's headlights would fan across the wall and we'd all hunker down, preparing to be extremely interested in whatever we were doing. He'd walk in and stand somewhere, his head in the light. My mother would say, "There's sloppy joes," and he'd fix himself a plate. They seemed to have contests at ignoring each other, which my father always won because he was genuinely oblivious.

He'd sit down on the couch behind us with his plate on his

lap, and I'd say, "Hi, Dad," turning around so he knew I'd spoken. "Hi, honey," he'd say, and maybe Carol would trot over to him and want the ice out of his Coke. But I was too old for that, and I knew by now it wasn't wanted. So I propped myself up on my elbows and drank in the TV. Its great eye bathed me in color. I watched *The Monkees, I Dream of Jeannie,* and *Rowan and Martin's Laugh-In.*

Sometimes the news came on, war news. I remember this occasion because it was the week before Halloween and I was trying on my costume. I was a devil, with red tights and a plastic pitchfork and a head with horns attached. Carol had a ballerina costume, but she was too little to go out in it. I was twirling the pitchfork and making devil noises, which I took to be sinister laughs. My father told me to pipe down once the news came on.

We saw planes, B-52s with blunt bulb noses and hammered metal skins, perhaps inhabited by some of the Chanute airmen my mother had known. There was a lurching view of treetops that could have been anywhere, shot from the plane, and a river, and then the trees went in an instant to billowing orange flame. I couldn't think why you'd have to burn the trees. I tried to imagine our town, each tree a plumey torch overhead, and it didn't seem like anything that would make you surrender.

Then the film changed. My mother was out of her chair. "We don't need to watch this."

"Leave it," said my father. On the screen there were some dead people, Vietnamese dead people, in a field. The camera traveled slowly so you could see how broken they were.

My mother stepped in front of the screen. "Girls, it's bedtime."

"Get out of the way," said my father.

"Other people live here too. You might remember that. You might show some simple human decency."

My father said, "Has it ever occurred to you that every word you say is completely ignorant?"

"Barbara," my mother said to me, "take Carol upstairs and get her pajamas on."

Carol whined, and I grabbed her by the elbows. I pushed her up the stairs from behind. She kicked at me and I pinched her arms in their fattest, reddest part. When she screamed, I sneered, "Baby," the worst thing I could call her.

I buttoned my sister all wrong into her things, and she squalled about that too, and finally I left her in her room, pulling the eyelashes off one of her dolls. I was still in my devil costume. I squatted at the top of the stairs. My father was being loud. "Get a good eyeful," he said. "Your tax dollars at work."

"I don't understand you anymore," my mother said. "You act like you're happy about every horrible thing."

"Right. I'm in ecstasy. Everyone should be this happy."

"You aren't over there. You don't have to think about it."

I don't know if he heard her or not. He said, "This is a lunatic asylum. The whole befucked country."

He started upstairs then, something I didn't expect. He didn't expect me either. He stopped a few steps away when he saw me, his head level with my feet. Growing his hair out made him look shabby, dangerous, and the scar over his eye could have been something he'd gotten in a mere disreputable fight. To go with my costume I had a black crayon mustache and goatee, and black devil eyebrows. We stared at each other. We both could have been lunatics. "Baby," he said, "don't listen to me. I don't know anything."

My mother began spending a lot of time with one of her girlfriends, Judy Maxey. Judy was older than my mother. She had deep hinged lines around her mouth and eyes, and pixie-cut hair with a little pouf on top, and silver eyeshadow that made her look like an oncoming automobile. I didn't like Judy because she made a big deal out of saying things in front of me in an arch, hinting way that I was not meant to understand but usually did. "She's telling everyone she's p-r-e-g," she'd say, or, "He thinks he's hot snot on a telephone pole, but he's only a cold you-know-what on a toothpick." Judy was separated from her husband, Roy, but sometimes they got back together. Judy also had a boyfriend, Lance, and Roy had a girlfriend, Anita. Things had been arranged like this for some time. They liked all the fuss. They liked standing toe to toe in alleys, flexing and shouting, and driving their cars into each other's cars, and always being angry at the same people, though in different sequence.

I didn't like my mother and Judy being friends. Judy was common, and she meant no one any good. Judy worked in Arthur, at one of the banks. She said the Amish were cheap and never left tips in restaurants and their houses were dirty. She said they were as thick as two planks and didn't know thing-one that went on in the world. I didn't believe any of it. I wanted them to be different from everyone, and exactly like themselves, forever. I wanted people to know who they were and to stay that way.

Judy never visited us when my father was there, and if he came home when she was over she got very cordial and bright-eyed, like she knew secrets about him, things my mother shouldn't have told her. My father didn't seem to like to find her there. She was always asking him questions, stupid ones, anything to snag his attention: How was work, cold enough for you, did he hear about her old car? Uh-huh, my father said. It was like a mean kind of flirting, nothing my mother should allow. But my mother just sat there looking snooty and letting Judy say things.

"Been up at House of Chin lately?" Judy had a cigarette going and she flourished it.

"Not lately," said my father. This was how I found out that he was spending some of his lost time up at the university. House of Chin was a Chinese restaurant, one the students went to. In good weather you could drink outdoors on the front porch. I didn't know why it was something Judy had to be sly about, or my mother angry.

My mother and Judy slit their eyes at each other. My father opened the refrigerator and stared into it. Talking to his back seemed to embolden Judy. "How's the peaceniks?"

My father hadn't heard her. He straightened up and closed the refrigerator door without taking anything out. Because the rest of us were there, Judy had to repeat it. "How you like those peace-niks?"

My father turned his head so that the blue beam of his stare bore down on us. I couldn't stand it anymore. "What's a peace-nik?" I asked.

Judy said, "You know. Like beatniks and sputniks."

"Peace demonstrators," said my mother.

My father said, "It's a word ignorant people use. People who get all their opinions sitting on bar stools."

"That wasn't called for," said my mother.

"What's called for? I'm supposed to put up with this? Who the hell is she anyway?"

Judy arched her throat back to blow out smoke. It had the look of something she practiced in a mirror. She said, "One thing I'm not. I'm not no traitor."

"Depends," said my father. "Does switching beds count?"

"You will apologize," said my mother.

"In a pig's eye I will."

Judy scooped up her keys and lighter. Her jaw was set in a horseshoe shape. "Judy, I'm sorry," my mother said.

Judy waved it off. She said, "It's these children I pity. The things they'll have to live down." Then she went off to talk about us.

This time my parents didn't send Carol and me upstairs. My mother said, "I won't live like this anymore. You do anything you want and no one else matters."

"Can it," said my father.

"You hear just fine when it suits you, I notice."

My father said, "Whatever it is you keep wanting from me, I haven't got it. Leave me alone."

"What is it you can't tell us," said my mother, not sounding angry anymore. She sat down at the kitchen table, weeping. Carol and I cried, pressing in on her. We wanted him to feel bad. It was one thing we could still get from him.

But it horrified us when he began crying too. The tears came crooked out of his scarred eye. They traced around the ridge of his cheekbone and soaked into the soft hair above his ear. It was a terrible thing to see so close up, as if the parts of his face had lost all connection. My mother rose out of her chair, with us still hobbling her, and they hugged, and we all stayed that way for a while. Someone's stomach growled, just above my ear. It was extraordinary to stand so close to them and hear the speech of their bodies. It felt embarrassing but hopeful.

There was a better time after that, when they tried harder with each other and things were more cheerful. Judy didn't come over anymore, though she and my mother kept up a subterranean friendship. My father spent more time at home, even if he still wasn't much company. Christmas came; my mother made felt ornaments and baked sugar cookies. My father strung lights and took blinding flash pictures of us sitting in heaps of crumpled wrapping paper. It was one of those truces in the war between my parents, shallow-rooted and nervous, with all of us trying hard to believe this was our real life.

The winter wore on, with its low skies and accumulations of gray ice. The sun balanced on the frozen lip of the earth as if it too would rather be somewhere else. On campus there were demonstrations, and boys burning their draft cards. My father absented himself from us again, and it was understood that this was where he went. He looked like one of the students now, shaggy and foreign. My grandfather called him Jesus Christ, because of the hair, and officially fired him from the implement dealership, although he continued, unofficially, to give us money. My father brought home strange books and newspapers, pamphlets from the Young Socialists' Alliance, homemade broadsides with cartoons of jack-booted, pig-faced police.

When he and my mother wanted to argue now, they argued about the war. My father was full of ammunition. He'd call my mother to account on the intricacies of the Gulf of Tonkin Resolution, or SEATO, asking her in a challenging, sneering way, if she thought one or another thing was right, or legal. "Why are you asking *me?*" my mother would shout back. "Did I do any of that?" If he badgered her enough, she'd retreat to the declaration that the president must know things that we didn't, and that was why he did what he did. It drove my father wild. "The president knows *bullshit.* New, improved, extra-strength, easy-pour bullshit."

I didn't understand how people could go from being one thing to the exact opposite. I didn't understand it because it had not yet happened to me. I thought my father had suffered some shameful wound that made him turn against everything, and now he hated us too for reminding him of who he used to be. Although I didn't want to agree with Judy Maxey about anything, I thought she was probably right when she said my father had something knocked loose in his head from the war. She suggested my mother might be able to get money from the government because of it.

In early March the air softened and the fields began to bleed through the snow crust. There was still plenty of winter left, and a steady discouraging wind that tried to peel your ears away. At about this time my father began taking me along with him on car rides. We drove nowhere in particular, following the grid of roads beyond town. You could go miles in any direction without seeing a natural landmark, hill or river or woods. There were only the things that had been built, and the fields laid down like rugs.

I sat in the front seat and gazed out at the remnants of winter-blasted cornstalks. Crows squatted on the edge of the road, feasting; they rose up grudgingly as the car passed. I mistrusted these rides. I knew my father was trying to make things up to me, and I was too proud and sulky, after all this time, to let it come easily. My father said, "It's so green in Vietnam. In the jungle you can hear water all around you. It falls from leaf to leaf and it never reaches the ground. Just turns into steam. You can stand there and breathe in rain."

"Uh-huh," I said, refusing to be interested. I kept my sad eyes on the window, not wanting to be tempted by his green alien country.

"They have mountains. Waterfalls."

I nodded, though I didn't want to keep agreeing with him. I knew that he wanted my allegiance. He wanted me to like him, and in some way that would prove he was right about everything.

He'd ask me if I was hungry, did I want to stop for anything, and I always said no. He played the radio, and I tried not to like that either, although I did. We passed solid red and white farmhouses, and if the names on the mailboxes were Amish—Yoder, Schrock, Jess—if there were horses standing about in a mud lot, and a man in black breaking the ice in a water trough, then I'd twist around in my seat, hoping to see more. I imagined women presiding over enormous orderly kitchens, serving up breads and meats and pies to men who had spent all day at serious work and expected to be fed, all of them godly and contented, at peace.

One Saturday morning my father pointed the car north on Route 45, and I knew that we were going to the university. He said, by way of explanation, "I have to go talk to some people." I didn't like the sound of that. I didn't know my father knew any other people. My stomach went cold at the thought of meeting them.

The street was one where students lived. You could tell. The houses had old couches set out on the porches, stuffing exploding through the upholstery. There were cats stalking everywhere, and thin cotton curtains at the windows, and last year's morning glories twisting on strings along the porch railings, and beer cans in the yards. I knew it was no place my mother would want me to be.

The house my father led me to was small and covered in cedar shingles, the kind that always made me think of rainy days. He knocked and the door opened and he steered me ahead of him, his hands on my shoulders.

Voices rolled above me. I kept my eyes down. I didn't want to see more than I had to. The walls were painted flat bright colors, like poster paints, blue and turquoise and orange. The shades were drawn against the daylight and the lights were on. The house had a closed-up, indoor smell, a winter's worth of furnace and laundry, thick and sweetish. I wouldn't have said the house was dirty, only that things were pushed up against the walls rather than put away, and the carpet had a lot of history to it.

We sat down in the kitchen. It was a kitchen although there was a sofa along one wall. "This is Lanny. This is Bunny," my father said. Lanny and Bunny said hello, and I muttered something. They wanted to be nice to me, I could tell. The idea of a child in their house intrigued them, probably because they were children themselves, or not much older. Bunny asked me if I wanted some ice cream. I still didn't want to say an outright yes to anything, but I shrugged in a way that was meant to be yes. Bunny dished out strawberry ice cream into an empty margarine container. It was the closest thing to a bowl she could find. It bothered me that there was a couch in the kitchen, and that I was sitting on it and that there were stacks of paper bags and wet newspapers on the counters and that I was eating out of a margarine tub.

Both Lanny and Bunny wore jeans and homemade-looking pullover shirts with uneven hems. They called my father Don, which bothered me too, though I don't know what else they might be expected to call him. I didn't want my father to have these friends, people he would like better than us, his family. He looked like them now, in his old slick jeans and lumpy parka.

Lanny said, "Man, it's going to be a time."

My father said, "I'm up for it. Whatever happens."

They were all excited about something. They grinned at each other, and once in a while the grins landed on me, just because I was sitting there. I jumped up and stood by the door to get out of the line of fire.

Bunny said to me, "Want to see our kittens? There's four of them."

There was a room with a mattress on the floor and nests of

clothes. The kittens were curled up in the blankets. They were orange and black, like wooly caterpillars. I petted them and they mewed and stretched. Bunny sat beside me. She said, "Their eyes aren't open yet. They're only two weeks old."

Bunny was pretty, with long, dark gold hair and brown eyes and a white smile. I liked her, even though I didn't want to. I wanted to ask her if she and Lanny were married, just to hear her say they weren't. The clothes tangled on the floor didn't look like married people's clothes. A kitten curled around my finger, trying to nurse on it. I said, "My mother doesn't know I'm here."

Bunny gave me a thoughtful look. She had the prettiest eyes. She said, "Maybe you don't have to tell her. You don't want to get her upset."

I nodded. I was a little ashamed of myself for agreeing, for so easily turning against my mother, but I felt relieved too.

Lanny stuck his head in the door. He had a beard, one of those itchy-looking beards. "Let's roll," he said, and then we were all getting coats and trooping out the door. My father started the car. Lanny and Bunny got into the back seat, which was another thing that made me uneasy, having them in our car. It was my grandfather's old car, a big springy Buick with tan leather seats and dashboard lights of chalky luminous green. My grandfather wouldn't have wanted them there. But by now I felt guilty and complicit, as if I'd decided something by my simple presence, or rather, it had been decided for me.

We drove to campus, to the Union, a building I knew because of the bowling alley in the basement. "Go with Bunny," my father told me. "I'll be along later." So I got out, and Bunny held my hand, and I trotted through the double set of doors and inside. Just like that, without thinking twice about it.

I liked holding hands with Bunny. She had on white knit gloves. It was like petting the kittens. Every so often she'd smile down at me. It made me feel dreamy. I knew that whatever happened she wouldn't let me get lost or hurt. I trusted her because she was pretty and had been nice to me and I wanted to be like her. I trusted her in a way I did not trust my father, and of course I had already betrayed my mother. It was just me and Bunny now, walking through the crowds, and if someone had told me I would live my life from now on in the cedar-shingled house with Bunny fixing me things, I would have accepted it without surprise.

We came out the back door of the Union, to the grassy space that opened up behind it. It was crowded with people, pressing right up against the doors. Bunny had to squeeze and shoulder us through. There was a voice coming over a loudspeaker, a shrill splitting noise, and I knew this was why we had come, and now I was uneasy.

Bunny led us some distance before we could find a place to stand. The loudspeaker voice went straight through me. "Choose sides now," it was saying. "Rage is growing like an alligator in a sewer."

I couldn't see the man talking. I looked up through people's shoulders. I was glad no one was paying attention to me. I felt the way I always did in a crowd, horribly visible, anxious to submerge myself. The air was milky and luminous, overcast and diffused, so that everything had a shadowless clarity. I felt Bunny's hands in their soft mitts resting on my shoulders. The faces around us were settled into listening. People shifted their weight and jostled. I wasn't afraid of the students the way I would have been anywhere else. It was like being in the middle of a herd of large mild animals.

My father's voice rose out of a wave of shouting from the crowd. The speakers made it sound tinny and whistling. My father said, "The people of Vietnam are not your enemies. The children of Vietnam are not your enemies."

Bunny said, "Can you see?" I couldn't. She moved us up a little ways. I saw the crown of his head and the pale sky reflected in the glass windows behind him, but I still couldn't see his face.

My father said, "I've been a soldier and I've lived a soldier's life. I loved the army. It had a rule for everything. It had a system.

You had it knocked. But nobody tells you what to do when the rules go belly-up and start to stink. I followed all the orders. The first time I killed a man, I cried. The other times I got drunk. I don't know if any of you out there have ever killed anyone."

In the silence you could hear faraway noises: a plane overhead, traffic.

"When you kill, it's like filling your mouth with dirt. I don't know how else to say it. You turn into death yourself. There should be some damned good reason to kill a man. A child. Its mother."

I drew in my father's voice like breath. I swallowed it down. It was both holy and awful to hear him saying such things.

"The war's back home now. It's blowing up in our faces. People are enemies everywhere they go. We hate each other for the things done in our name." There was a spike of feedback and my father's voice climbed down from it. "I've been told there's a man over there taking my picture."

The crowd made a noise like wind in a tunnel. My father said, "Ever wonder what a subversive's file looks like? Ever wonder why you're an enemy?"

I wanted my father to keep talking. I wanted to hear him say something about me in his new electric voice. I thought that if he said "my daughter," then whatever followed would be his heart's truth, and I would know what he thought about me. But there was some commotion up front, and people craned and pushed toward it. Bunny crossed her arms over me and pressed me into her legs. The microphone sang out, an amplified tuneless shriek. "There's some friends of mine," Bunny said. "We'll all go get some hot chocolate. Would you like that?" Behind us people were beginning to circle, running. The crowd was turning on its axis like a pinwheel. It was that fluid moment when anything can happen, panic, flight, or simple dispersal, but Bunny walked us out of it so quickly, I was hardly aware of it. Nor did I think to worry about my father, though I might have.

Perhaps because I had not worried, everything turned out all right. Bunny and her friends and I sat in the Union cafeteria, and I had hot chocolate and a cinnamon roll. After a while Lanny and my father joined us. We dropped Lanny and Bunny off at their house, and my father and I drove home in the sunless late afternoon.

Fog was rising from the low places in the melting fields where the snow still hung on. My father asked me if I was tired, and I said, "A little." I was glad to be in the car again, with its familiar bath of hot air washing over my feet, and the glowing green dashboard lights. Now that we were back in the car everything was ordinary again, as if the rest of it had not happened. My father looked like he always did when he drove, preoccupied, a little stern, hands on the wheel at ten and two o'clock. He was a good driver. I said, "Who was it you killed?"

He didn't answer, and I thought he hadn't heard me. Then he said, "I don't know who they were. You don't ever." And a little while later he said, "You're old enough to remember this, aren't you?" We didn't say any more about it. We reached home at dusk, and I ran into the house ahead of him, and within a year my father moved to Phoenix, Arizona, as far from a jungle as you can get, and that part of our life was over.

I thought the war between my parents and the war on television would both go on forever, without conclusion, in ways we were all used to and which we had already adapted to. When first one, then the other, came to an end, everything changed. There weren't enough rules left to know what to expect of the world. I don't think that's such a bad thing, not anymore, at least. When I was a child I thought you chose one side and stuck with it. The day I heard my father speak I learned how allegiances can change: all at once, without decisions.

My mother remarried and made a new life for herself, as they say, although she continues to be my mother. She's brisk and resilient and ordinary, and sometimes I think she might have made a better soldier than my father, just as I might have made a better son than a daughter, and claimed a different territory. I talk to my father every now and then. He has a hearing aid and a special telephone headset that amplifies sound. He says things are OK with him, things are fine. It's the way we talk best, through wires and machinery. It's the only way we can talk to each other, across distance. We still don't say that much, but we don't expect to. The old grievances, failure, and shame are turning into history, inch by inch. Every time my father picks up the telephone to call me, he's telling me he's sorry. Every time I answer, I'm telling him the war is over.

three
SPIRITS

ANTARCTICA

Because the daughter and son-in-law were off touring Antarctica, it was the granddaughter who drove the old lady out to inspect the nursing home. The granddaughter had been sleeping on the grandmother's couch for a week, making sure she didn't forget her medicine, making sure she didn't fall down and hurt herself. There was an enormous black bruise, like a sack of blood, on the underside of the grandmother's arm. This was from the time she fell into the glass coffee table. Then she had fallen out of bed and broken her back, compressed the vertebrae, although apparently you could do that and still walk around. The grandmother said the pills made her sick and dizzy. She took so many pills, they went off inside her like bombs. There were reactions, interactions. When she forgot to take her pills, she felt sick in different ways. She'd had bad spells before, but now it was apparent things were not going to get any better. The doctor said the grandmother was going to need more care from now on. This was how he spoke of it, needing more care, rather than saying diapers and bibs and the end of the line.

The grandmother said, "I can't abide any food that has the animal on the package, looking like it's happy about being eaten." She was talking about the sausage the granddaughter was fixing for breakfast, the grinning cartoon pig dressed up in overalls and brandishing a pitchfork. "Like Charlie the Tuna. Is he still on? Who are they trying to fool?"

"Nobody. Would you rather have oatmeal? Raisin bran?"

"Don't fuss, dear heart. Tell the truth, you can get tired of food. It's one of those things people always think should make such a big difference."

The granddaughter forked the grandmother's sausage onto her own plate. The granddaughter's name was Evie. She was short and round, with close-cropped brown hair and a sweet face. Evie felt bad about the nursing home, as if it were something cruel she was doing on purpose. But what else was there? The grandmother didn't want to be a burden. Evie couldn't keep taking time off from work, nor could the grandmother be expected to move into Evie's apartment, displacing Evie's fifteen-year-old son onto the living-room couch. The daughter and son-in-law, Evie's parents, had a big house full of aquariums and La-Z-Boys and burglar alarms, but the grandmother didn't want to live with them. "Who would I ever see there? Nobody but the dog." Evie's brother lived in New York City, where no old lady ought to go, and there was the sister who nobody talked about, currently residing in Killdeer, Montana. The grandmother was ninety-five, too old to go anywhere new anyway. Ninety-five! She had been alive for every year of the century. When the *Titanic* went down, when Grandpa fought the Great War. When the Twenties Roared. The Great Depression,

Hitler, the atomic bomb, I Like Ike, Vietnam, Nixon, men on the moon, computers, AIDS, the works. The grandmother remembered history perfectly. It was the right-now part she wanted to forget.

The grandmother had been living in a seniors' apartment complex, a nice place, with security, new carpeting, flowers in the lobby. There were emergency buzzers in the bathroom and by the bed. Every morning when you got up, you hung a GOOD MORNING sign on your door, to show you were still alive. The grandmother had girlfriends, and they often got together for cocktails before dinner. They drank bourbon, which always seemed mildly alarming and rowdy to Evie. Bourbon was probably not allowed in the nursing home.

After they finished breakfast, and Evie had set the dishes to soak, the grandmother took up her cane and they snailed out into the hallway. The apartment complex had the world's biggest, smoothest elevators, to keep the old people from getting claustrophobic or losing their balance. Evie installed the grandmother in the front seat of the car, the way you'd wrap a fragile package for shipping. They got on I-80 and headed north, toward Roseville and Citrus Heights, those fragrant names that diminished into freeway exits. The downtown skyscrapers were planes of dented light, receding. It was winter, November—that meant it was summer in Antarctica, more or less—and the shallow California fields had greened up so that they were the color of boiled vegetables. It was chilly, and a high fog made the sun a brassy smear. Traffic slogged along on both sides of the highway, a dull herd. The grandmother, who was tiny, who shrank down a little more each year, pointed her chin over the dashboard, pretending to take an interest.

Evie said, "It's supposed to be a nice place. The pictures were nice." The nursing home had sent a brochure. It showed a garden full of lilies-of-the-Nile and oleander, and hearty-looking oldsters, people who didn't need a nursing home in the first place, strolling the paths.

The grandmother reached over and petted Evie's hand. "I'm sure it's nice enough, dear heart."

"If it's not, we'll find one that is. We'll build our own from scratch. You don't have to decide anything. We're just looking."

The grandmother said, "There's no real trick to getting old. Not if you've already done everything worth doing."

"When Mom and Dad get back, we'll sort the insurance out. They've got all the insurance stuff."

"Did your folks go someplace?"

"They went to see the penguins, Grandma. They sent a post-card."

"Oh shoot. I knew that. Penguins. I bet those things can bite like the dickens."

The daughter and son-in-law were always going to places you'd think were only names on a map. Tahiti, Gibraltar, Tasmania. For the Antarctica trip they had boarded a ship in Tierra del Fuego. The ship brought them to within a mile of the continent, where, because of the difficulty of navigating the ice shelf, they'd ride a Zodiac the rest of the way in. They would disembark at Little America, in the Bay of Whales. They'd bought expedition-weight long underwear, field-tested parkas, and boots and goggles. At least it was not one of the places you had to get shots for.

Evie thought it was strange that they had tours of Antarctica now. Her parents only went places on tours, first class, and were scrupulous about their comfort. Still, the Zodiac impressed her. It seemed more like what she imagined travel ought to be. When her parents weren't going to other countries, they went on rallies with their RV club, to Mexico or Tahoe or Las Vegas. They set up barbecue grills and brought out lawn chairs and American flags and schnauzer dogs. The name of the RV club was the Rambling Wrecks. The parents had a bumper sticker: WE'RE SPENDING OUR CHILDREN'S INHERITANCE.

The nursing home fronted a busy street, the trailing end of a shopping district. Evie didn't much care for that, but the grandmother said bravely that she liked the idea of taking herself out to the Walgreen's. The nursing home was called the Heritage Center. It was one story, like a motel, built of pinkish brick with white columns. A strip of green lawn with a sprinkler whirling. Inside, Evie sniffed the air suspiciously. She knew about the smells.

The place was nice enough. Nice nice nice. A lady from the office squired them around. There were potted plants. A room with a piano. A bulletin board with HAPPY THANKSGIVING and a cutout turkey, like a schoolroom. Everywhere you looked there were wheelchairs loaded up with papery old people. In the rec room a cheery aide directed a circle engaged in batting an oversized balloon which kept falling to the floor. The dining room smelled of steam and warm milk, but that wasn't anything bad. The office lady talked about nutrition, the Saturday-night movies, the capable nursing staff. The garden looked crabbed in the dull sunlight, a cement maze interspersed with shrubs.

"Vegetables," the grandmother whispered to Evie. "Everybody here is one of your basic food groups."

In a room, in a bed heaped with pink afghans, an old lady stared out at them. Her head looked like an egg gone soft. There was a little fluff of white hair and a tiny face, the mouth hinged open in an O. "This is Mrs. Folkstone," said the office lady. "Mrs. Folkstone's our pet. She's been with us six years. How are you today, Mrs. F.?"

The O was now a Q. Mrs. Folkstone's tongue was in evidence. Her voice was a cracked flute. "They took my hearing aid."

"You're such a silly girl," said the office lady.

"Took it and hooked it up to the air conditioner. That's why I'm freezing to death."

Evie looked at her grandmother. The grandmother's eyes were closed, as if she was sleeping, or weighing a complicated thought.

When they were back in the car, the grandmother said, "I bet you think I'm an awful sissy."

"Of course I don't."

"I suppose you could carry on a conversation with the nurses and such. If they weren't hateful."

"We'll find some other places," said Evie. She knew the place they'd seen was probably the best you could hope for. She felt old herself, old and remote, as if everything sad had already happened and she was watching it from the far side, as if today were already a memory. She loved her grandmother, who, Evie always said, could do anything from butcher a hog to serve tea to the queen of England. The grandmother had lived on a ranch in the Central Valley, she and Grandpa, harvesting oranges and olives. She'd raised four children and buried two. Driven a truck over the Donner Pass in a blizzard, and swum in two oceans. When Grandpa had his stroke and turned simple, she was the one who hauled him in and out of the bathroom, kept him clean and decent, walked the groves with a shotgun, sent her children to sell baskets of fruit on the highway. All the stories Evie had grown up with. Now the stories were slipping away, like the stream of freeway air outside the car windows.

She reached for a story. "Do you remember when we were little, and our old dog Tigger got into the ant poison, and we all had to take him to the vet? And you told us dogs were tough, you couldn't kill them if you tried." What a thing to talk about. She couldn't believe she'd come up with that one.

"Tigger?" The grandmother's chin pointed down.

"The little yellow one. His ears flopped over." Evie saw him clearly, a comical, self-important dog. "Mary Ann named him. From the Pooh stories."

The grandmother had sagged into sleep. Evie supposed what she'd really wanted was to talk about Mary Ann. She wanted to talk about her before it was too late.

Evie had gone to visit her sister this past summer in Killdeer, Montana, the first time she'd seen her in nearly eight years. Mary Ann's husband was a Presbyterian minister, and they had trekked from one surly congregation to another in bad or worse places.

Ellensburg, Washington. Vernal, Utah. Thermopolis, Wyoming. He was apparently not on the ministerial fast track. Now they were in Killdeer, which was part of the Golden Triangle, Mary Ann had said. This confused Evie, who'd thought the Golden Triangle referred to opium smuggling in places like Burma. But Mary Ann said it had something to do with wheat growing.

Evie drove north from Great Falls, seventy miles of wheat fields and windy sky. Somewhere up ahead, not very far, was Canada. The only thing lonesomer than the wheat fields was the town itself, three narrow blocks of downtown, a grain processing plant, a Western-wear store with a full-size fiberglass palomino out front, and a huddle of houses in treeless yards. Evie followed Mary Ann's directions, four streets deep and left two blocks.

Her sister, whom she would have recognized anywhere, stood in the driveway, as if she had known the exact minute Evie would arrive. Someone she imagined to be her brother-in-law, the minister, was peering into the garage.

Evie parked, got out, and hugged her sister. Mary Ann was thin, an armful of bird bones. She had always been thin. Evie was blubbering a little. "Oh my God, it's really you, it's still you, oh God, Mary Ann."

Mary Ann detached herself, smiling her thin smile. "You found the house OK?"

Evie said yes, she had. A little awkward now, since she had gotten too excited. "What a nice place you have." The house was so ugly that any such remark could be taken as sarcasm. It had weeping green shingles and dinky windows.

"The church pays for it." Mary Ann shrugged.

At the end of the driveway the brother-in-law pulled the garage door down and darted through the back gate.

"Byron has a meeting," said Mary Ann, leading the way to the front door. "Jessica's at Brownies. I have to go pick her up in a little."

The brother-in-law reemerged from the backyard, his mouth

working in a mutter, and headed for his car. Evie tacked sideways to intercept him. "Byron. I'm so glad to finally meet you."

He inserted his hand into her outstretched one, his gingery face scowling at the ground. "Membership committee," he said. "It's always something."

Inside, Evie asked to use the bathroom. She sat on the toilet, staring at the blue plastic shower curtain and its pattern of sea horses. The house was so small, she could hear Mary Ann opening kitchen cupboards on the other side of the wall above her head. For the life of her she couldn't pee.

"Evie?" Mary Ann spoke from the other side of the bathroom door, about eighteen inches from Evie's knees. "I'm going to go get Jessica."

"Sure," said Evie. When she was alone in the house she walked through the rooms, not exactly spying, but looking at things in a way she would not have otherwise. There was a heap of laundry on the bed, waiting to be folded. Some stuffed animals in fluorescent colors. She was hungry, but the refrigerator held mostly plastic bowls and plastic-wrapped bundles, mysterious, darkly beaded with moisture, unidentifiable. A framed scroll on the living-room wall: Where There Is Love In The Heart, There Is Joy In The Home.

Mary Ann came in from the garage, pushing her daughter ahead of her. "Stand up straight. Come say hello to your aunt." The little girl wriggled away and bolted for her bedroom, slamming the door.

"Jessica, what did we talk about in the car?"

"I don't want to have an aunt. She's too fat anyway."

"Jessica Lynn *Morr*ison."

"I brought her a present," said Evie weakly, reduced to bribery.

"I want a Barbie. And a monkey." From the noise, it seemed she was jumping up and down on the bed.

"I'm afraid we don't have a lot of company," said Mary Ann, by way of apology.

"It's all right." Evie was embarrassed, as if her sister's family should not be available for public display. "It's OK if she's shy."

The bedroom door opened. The little girl's dour face peered out. "I am not shy."

Things got better after that. Evie had to take into account they had never seen anyone from Mary Ann's family before, that fabulous bestiary. They were naturally mistrustful. Mary Ann and Evie sat together, drinking tea. The minister had taken his daughter out for ice cream. Evie examined their four hands on the kitchen tabletop. Both of them had small blunt fingers, like those rounded-edged scissors they give to schoolchildren. She wouldn't have guessed their hands would still look so much alike.

"So what do they say about me?"

"Nothing. What did you expect?"

"Denial," said Mary Ann, wisely. *Denial* was one of her words now. It had something to do with their mother always being nice. Nice nice nice. The mother set the table in August with her Christmas dishes: plates, bowls, butter dish, napkin rings, salt and pepper shakers, all ornamented with Santas and holly. You were not allowed to find this funny. You were not allowed to remark on it at all. You were not allowed not to be nice. It was the mother who wrote the postcards on their trips: *The weather has been a little cold, but we are enjoying the beautiful scenery. Tomorrow we are going on a tour of the Old City.*

The father was supposed to stay away from sugar and caffeine. Sugar and caffeine made him irritable. The mother experimented with carob and fructose. When the father was irritable, you had to stay out of his way. If his food was wrong, he might pick it up and throw it. If the children tried to be smart with him, they were asking for it. Their brother was the worst one, the biggest smart-ass. The father dragged him down flights of stairs by his ankles, so his head bumped bumped bumped like a gourd on every step. The father kicked with his shiny black shoes. Slapped and punched and screamed. They made him sick. Evie was a fat pig. A lard-ass.

Look at her. Was there anything she wouldn't stuff into her fat pig face? He pulled out a fistful of her hair so that she would be just as ugly as he said she was. Mary Ann had a nervous stomach. She was a mealymouthed complainer who thought she deserved special treatment. Well she didn't. Nobody in this house was going to get special treatment for whining. If she wanted to throw up, fine, go ahead, see how far that got her in life. They were all going to learn a lesson or two someday. The father sulked majestically. The mother coaxed him with new recipes. There was an accident where the brother's arm was broken. The father had his business and the serious worries that went along with business. It was understandable he had a lot on his mind. The sisters stayed upstairs in their bedrooms and listened to the furniture splinter.

That was how they had grown up. It was bad enough, wasn't it? But the other. Evie could not get her mind around the other. "I don't think it happened to me," she told Mary Ann.

"I didn't remember it either, not for years and years."

"I don't understand. How can you start remembering all of a sudden?"

"It was when Jessica was getting potty trained, when she was getting interested in the potty. I'd get these weird feelings like panic attacks. I started throwing up again. It was something about the potty. Something that was done to me then. When I was that little."

"What . . ." Evie stopped, sick, her mind crawling.

"Look, I can't show you a movie. I can't prove anything. But why *wouldn't* he do it? He did enough other things with his hands."

Their own hands, resting on the cloudy Formica tabletop. "I'd know if it happened to me," said Evie. But she wasn't so sure. Could the body remember what the mind could not? It might be waiting to ambush her, squatting in the corner of her vision when she turned her head or looked in a mirror. Mary Ann was right, he had done enough other things. Could you really say this was worse? Yes. It was the worst thing.

She was four years older than Mary Ann. Maybe she had already been too fat. It was one more way he would not love her. That was terrible to think, the saddest part of all, that this had anything to do with love. She said, "He must remember it. How could he not remember?"

"Because he was always drunk. He's an alcoholic, you know."

Evie considered this. She had never really thought of her father as an alcoholic before, but it made a kind of sense. *Alcoholic, dysfunctional, abuse.* Those were some more of Mary Ann's words. She got them from the therapist. It made Evie feel stupid and cowed, not knowing the words. The therapist was the one who helped Mary Ann write the letter. Mary Ann got up from the table. "I want to show you something."

Evie followed her to the bedroom. Mary Ann dug in her closet and brought out some pieces of poster board that were stored against the back wall. She pushed the laundry on the bed aside and laid them flat next to each other. "These are something I've been working on."

They were collages, cutout pictures overlapping and glued into place. In one corner was a horrible dead-fish-looking thing, except it had arms and legs, and a face, or what was left of one. Bump of a nose, teeth showing in an eroded grin or scream, black rags of skin peeling away.

"What in the world is this?"

"It's the Ice Man. The one in the glacier. I think he's Bronze Age."

There was a picture of a house, ordinary enough, but a howling ghost looked out from one window, and flames sprouted from the roof. A tangle of creeping things, like salamanders, at the base of black lowering cliffs. Shadows in the shape of claws, lake of dark blood. If you fell asleep and dreamed about hell, it might look like this.

"I get them from magazines," Mary Ann was saying. "*Smithsonian*'s a good one."

Evie didn't like to think of her sister going through pages, scissoring out pieces for her nightmares. "What's this supposed to be?" A white bird flying, a speck in a lurid sky above a car accident.

"That's the Holy Ghost. I wanted there to be a little bit of hope, you know?"

No one had ever told the grandmother about the letter. After all, she was an old lady. There was no reason to upset her. Evie got off the freeway and drove down another traffic-choked highway. The fog had burned away and the sun was beginning to batter the cement, the ugly litter of strip malls and parking lots, the glass and metal world that sprang up like a rash when no one was looking. The grandmother woke with a jerk and blinked. "Where are we going now?"

"Back home, Grandma. Did you want to stop for anything?"

"Home. Where you hang your hat, I guess."

"I'm sorry this is all so hard for you."

"You're my sweetest sweetest girl."

"Oh, I don't know," said Evie, feeling helpless. It didn't do any good, being sweet. Nothing she did or said made any difference. And maybe she was not really that person, the person everyone thought she was: helpful, anxious, ineffectual. Maybe that had only been the path of least resistance. She might have been twisted into a certain shape, like an ornamental hedge.

"Grandma, do you remember much about being a little girl?"

"Sure I do," said the grandmother, crossing her thin ankles in their flesh-colored elastic stockings. "Lots of things. You'd be surprised. It wasn't that long ago."

The stoplight in front of them went red. They sat, inhaling brown exhaust. Traffic was scarcely moving. There must be an accident or something up ahead. When the light turned green, Evie had to change lanes, something she did with reckless desperation, as if she were a trapeze artist grasping at a swinging bar. Someone behind her honked. Her stomach squeezed, hungry again. That soft and greedy part of her, like a secret she could never keep. Why couldn't she hate food, like Mary Ann? "Tell me about Grandpa," she said. "Before he had his stroke, I mean. What was he like?"

"All these questions. Who are you, Oprah? Well, it wasn't all roses. The war made him gloomy. Like he'd never come all the way back from it. I married a war relic."

"Like my dad."

"What? Oh yes. Different war."

"I guess it would change somebody's outlook."

"Not for the better."

"Dad was in the Pacific. Bombing people." Evie made her voice brighter, since the grandmother seemed to be losing interest, listening to something inside herself, perhaps, some flutter or ticking in her blood. "Grandma, are you feeling OK?"

"I think I need my pills."

"We'll be back home in just a little," said Evie, although the traffic was still as thick as a stew. She cranked the window down and wrinkled her nose at the poisoned air. The grandmother was asleep, just like that. Her mouth hung open and her eyeglasses had slipped. What if she died right here, on this ugly street? What if she was already dead? But of course she wasn't. The grandmother stirred, righted her glasses, slept again. The cars up ahead of them bumped forward.

Did you know that seventy percent of the world's water is frozen in Antarctica? The mother's last postcard. Even in summer it was cold there, zero. In Antarctica you could walk right up to the animals. They hadn't seen enough humans to be afraid of them. There were all sorts of birds and animals, lots more than you'd expect. Giant albatrosses, petrels, shearwaters. Blue whales, sperm whales, killer whales. Seven or eight different species of penguins, all of them waddling and preening and taking themselves seriously. There were elephant seals and leopard seals and fur seals. The seal lay on the ice in a little fur bundle. Her father approached with his video camera, walking in a crouch so he'd be down on its level. His shadow inched ahead of him. "Run," Evie told the seal. The traffic's slow parade stopped altogether. She was being completely ridiculous.

Her father was old himself now. He had a shiny pink rubbery face, like an old baby's. His eyes behind his glasses blinked in perpetual hectic motion. He hadn't hit anybody in a long time. He was too busy with the trips, with going and coming back and planning the next one. "Watch this," he'd say, increasing the volume on the video. He was getting hard of hearing and played everything loud. He had three different remotes and he kept clicking them up and up. There was footage of gift shops, formal gardens, scenery jumping along outside of bus windows, the mother hauling suitcases. He played the videos all the time.

It was curious, watching the world through her father's eyes. Those merciless stretches of boredom, the sudden epileptic shifts of focus. "Watch this." What were you supposed to see? Sometimes she thought she didn't know one thing about him, or he about her. No matter what he'd done. She couldn't stand thinking about that. It left a bruise on her mind.

Her last day in Killdeer, Montana, she and Mary Ann drove to a little park, a stretch of willows lining a creek. A wind kicked up yellow dirt, and there was the distant sound of a tractor. "I need to tell you something," said Mary Ann. "I've been remembering some other stuff. Ritual abuse. I think I'm justified in calling it that. It was when we went on camping trips. Aunt Greta and Uncle Jim were there. They'd all be sitting around the campfire, laughing at me. They made me eat something burned on a stick. Babies. That's what they called it. Burned babies."

Evie felt the ground tilt beneath her, moving slow as syrup.

"You don't believe me."

"We toasted marshmallows and hot dogs."

"You think I'm crazy."

"Do I have to believe everything?"

"You're the only one I care about," said Mary Ann. "The only one I really love. Do you know that?"

"Yes." She did, somehow. She'd always known it.

"Nobody else but you knows what it was like. Even Jack. He was a boy. It wasn't the same for him."

"I can't say it happened. I can't say it didn't. I just don't remember."

"It was all such a big stinking secret. Other people thought we were like them. We weren't. Nobody else even knows who we are."

Evie closed her eyes. Stripes of sun and willow shade fell across her face. No one had ever truly singled her out, loved her more than anyone else, except perhaps her son when he was young, and he'd had no choice. But it frightened her, this furious love. Mary Ann frightened her. "It's all so hard," she mumbled.

"You should pray for healing," said Mary Ann, yanking up handfuls of grass. "For God's grace and mercy."

But Evie didn't believe in God, whom she always imagined to be too much like her father. Bigger than everyone, and full of terrifying angers. She didn't know what she believed in anymore. Who she was. She was another secret.

There seemed to be something wrong with the grandmother's neck. Her head flopped against the side window. Her mouth hung open, like a bird's in summer heat.

"Grandma?"

"I don't feel so good, dear heart."

"We'll find a hospital."

"I don't want the doctors getting ahold of me. Them and their old pills."

Evie inched toward the curb, trying to pull over, turn, think. Should she stop, call for an ambulance, keep going? She swallowed the thick panic that rose in her throat. There was no one else here. Whatever happened would be her fault.

"Which one are you?"

"I'm Evie, Grandma."

"I knew that. My head's just all soupy."

She managed to turn onto a side street. The grandmother made a snoring noise, although her eyes were open. Evie trod on the brakes and the engine bucked and died. "Grandma?"

"That's not my real name." The grandmother gave her an almost crafty look.

"I can call somebody. We can wait right here and they'll come get us."

"No."

Evie started to explain again. But the grandmother kept saying no, as if her mouth was stuck on it.

"No what?"

"No doctors." The grandmother began to cry. Tears came hurtling from her. She paddled at the air with her hands. "They'll put me in the hospital. They'll drain everything out of me. How old do you have to be before they leave you in peace?"

"All right, shh. Nobody's going anywhere. We'll just sit right here for now." Evie's heart broke and broke. The street they'd come to rest on was residential and stately, with pretty stucco houses and yards full of ferns and late roses. She could imagine herself living in such a place if she was a different kind of person with a different life.

"Am I going to die?" asked the grandmother, balling up Kleenex.

"Not right now."

"Oh." That seemed to calm her. She trailed off into sniffling.

Evie rolled the windows down further. A little mild air filtered in. The grandmother said, "Don't tell your mom. I'm leaving all my money to you."

"You don't have to do that." Evie was unsure if the grandmother had any money. "Why don't you want to tell Mom?"

The grandmother winked. "There's lots of things she don't tell me."

"What do you mean?"

"Lots and lots. Where is it they went? The North or South Pole?"

"South, Grandma. They went on the boat. What things?"

"They aren't coming back."

"Oh, Grandma."

"Like the other one." Again the crafty look, as if the grandmother was peering out from behind a rock or a tree. "Did she die?"

"You mean Mary Ann? Of course not. Nobody died."

"She went off on a boat and it sank."

"No, she didn't. She's in Montana." She wanted to follow the grandmother to wherever she'd gone, drag her back, make her listen. "She wrote a letter to Mom and Dad and said she wasn't going to see them again because Dad physically and sexually abused her."

"Did I know that?"

"No, Grandma. He did all sorts of things nobody told you about. Once he held my head underwater in the bathtub. He used to whip Jack with a belt. I think he hated us."

"Which one is Jack?"

She was too late. Everything had happened too long ago, and none of it would ever change. She looked around her, at the pretty street where she did not live and never would. The grandmother was looking at her sweetly. "I bet you're somebody I know."

"That's right."

"I'm sorry I'm being such an old nuisance."

"You're not any such thing."

Evie started the car. The grandmother said, "Tell me a little about yourself. This is all so embarrassing."

"I'm Evie."

"How do, Evie."

Had her father really hated them? All her life she'd imagined that he must love her in some way she did not recognize. All her life she'd tried to puzzle it out, explain, excuse, understand him. Maybe it had been simpler than that all along.

She began again. "I was the only child of a beautiful young couple. When I was just a baby we went on a cruise around the world. The ship hit an iceberg and sank. My parents and everyone else aboard were lost."

"You're making this up," the grandmother said, wagging a finger.

"I washed ashore on a glacier. A creature called the Ice Man found me. He took me back to his cave and that's where I grew up. He fed me whale meat and raw fish. Somehow I always knew it was the wrong food. The Ice Man frightened me with his roaring and his cold breath. One day I was on the edge of the ice when the sun came out and shone so warm that a piece of ice broke loose and I floated away. I wasn't scared, because right then I remembered I came from a different place, a place where there were other people. I floated a long way, until the water was warmer and the ice melted. I swam on to a beautiful coast where orange trees grew. I made some friends there. I had a little boy. I got a car so we could go for rides together."

"That's a nice story," said the grandmother. She shifted in her seat, getting comfortable. "Is it lunchtime yet?"

The Holy Ghost was a great white seagoing bird of prey, high in the glittering frozen sky. It spread its wings like arms. It descended like a bolt.

THE LOST CHILD

Come away, O human child!
To the waters and the wild
With a faery, hand in hand,
For the world's more full of weeping than you
    can understand.

                          —William Butler Yeats
                          "The Stolen Child"

The boy could hardly remember a time when he had not been in
the car. The car and the driving hadn't really made him forget; they
just made it hard to believe there was anything else in the world
except them. It was night again. He no longer watched the beads
of light in the distance, though they'd fascinated him at first. He
liked the way they swam out of the darkness and traveled along
with them; he liked the way they disappeared all at once, as if
dropped into a pocket. (That was the hills, she said. He couldn't
tell if there were hills or not.) For a while he had imagined the
lights to be stars, whole constellations that revolved and winked
while the car flew through the sky. Because it was sort of like
flying, the air rushing all around and the blackness. He could lean

his head against the glass and listen to the small ticking noises of the car and watch the green half-light from the dashboard. And these things changed so little, the inside of the car was so enclosed and separate, the outside so black and formless, all of what happened had been so very strange that flying would have seemed no stranger to him.

But now he was too tired to pretend any longer about spaceships or magic carpets, and he was cold. He was still wearing his pajamas, which embarrassed him a little. You couldn't really tell they were pajamas until you looked up close. They were blue, dark blue with red cuffs. He had his jacket and sneakers too, so he supposed he looked dressed. But it felt funny. He knew he was sort of dirty too. When he lowered his chin to his chest, there was a smell. The blanket she'd given him itched, but now he wrapped it closer around him.

"You're cold," she said, without looking away from her driving, and the boy said yeah, he guessed he was, a little. She reached over and fiddled with something so a stream of noise and heat blew over his knees. Immediately he felt better, warmer and sleepier. "See," she said. "Don't I know what's good for you. Don't I just."

"Uh-huh," the boy said politely. It was easiest to agree with her. It was easiest when she was in a good mood. Besides, he thought she really did want him to be happy about things. She wanted him to be happy for her.

She was in a good mood now. The boy curled up on the seat so he could watch her without her knowing it. The radio was on, and she sang along under her breath, tapping her fingernails against the wheel. When she sang like this she made a pouting shape out of her mouth, then smiled and tossed her hair. She was pretending to be someone else, a singer on a stage, someone pretty.

The songs sounded the same to the boy, all mush and yodeling and hard, high voices. These songs played in every place they'd stopped for food or gas; sometimes it would be the very same station, coming out of a little radio on a counter or from a car parked next to them. It was a whole separate world he had never known about before, this place where the radio always played and the people talked like the songs. He had heard some of the songs so often by now that he was starting to recognize them, starting to learn the words. Whenever that happened he held his breath and tried to think of nothing at all, tried to squeeze the songs right out of his mind. He did not want to remember the songs or the things that had happened along with the songs. He had a feeling that if they became a part of him, if he gave in to them, then everything else would get even farther away.

Farther and farther. He had not really forgotten anything. He was holding tightly onto something that felt like a big rubber band stretching between there and here, home and all this that was not home. As long as he held on tightly enough it could only stretch so far. Then it would snap back and pull him home with it, and in the meantime he could not think about it or let go of anything.

"Here," she said suddenly, interrupting her own singing. "I bet you're hungry. Have you something to eat." She fished in one of the bags in the front seat and there was the sound of tearing plastic. "Here."

The boy ate, because she got mad when he fussed about food. He wasn't hungry, and the doughnut she'd given him was a kind he didn't like. It had crunched-up peanuts stuck all over it, and the sugar made his teeth hurt. "Thank you," he said, and held the part he couldn't eat below the blanket where she couldn't see. "Where are we?" he asked, to distract her.

"Tennessee."

"What's that?"

"Tennessee?" She said it TEN-uh-see. "That's a state. Like Pennsylvania's a state."

"I live in Pittsburgh," he informed her.

"I wouldn't worry about that if I was you." The way she said it wasn't mean, but he decided to be quiet.

He lay back and watched the lights and shadows bump against each other on the ceiling of the car. He wondered if he could call someone and say I'm in Tennessee, come get me, and if they would know where that was and if they'd be mad at him. He figured they would probably be mad. And after that he must have fallen asleep for a minute, because when he opened his eyes again, he felt hot and startled, the way you did after naps. There was still the peanut taste in his mouth, gone sour. She was talking, telling a story. He must have heard some of it in his sleep because he understood right away it was a story about when she was a little girl:

"We went on this water ride. It was paddleboats shaped like swans, big swans, with a place to sit in the middle like you was riding on their backs. It was so pretty, all this green water and the swans pink and white. You could stick your hand right in the water and feel it slide past. I didn't ever want to get off, when they made me get off I cried. And my mamma said, Fay, you will surely have to learn which things in life is worth crying about."

"Is that your name?" the boy asked with sudden interest. "Fay?"

She turned toward him so sharply that he thought the car swerved, though in fact it hadn't. "Did I tell you my name?" she demanded. "Did I tell you to call me anything?"

"No."

"No what?"

"No, ma'am."

She gave a little snort and turned away from him. Her mouth was thin and her eyebrows looked madder than usual, but nothing else came of it. And when, after a while, he told her he had to stop, she pulled the car over to the side of the road without saying anything.

He got out and stood by the rear wheel of the car, turned away from it so she couldn't see. It was another thing he was beginning to get used to, stopping to go to the bathroom like this, though the first time he'd cried and said he couldn't. "Well, hold it then," she said indifferently. He couldn't do that either and so he went ahead, crying, splashing himself a little, and when he got back in the car she said, "If that isn't pitiful, a big boy like you afraid to pee. You're going to have yourself one tough time in this world, mister."

Now he shivered, looking around him. It took a while to see anything; it was all just different kinds of black. Then gradually the hills took shape against the sky. They were not so very steep, but the road followed such a winding path between them that you stood in a small bowl of darkness, unable to see beyond its rim. The road itself was narrow and it was a long time since they had passed through a town, or even seen another car. Now he could make out the road surface more clearly. It was gray and smooth, and quiet, just like everything else. There was only the rumble and cough of the waiting car. But it was a listening kind of quiet, as if they had interrupted something that now sat back to watch them.

Thick brambles grew right down to the edge of the road. Scrub trees climbed beyond them. There were things in there, he was sure of it. They lived there. Exhaust from the car's tailpipe curled around his ankles, and his own drizzle steamed against the asphalt. It was lonesome, it was all the lonesomest place he'd ever seen. He didn't like to think of anything that lived here in such cold and darkness. It made him feel too much like one of them, something wild and afraid; it made him feel lost beyond all finding. And when he heard a noise racing toward him, and a light was thrown into the sky too quickly for him to hide, he screamed out—even though it was only a car, receding now into pink taillights and droning.

She opened the car door then. *Fay? Was that her name, Fay?* "I haven't got all night," she called out, and he realized that she hadn't heard him. Either he had only imagined himself screaming that loudly or she'd missed it in the intersecting noises of the car.

"Get in the back," she directed. "Go on to sleep now." Her hair, all its puffs and tangles, nodded at him from the front seat.

And he did sleep. At least some of it was sleep. He had a

dream, although it started out not as a dream but exactly as something that had happened that very day. They had stopped somewhere to eat. She sat at the counter drinking her coffee and laughing with the man who worked there. Propped over her elbows, laughing, she looked the way she did when she sang along with the radio. The boy slid off his stool. He was aware of the food he had eaten thickening in his stomach, of her teasing voice just on the edge of his attention—oh you are so funny you know I was born at night but it wasn't last night—and of the smell of raw new wood. The place was all of wood. It had a plank floor and a roof like a barn. There was so much in it: mugs and hats and T-shirts and moccasins and boxes of dry-looking cellophane-wrapped candy and ashtrays and flags and pillows and jars of honey in the shape of bears. It was all too much; it exhausted him just looking. He stood solemnly in the middle of an aisle, trying to decide if there was any of it he ought to want.

Then she was skidding around a corner, stopping fast when she saw him. "*There* you are." A paper napkin floated from her hand like a banner. She swooped down at him and he made himself very small, waiting. But she only hugged him, hard and so close up he could smell the hot, burned-coffee taste from her mouth. "I ought to beat the living Jesus out of you." That puzzled him, the idea of something living in him, but then he saw that whatever it was she wasn't going to do it; she didn't mean it one bit. He understood that she was afraid someone had stolen him the way *she* had stolen him. It made him feel a little sick, thinking of himself like that, as something so easily taken away.

"You pick out something," she said when she released him. "Go on. Pick out anything you want." She gave him a little shove, impatient for him to enjoy himself.

So he picked something, and she shooed him over to the counter and said to the man, "Young ones. It's always they pester you for stuff," in the same voice that didn't mean it. She was bragging, she liked pretending to complain about him.

"Good for business," the man said, and she said that boys would be boys. Their voices grew far away and adult; they were no longer talking about him and he lost interest. The man leaned down toward him and here was where it turned into a dream. You shouldn't make your mother worry so much about you, the man told him. The boy said he was sorry. The man looked at him sadly. He was a small man with hair pushed up into a crest on the top of his head. A radio was playing; maybe it had been playing all along. The boy knew the song. A man and a lady singing something mushy. But now she had gotten right inside the radio, her and the man from the store, or else the radio was all around them. The two of them were singing right at him and smiling tenderly, and when they were done, the man said, See? She even looks like you.

She does *not*, the boy said, and that was when he woke up. The car was stopped and it was morning. She was asleep in the front seat. Stretched out like that and not moving she seemed even skinnier, like all the air that kept her talking, singing, getting angry, had gone out of her.

They were parked in a little sandy space, a loop of road with a picnic table and trash barrels off to one side. The hills had flattened while he slept. Now there were pale fields and darker trees, pines, making borders between the fields. The boy regarded it all incuriously. He was getting tired of seeing so many things he had never seen before.

Cautious now, without making any noise at all, he leaned over the edge of the front seat to study her as she slept. (*Fay?*) She lay on her side, curled toward the seat, and her mouth gaped open a little. Her hair was black and always seemed to have just exploded into whatever shape it took. When you looked at her teeth you saw spaces in between them. He didn't look one bit like her and never would.

He caught sight of his own face in the mirror then. It interested him; he leaned forward to study it more closely. He looked like he always did. Satisfied, he crossed his eyes. He rolled his lower lip out, he pressed a finger against his nose so it was a pig nose. He grinned enormously, showing all his teeth. And when he stopped and looked again, it was still his face.

Here is what had really happened in the store instead of the dream. The man had leaned down to him and asked him how old he was. "Six and a half," the boy said. He'd spoken without thinking; after all, that was exactly how old he was. But now he was afraid he'd gotten it wrong. He couldn't look at her. He looked instead at the tins of fancy nuts below the cash register. "Six and a *half*," the man said. "Now that's pretty old. What's your name, son?"

He couldn't say anything. He was afraid of getting it wrong. He saw the man beaming at him, he heard her shifting her weight, quick quick, he knew that he was supposed to answer. But he couldn't start, and the longer he waited the worse it got. "I," he said, and that was all he could manage before the tears began. They were big heavy tears, and he let them roll all the way down his chin. From habit, he stuck his tongue out to taste them.

"He's shy," she pronounced. He felt her moving up behind him and felt her two hands come down on his shoulders, two exactly equal weights, like twin animals. "Who'd think such a big boy would carry on so. His name is Jason Jerome."

"Jason Jerome?" the man said in a kindly voice. "Is that your name?"

"No," he said, but by this time they both just laughed at him. She led him out to the car and once they were driving again she said, "Jason Jerome. Say it out loud for me. Jason Jerome."

"Jome." He was still crying.

She sighed, a sound of heavy patience. "I am trying not to lose my temper," she said. But when he didn't stop crying she got out her Kleenex and made him blow. "You'll get sick, carrying on like that."

"I don't care," he said in between the messiest parts of the crying. He could tell she was worried. He made himself cry harder, more strategically.

"You want some licorice? Look here."

He shook his head. He felt a little sorry for her that she didn't know more of what to do.

"I'll tell you a story," she said, and that sounded almost interesting, enough so that he took a big, satisfying sniff and waited, looking up at her.

"All right," she said. "This is a story about, ah, a dog."

"What kind of a dog?" he asked suspiciously.

"A magic dog." She was making it up as she went along. "He was magic because he could talk."

"So what did he say?"

"Hush up. I'm getting to that part. His name was Harry. Harry the Dog. Nobody knew he was magic except this one little boy."

"And what was his name?"

"Frank," she said, more promptly now. It was coming faster to her as she went along, or maybe she was just good at making up names. "So Frank and Harry the Dog lived together."

"In a house?"

"Of course in a house. In a house all by themselves."

"Who took care of them?"

"They took care of them*selves*. Say, you want to hear this or not?"

Yes, he said he did, and the story went on from there, about how Frank and Harry the Dog took a vow, a blood vow, to stand by each other thick and thin even if the whole world went against them, and how one day they went out to see what they could see. The boy listened, but the best, most amazing part was already told, as far as he was concerned. How they lived all alone together in their own house, nobody but themselves.

"So how did you like it," she asked sometime later, after she'd led the story through many dangers and adventures and escapes and brought it, triumphantly but a little abruptly, to a happy ending.

"I want a dog," he told her.

"I ast if you liked the story."

"Uh-huh. I want a dog."

"Well I don't have one in my pocket, do I? You'll get a dog soon enough."

"When?"

"When we get where we're going."

"Where's that?"

"You ever get tired of asking questions? It's when I tell you we're there."

He had not been displeased with this answer. He'd sat back, trying to decide just what sort of dog it was he wanted.

Now, this morning, he looked around him and wondered if they were there yet, the place they were going. He hoped not. There was nothing here at all. Even the sky was nothing. It was gray and thin and looked like rain could leak through it at any moment. A pick-up truck with a heap of lumber in the back chugged along on the road behind them. The boy tried to interest himself with it but that only lasted a moment and he fell back against the seat, totally bored.

He wanted her to wake up. Experimentally, he kicked at the front seat, a light, scuffing sort of kick he could pretend was accidental. Nothing. He kicked harder and waited. Then he began a series of small impatient rustlings and exhalations, pausing every so often to see if they worked. More nothing.

He peered over the edge of the seat once more. She hadn't moved, not even the shape of her mouth had changed. He listened to see if she was breathing and she wasn't. She was dead. "Fay?" he whispered. Her eyes looked dead too. They were closed tight and the space below them was blue and sunken. She would never wake up and he was left here all alone with nothing. This time he screamed it, spitting a little. "Fay! *Fay!*"

She was awake all at once, her shaggy head bolting upright,

whirling around as if she didn't see him. She said something you were not supposed to say, very fast, and when she finally focused on him, she said "Chri-i-ist," in a whole long breath, and gave him a wondering look.

He supposed he should be afraid of what she would do, but he was mostly relieved. "I thought you were dead," he said.

She must have still been asleep. She only stared at him. The corners of her mouth were white and cracked-looking. "Well I ain't, am I?" she said finally.

"I didn't want you to be," the boy told her.

She was waking up now, digging the sleep out of her eyes. "I'm too mean to die. An' too young."

"How old do you have to be? To be dead."

"Just old."

"So how old are you?"

"Guess." She yawned enormously.

"Come on."

"No, guess."

"Twenty-one."

"Hoo hoo hoo." She was laughing in the middle of the yawn. "Hooo."

He smiled a little too, out of politeness, though he didn't much like being laughed *at*.

" 'I turned twenty-one in prison, doing life without parole.' That's a song. You know that one?"

When he shook his head, she said, "Never mind. You can take my word for it." It seemed to put her in a good mood, whatever it was. She told him they would go get breakfast and he could have pancakes. He settled back, happy too. He liked pancakes.

Later that day, toward evening, after they had driven and driven nearly beyond boredom, he asked her again where they were going. It had been spattering rain all day, big drops that made freckles in the dust of the windshield. Everything had been the same all day.

"We're almost there."

"We are?" He looked around him anxiously, trying to see. It was growing dark fast now and the rain was coming on harder out of a big pile of brown and purple clouds. "Where?"

"I said almost."

The road was as thin as a finger. The pines closed off one side of it. He watched their trunks blink past him and blur together in the darkness. Then the road turned and dove through the middle of the trees and it was all darkness except for the headlights pulling the car after it. The boy was about to pester her some more when the car swung into a long driveway. At the end of it was a cleared space and a long, block-like white house.

He couldn't see much through the lines of rain, or maybe there was just not much to see. Over the sound of the car came the racket of excited dogs. They circled and pranced and sniffed and yapped and she had to roll down a window and holler at them. "Wait here for me," she told him, shutting the car off and getting out. The dog noise followed her as she trudged up to the house.

He waited there a long time. The rain was melting the windshield, making it bubble and stream. What if she never came out? He would be afraid to go in after her. The dogs had quieted. One of them came and scratched at the window. He saw the pads and nails of its feet spread out on the glass, like a handshake. He scratched back and the dog's nose struggled up to the window. "Hi, dog," he said, but it bounded away.

The driver's door opened. The light made him squint. It was her, Fay, and behind her another woman, and the dogs behind them, all dripping with rain.

"Wake up now," said Fay, though she must have known he was not sleeping. "Wake up and say howdy."

The other woman pushed past Fay and stared in. She was old. She stared hard at him, then said in a slow, tired, meant-to-be-heard voice, "Tell me I am not seeing what I see," and then she sighed and said, "Come on then, boy," and lifted him right out of the car. Fay was saying he was half asleep.

"Half dirt's more like it," said the old woman. "You ever wonder as to what color he is?"

She was strong, she carried him straight through the rain and inside to the bathroom, too fast for him to see anything. She set him down and started water running in the bathtub. Her hair was the color of pencil lead and when she knelt in front of him he could see how wide the part down the middle was, wide and ragged at the edges. Her fingers as they skinned his pajamas off were hard and dry and brisk, like they'd done everything a hundred hundred times before. Not like Fay's, he thought. Fay was standing in the open doorway, looking in.

She said, "Don't fuss him to death, Mamma."

"No child ever died of a bath."

"Or of needing one either," Fay said, but the old woman paid no attention to her, just went on with him, lifting him into the bathwater. After a minute Fay stomped off somewhere, mad or pretending to be mad.

"Hold still," the old woman murmured, looking at him in a distant, abstracted way, as if all she saw of him was the dirt. "Close your eyes so's you don't get soap in 'em." (*Mamma? Her mamma?*) They didn't look alike either. Fay didn't look like anyone.

Later, dressed in somebody's old undershirt that reached to his knees ("I don't suppose he come equipped with clothes, or a toothbrush, nothing silly like that"), he lay bedded down on a couch and listened, thrilled, while they argued about him. They were in the kitchen. Laundry machines lopped and rolled, and their voices came to him only in the quiet parts.

No. He kept hearing that from both of them. Then Fay said, "She's real sick with the cancer, and she had to go in the hospital. And his daddy he beats up on him. So she didn't want him to find him, so I have to take care of him till she's better."

The enormity of the lie made him want to leap up and tell them. *He does not, she is not, my mother is not sick*—but he was too fascinated.

"You couldn't take care of a cat. Never could."

"So you've been telling me all my life."

"And so I've been right. Just look at you."

"That's why you know everything there is about kids. Yours turning out so well and all."

He missed some of it then. The next thing was Fay's voice. "Ask him, if you don't believe me. You go ahead and ask him yourself if he likes me."

"One child looking after another."

"Just ask him."

"What he likes is nothing to do with it. I'm asking who loans out a child like a newspaper."

"People do what they have to do," said Fay.

"Some people got no common sense."

"And some got no natural feelings."

"Oh I know. Everything has ever happened to you works out to be my fault. I guess that's why you bring this boy here, to show me you can make a mess of him too."

He lost their voices again in the sanitary hum of the dryer. It was still raining. He could hear it on the roof, a thin drilling sound. He wanted to sleep but he couldn't, everything was too strange. The house smelled like a closet. And it was full like a closet: boxes, shelves, picture frames, piles of folded clothes in corners, furniture on top of furniture, curtains over curtains. It reminded him of the store, except none of it was new. He was afraid of something falling on him. He wondered how the old woman moved around without things falling. He imagined her hiding things, making paths, so no one but her could move or find anything.

Was it still Tennessee? He would have to ask Fay.

Where's my mother?, he'd asked her, and she'd said, Away downtown. She sent me to get you, she wants you to come with me.

He hung in the door frame, staring out at her. She looked like no one he'd ever seen before. I have a stomachache, he said.

I know. We're going to the doctor. Your mamma wants me to take you to the doctor. Hurry up now.

She was inside then, and the sight of her rooting through the coat closet was so odd it didn't occur to him to be frightened. Her every move sent hangers rattling down to the floor. She had a cowboy hat balanced on one part of her hair, and her legs in blue jeans were long and skinny, like a horse's. She looked more like a horse than anyone he'd ever seen.

Get your shoes, she told him, and she shoved them on him without bothering to tie the laces, and she pulled him by the hand out the front door and down the driveway. He forgot about his stomachache. There wasn't time. When the car began to move, he looked back at the house, nodding at it like it could see him too. It looked like it always did. Wouldn't it always look the same, wasn't it still his house even if he wasn't there? When he thought of it now, he wasn't sure. Maybe it looked different when he wasn't there.

Where's my mother? It was a long time later and they weren't going anywhere that he knew. Where's my mother and who are you? I don't like you, he said, because that was the worst thing he could think of to say. You smell bad.

Her hand in front of his face was as big as a board. It was hard like a board too. It was the only time she'd really hit him, but nobody had ever hit him that way in his life. They'd scared each other. The blood had scared her. It was one thing she couldn't tell him to stop doing. So now she only pretended to hit him. Maybe he could pretend it hadn't happened at all.

Who are you, why did you come to my house for me? He wanted to ask but he didn't. He was afraid of what she'd say. He was afraid they'd told her to come get him. If they wanted him back why hadn't they come after him? What if his mother really was sick, like Fay had said? Maybe he'd done something really bad without knowing. Once he let himself start thinking like this he couldn't stop, and the thing that felt like a big rubber band stretched and stretched until it might break entirely. What if the house changed while he wasn't there? Where was the car going?

He woke up then, he hadn't known he was asleep until he woke up. It was too dark to see anything. There was just his heart, going so hard and loud he might have been inside it, and not the other way around. He waited until it slowed and the darkness sifted enough so he could make out the shape of the room. He was lying all curled up beneath a pile of heavy blankets, on the couch where they'd put him. He guessed he'd only dreamed of being in the car. He was tired of trying to figure out which were the dreams. Either Fay was a dream or home was a dream. There wasn't enough room in him for both.

He kicked at the blankets. There were way too many of them and they smelled stale, like the rain had gotten into them. He was wearing his pajamas once more. Maybe he'd only dreamed wearing something else.

He listened a while longer, and when he didn't hear anyone, he knelt on the couch and looked out the window behind it. A little gray light—sun or moon, he couldn't tell—made the sky soft. He could see the pine woods beyond the bare mud of the yard. The trees were solid black, and though it had stopped raining, water dripped from them. He could hear it in a hundred secret places. Everything else was quiet. He wished he was out there too, in some secret place where no one could find him.

Someone was coming. He got down as quick as he could and pretended to be asleep, though he was never very good at it. He tried to be too artistic about the breathing, even put in snores.

So this time he was just quiet. It was Fay, he could tell from the skittery sound of her feet. She bumped into something that bumped back, and he heard her fussing at it in an unserious sort of way. Then she was sitting on the couch, down at the far end, watching him. Maybe he looked dead like she had looked dead. He had a funny feeling that no one in the house was really asleep, not Fay or himself or the old woman either, lying somewhere listening to everything.

Any minute he expected her to poke at him and say she knew he was faking. But she only sat. It went on so long he thought he was going to have to move or breathe and give himself away, but then the couch creaked under her weight. Her hand, just the heat of it, passed over his face. Not touching. He thought she was afraid of her hand. She was afraid always of it doing the wrong thing. *I'm awake,* he wanted to say. *I'm awake and you don't have to worry about hurting me.* Instead he yawned, like he was just waking up.

"Are we going somewhere?" he asked.

She just nodded. He could see the shape of her hair against the window. It was good they were leaving. He'd decided he didn't like it here, even if there were dogs.

"Hush now," she whispered, though he hadn't been loud at all. "We're going away right now."

She scooped him up in one of the blankets, staggering a little, the blanket edge catching on things as they went. Outside it was still gray and dripping. The dogs sniffed amiably at them and only barked when the car started, for fun's sake. It was enough noise so the old woman must have heard them, but the house didn't try to stop them at all. He looked back for it once. The trees hid everything.

"Fay? Will you teach me how to drive the car sometime?"

It was later that same day, and he had been thinking it might be more fun sometime if he could drive. He could go fast when he wanted. He could play the radio if he wanted. It was good to be back in the car. It was all just like he remembered it.

"Sure I will. I can teach you all the tricks."

"What tricks?"

"Well if I come straight out and tell you, then they're not tricks anymore."

That made sense to him. He figured the best tricks were the ones nobody told you at all.

"Fay?" he asked again, because she didn't seem to mind him asking things. "What do you do when you're not in the car?"

"It's called walking. Ha ha."

"Come on."

"Lots of things."

"Like what?"

"I go out and get money. I get money from people who like to give money away."

"Oh. Fay?" This time she said What, like this had better be the last one for a while. "Do I have to tell people my name?"

She thought about it. "I guess not. This is America, ain't it?"

That made him happy. He bounced up and down on the seat until Fay told him to quit. After a while it would be dark and the lights would be there. The lights were like friends. If you went to sleep and woke up again, you knew there would still be the lights and Fay, always driving.

They were going to Florida; that was another state. It had the ocean and the palm trees. Fay was telling him this as part of a story. The story was about the two of them, him and Fay, and how they went to Florida and lived on a boat. Boats were better than houses anytime. The boat was called the Swan because it looked like a swan. Fay bought him a cowboy hat like hers. She taught him how to sail the boat. Sometimes they fished and had fish for dinner. When they got tired of one place, they picked up and sailed to another. When they got tired of their names, they made new ones. Nobody bothered them. Nobody needed the names except them.

THE RICH MAN'S HOUSE

It was a rich man's house, designed for expensive recreation and daily luxury, the home of a family with strenuous hobbies and social tastes. But the rich man's wife had left him two years ago, and his children were grown and never visited. The pasture where his daughters had kept their horses was consigned to weeds. No one lobbed balls on the tennis court or showed off on the three-meter diving board. The rich man himself came home late at night and left again at sunrise for his office in the city. I'd see his big smooth car gliding up the driveway, and the wrought-iron gate opening by remote control. Two huge electrified lanterns were set in the stone archways of the entrance. There were nights he didn't come home at all and the lanterns stayed lit, pale filaments burning thinly in the daylight.

Beyond the entrance was a brick courtyard and a fountain (dry), and the triple doors of the enormous garage. Artful landscaping kept the eye from penetrating farther, but there was a suggestion of balconies, verandas, crystal chandeliers suspended in magnificent space. The house was visited regularly by a Mexican maid, by ranks of gardeners, and by workmen engaged to drain and fill and regrout the swimming pool, or pour new cement, or other projects which split the air with saws and drills. Each Tuesday morning a truck from a private water company drove up, carrying plastic water jugs like blue jewels. Each Thursday evening his pristine garbage cans were set out at the curb, and each Friday morning they were whisked back inside. Leaf blowers whined, sprinklers pumped nets of mist onto newly laid sod, panel trucks arrived to disgorge materials, all in the owner's absence. The house made me think of Egyptian pharaohs and the armies that labored building the pyramids.

The rich man's name was Kenneth Dacey. I knew him because I lived next door, the way next door was figured in our rural part of the county. My husband and I had rented a cottage on the parcel of land next to his. My husband had gone away, but I was staying on, at least for now. Kenneth Dacey introduced himself when we moved in, and we waved to each other in passing, and once or twice we'd traded opinions on the weather or marauding deer. But I'd never been inside his house, or he in mine, until the morning he appeared on my front porch, asking if I'd feed his cat.

I peeked at him through the kitchen window before I answered his knock. He was wearing his weekend clothes, a plaid western shirt, sheepskin vest, jeans, boots, a belt with an oversized silver buckle. He was a big bald pink-skinned man, nearly sixty, I guess, with watery blue eyes and a little fair mustache. Those clothes always managed to look like a costume on him. "A banker playing sheriff," my husband used to say.

I opened the door, arranging my face into an expression of surprise and pleasure. I'm one of those people who fall back on niceness when I don't know what else to do. "Good morning," I said to Dacey. I never felt comfortable first-naming him, and I usually avoided calling him anything at all, like an in-law or a repairman.

He said good morning, and then we said it would be a fine fall day once the fog burned off. We turned around to admire the morning, since it was something we both agreed on. The hills of blond grass rose on each side of the valley floor. Oaks and eucalyptus grew on the lower slopes. A ledge of granite and four tall pines crowned the highest hill. The air was milky, and these pines seemed to advance and retreat as the mists shifted. Way overhead was a patch of blue sky, a promise.

When we'd finished with the view we were obliged to turn back to each other again. In a moment more I would have to invite Dacey inside. My husband had been gone for three months, and my house no longer looked as if a man lived there. That's how it seemed to me. It was like my tongue sliding over a row of teeth and coming to rest in an empty space.

But he got down to business then. *Business;* that was what brought him here. He was going away for the weekend, and would I mind feeding his cat? I said I'd be happy to. It seemed like the sort of thing a neighbor ought to do, something social and human, conditions I should aspire to. He said if I had a minute he'd take me up to the house and show me what had to be done.

It was our longest conversation ever, although I'd lived there for a year and a half. We were both people who kept to ourselves, maybe for the same reasons these days, a combination of loneliness and pride. But then I'm always too ready to ascribe my own motives to people and to make assumptions. That's what my husband told me, during that period of our marriage when it was important to him to inventory my flaws. Kenneth Dacey angled his body away from you when he spoke, which could have been from rudeness or shyness or both. His loose pink face was the face of a baby surprised to find itself grown old. An unthinking face that gave no indication of an inner life. It was hard to imagine him deliberately acquiring a family, or maybe he had simply allowed that to happen to him over time.

I grabbed my jacket from the hook and walked with him up the driveway. There was a pickup truck parked just outside the gate, and the usual racket of hammers and shouted instructions. It was curious that with all his gangs of tradesmen and hirelings, he couldn't find one of them to feed a cat. It's possible he meant to make me a kind of employee also, and was the kind of man who was most comfortable with human relationships when they could be mediated with money or obligation. But I didn't think any of this until later.

We reached the wrought-iron gate, and Dacey gave me a key that unlocked a side entrance, a foot passage across the bridge spanning the creekbed. It was the same creek that cut through the back wilderness of my lot, though at the end of this dry season it was only a heap of tumbled gravel and a few patches of soft mud. Once I was inside the gate, I could see that the garden was another kind of construction zone, with heaps of wood chips and black plastic sheeting everywhere. A statue of St. Francis blessed three bare rosebushes.

"All this," said Dacey, waving his hand to indicate the litter of wheelbarrows and rakes and bags of topsoil, "this was supposed to be finished by now." He shook his head, speculating darkly on the wrongs of contractors. I made the appropriate sympathetic noises. But I wondered what was so complicated about the project, when Dacey could, if he chose, arrange for giant palm trees to appear in his yard overnight.

He showed me how to operate the double locks on the front doors, and the code that disarmed the burglar alarm. I was imagining myself ringed by floodlights and sheriff's deputies, with no better alibi than a can of cat food. "All the glass is wired too," said Dacey. "Break a window, they'll get somebody out here in four minutes, guaranteed."

"Really." My voice sounded faint and false. It was oppressive, the effort it took to admire things. We were standing in the entryway, which was two stories high. Suspended overhead was the crystal wedding-cake chandelier you only imagined from the road. It was an odd choice to go with the paneled walls and clay-colored floors, like an argument nobody had won. There was a curving staircase leading up. Dacey climbed it first, and I tried not to watch the elephant-like rolling of his denim hindquarters.

"Living room," he said at the top. There was a large, stiffly decorated area, and a dining room opposite. I explored both of them later, when I had a chance to spy them out. They were fusty, old-fashioned rooms with brocaded sofas and ponderous lamps. Swags of stiff draperies hung at the windows. There was a nearly concert-sized piano, and a formal array of family photographs, sailing prints, ornamental brasses. The dining room had a table that could have been used for board meetings, and a book of racing prints propped up on a stand, opened to a page showing *Man o' War*.

But Dacey walked straight past all this, as I guess he was accustomed to doing, back to the kitchen and den. This was one large room, with glass doors leading out to a deck. There was a recliner, television, an aquarium full of fish, a telephone desk with a pile of receipts and stray papers, like you'd find in anybody's house. He opened a cupboard to show me where the cat food was. Everything on the shelves was tidy and monastic, the kitchen of someone who never cooked: cereal, packets of instant soup, crackers, muffin mix, a box of neglected raisins, a tin of anchovies. I was so used to admiring things by now, I had to stop myself from exclaiming over his groceries.

"Now you probably won't even see Jake," he said. Jake was the cat. "He stays outside. I could leave all his food out before I left, but the raccoons would get it."

I repeated, idiotically, that I was happy to help him. I asked where he was going for the weekend.

Dacey blinked at me, as if I'd committed some trespass, and he'd found a reason to dislike me. But he said, "I've got a cabin up in the foothills. Going to do some fishing. Your husband like to fish?"

"No," I said.

Dacey raised his eyebrows, as if he couldn't imagine such a thing. Our conversation stalled, then went belly-up. We stared at each other for a moment more. I couldn't remember meeting anyone who damped down human speech as Dacey did. He showed me downstairs again, and we repeated our politenesses, and then I was outside, breathing in the cool morning air.

I hadn't lied, technically, about my husband, but I'd missed some chance to tell the truth. I wasn't sure if that had more to do with Dacey or myself, with his coldness—I put that name to it— or my own sulking. He didn't know or hadn't noticed that my husband no longer lived here, and I hadn't bothered to inform him. Maybe I didn't like the idea that the two of us might have anything in common. When I got back to my house, it had a welcoming look to it. Your own unhappiness is always preferable to someone else's, just as you sleep better in your own bed, even alone.

A little while later I saw Dacey's truck, a big Silverado that he used on weekends, rumble down the driveway. And later still, after the workmen had all gone home, and the sun had dropped behind that ridge crest, I took the ring of keys he'd given me and headed toward the iron gate. I thought how strange it was that he'd entrusted his house to me, whom he hardly knew. Maybe he didn't have anyone else, or maybe I was so insignificant as to be harmless.

That first visit I didn't stay long or poke around much. I left out food for the invisible cat, and strolled through the rooms I'd already seen, not touching anything. The fading sunset light and the huge emptiness of the place oppressed me. It was like wandering alone through a monument or a tomb. A corridor upstairs led to what I guessed was a wing of private rooms, and there were other doors that wouldn't give when I put a cautious hand to them.

The ceilings in the hallways had panels of some thin reflecting glass, and it wasn't hard for me to imagine that Dacey, with his fondness for security, might have mounted cameras up there.

Still, he couldn't blame me for looking at the pictures. You were meant to do that. There was no photograph of his wife, but there was one of someone's elderly parents, looking timid and glassy-eyed. Dacey himself, posed in one of those elaborately casual shots where the photographer has attempted to do something expressive with the hands. And a large portrait, big as an oil painting, of Dacey's children: two teenaged girls—twins, it seemed—with glossy chestnut bobs, and two younger boys, grinning and freckled. I looked for family resemblances among them but there wasn't much, only the expression of glazed constraint common to overdressed children. From the hairstyles, I guessed the portrait was at least fifteen years old. They'd grown up in this house but they'd left it behind them. I looked at the portrait again, this time for clues, hints of their future flight. Were they happy here? I wasn't acquainted with any rich people. I didn't know if money made them unhappy in interesting ways, as it did on television. The faces in the photograph told me nothing. But their spirits were all around me, those shy childhoods, fluttering like trapped moths.

I was beginning to spook myself. I turned on the entrance lamps as Dacey had instructed me, locked and double-checked the doors, and walked up the driveway in the clear evening light. There was a little gold half-moon, like an earring, already high in the sky. The air was calm and smelled of wood smoke. I wished that my husband was waiting for me inside, that we could open a bottle of wine and I could tell him about Dacey's house, how it made me feel, how any place so fortified and empty was somehow wrong. I imagined scenes like that more and more, and remembered less and less of the things that had really happened between us. It was a different phase of loneliness, the one that came after the sharpest edges had worn off.

The next morning, Saturday, I was up early. I didn't really have to feed the cat—once every twenty-four hours was enough—but I wanted to turn the lights off, make sure nothing had burned down or gone amiss. I felt some anxious responsibility for the place. And I wasn't above nosing around more, although I wouldn't do anything crude like drink Dacey's liquor or make long-distance calls from his phone.

The morning light turned the rooms ordinary and unremarkable. The cat, or something, had cleaned out the food and I filled the dish again and changed the water bowl. I stood on the deck and looked out. I saw, a little ways up the valley, the line of the creek and the higher ground where deer and wild turkeys ranged. When I lowered my eyes I saw the ragged horse pasture and some pipe corral stalls. A boat trailer and a long-dry skiff had come to rest there, abandoned projects on abandoned land.

Then, closer in, there was the turquoise oblong of the swimming pool, and the chalk-lined tennis court, surrounded by strips of hyper-green sod. An L-shaped structure on one side of the pool deck, and a larger building with skylights in its roof. Everything below me was in deep blue shadow, with the sunlight just now touching the wood at my feet. Something moved in the shadow. A man looked up at me. "Morning," he said.

He was grinning. I don't know what my face was doing. I said, "I'm here to feed the cat." I don't know why I felt I had to explain myself. I could have just as easily demanded to know what he was doing there.

He came to stand at the border of the shadow, so he had to shade his eyes to look up at me. "Thought maybe you was his girlfriend."

"I live next door," I said, as if that ruled out my being anyone's girlfriend. He nodded, then seemed to lose interest in me. He walked across the deck, whistling, and unlocked the door to the pool house. I heard him rummaging inside, and noises of metal shifting against metal.

So he was a workman of some sort, and I didn't have to worry about him. But I was unsettled, as if I'd been caught actually rummaging the house, instead of just contemplating doing so. I locked the glass doors and went downstairs.

While I was securing the front door I heard him behind me, dragging something heavy. I turned around and he said, "Work's never done around here."

I said I could believe it. There was a hunk of metal housing on the deck, some part of a filtration system, I guessed. We both regarded it for a moment, as if it would explain us to each other.

"Does anybody ever swim in that pool?" I asked. I don't know why I was talking to him. It had something to do with the early-morning quiet, and the two of us there alone, and the blue unmoving water. Everything we said sounded like a secret.

"I do. When nobody else's here." He grinned at me again. He had a thin, mobile face with curious light, soft eyes, and a lot of feathery gray hair. There was nothing handsome about him but I kept sneaking glances at him. Scruffy, with that light-bodied, underfed look you see in some workingmen, as if they wear themselves down to smooth-running levers and pulleys. Blue jeans and a T-shirt whose fabrics had been sweated through and washed hot and fried in the dryer. He was maybe thirty, too young for the hair. These days I watched men the way you might an unknown species of bird, observing markings and calls, trying to determine their range and habits. Since my husband left, I didn't trust anything I thought I knew about them.

He said, "You ever see his playroom?"

"His what?"

"This here." He walked across the deck to the peak-roofed bungalow, the one with the skylights. It was made of blond wood and glass, and sat in its own sunken deck. He turned and waited for me at the door, like a host.

Inside there was a pool table, covered with a piece of crushed velvet, gold-colored and tasseled at the ends. The table itself was claw-footed, oversized, an antique of some sort. I said, "Does anybody ever use this?"

"When nobody else is here . . . ," he began.

I shook my head, pretending to disapprove of him. There was a Ping-Pong table, and a model-train track that folded down from the wall, and a croquet set, and a poker table with stacks of chips. There was a wet bar in one corner. "I don't believe this," I said. It was too much. Nobody would ever be able to have this much organized fun. The room smelled of sawdust and plaster. Black wires dangled from the ceiling, and in one corner was a push broom and a small pile of construction trash.

"This is all new," I said, marveling. The sun was pouring in through the skylights and the room was turning hot.

"Remodeled."

"Why does he need all this? Why would anyone?"

"It gives him something to do, I guess." He patted down his pockets for cigarettes. "Gives me something to do. I'm Jesse."

I introduced myself and we shook hands. He said he thought he'd seen me from time to time, unloading groceries or at the mailbox. He hadn't really thought I was Dacey's girlfriend. That was just kidding. He worked for Dacey off and on, doing repairs and construction.

"I don't know him very well," I said. "Mr. Dacey." The sun was drilling straight into my scalp. It made me feel sleepy, like everything in me had slowed way down.

The man, Jesse, was squinting at his cigarette, angling it toward the small flame. He turned his head away to blow out a stream of smoke. Sometimes the simplest things men did seemed like magic tricks to me.

He turned back again. His eyes were gray. It had taken me that long to look at him straight on. "Isn't he a work of art, that guy."

I said I wouldn't know about that.

"He's got some house."

I said, "I wouldn't live here if you paid me."

"You seen it all?" I shook my head. "Well, come on."

Jesse had his own set of keys. I followed him inside without thinking twice about it.

Downstairs there were two guest bedrooms, neat and unused, and a locked door that Jesse said was an office, "Where he wheels and deals and steals." Beyond that was an exercise room, complete with weights and a stationary bicycle and those elaborate machines that make you think of scientifically engineered torture chambers. I didn't ask Jesse if Dacey ever came down here to work up a dutiful sweat. (The image of him, pink and sagging, pedaling away in furious stasis, was something I didn't care to dwell on.) By now I'd caught on that for Dacey buying was the equivalent of, or the substitute for, doing. If Dacey had been more personable, I might have felt sorry for him. I wouldn't have wanted anyone in my house, doing this to me.

There was an overclean workroom with a tool bench off the garage, and Dacey's big navy blue Lincoln, and a little green MG I'd never seen him drive. Jesse held a hand over the curve of a headlight, the way another man might cup a woman's breast. "Now this is the only thing he's got that I covet." *Covet*, a Bible word. It sounded strange in anybody's mouth, and in all that echoing cement.

We climbed up to the second floor. He steered me toward the wing I hadn't seen, and pointed to the deck outside. "The royal hot tub."

It was a big six-sided affair, with a tight-fitting lid like a stew pot. Jesse said, "You should come up here sometime, check it out."

I did something—shook my head, I don't know—and moved away from him. I didn't like him saying that. I was thinking I didn't know him at all.

"Hey," he said. "It's a joke."

I muttered something like all right, never mind. It was the wrong place for maidenly sensitivities, or maybe I'd acquired them too late. I couldn't believe I was doing any of this.

Dacey's bedroom was a big unadorned chamber—like a hotel room—with a separate dressing room littered with magazines and stray coins and cardboard packs of batteries, with unpaired shoes, an elaborate silver-topped tankard of the kind no one ever uses for drinking, a miniature TV, binoculars in a pebbled leather case, more. His bathroom was all onyx and dark green, like an underwater chamber, with a sunken tub. The towels were oversized, the same funereal algae color. Nothing was unclean, but the suite had a stale, burrow-like quality to it, the one place where someone really lived.

His sons' rooms were across the hall, connected by a more utilitarian bathroom done in earth tones. There was no furniture here, only open cardboard boxes disgorging lamp bases, an electric space heater, ladies' handbags, throw pillows, curtain rods, shoe trees, all manner of pawed-over and unloved items. Jesse said, "His missus packed up all this when she left. Never came back for it."

"What was she like? Is she like, I mean."

"Nice lady. Nervous sort. She always looked like her belt was too tight, maybe."

I laughed at that. We were standing in front of a mirrored closet door and our reflections faced us. I looked into the mirror while I was still laughing, and I hardly knew myself, much less the man standing next to me. I closed my mouth and my familiar image returned: skittish, with my hair too ragged, legs too lumpy, all the things I wanted to reach out and brush away. The man beside the woman said, "Pretty." I saw his mouth move.

"Don't talk to me like that," I said, looking at him now, not the mirror.

"Sorry." He turned his palms upward and raised his eyebrows to indicate harmlessness. I was annoyed because I thought he was making fun of me. I didn't think I was pretty.

"I saved the best for last," he said, opening the door at the end of the hallway.

Twin canopy beds, decked in white ruffles, stood at opposite ends of the big L-shaped room. Each was freighted with stuffed animals. There were owlish-looking teddy bears, plush rabbits, happy tigers. Two white and gold desk sets shared a wall. One corner, the L end, was set up as a parlor, with a loveseat and a television.

Jesse said, "Which do you think he liked better, those girls, or his boys?"

On the walls were formal displays of medals (horsemanship, swimming), school pennants, heart-shaped picture frames, a program from a production of *Brigadoon*. All of it prim and fixed, like a museum of girlhood. "Unreal," I said. I walked to the center of the room. A single thread of spiderweb broke across my face.

Jesse said, "I mean, how far back would you want to go, if you was them?"

Each end of the room opened into a dressing room, with its own sink and vanity table, ruffled skirts and pretty little lamps. The rooms smelled like old powder.

"All his kids were adopted," Jesse told me. "If you're rich enough, I guess you can buy anything."

I said I'd seen enough. The house was stale and sad, arrogant and wrong-headed, even ugly. We trooped downstairs and I waited at the front door while Jesse set the burglar alarm.

"Can you imagine doing this," he said. "Every time you go in or out, you have to get permission from yourself."

"There's nothing here I'd want to steal," I said.

"Sure."

"I mean it." It irritated me that he might not believe me, but it wasn't the kind of thing you could prove.

"Well, back to work. Nice meeting you." I said it was nice to meet him too. He nodded and turned abruptly away. A minute later I heard him banging away at the hunk of metal again. I didn't know what to make of him. Odd duck, my husband would have called him. It was one of the things he said that I still heard from time to time.

I fed the cat again the next morning without seeing anyone. Dacey would be home that night and I wouldn't have to worry anymore about his grandiose bathrooms, his ignorance, his lonesome money.

My husband and I loved the valley. We'd moved there from our perfectly unremarkable suburbia, from traffic and hyperkinetic televisions and shopping malls and streets with fragrant, ultimately disappointing names: El Paseo Drive, Vista Del Sol. We moved because we had ideas about tranquility and solitude, nature and space, about a worthwhile life lived genuinely. It would be easy to make fun of those ideas now, or at least to treat them ironically, as untried romanticism, but I can't. I still believe they are good ideas; we just weren't good people to carry them out. But we didn't know that at first. We felt brave and lucky. The landscape's moods and weathers thrilled us. There were sharp-edged winter nights when the air was clear and the stars were as big as fists. One cold morning we stepped out on the front porch and saw an extraordinary thing: a bare tree with six turkey vultures perched in its branches, their wings spread out to warm in the sun, like black laundry. We loved the green rains and the yellow summer days when every dry wind could be the sound of fire.

I say *we* but I can't assume that anymore. I can't say for certain how he felt about anything. Maybe he never really loved those things, or maybe he changed his mind, like he did about me. He'd been mistaken in his first enthusiasms. Or he'd been deceived by me and by the life we'd chosen here. We'd misrepresented ourselves. We'd made false pretenses, raised his expectations and then failed to meet them. I think it scared him when he found himself feeling ordinary, bored or fretful or adrift. The new life was meant to change all that. And I was supposed to have been someone more interesting, but that seam in me played out quickly. I'd disguised my limitations and my unglamorous plodding nature behind intricate shimmering veils. I didn't recognize that version of myself, both cunning and dull. All I'd ever wanted was for someone to know me so thoroughly that I could love without apologies. Now it seemed that neither of us had known the other, or ourselves.

Monday morning the lanterns in the stone arches were on, as

I'd left them, but I imagined Dacey had come home late and didn't think to turn them off. Before I left for work—I was still working in town, at my office job—I walked up the driveway, hoping to surrender the key. The upstairs windows were open and throw rugs were draped over the balcony railings. The doorbell chimed over the racket of a vacuum cleaner. The Mexican maid came to the door and shook her head when I asked for Dacey. I couldn't tell if she was denying knowledge or language or both. She kept shaking it when I tried to find out if he'd been there at all. When I stopped asking questions she shut the door again.

The maid's car was gone when I came home late that afternoon. The electric lights were beginning to reassert themselves when I thought about the cat, and whether he'd been fed. I set off up the driveway to Dacey's. It was becoming easier all the time to go there, like any habit. The house smelled of polish and atomized cleansers. I climbed the staircase, wondering what it was designed for, whether the twins had posed there with prom dates, wearing white net dresses and corsages.

In the kitchen I scooped up cat food, then walked out to the deck. I wasn't even looking for the cat—I'd pretty much given up on ever seeing him—when he came pattering around the corner of the deck, uttering little cries of reproach. He was a tiger cat, gray and rangy, and he let me stroke his back while he ate. "Jake," I said. I felt his ribs, and the greedy mechanics of his eating.

The phone rang. It was just inside the door, and the sound of it made me jump. After two rings an answering machine clicked, and Dacey's taped voice instructed callers to leave a message.

There was a silence, full of hesitation and listening. Then whoever it was hung up without speaking. Under my hand the cat thrummed and purred. I was glad he was there. The house was too full of ghosts, and each day I woke up to the ghost of my marriage, and there were times when it seemed I had only a remembered life. The cat at least was solid and real, even though after he finished eating he bolted away, escaping me.

Dacey didn't come home that night either. When I returned

from work the next day the man Jesse appeared at my front door. That in itself seemed remarkable, as if I'd come to believe I might have invented him or conjured him up. But here he was, planted on the front porch, running a hand through his hair as he spoke. Dacey was missing, he said, or at least overdue. Dacey's office had called him, Jesse, to see what he knew.

"He was going fishing at his cabin," I said. "That's what he told me."

"Well he never got there. Least, nobody's seen him."

We watched each other thinking. The sun was tangled in the low trees across the road and the light from it was as level as a ruler. I said, "Two days. That's not a long time."

"It is for a money man not to be calling his office."

"Oh," I said. I was retrieving and dusting off the words used in such situations: misappropriation, embezzlement. "Do they think . . ."

"They don't know what to think. They didn't say anything to me. I could just tell."

I was turning over this new picture in my mind, Dacey the conniver, fiddling accounts, doing whatever it is you do to move a line of zeroes from one piece of paper to another, turning all that unreal money into something you could pocket and run off with. There was the way he'd looked at me when I'd asked him where he was going. It made sense, until I imagined him lying dead in some creek or canyon, and that made an equal amount of sense.

I said, "I guess I'll keep feeding that cat."

"I guess."

Jesse was looking behind me, through the half-open front door. "This is a nice place," he said.

"Thanks." I was trying to fill as much of the doorway as I could. I shaded my eyes with my hand. Everything was rimmed with red sunset light.

"Where you think he went?"

I don't know why I thought he meant my husband. I said, "I don't know. I'm sure that's the whole point, for me not to know."

Then he was confused, and I had to explain, and then I was confused and embarrassed in turn. We sidled around on the porch a bit. "Sorry," Jesse said.

"You didn't do anything."

"I mean, sorry for you."

I had to squint to see him. His hair was all sunset and his eyes were chips of light. He said, "What's he like, your husband? Tell me about him."

"I don't know him anymore. I don't know him any better than I do you."

When he moved closer I could smell the boiled cotton of his shirt, and the day's heat soaked into it, and his skin's salt. I stepped forward, closing the door behind me. "Not in here," I said.

Dacey didn't return the next day or the next. After a week had gone by the local papers carried stories about the search for him, identifying Dacey as a "prominent investor and businessman," indicating, in glum neutral journalese, that the investment firm's records were being examined. The Silverado was found in a highway rest area on I-5, a hundred and fifty miles north of Los Angeles. Just the truck, no helpful matchbooks or bloodstains or negotiable securities. Dacey himself had been magicked completely away.

After the first week the Mexican maid stopped coming, as well as the rest of the workers. The garden is left in unfinished half-splendor, although I water the rosebushes, and Jesse keeps the sod green. I bought a new bag of cat food when the old one ran out. We coaxed the cat inside and he prowls and sniffs the rooms and makes himself at home on the upholstery. I do my laundry in Dacey's big old-fashioned machines, even using his soap powder and bleach. For a time the phone still rang, then one day for some reason I picked it up, and the dial tone was gone. Jesse has other jobs now, but he comes by at the end of his day, and often spends the night. I assume he has a different life outside these gates, one he doesn't talk about, one I don't need to know. We float in the pool, me wearing the matronly bathing suit he teases me about. It's October now, but still blazing warm at times, with a sky of blue enamel. I still go to my job, and do errands, and fill up my day with ordinary things. It seems that part of my life will go on without changing while we float in the blue water under the perfect sky.

We talk about Dacey, Jesse and I, and what might happen to the property. Nothing, Jesse says. Nothing until Dacey turns up either dead or in Brazil, and even then nothing for a long time. Everything Dacey owns will be in legal paralysis. The house will be like Sleeping Beauty's castle, hidden behind a briar hedge of suits and injunctions. We will intercept the water and power bills somehow, keep things up and running. We can probably stay here for a long time, as long as we wish. Each night we sleep in a different bed; anything we wish for, towels or ice or firewood, the house provides.

Dacey is either living his new life on some palm-edged shore, or else the silver buckle of his belt tarnishes under a layer of leaf mold and dirt. Just as my husband is either a man who loved me or one who never loved me, just as I am either an ordinary woman or one who inhabits a secret. Stepping out of character, people call it, but that's not really the case. It's more about abandoning the house of our unhappiness, about the spirit moving on. Sometimes the house is really a house, and sometimes it's a body—our own or someone else's—that we leave behind. I'm convinced that Dacey wanted to leave, unbuild the life he had here, whether he knew it or planned it out, and that in the same fashion he chose me to inherit it.

Just yesterday morning I saw three wild peacocks, escapees from someone's misguided notion of an estate, dragging their tails across the old horse pasture. I clucked to them, wondering what you did to make them raise their fans, but they scurried uphill out of sight. When I went to bed that night, there was a long soft feather on my pillow, a single green-gold-blue eye. Jesse found it for me, a free treasure picked right up off the ground, then given away.

POOR HELEN

She wore hats. That was one thing wrong with her. Not the kind trimmed with roosting birds or rubber grapes, nothing grotesque. What was wrong with her involved finer distinctions. The hats were expensive, good quality linen or felt or straw. But nobody wears hats like that except in magazines. Nobody wears a pink witch's hat to sit in an empty bar at two in the afternoon. That was one place you'd see her. She'd be drinking a drink the same color as the hat. And her fingernails or her shoes or maybe the beads around her neck, they would be the same (or a coordinating) shade of pink (or melon or red or bronze), and the effect of all these careful ensembles was that she always looked like she was trying to get picked up.

Her name was Helen Harper. She was in her forties, a little
fair, freckled woman, aging badly. She had the face of a middle-
aged girl, a pretty doll's face embedded in flesh. Unfair, how your
genes can ambush you like that. A seed waiting to sprout into
unwanted growth. There was a good deal that had been unfair in
her life. Poor Helen, people said, meaning she embarrassed them.
Meaning they *understood,* and God knows she deserved their sympathy, but in the same circumstances they rather hoped they would
behave better.

If such a woman chooses to wear white trousers that inflate
her rump like a balloon, or high heels that make her clump and
totter, if she drinks alone, if she drinks too much and looks like
she's trying to get picked up and maybe she does get picked up
from time to time, well, why should anyone care? You could almost admire her. If the world preferred you to sit home being gen-
teel and unobtrusive and lonely, you told the world to bugger off,
and good for you. But in fact women who knew her thought of
Helen most often when they faced their own mirrors. They would
contemplate adding the extra scarf or belt, the extra touch that
jingled or jangled or dangled. And they would say to themselves,
No, Helen, and put it away.

You saw her strolling along the sidewalks, aimless and solitary,
the hats and the airy bright clothes making her resemble a small
ship under sail. You saw her in bars, waving to someone. She knew
most everyone, it seemed. A friend would invite her to sit down.
Helen would shake her head, beaming at them all. "Oh no, my
dear, I need to get a table. I'm with a man, can't you tell?" She
smiled and her little hands fluttered. Everyone had been invited
to listen and watch. Oh well, Helen's friend would say, in that
case . . .

"Wish me luck," said Helen, and her friend did so. They might
have winked. The friend laughed. Ah Helen, there's no stopping
you, is there? "Not tonight there isn't, darling, well, toodle-loo."

And when the man showed up, brandishing their drinks before

him, you looked to see just what was the cause of all this public girlishness. The men were always wrong. Like the hats. Too young or too old or too drunk. This one was dressed entirely in denim and his hair was long and careless. He was younger than Helen, but like her he gave the impression of being too old for what he was wearing. He looked unemployed. A funny thing to think, but he did. The two of them sat down and the man talked and talked. You couldn't hear everything, but you could tell he was serious, deadly serious about it. He was talking about his Theory of Life, or Art, or Capitalism. Something immensely serious and boring that he always talked about and no one ever listened to. Helen was listening to him. She was leaning across the table looking earnest, in the way such conversations oblige one to demonstrate earnestness. Earnest with a little edge of something else, impatience or panic, so much talk, he was so serious and boring, was her luck running out?

Another night, a different bar, this time with a band and dancing. It was crowded on the dance floor; it was one of those places where you dance around stray tables and cement poles. Every so often the crowd pitched and yawed, and you'd find yourself peering at someone's teeth or hairdo or flailing arms, too large and close up, like sitting in the first row at the movies. Music fragmented too, a mix of yodel and chirp and boom. Helen's face thrust itself up from the crowd. She was leaning back on the arm of her partner, her eyes rolled upward in ecstasy. She looked breathless, sweaty. You felt as if you'd stumbled into someone's lovemaking. Just for an instant, then the crowd pushed her away again. Poor Helen, you thought. Even when she seemed to be enjoying herself. Poor Helen.

She had a husband and children at one time. You don't exactly lose children in the same way you lose a husband, but for all practical purposes she didn't have them anymore either. The husband went first. It was religion that did it, not the usual things. Or maybe it wasn't religion exactly; maybe it was another kind of genetic ambush, another seed sprouting up wrong. Anyway, Danny Harper had been raised Presbyterian or Methodist, something mainline like that, and none of it had ever caused him any trouble, none of it crossed his mind more than twice a year. Then at the age of forty, for reasons he was to spend the rest of his life exploring, he began having religious hallucinations. The devil appeared behind him in the bathroom mirror as he shaved, a companionable presence pointing out spots he missed. Jesus floated in the evening sky above the power lines. He was large and flat, like an advertising banner. Danny stopped sleeping. He wept in public. He took to sitting up all night in a Catholic church where that sort of thing was allowed.

One night he came home instead. Helen had started sleeping on the couch downstairs in front of the TV. It was less lonesome. The whole house stank of unhappiness and dread these days, as if the rooms were sponges soaking up dirty water. The children had already begun the vanishing process they would perfect in later years. They stayed overnight with friends, they went on excursions with the Scouts and athletic teams. Helen was alone. She had been dreaming of sleep. She got so little sleep these days that she was always greedy for more. She dreamed the weight of her body and the weight of the air surrounding it. She dreamed the little wet snoring noises she made into the pillow. Danny woke her when he turned the TV off.

"Wake up," Danny told her, not unkindly. He was excited about something. The skin beneath his eyes had pouched alarmingly in the last few weeks, and the eyes themselves were cracked and overbright. Helen sat up and let out a big, sticky yawn. He was busy turning on all the lights in the downstairs rooms. "What," she said, trailing after him. "What's so important, Danny, that I have to get up?" She wasn't a bit afraid of him in his madness. He wasn't anything to be afraid of. These days she found herself talking to him as she would a child, with a heavy patience that approached boredom.

He was occupied with the dimmer switch in the dining room, twiddling it to get the right intensity. It was a very nice house they lived in, well-equipped with things like dimmer switches. "One minute," he murmured, making the little electric flames in the chandelier leap and shrink. "Where are the kids?"

"Asleep," Helen said. It was the easiest answer, and it was probably true.

"It's getting late," he said somberly, standing now in the center of the blazing bright room.

"I guess so." She thought it could have been any hour of the night or morning, she couldn't tell.

"I mean *late*. We have to say the rosary. Everybody does, or the world's going to end."

No shit. That's what she felt like saying. There was really no point in getting angry. No point at all. She'd been through all that with him by this time and most other things besides. "And who told you that, Danny?"

Helen was prepared to hear anything from him, but he answered simply that the priest at St. Joseph's told him. They had been talking and he, Danny, was thinking of converting. The secret of the rosary was revealed in 1917 by Our Lady herself.

"That's stupid," Helen said dangerously. "That's stuff they scare little kids with." So he was picking up dogma now, stray bits of creed, where before it had been only his personal visitations. Helen felt saddened. How banal madness was, finally. She never would have believed it, it was almost the biggest surprise of the whole misery, that the delusions of an intelligent man were not themselves intelligent. What had she done to deserve this? She was religious only in the sense that she believed in punishment.

"Well, maybe people ought to be scared," said Danny reasonably, then. "Pray," he coaxed. "We should both pray."

"Don't be dumb. It doesn't mean anything to me, it wouldn't work." She wasn't sure herself what she meant by "work." He wasn't listening to her, of course. These days he only really listened to what he wanted to hear. Helen still couldn't bring herself to believe there was not something cunning and voluntary about him, that he had wanted to be a child all along, a wheedling impatient child demanding her attention.

He had not wanted to be her husband, and so he became her child. He no longer wanted to be her husband. Something she had not told the doctors, though they'd certainly asked. Had they been having normal marital relations? They said it just like that. Doctor-talk. Why yes indeedy, she told them. Lied like a trooper. It was none of their business. It was your own pain and you didn't go turning it over to doctors. She understood it better than they did anyway. All this religion—*crap,* that's exactly what it was—it all had to do with Danny not wanting to be her husband.

Danny was kneeling on the rug, mumbling into his folded hands. He didn't seem too distressed at the prospect of the world ending. He looked pleased; he looked both exalted and silly. Helen saw right then and there why people, and not just crazy ones, were always so fond of announcing the end of the world. They didn't want life to go on without *them.* The world would end, slam-bang, and they wouldn't miss any of the party. "You don't even know the stupid rosary," Helen said.

His lips popped and curled around the prayers. His bald spot glowed like a halo. His hair needed washing. The clothes he wore would have marked him as a madman even if nothing else did. She watched her husband's heels knock together on the rug. He smelled. He actually smelled. It was not him at all, she was furious with him for no longer being himself. She could not escape the feeling that he was hiding from her, refusing to be himself, her husband, a man who had loved her.

"Get up," Helen said, then screamed it. She grabbed at the cloth over his shoulderblades. He'd lost weight and it seemed an easy place to hoist him by, those protruding bones, but he was still heavy beyond her strength. He only looked frail. She stumbled, tugging at him. She hit him on the back, flat-handed, and he hunched over, turtle-like. "Goddamn you. Goddamn you." Goddamn Danny. Goddamngod.

She was on the floor beside him, weeping. Danny's voice tickled her ear. "God understands a lot more things than we do, Helen."

In time he was institutionalized and given enough drugs so that he no longer talked about God or anything else, and there he stayed. Helen got by. She took a job at a travel agency. She sold the well-equipped house and moved into an apartment with her younger child, a boy. Helen's daughter, after many arguments, had moved in with a boyfriend. A wild girl, but her wildness was only the fashionable sort. The daughter wore her hair in a sporty, punkish wedge, and smoked like a dragon, and tried to talk even tougher than she was. She was a smaller version of her mother, translated into a younger style.

There were bad stories about the boy. When he was twelve, he did something to a little neighbor boy, something so bad that even the stories were vague. Helen sent him to a counselor. It didn't take. When he was fourteen, he threw some chunks of concrete from an overpass at cars below, although he was caught before he could kill anyone. He officially entered the juvenile justice system at that point. It was an endless series of hearings and petitions and programs, somewhat like being swallowed and digested by a snake. The boy was not easily digestible. He got into other, less exotic trouble from time to time, things like drugs and skipping school. It was a long snake, a long process, and there was a period of several years while everyone waited to see if the kid would get his act together. Or would he become one of the legion of sullen, expendable young men who washed out, bought it, in car wrecks, drug ODs, or penitentiaries. Were there always such great numbers of expendable young men, or was it some modern disease?

So this was how she came to be a woman alone. For all intents and purposes she was alone, even when the son was at home rather than off being incarcerated or programmed. She had time on her hands. She went out often. There was always a chance that something would happen. She was willing to take chances. That was something she prided herself on, something she toted up as one of her assets, the way another woman might give herself credit for having good teeth or hair. Helen never saw why *adventuress* had to be such a negative word.

There was a bar she liked because it drew a good crowd, the right sort of crowd. That is, she was unlikely to run into her daughter there. It was windowless, like all really successful bars, so that it was a little enclosed world of its own with constant weather and kindly light. It was called the Roost. Helen knew the bartenders. She made it a point to know bartenders and to be amiable to them, and they in turn were nice enough to her. After all, she never caused trouble for anyone but herself.

Helen was there at the Roost one evening in September, early, about seven. There was nobody except her and the bartender and a young couple she didn't know and a man she did named Leon. She said hello to Leon and sat a couple of stools down from him. He was an old man, old at sixty, with a really horrible precancerous cough—thick, liquid, full of spit and spongy bits of lung. Helen liked him. They could keep each other company or leave each other be, as needed. Leon didn't show up here to chase women anyway. He came to forget about things like the unpleasant prospect of drowning inside his own chest.

Leon told Helen she looked mighty sharp tonight. Helen smiled and said thank you, and nodded at herself in the mirror behind the bar. She was black and white tonight. Black linen suit with a deep white collar and a necklace of big chalky pearls. The wings of the collar were nearly as wide as her shoulders. The space where the pearls hung was so neatly framed and presented, it reminded one of the picture windows of certain houses, where swags of draperies surround a single ornate lamp. Helen's earrings were black, in fashionable melted geometric shapes, and she wore a little white boater hat.

She was drinking a margarita. Just sipping at it. She didn't want to get tiddly, not this soon. She felt good. There were some nights when her body defeated her no matter how diligently she shored it up or ministered to it. But not tonight. She felt trim and comfortable inside the black linen, and she had on a new silky black slip that whispered when she crossed her legs. Again she nodded at the mirror. She liked the black and white. She reminded herself of paintings by Somebody. Paintings of Parisian ladies at the turn of the century, ladies with upswept hair and mouths like crushed roses, dressed in smart, whimsical clothes, striped silks and ribbons and little veils. They sat in cafés looking languid and elegant, gossiping and flirting and getting tiddly on whatever it was they'd be drinking. Champagne? Her sister adventuresses. Helen ordered another margarita.

She hadn't seen him come in, the man now sitting next to Leon. She was first aware of a kind of indirect heat, the way you sense sunlight through closed eyes. He was sitting next to old Leon, talking to him, with one empty bar stool between him and Helen. How had she missed him? She always kept an eye out, she noticed anyone interesting right away. Oh, he was interesting. Helen was aware of a current of little subterranean, surreptitious motions, the two of them shifting in their seats, realigning their bodies as a preliminary to speech. Good. He'd noticed her too.

Helen waited, composing herself. He looked like a nice man. There had to be some nice men in the world, didn't there? It was mathematically impossible not to trip over a nice man sooner or later. She didn't dare check her makeup or preen. She remembered nodding at herself in the mirror. That was how she looked. The jaunty little hat. Gay Paree. She looked fine.

"Heya, Helen." Leon talking to her. She turned toward him, not pretending to be startled, which would have fooled no one. "Helen, this is my friend Curtis. Curtis, Helen."

Curtis said it was a pleasure. Helen gave him the smile she'd been working up. Pleasure. A set of shoulders on him, she noticed straight off. Fortyish. She turned back to her drink, knowing there would be another little interval of Not Talking before the Talking began. A nice man? Why was that so much to ask? So many men were not nice. Sometimes she felt they all must have gotten together in advance, these men, and decided what a swell trick it would be to pretend at first they were normal agreeable responsible people. On an evening not long ago, her escort had urinated in the lobby of a restaurant they were leaving. Helen didn't pray to God, of course, but she might have said to Someone, *Please let this one work out.*

"Are you ready for another drink?" the man called Curtis asked her, and this time she was startled, genuinely. She'd been so intent on the thought of him that she'd nearly forgotten the physical fact of him.

"That would be nice. Thank you." Smiled again, told herself to get with the plan, pay attention. She was spacing out, at the very moment she needed to be all brightness and charm. Helen watched him order the drinks, saying something jolly to the bartender, reaching for his wallet with a big square summer-tanned hand. Big square chunky gold watch. No rings. He was moving to the seat next to her. She wasn't sure she wanted him to do that just yet, but he made it look all right.

Oh, nice enough so far. But she felt unexpectedly weary with the whole business. The gamesmanship, the jockeying for position. Helen knew you were supposed to get all energized and breathless at the prospect of courtship, the teasing and maneuvering, the chink of the foils, and so on. Well sometimes. But more and more lately it only made her tired, adventuress or not. It only made her wish it was all settled somehow. She missed that about her marriage, if nothing else. The comfort of taking each other for granted. Sometimes the heroic effort it took to arrange and rearrange and coax and prop yourself up seemed just silly, you wished that were settled some way also. . . .

Meanwhile, here was this man she must talk to, and talk to in a fashion that was piquant, provocative, challenging, whatever.

Helen smiled at him over her new drink and opened her mouth to speak, but it was Leon who beat her to it. "Now Helen." He had to stop and give one of his horrible liquid dead man's coughs. "Now Helen, don't you believe anything this old boy tells you. I know him too good." Another coughing fit. Lord, the man sounded terrible these days, like a blender churning up mud. "Haargh. Agghagh. This old boy, he tells six lies before breakfast, just for practice. And with the ladies he's shameless."

"Is that true?" Helen asked gravely, and Curtis made his face very innocent.

"All goddamn lies," he said, and they both laughed. Old Leon's teasing gave them something to unite against. They would refuse to be embarrassed by it. "Helen," he said, meaning, did he get it right, and she nodded. He had nice skin. A tan melted down to gold. She liked the size of him too, she liked big men. She liked everything about him so far. Helen said she bet people called him Curt, and Curtis shook his head and said he bet they didn't. Not more than once, at least.

"Have you known Leon that long?" Helen asked, because it was her turn to say something.

"A little while. Long enough for him to make up stories on me." He laughed at that. "OK, Helen. Give. Tell me all about yourself."

"I work in a travel agency. Your turn."

"I'm a traveler."

"Cute."

"I am," he protested. "I mean, a traveler, not cute. Ha. So, do you like being a travel agent?"

"I'd like it better if people ever went anywhere interesting, like Istanbul or Australia. They don't mostly. Boring." At the risk of being boring herself, she could have gone on and talked about the yelping phones and the airlines that changed fares every five minutes so you never knew the prices and people gave you hell about it. And the bitches she worked with, not a one of them wouldn't walk over your dead body if they saw it lying in the street. She put a lid on it, and tried to think of something interesting to say. She was so off tonight, so tired. . . .

"So where do you travel?" was the best she could come up with. She wanted to know if he was some salesman type, somebody just passing through, and she shouldn't get her hopes up.

But he said he was in insurance, commercial and industrial insurance, and he traveled a bit checking out claims, but he lived right here in town. Helen considered the possibility that he was lying, then she shrugged it off. She let herself relax and drift while he talked. She nodded and smiled and sipped. She wasn't a bit interested in insurance, but she supposed somebody had to be. As if you ever really knew when your airplane was going to drop out of the sky, or somebody's car leave the street and knock you down like a large untrained dog, or whatever else. Helen knew the answer to that argument was statistics, but she knew also what she thought of *them.* So she smiled and sipped and nodded at the right places, and all she was really aware of was the dazzle of glass behind the bar, and the crowd noise which sounded exactly like a normal conversation stirred and stirred until it broke into bits, and her own pleased sensation of sitting with a man who was paying attention to her. Talk about your risks. Just who would he turn out to be anyway? Her heart's desire. A nonbather. Nothing at all. The way she lived, Helen decided, was not insurable. She very nearly missed what he said next, would have missed it if she hadn't been half-listening for it all along. He asked if she'd ever been married. A fine-looking lady like herself.

Helen smiled in a way that was supposed to be breezy. "Oh, but I am still married. He's just not on the premises. He had a mental breakdown. I drove him crazy, ha ha."

Curtis was looking polite about this, the way people tended to look polite, and rather sorry they'd asked. Helen hurried to say more, because she wanted more than that from him. Didn't she deserve to tell people, didn't she deserve some credit or sympathy?

She'd begun all wrong, she supposed. She didn't like that part of herself that turned Danny into a kind of trick, a bar story, an anecdote that could make her more interesting to strangers. It kept coming out of her like Leon's cough, something nobody wanted to hear but you couldn't keep down. She had to talk about it and it wasn't anyone's fault, just another unfairness, that she could never find the right words or the right people to tell it to.

So she began again, frowning: that was the better way to look. "He's in a mental hospital. He's been there almost three years now."

"Hey, I'm really sorry, Helen. Wow. Are they helping him?"

"Not so's you'd notice."

"Listen, I don't want to make you talk about it if—"

"No, that's OK. I don't mind." She took another pull at her drink. She did not have to pretend to bitterness for very long. "It's just that doctors don't know why things like that happen to people. Nobody does. But they can't own up to that, they always have to be doing something—"

"And the cure's worse than the disease."

Helen nodded. She had hardly noticed his interruption, it was so exactly what she meant to say herself. "I wouldn't let them do shock therapy. They have to get permission now, did you know? But I wouldn't let them do anything like that."

"Of course you wouldn't."

"You try and think of everything," she said vaguely. "You try not to make mistakes."

They were quiet then, and the noise of the bar rose up around them, as if it had not been there all along. She was aware of Curtis next to her, drinking—Scotch?—and waiting to see what she'd do now. Helen closed her eyes. She didn't want to think about him for a minute. The jukebox was playing a song Helen recognized as one her daughter used to play, one of the songs that swarmed around her head like a flock of amplified bees from the various metallic hives. Radios, stereos, Walkmans, blast boxes: Helen could never quite keep them all straight, couldn't remember how her children had acquired so much noisy and sophisticated electronic gear. Nor could she remember the name of the song. It was one of those tough-boy songs, all screaming and mean guitars. She couldn't tell it from all the other songs like it. And the boys who sung them were all skinny and sneering, and the names they gave themselves you couldn't keep straight either, because they were only chosen because they meant nothing at all. Helen found herself wondering where her daughter was at that very moment. Out doing something wicked, or at least noisy, she supposed. Her tough daughter and the boy she said she was in love with. Yes, love, the daughter had insisted, furious, when Helen made the mistake of doubting it out loud. You're too young to know what that even means, Helen said, knowing as it came out of her mouth it was the exact wrong thing to say. Oh sure, Mom, when do I get old enough to really screw things up like you, way to go, screw up your own life and everyone else's. You always have, you know, even when I was little, I didn't believe anything you said because you talked so much, don't you ever get tired of not knowing what you're talking about?

"Excuse me," said Helen. She slid off her stool and headed for the ladies'. She was about to cry and for all the wrong reasons. It wasn't on Danny's account, or her daughter's, or anyone she really ought to cry for. It was because of this man she didn't know and couldn't tell from any of the others, and herself saying the same things she said to the others, passing her pain from hand to hand, making it commonplace, and *love* was the exact wrong thing to say.

When she returned to her seat at the bar Curtis was looking concerned, like she knew he would. Whether he only looked that way out of manners or strategy, she didn't care. Whether he was anything she wanted him to be, it didn't matter. She was too tired of it all. Helen sat down and smiled at him to show she was perfectly all right, she wasn't some hysterical type he had to worry about. "Mud in your eye," she said, hoisting her glass.

"Hey, Helen. I'm sorry about your husband. That's really a rough one. Man."

"Well, it happens."

"He didn't get . . . violent or anything, did he? Listen, never mind, it's none of my business. I'd just hate to think of you—"

"Oh no," said Helen. "It wasn't like that at all. He never laid a hand on me." She ducked her chin so he couldn't see her smirking. It was sort of funny.

"The only crazy people I ever knew, they were either born that way or got that way because they were old. Like my old grandma. She got on this thing about food, hiding food. Six-month-old tuna salad in closets. Nasty. But she was just old."

"He wasn't old. Isn't. My husband."

"Sure. I mean, unless he was a lot older than you. Listen, you want to talk about something else? How did we get started on this anyways?"

"He saw things and heard voices. He was one of those." Helen was speaking carefully, just on the edges of the liquor, as if she was balancing just on the edge of the glass. It was one thing she could do for Danny, she thought. Talk about him right. She saw Curtis looking at her, trying to figure her out. Probably wondering if she was crazy too, or about to start off on a crying jag. She didn't blame him but she also didn't much care what he thought. Who was he anyway? Nobody. Everybody. She wasn't going to worry about him. Helen saw him visibly decide to string along with her, what the hell. He smiled and moved a little closer to her, not moving much, but enough to mean something. He put his heavy arm on the back of her chair. The fur on the arm was gold on top where the light hit it, darker below.

"What sorts of things did he see?"

"Oh. Religious things. Are you religious, Curtis?"

He laughed a little at that. Funny, Helen had noticed, how people were more embarrassed talking about religion than about sex. "Me? How did you put it. Not so's you notice."

"Well my husband wasn't either, until all this. One day he comes home from work and tells us—the kids and me, I have two kids—he tells us the Lord is going to smite down all wickedness within our lifetime. He says that, *smite*. We're at the dinner table eating barbeque sandwiches."

"You're kidding."

"That's what I told the children. Daddy was making a joke. Oh boy. They knew better."

"Was it one of those preachers, one of those cult things?"

"Nope. All his idea." Helen set her glass down precisely in the center of the cocktail napkin, on the little moist ring it had already made. She had to remember things precisely. "Stuff like that kept happening. I tried talking to him. That was a mistake. You can't talk somebody out of being crazy, you know? He told me heaven and hell were real places, like Dallas or Boston, and people could think whatever they wanted. He knew better. The nuttiest thing was, you could almost believe him, I mean, he was so damned intense about it. You could almost believe him until he started talking about Jesus telling him to wear his seat belt."

"Told him—oh man. Oh man, I'm sorry, Helen, I don't mean to be laughing—"

"Go ahead. It's OK. You think I don't know how it sounds?"

"Oh man."

"There was a lot more like that. Just plain silly." She still didn't think she'd explained it right. "But you know, he wasn't trying to be funny . . ."

He was instantly not laughing, and Helen wondered if it was the laughing he'd pretended, or the not laughing. "Oh sure. It had to be something serious going on with him, that kind of stuff—"

"He was afraid of dying," said Helen, and she watched his big square suntanned face stop moving all of a sudden, as if she'd finally said something that really interested or really shocked him, found him out somehow. She examined the watery green remains of her drink, the little wet glass world in its orbit of soggy paper as if it too would change on her. Everything changed once she said

it, because she had not known it was true until the moment it came
out of her mouth.

"Well," he said finally. "Isn't everyone?"

"I'm not sure. I'm not sure everyone should be."

"Just what do you mean, Helen?"

Helen felt his arm graze her shoulder. The hair gold on top
and black underneath, like a storm cloud. She leaned away from
the arm slightly, politely; she didn't want to hurt his feelings. "I
guess I mean, dying is something that happens to everyone."

"No," Curtis said. "That's not what you meant."

"You're right. I didn't." It surprised her a little to realize it.
Helen smiled up at him from under her lowered eyelids. He was
smiling too. Something gold far back in his mouth, winking at her.
"So," she said. "What did I mean, since you're so smart?"

"Maybe you meant some people just give in to it. Some people
give up graceful. Is that sort of what you meant?"

"Oh yes," Helen agreed. It was so nice to have someone understand her. She tilted her head back to look him full in the face,
but something was in the way. The brim of her hat? His arm? His
face was too close to hers, she could only see parts of it. Teeth as
big and blank as billboards. "You know," she said, "you can get
tired of anything."

His voice was somewhere at the back of her neck. She kept
turning to try and get it in front of her, but it was too close. "Since
you brought it up," he said, "I don't mind talking about it. You
know I always like to meet a lady who's interested in serious conversation. A lot of folks won't talk about things that scare them.
Like something's going to hear them and come after them. Ha.
Anyway, it's something to think about, the different ways people
cash in when it's their time. Some are more sensible than others.
They don't kick up a big fuss or get to boo-hooing about it. They
behave themselves. And you know, Helen, you have to admire
them for that. I mean, it shows some class."

"Class," she repeated, by way of agreement. Her eyes strayed
to the mirror, then skidded away hastily. How had her hat gotten

so crooked? It was pushed down low over her forehead at a rowdy angle, for all the world like a drunken sailor's. She moved one hand up the side of her head, as if she were only adjusting her hair, and gave the hat a good yank. She tried the mirror again, this time out of the corner of her eye. It was OK now. But how mortifying, how long had she been sitting there like that, why hadn't anyone told her? Now she examined the other faces in the mirror, the people lining the bar and milling behind it. When you saw them in the glass like that it was hard to connect them with all the noise they were making. The mouths moved but the noise came out of somewhere else. Nobody was looking at her, which was a relief. Where was old Leon? She didn't see him anymore. He must have gone home. That bothered her somehow; he should have said good-bye to them. She turned back to Curtis. He was paying the bartender for new drinks.

"I don't need a drink," she told him. "Really."

"Just a quickie. One for the ditch."

"Are we supposed to go somewhere?"

"Sure. Istanbul."

"Cute." She was drinking now, though she couldn't really taste it.

"We can go wherever you want to, Helen."

"Dallas," she said, and laughed because it was all very funny. In the mirror her mouth moved, but she hadn't said anything.

"A woman like you," Curtis was saying, "is something special. I marked it right away and I asked to be introduced because I wanted us to meet proper. I wanted to show some respect. You have a style to you. You deserve the best there is, because you got class."

What is it people deserve? she wanted to ask him, but she didn't since she would have had to explain too much. She meant, was there somebody who decided these things? You always wanted to think so. Maybe he was just flattering her, the same way he might have told her she had pretty eyes. Something he'd know she'd want to hear. *Beautiful lady, be comforted. Somebody some-where is keeping score. Somebody measures these things out. Pol-icies are honored. What we call luck is just another way of saying whether or not you get what you deserve.*

"Drink up, Helen honey." He patted her shoulder.

"Already?" She was a little disappointed, a little regretful now that it was time to go.

"Yup. We got to beat feet."

"Oh all right." She couldn't remember if she had a purse or not. She supposed if she didn't have it, she didn't really need it. He helped her get down from the stool, chuckling a little, and she leaned into the nice solid warmth of him. It was slow getting to the door because of all the people. Good-bye, she called to every-one, good-bye, good-bye. Quite loudly, she thought, but no one seemed to notice her at all. The sound had been blotted out some-how, like the empty balloons that came out of people's mouths in comic strips.

"Why, you've gotten me drunk," she said when they were finally outside. It was solid blind black; she couldn't see a thing. And colder; she reached for her elbows and hugged them.

"You ain't drunk," he said from somewhere to one side of her. "Don't you know as long as you can worry about being drunk, you ain't really drunk. Foolproof test."

"I didn't know that," said Helen. His car was nice. She couldn't tell what kind it was but the seats felt good and smelled good and the engine hardly made a sound, that's how nice and smooth and easy it all was. He must be a good driver. "Here's some poetry," Curtis was saying. "I bet you wouldn't figure on me knowing po-etry, would you, but I do:

> *He is not drunk who from the floor*
> *can rise again and drink some more.*
> *But he is drunk who prostrate lies*
> *and cannot drink and cannot rise.*

You like that? I made it up."

"You did not," said Helen, smiling, pleased because she knew this kind of teasing talk. She knew all about it. It was nice when you finally found the right words for something. It was sort of cold even inside the car and she thought about asking him to turn up the heat. She liked having men do little things for her and fuss over her. And she could be good to them too. The teasing they liked and laughing at their jokes and looking pretty for them—

Where was her hat? She didn't feel it anymore, and in a panic she groped for it. "It's OK, honey," Curtis said. He knew right away what she was worried about. "You don't need it." And then she understood he had taken it off for her, it was all right. "You don't need this here either. Lift up your arms," he directed in his kindly voice, and she did so, wondering only how there managed to be so much room in the car. Maybe they had finally gotten to where they were going. And you don't need this, he kept saying, or this or this. She marveled at all the things there were to take off. Her clothes and then her necklace and rings and even the earrings from her ears, every scrap. What a funny feeling it was. She tried to move her legs, a paddling motion, but they were too far away. You don't need this or this. Legs or arms, muscles or bones. Undressing always so much easier than the fuss of dressing up. *Beautiful lady*, he comforted. *The mirror is empty.*

Danny, she thought, though she knew he was not the one there with her. She tried to rise up on her elbows but there was nothing to balance on. Skin was just like clothes, it wore out too, and maybe he'd had the right idea all along. Old crazy holy Danny. Why touch what didn't last? If there was something that lasted, you couldn't touch it; you could only reach. *Oh Danny,* she said, as if that would be enough to explain everything to him. She was through worrying about words, *no* or *please* or *love*. You didn't need words either. She tried to rise up one more time before *up* vanished too and she didn't have to do anything at all.

FOREVER

"You know how long it took me to use a knife again?" The mother held up her empty hand, as if it could testify on its own. "I couldn't slice a tomato, carve meat, anything. I'd shove it away from me."

The reporter's hand held a pen. He had a notebook as well as a cassette recorder, and every so often he wrote something down. "What are you writing?" the mother asked. "What did I say?" The reporter showed her. He'd written the word *knife*. That was all. It was a note to himself, he explained.

"It's always in the back of your mind," said the mother. "It comes out in ways you don't expect. Like if I see a TV commercial with a little girl in it, it don't even have to look like her. It still sets me off. Is this the kind of thing you want, Mr. Hughes?"

Hughes said yes, this was fine. He said she should talk about anything she felt like.

The mother said, "I am only doing this because it might help jog somebody's memory. Or whoever's out there, it might make them come forward."

The mother sat on the living-room couch, which was covered with a tasseled bedspread. The mother's name was Bonita Poole. Hughes knew from his notebook that she was forty-four years old, divorced, and worked in a factory that made packaging materials. Next to the mother on the couch sat her oldest daughter, Joy. On top of the television set was a picture of the daughter who had died, and an arrangement of dried roses. The roses came from the funeral, the mother said. They were pink roses, faded to the color of old paper except at their tips, shedding petals when nobody was looking.

In the photograph the daughter had a waterfall of poufy hair arranged over one shoulder, and a smile that pulled up one corner of her mouth. A wise-guy smirk, as if she'd mugged and giggled and stared the camera down, not really wanting to have her picture taken. Her name was Kelly Poole and she was eighteen when she died, one year ago minus ten days.

The mother saw Hughes looking at the picture. "Pretty, ain't she? Those big brown eyes. She favored her dad that way."

Mrs. Poole and Joy were stamped out of a different mold— fair, with sketched-in eyebrows, and faces as broad and plain as pie tins. Joy was twenty-seven. She looked like she'd stopped being young some time back, almost with relief. Young had probably never suited her. She was hard around the mouth and soft everywhere else. Flesh mounded up under her T-shirt and stretch pants. Just by sitting, she projected grievance, the unfairness of being large and unpretty and having a sister who'd been raped and murdered and pushed into a ditch off a county road. Joy reached up and adjusted the plastic clip in her mother's hair, absently, as if it were her own head.

Hughes thought, as he often did in the homes of the poor, of expensive magazines, department stores, and banks—everything that implied this room did not exist. But here it was in all its gaping ugliness, turning the lie around; it was as if nothing else was real except for it. The living-room walls were painted a deep, flat unconvincing blue. Water stains dripped down from the corners. Plastic curtains hung at the cloudy windows. The kitchen was at the other end of the main room. Boxes of cereal and crackers were lined up on the counter, along with scouring powder and a jar of iced-tea mix. The refrigerator muttered, laboring. Two ceramic plaques in the shape of preening roosters hung over the kitchen table. The smell in the house was of something burnt, with an overlay of cheese.

"Tell him about the phone calls," Joy said. It was the first time she had spoken. Hughes waited, but the mother shook her head.

"That stuff don't have nothing to do with Kelly. It's just ugly."

"People are sick," said Joy. "We got calls right after the funeral. People hanging up on you. Or saying things."

"That's enough," said the mother. "Like I said." Joy sat back on the couch, her mouth closing down over another grievance.

"Tell me about the psychic," suggested Hughes. The psychic had told the police where to find the body. The psychic was one of the things that made the case newsworthy.

"Oh, him. We kind of gave up on him."

"He moved to Cincinnati," said Joy. "He was regular-looking. He could of been somebody's grandfather." Her tone implied that this was one of his failings.

"They give him a sweater of hers. Like a bloodhound. He knew to find her near water, the borrow pit." The mother closed her eyes. Hughes had seen the police pictures of the body. He hoped the mother had not.

When she looked up again she said, "He can't help us with who did it. It's like the trail's gone cold. Like he can't find her spirit. Do you think people get more dead as time goes on?"

Hughes said he didn't know. He was unsure of what the mother wanted him to say, and unsure of the whole notion. Yes, he might have said, if he'd thought about it. The dead become more dead. They recede from us little by little, down a long corridor. They forget their names before we do.

But the mother didn't want an answer. She said, "He give me all these numbers that were supposed to be license plates of cars. For a while that's all I did, was drive around looking for those numbers. I had all these little scraps of paper everywhere in the house. One day I looked at them and said, What is this? It was getting out of hand. Sometimes I sit and try and make my mind clear, to see if something comes to me. You'd think if anybody would feel something, it'd be me."

In his notebook, Hughes saw he had written the word *psychic,* followed by a question mark.

"Her father lives in Florida. I had the police call him. We haven't seen him since nineteen seventy-nine. He didn't come to the funeral. He never kept up with her or his other, that's Pete. It's like he never had a daughter. It's like a car he sold a long time ago, then somebody else wrecked it."

Photographs of the mother's six surviving children stair-stepped their way across the living-room wall. Some were tow-headed and jowly, like Joy, others darker, more angular. Distinctive features—a receding chin, freckles—emerged, then extinguished themselves, a schematic representation of the marriages, three of them. Someone else might have asked, reasonably, why Mrs. Poole kept on marrying, kept having children, but Hughes thought it was because Mrs. Poole took life seriously. Hughes liked Mrs. Poole, which was different than feeling sorry for her.

"Do you want an orange soda?" she asked. "I run on so much, I didn't think to offer anything."

Hughes said thank you, but not to bother. He closed his note-book. His hand rested on the cassette recorder, waiting and delicate.

"I almost forgot you had that going," said the mother. "Did you get enough for your story? There's a lot more about Kelly, but I don't know if it would be good in a story. She liked baking cakes, fancy ones, with the decorations. She loved kids, she was great with them. Oh I don't know. What else can I say except she was my daughter. That night she had on a new red jacket they never found. That and her keys. It's another thing I look for now. Some-body wearing that jacket. I know that don't make sense. It's the exact same jacket you can get at the mall."

Hughes made his thank-yous. He eased out the front door and stood looking at the square of lawn, the clumped brown grass that had already stopped growing. It was the end of September, a bright dry season, when everything in the landscape bleached out. The sun had a squint to it, flattening the shadows. White weeds lined the ditches. Leaves faded and curled under. A dry wind made these leaves click together, and spun the petals of a plastic sunflower stuck at the edge of the lot. A clothesline hung along one side of the porch, freighted with white cotton socks, striped bath towels, T-shirts, stretched-out underpants. The cloth made stiff ridges around the clothespins, as if everything had been hanging there a long time.

The grass reminded him of something. He decided it was the petrified flowers inside. On the street the car he'd come in was parked, a heavy, shining car that made the small frame houses look stoop-shouldered, flimsy, and wrong. He could see the photogra-pher sitting behind the steering wheel, his head back, dozing.

The front door opened again and Joy came out. Hughes couldn't tell if she'd wanted to find him, or if it was an accident, his standing there a minute too long. She didn't seem startled at encountering him. She said, "So what are you going to say about us?"

"It depends on how much space the editor gives me." This was true, although it didn't answer her question.

"Uh-huh," said Joy. She folded her arms over her chest. The cool wind roughened her skin, bringing up pebbly goosebumps. "She was my half-sister," she said. "Kelly was. My dad was named Jim Harney." Everything she said managed to convey deep suspicion, belligerent disbelief.

"You mentioned phone calls."

"I wasn't always the one to answer. The times I answered it was some guy. He'd say, 'Hey, I did her too, and she was good.' Talk like that. And a lot worse. That's what my mother had to listen to."

"I'm sorry," said Hughes. There was a place in his mind where he sealed away the knowledge of such things.

Joy kept talking. It was as if only certain words fit the shape of her mouth, words she had not been allowed to say inside. "She grew up flighty because she was spoiled. She had to have everything: clothes, a car. She got in trouble once, she was going to have a baby. Mom had to pay for that too. She used to walk around the house without all her clothes on, just to show off. You could see her ending up like she did. I don't care how that sounds. She knew too many boys and they were all supposed to pay attention to her. But she was my own family. I knew her all her life, beginning to end."

"I'm sorry," Hughes said again. He wanted to leave now, to get away from this world of women and their dense, intricate griefs. He looked out past the crimped grass and the gleaming ovals of light reflected in the surface of his car, to the end of the block where the road broadened out into Main Street.

"If they found out who did it, I would do anything. I would cut off parts of him."

Hughes didn't respond. Joy said, "You live in Chicago, don't you?"

"The suburbs," amended Hughes, then wondered what possible difference it would make to her.

"You wouldn't come to a place like this in a million years except for Kelly. She was always fussing in the mirror. Like she had to be so pretty. Well, she's dead now because she was pretty and somebody wanted to get her. And you're only interested in her because she's dead."

Hughes had never wanted to kill anyone. He considered himself deficient in hatred, or perhaps murder came from something different, something cooler to the touch. He had not wished to kill, even in his imagination, his ex-wife in the last ruinous weeks of their marriage, nor drunks who had stood toe to toe with him in parking lots, nor any of his professional enemies, men who had lied or undercut him. No treacherous friend, no figures of fairy-tale malice from his childhood. (Hughes had grown up in a place called Licking, Missouri, and he wouldn't have gone back there in a million years.) He was as incapable of the thought of murder as of the deed. He recorded the words of those who were capable of both like a sighted man running his hands over braille.

Superior, Indiana, was another small town burdened with a whimsical name. On its Main Street, two closed-down gas stations faced each other from opposite corners. At one the corroded pumps still stood, nearly paintless, sinking into cracked cement. At the other they'd dug out the fuel tanks and covered the lot with gravel. (The new gas station, a self-service franchise that sold packaged sandwiches, milk, and doughnuts, was two miles away on the highway.) It was a town losing ground by both inches and leaps.

There was a Red Star Market, an auto body shop, and two churches built of the same liver-colored brick, one for the Methodists, one a United Church of Christ. A row of false-front buildings, empty except for the Honeybee Bakery. A gift shop that accommodated a post office. A new flat-roofed minimall housing an insurance agency and a Laundromat. There was a pizza restaurant, a feed store, a tavern that sold hunting licenses, and a white frame cottage tricked out for antiques.

"Small town values," the photographer intoned, as he steered the big car through the quiet streets. "Deep roots. America's rural heritage." The photographer's name was Jencks, and his ambition was to take celebrity portraits. He was a young man, about the age of Mrs. Poole's daughter Joy, Hughes figured. He wore clothes that Hughes, who was closer to Mrs. Poole's age, found affected: everything baggy and drab, expensive garments meant to look like they came from thrift shops. His hair was combed back with some product that kept it looking wet. Jencks said, "They'll never use a tombstone shot. Too kitschy."

"Your talents are wasted on us," agreed Hughes. He had stopped paying attention to Jencks sometime during the hundred-and-sixty-mile drive from Chicago. "Turn here."

"It is kind of pretty," offered Jencks. "It could be on a calendar for an insurance agency."

The shade trees showed spots of pale yellow, pale orange, and copper. Some yards had shining green or blue reflector balls set on pedestals, objects Hughes had not seen since his childhood. Tomato plants and cucumber vines hung on in the gardens. There was a dusty bloom laid over everything, the kindly aspect of decay.

"Tell me again," said Jencks. "Why are we here? What's the big draw?"

"Mrs. Poole wrote the paper a letter."

"The paper with a heart," said Jencks. His face went slack, as if he had surprised himself and said what he meant.

A young man sat on the front steps of a house on the corner. In spite of the cool weather he was shirtless, his lean, elongated chest looking nearly anatomical, a working model of ribs and muscles. He wore blue jeans and scuffed black boots. His hair was shaggy, the color of broom straw, and in his shadowed face his eyes were unexpectedly light and piercing, like a malamute's. He and the reporter traded stares for a moment before Hughes was borne away. If someone besides Jencks had been in the car, Hughes would have said what he felt, that Kelly Poole had been killed by a boy exactly like that, or maybe that same boy: young, bored, fitfully employed, knowing nothing of himself or anyone else, and with a talent for meanness.

The cemetery was a long mile outside of Superior, beyond the remains of a lumberyard. It occupied the grounds of a disused church, the ancestor of one of the new brick constructions in town. The old church was white painted board, outfitted with a steeple, and coming unknit at all its angles. The graves were laid out in rows, like corn. The oldest stones went back to the end of the last century and were smooth, nearly featureless, the dead who had become entirely dead. Some of the plots were ornamented with bits of ribbon, chrysanthemums in coffee cans, or artificial geraniums. "This is so *sad*," said Jencks, indicating the foil-wrapped flower-pots, the crosses made of wire and tissue rosettes, the thick-grimed plastic petals. By that, Hughes thought he meant it was in bad taste.

"Where is it you'd like to be buried?" asked Hughes, wanting Jencks to shut up. He'd found Kelly Poole's gravestone. It was pink granite with two interlocked hearts, and FOREVER chiseled above the name and dates. There was a grain or sheen in the stone, something that sparkled.

"Hearts," said Jencks, meaning it as a comment.

"She was stabbed in the heart," said Hughes.

Jencks went back to the car for his cameras and worked in silence, kneeling, focusing, squeezing off shots. The cemetery was on a rise, and Hughes looked around him in all directions, back east toward town, north to the railroad tracks and the tree line beyond, south across a chewed-looking hayfield, then west, where the small white sun was lowering itself behind a knobby hill.

"Finito," said Jencks, packing his equipment into its stiff leather cases. He already had pictures of Mrs. Poole and her house, a copy of Kelly Poole's portrait, and other, possibly useful shots of Superior and environs. "We gone."

"Take me over to Anderson," said Hughes. Anderson was twenty miles away, the nearest metropolis, where people went when they needed a doctor or a bank, shoes, refrigerators, jobs. "I want to get a rental car."

Jencks said, "I feel obliged to point out that you already have a rental car."

"You're going back. I'm staying overnight. I want another crack at the boyfriend." Hughes was pleased to think that he'd just had his last conversation with Jencks, although Jencks said a few more things. "Mmn," said Hughes. "Mmnhm." At the rental-car office he fished his things out of the trunk and gave Jencks his sunniest smile and wave.

Hughes equipped himself with a motel room and a fried-chicken dinner. He called in for his messages. He tried to reach Kelly Poole's boyfriend at the number Mrs. Poole had given him, but got no answer. He set up his laptop computer and reviewed his files. More and more, he liked working outside of the office. He preferred these assignments to transcribing the accusations of one politician against another, or reading the entrails of press releases. He liked being alone in utilitarian rooms and eating out of paper bags. He searched out opportunities for solitude. He had been a reporter for most of his life, and sometimes he seemed to himself like a stirred cup—or a gong beating in a metal chamber, too full of noise and push and other people's stories: grand, indifferent, tragic, or vapid. Every chord in him had been struck over and over, until the strings were loosened. There was nothing that could not be hyped up, sentimentalized, made obvious and meaningless.

But he liked Mrs. Poole. If he had been a different kind of man, he would have said "God bless you," or something like that, on his way out the door.

Kelly Poole's boyfriend's name was Dean Kinshaw, and he ran a car wash and detail shop in Anderson. Hughes was there early, before it opened. It had rained just before dawn. Puddles reflected the moving sky, which was the color of cement and bruise. Cold fogs rose up. The car wash was built of white cinder block and occupied a triangle of space on a commercial artery. Traffic rolled and braked. Hughes sat in the front seat of his rental car, curling his fingers around a coffee cup, breathing in steam and exhaust.

There was a billboard overhead, one he'd seen a number of times since yesterday, an advertisement for a counseling center. LIFE IS HARD, it stated flatly, next to a starkly lit picture of a spectacled man gazing at some unseen inward blankness. The line of his mouth was thin and sealed. Only now did Hughes recognize it as his own face, enough like him to be a photograph. Or rather, it was his face as it might appear if no one else was watching it.

A maroon panel van pulled into the driveway, all its doors seeming to open at once. A small man and smaller woman emerged, followed by three children who seemed to be nearly the same age and size, like a nest of mice. The children carried expedition gear: a portable television, a cooler, paper sacks, gym bags.

Hughes stood in the office door until someone, the woman, noticed him. The children were already strewing their goods around the shop, unhooking the vacuum cleaner hoses to use in tug-of-war, feeding quarters into the pop machine, preparing for their day just as seriously as the adults. When the woman nudged him, the man stubbed the end of his cigarette into the concrete and crossed the room. "Help you?"

Hughes introduced himself and gave the name of his newspaper. It was a weighty name, one that most people were unused to encountering in the flesh. It intimidated them, or got them defensive and riled up. Dean Kinshaw reached for the cigarette he'd been smoking and found it missing. He was older than Hughes had expected, in his late twenties, undersized, hollow-chested, black-haired, and pale, with a slight, angular, handsome face. The stray seed of some lost black Irishman, grown up among weeds.

"I know why you're here," Kinshaw said. "Bonita called me. She's all excited. I don't see what she expects to come of it. Talk. There's things you shouldn't have to keep saying."

Hughes suggested getting a cup of coffee. Kinshaw shook his head. "Let's make this one quick."

"Would later today be any better for you?"

"Never would be better for me," said Kinshaw. He fished in his breast pocket for a new cigarette, setting off a rattle of cellophane. "I smoke too much," he offered. "Regular chimney."

"Everything's bad for you," agreed Hughes.

"I worked nights then. That night. You know that already, I bet. I was over at the foundry. I quit because my nerves went out. I still can't do a lot of things. Like drive. You know what I mean? They put you back together with pills, and the pills make you sweat and pee funny and bite your tongue until it bleeds. Just so you know where I'm coming from. I don't see what good a newspaper is here. No newspaper ever raised the dead, last I heard."

Hughes thought of the stream of letters the paper got, the lost and losing causes, petitions for redress of grievances, prayers, confessions, accusations, cranks, victims, unsung heroes wanting to be sung, miracle seekers all.

"Do you believe in God, Mr. Hughes?"

Hughes glanced at him, but there was nothing belligerent in Kinshaw's face. He was only serious and remote, gazing out the open door.

"No," said Hughes. "Not lately, I don't."

"Well I do. I have to. Because God's the only one who can really kick ass."

Kinshaw leaned in over his lighter. The small flame hollowed out his narrow, handsome face. Hughes felt sorry for Kinshaw, which was different than liking him. Weakness always made him sorry. He thought of Kelly Poole watching Kinshaw just like this, bent over his cupped hands. Hughes tried to make himself quiet inside. He wanted his mind to be as a tree branch is to a bird, he wanted to coax the vision closer, see what she'd seen in all the faces she'd known. Kinshaw straightened, calling, "Sharon."

The woman detached herself from the telephone and came to stand beside Kinshaw. She had short brown hair and a round shy face. "This is Sharon. We're together now. She knows everything about me."

Sharon's children had the television hooked up and were piled in front of it watching a show, ignoring the adults. Kinshaw said, "Life goes on. Maybe that sounds cold. I can't tell you what you come to hear. I can't keep dwelling on it. It could have been anybody did it. That's how I look at people now. Like they could be the one. Everybody. Kelly was tough. She fought him hard. Her shoulder was dislocated. I've already gone and said too much."

"Life is hard," said Hughes, to no one. He was back in his car, driving the two-lane highway from Anderson to Superior. "Life is hard, and then it goes on." For some, he added silently. The weather had shifted overnight from dry to damp, the first step down the long slope that led to winter. A shrill, unfriendly wind scoured the corn stubble and shredded the leaves.

Kelly Poole hadn't liked her boyfriend working late shifts. She'd complained about it to her girlfriends. The last night of her life she'd left her mother's house at ten o'clock. She was bored and fretful, and sometimes kids she knew hung out at the Denny's seven miles away. It was a school night, but she and her friends weren't very serious about school. They were seniors, and were not expected to take it seriously.

At Denny's she sat in a booth with two other girls, ordering diet Cokes and fries. There was never anything to do nights, they agreed. This *place,* they said, rolling their eyes. If they lived anywhere else in the world, there would be something to do. Kelly said she was thinking of skipping school the next day. She borrowed three dollars for gas to get home. She yawned and contemplated the tabletop universe of crumpled straw wrappers, circles of damp, the smudged creamer, the cradle of pink saccharin packets, everything familiar and unremarkable, begging to be noticed for the last time.

They left Denny's at eleven-thirty, trotting across the parking lot with their hands in their pockets, shivering. Kelly hopped on one foot, looking for her keys. Her friends waited in their car, the engine running, while she went through a pantomime of exasperation: *Do you believe this, how dumb, I mean, really dumb.* Then she dredged the keys out and held them up in triumph.

Hughes stopped his car in front of the Red Star Market, with its banners advertising pork and beans, heads of cauliflower, dish soap. Two pickups were parked by the feed store, and an old woman with a head scarf like a bandage was entering the Laundromat. Wood smoke rose from a chimney down the street. The life of the town had retreated indoors, like a green plant set in a silent room.

When he stepped into the wind he tasted stinging grit. He pushed open the door of the Honeybee Bakery, with its smell of sugar and radiator heat. He took a seat at the counter, nodding at a table of men in windbreakers and caps. He blew on his coffee, waiting. These days he waited out stories, where in years before he might have pursued them, forced them, asked too many questions. Now he had more patience. He was a tree branch, and the story was his bird.

In the mirrored panel behind the counter he saw, as he'd known would happen, one of the men at the table get up and approach. He knew how small towns worked. The man leaned his backside comfortably against the counter. "You're from the newspaper."

Hughes introduced himself and shook hands. "Bob Larrabee," the man said. "Care to join us?" Hughes piloted his coffee cup to their table. There were five of them, substantial men with solid handshakes and meaty, weather-beaten faces. Hughes edged into a seat and they shifted heavily to accommodate him. "Plenty of room," one of them said. "Don't let Art here crowd you."

Everybody laughed. Art was the only one of them you might have called thin. There was a silence. They seemed embarrassed. "Terrible business," said one.

"It was my field they found her in. I got to say, I wish she'd ended up anywhere else. Gives you the cold chills."

Another silence. Another man said, "All this time, and it's still going on. Still in your face."

"No good ever come of that family."

"Bonita's all right. It's those kids. That girl and the two after her."

"Kids run wild these days."

"You got to feel for Bonita. She was on her own."

"You see," said Larrabee, "this isn't the city. People don't do each other like that. We never had the newspaper here before."

"It's always been a good place to live. Still is."

They were waiting for him to second this. "It's good to get out of the city," he offered. "See some open space." He felt them considering him. "I grew up on a farm. Used to show polled Herefords." This was an exaggeration, but one he thought he could handle.

He let the information settle. "What do you think happened to her?"

"She got into somebody's car. Or was made to get in."

"She stopped at Supergas. The boy there saw her. So it wasn't her car quit on her."

This time the silence was expectant. None of them looked at Hughes, but he felt them encouraging him, wanting him to say things for them. "You think she went out looking for trouble?"

"Maybe she was somewhere she shouldn't of been."

"Bad luck or bad habits."

The waitress, a lean woman in slacks and a sweatshirt, approached with the coffeepot. "I think none of you has an ounce of charity in you," she said. "I'm ashamed to know you."

"Now Hildy."

"It might have been your own daughter. Or it might have been your son did it. You don't know anything."

"I am buying this gentleman his coffee," said Bob Larrabee. "I don't want him to think we are always this ugly to people."

"Buy a steak dinner if it makes you feel better," said Hildy. "Maybe this used to be a nice place. It's not now."

Hughes took a last look at Superior. FOUR-H WELCOMES YOU. JOIN US FOR WORSHIP. HOME OF THE CHARGERS. YOUR STATE FARM AGENT. It was after four o'clock and the sunless sky was descending like the lid of a box. He was anxious to be back in his own world, where he was unremarkable and anonymous. Where evil was as diffused and impersonal as the soot drifting down from a smokestack. He touched the paper cone on the seat beside him. It made a bright, crackling sound.

He took the turn to the cemetery, glancing up at the narrow house on the corner. It was a beat-down yellow, the color of a yellow dog. The porch was a broken lump of cement, set at a little distance from the front door. At that moment the light-eyed boy came around the corner of the garage. He was wearing a denim jacket unbuttoned over a T-shirt. As before, he stared at the car, a long, wolfish, disinterestedly rude stare. In his hands were a loop of frayed electrical cord and an open pocketknife.

Hughes kept driving, his hands steady on the wheel, but he felt as if an alarm were ringing within him, as if the skin had been ripped from the ordinary surface of the world. If there had been anyone in the car, even Jencks, he would have said he was afraid he was losing his mind. He wanted to be the telephone voice whispering in Joy's ear: *him, that one.* But there was nothing he could ever say to anyone, and no one to say it to.

He reached the old churchyard and pulled in, listening to the small ticking of the cooling car. He considered the possibility that he had spooked himself. Nerves, just like Kinshaw, poor sorry bastard. He considered the possibility that he'd had a vision. That this was what a vision was, something neither verifiably true nor false. A fine veil of misty rain blew against the windshield.

He picked up the paper cone, got out of the car, and walked behind the church to survey the graveyard. A dark-haired girl in a red jacket stood at Kelly Poole's headstone. It took him a long suspended heartbeat to recognize her as Sharon, Kinshaw's girl-friend.

As he approached she turned her head and smiled at him over her shoulder, a small, welcoming smile. She was wearing an elderly oversized high school jacket with cracked leather bands at the shoulder. The maroon panel van was parked behind her on a dirt track.

"Hi," she said. "Didn't expect to see you again."

"I'm just now on my way out of town."

She pointed. "What have you got?"

He held the paper out to her, a little embarrassed. "Well look at this," said Sharon. The roses were cream-colored with an edging of yellow, heavy-headed, densely textured. "These are beautiful."

"I forgot a vase," he said, apologizing. He had not wanted to explain himself.

"It's no matter. Just lay them right there. That's fine. It's real sweet of you. Dean likes for her to have flowers."

"She deserved better than what she got," said Hughes. "Any-one would."

"That's exactly right," said Sharon.

They stood for a moment looking at the roses, and the sharp-cut pink stone with its skirt of clipped sod. "So what brings you here?" Hughes asked, just as if he himself had a reason.

"Oh, Dean can't come out here. So I do. For him, sort of. It's not a jealous thing with me. It's real peaceful here, don't you think? Some people it scares them. Not me."

"It is peaceful," he agreed. He felt himself calming. He wanted Sharon to keep talking. He thought this was what Kinshaw valued in her, calmness.

"Dean paid for the stone," said Sharon. "Did you know that? But he's never once seen it. He was in the hospital for the funeral. I think one reason he took up with me and the kids is there's so many of us. No matter what happened, there would still be someone left for him."

The fine misty rain blurred Hughes's glasses and beaded on the creamy skin of the roses. "Did you know her?"

Sharon shook her head. "She was so pretty. I've seen all her pictures. And full of spirit, like a little wild horse. He tells me all about her. She wasn't a bad girl, no matter what people say. She was just young. She was perfect the way she was. Put that part in the paper."

Hughes shook his head. "Ah, Sharon."

"Sure you can."

"Neither of us knew her," he said, not wanting to explain the strictures and requirements of journalism.

"There's different ways of knowing," said Sharon. She curled her fingers up into the oversized sleeves of the jacket. Her hair was darkening, clinging to her broad forehead. "It wasn't fair. She was just young."

Hughes felt sleepy. He felt as if he had been dreaming someone else's dream. The rain was softening the edges of things, turning the horizon into gray gauze, the fields into squares of light. The roses dripped with light. The boundaries of the world were indistinct. The dead were slipping through the tree line, through the soft fences of memory. His own death approached him, neither very far away nor entirely near. He recognized it with a certain relief, as he might recall the name of an acquaintance who had been smiling at him from a crowd all along. He was only one of the dead who were not yet dead.

"I should get on home," said Sharon. "He frets if I'm not back by dark. Drive careful. You'll have some real rain up north. If there's room in your story, put that he will love her forever."

PUBLICATION
ACKNOWLEDGMENTS

"All Shall Love Me and Despair" first appeared in *Mid-American Review*, Spring 1995, Vol. 15 (1, 2), and was later reprinted in *Best American Short Stories 1996*.

"The Little Heart" and "Fire Dreams" first appeared in the *New Yorker*, January 20, 1992, and October 24, 1988.

"Mercy," "Who Do You Love," and "The Amish" first appeared in *American Short Fiction* (26, 12, 13). "Who Do You Love" was later reprinted in *Pushcart Prizes XIX*.

"Heart of Gold" first appeared in *New England Review*, March 1991, Vol. 13 (2).

"Antarctica" first appeared in *Story*, Spring 1998.

"The Lost Child" first appeared in *Ploughshares*, Vol. 13 (3).

"The Rich Man's House" first appeared in *Ontario Review*, Spring 1995 (42).

"Poor Helen" first appeared in the *Carolina Quarterly*, Fall 1998, Vol. 41 (1).

"Forever" first appeared in *TriQuarterly*, Spring/Summer 1995 (93), a publication of Northwestern University.